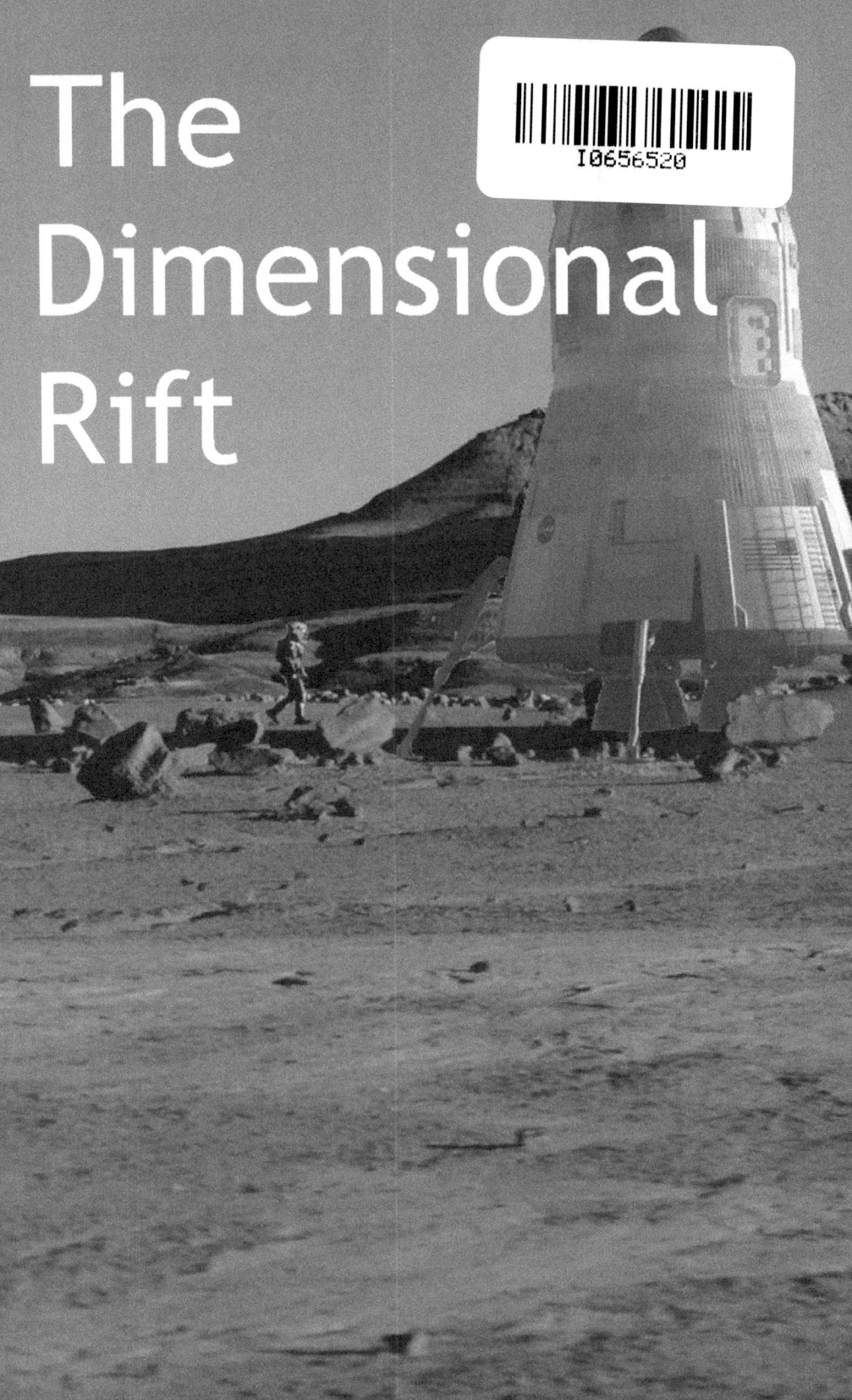

The
Dimensional
Rift

The Dimensional Rift

Rose Kincade

Kings Guards
PO Box 31015
Flagstaff, AZ 86003-1015

Printed in the United States of America

First Printing, 2012

ISBN 978-0-578-78792-3

This book is dedicated to two people who helped me find the straight and courage to follow my heart's dreams.
Leslye Anne Piper & Holli Rebecca Burnfield
Thank you, from the bottom of my heart.

Table of Content

Preface

HELLO, AND WELCOME TO MY first book of a planned mega-series. I started writing the first of my stories in 2010 and called it 'The Dragon Knott's: Beginnings' to correlate my dream diary into something others could follow. However, Before I could finish the story, I started having dreams of this new story, 'The Dimensional Rift.'

After Writing the first two books I decided to make them into a sing series. I placed the stories on a peer review site to see what other writers thought of my stories. Though they loved the bases of the stories, I was told they needed a lot of work in Grammar and Punctuations. Discouraged, I put works aside a focused on my third book and forth stories in the series.

In 2016, after moving all the way across the United States, and being encouraged by my new friends, I returned to college. I focused on additional English classes in addition to my regular major.

With all that I learned I went back to my original works and started reworking them. And this is the first of those stories.

This series opens in the year 2043, and the Earth's ocean levels have surged to swallow a third of the world's landmass. As a result of the rising waters, and with a population of over twelve billion people, Earth has embarked on a journey to the red planet known as Mars for the first time to start a colony.

Rose Kincade

Once *on the surface, they discover what appears to be
an American minivan that looks as though it has recently
crashed onto the surface and may ultimately have survivors
inside. The investigation into this remarkable vehicle
reveals far more than any of them are ready for, leaving
some in astonishment and the rest demanding answers.*

*The only occupant that can give any of them answers
happens to be a strange-looking alien creature discovered
deep inside this vehicle. Now, she must tell her story,
rescue her friends, and save tens of thousands of others like
her, trapped on the Earth in the hands of the many
different governments.*

I hope you enjoy the store you are about to read.

Prolog

Col. James Nichols

T IS A BRIGHT SUNNY MORNING as the sun steadily rises in the sky. Darnel lake shines with a luster-ish glow of brilliant blue-green water. The cool breeze is blowing north to the homes built along the lakeside, offering relief from the heat. A majestic eagle fly's high overhead, looking for its next meal. Circling high above, it catches sight of a middle-aged man sitting on a roof watching him fly.

It is June 14, 2043, as the phone starts ringing in Col. James Nichols cabin. Col. Nichols has been on leave for the last two months since the death of his wife. She died in an accident involving the experimental surveillance drone meant for the slated international manned mission to Mars scheduled later this very year. The drone had been intended to go to Mars to help find places of interest for the astronauts, areas for exploration on the upcoming three-year mission to the Red Planet.

The drone had done well in all the tests that it had been through until that fateful morning. But those in charge were not satisfied and decided to put it through a high-speed obstacle course that exceeded anything the drone would encounter on Mars. The chosen obstacle course was better suited for racing or attacking on Earth rather than for surveillance on another planet with half the air density and one-third of Earth's gravity.

Nancy had just finished her workout routine at the base's workout facility on that fateful morning in March. When she stepped out of the facility, the drone crashed into the front of the building, killing Nancy and injuring four others. The news of Nancy's death hit Col. Nichols hard, mostly because that night would have been their first anniversary since their daughter Emily died.

The phone starts ringing again for the fourth time that morning. Col. Nichols decides he should probably answer it, if for no other reason than to demand them to stop calling. After standing from his perch atop the roof, he knocks over several empty bottles of Vodka and Rum, causing them to go crashing to the ground below as he makes his way to the open window.

Tumbling through the open window, he somehow manages to land on the table with the phone, causing it to break, resulting in the phone to go sliding across the hardwood floor, disappearing somewhere under the bed while it is still ringing loudly.

"This is just Fucking great." He shouts as he forces himself up off the floor to hunt for the phone that is still ringing.

Laying down next to the bed, he rummages under it for the ringing phone. He soon finds a book with his wife's handwriting scrolled across the front. 'My Secret Life — My Dreams and Ambitions' he reads across the front cover. He lays there on the floor for several minutes, just looking at the cover of the book with his wife's fancy handwriting.

'My wife wrote this,' he thinks to himself, trying to remember if he had ever observed her writing in it before.

He is about to sit up and open the book when the phone starts ringing once more. Laying the book on the bed, he redoubles his search for the phone and soon finds it.

"HELLO," he shouts when he answers it.

"James? Col. James Nichols?" The voice on the other end of the phone responds. "I have been trying to reach you for the last few days."

"Who the *Fuck* is this?" James asks, emphasizing the word fuck as he speaks.

"Watch your language Col." The voice says, sounding angry. "This is Maj. Gen. Lupton, and you Col. are on recall starting immediately. You will report to X-ARC in northern Nevada on Monday morning, or the MP's will come and take your ass there. The choice is yours, Col."

"Yes, Sir. Maj. Gen. Lupton, Sir. I will be there." James says, holding a lazy hand up to his head in salute.

"Good. There you will find out why you have been recalled to active duty, and you will be briefed on the mission at hand." Maj. Gen. Lupton says before hanging up the phone.

James sits the phone on the bed before pulling himself up off the floor. He looks back at the window, remembering the past: remembering all the times that he and Nancy have spent out there, just watching the stars, contemplating the future of their daughter.

As though a shot had just gone off, James suddenly remembers about the book he found under the bed. James turns his attention to the book that is sitting just inches from his hand. He picks it up and begins to stare at the cover once more, longing to hear Nancy's footsteps marching up the hallway.

He debates for some time if he is going to read the book or not. He wants to know the types of things Nancy has written down, but he feels as though he will be violating her privacy if he reads this book. He knows she is dead, but if by some chance that the body they found is not Nancy's, he wants to be able to say 'honestly' that he has not read her special book.

James's mind goes through every reason why he should read the book, while his heart gives him every excuse for why he should not. This goes on for the next few days while he gets ready to head for X-ARC.

Finally, Sunday comes around, and James is ready to say goodbye to the house when someone knocks on the front door. Upon opening the door, James sees two MP officers standing there with a piece of paper in one of their hands.

"I am just about ready to leave as ordered. Why the hell are you here?" James asks the two MPs.

"Sir, our orders are to escort you to X-ARC. This is only for your protection." The guy on the right says, holding out his hand to hand James the paper and photo he is holding.

James takes the paper with the photo and sees the photo is a picture of himself. He then starts to read the letter:

Col. James Nichols
1412 North River Road
Las Vegas, New Mexico

> *It has come to our attention that a rogue individual may be in your area and may intend to cause you harm. This individual is considered extremely dangerous due to the fact he/she has even taken out whole platoons of troops single handily. Considering this, I have ordered Second Lieut. Brandon and Second Lieut. Marks to escort you to X-ARC for your safety.*

> *Signed*
> *Maj. Gen. Lupton*

James reads the letter several times before he closes the door. As he turns and walks away, the door opens, and the two MPs step into the house. They follow James as he makes his way up the stairs and into a latrine where he closes the door in their faces as he did downstairs. The two MPs stand outside of the door for several minutes, waiting for James to come out. Then without warning, they hear the horn of their car blaring, alerting them to some kind of danger. They start slamming themselves into the door, repeatedly trying to get into the latrine. After about the fourth slam, the door gives way revealing an empty bathroom and an open window. The two MPs run down the stairs as quickly as possible and out the front door to find James standing next to the car waving at them.

"We better get going. If you plan on making it to the X-ARC facility by tomorrow morning." James says with a smile on his face opening the driver's side back door and getting into the car.

The Two MPs look at each other with looks of incredulity. Dumfounded, they walk to the car too and get in themselves to start their drive to the airport. James makes it to the X-ARC facility by zero eight hundred hours Monday morning without any issues. Not even a delay at the airport for having a gun in his pack. James figures this is because of the two MPs escorting him, but he is not entirely sure.

After entering the main building of the X-ARC and taken to the top floor, James is instructed to wait in a large room on the third floor until they are ready for him. In this room, James can see several other people around the room. People are standing, sitting, and even lying throughout the room, waiting for their appointments. Except for James and an Army woman, everyone is in casual wear of one form or another. Most of which, James would identify as 'beach bum wear.' James decides that each of them must be there for some other reason than him. He concludes that he does not need to interact with them and finds a seat by the window. A window that looks out into the courtyard and the beautiful fountain that reminds him of his little girl, Emily.

Emily would be thirteen this summer if she did not go on that school trip that fateful spring day previous March. Nancy nor James blamed the school for not keeping a close eye on the group of girls as they took their group selfies at the edge of the Grand Canyon. They both knew that it was a fluke accident that an entire outcrop of rocks that had stood for over ten-thousand years had suddenly collapsed to the canyon floor.

James can still remember the pictures of each of the girls that managed to upload before their phones were destroyed. Emily's happened to snap a photo just a split second after the ground under their feet gave way, capturing the looks of horror on the girl's faces as their hair started to float upwards.

After some time passes, James pulls his mind back to the present and tries to focus on the situation at hand. Several more people show up before the first of them is called for their meeting.

Around thirteen hundred hours, the staff rolls in a large cart full of food for those waiting in the large room. James and the army woman wait for everyone else to get what they want before they stand to acquire some food for themselves. When they walk up to the table, they find that there is still quite a bit of food left to pick from, even though ravaged. There are crab legs, sausages, cheeses, shrimp, lunch meats, and even crackers and bread. After getting all they want, James and the woman walk over to a couch where they both sit to eat their food before James starts a conversation with the army woman.

"I am Col. James Nichols," James says, introducing himself.

"Hi, my name is Maj. Rebecca Thomas." The woman says. "Do you know why we have been ordered here today?"

"No. I have only been ordered to show up." James says.

"Same here," Rebecca responds.

The two talk briefly about where they are from before they finish eating in silence and do not bother speaking to each other after that. Both James and Rebecca sit there in silence, only standing from time to time to stretch their legs, stretching them by walking a few laps around the room and then returning to their seat. Everyone else in the room has gone, and no new people arrive after nineteen hundred hours.

Shortly after nineteen-thirty hours, Rebecca is called for her meeting, leaving James alone in the room. Until this point, each person had been called for their meeting between twenty minutes and half an hour from the previous person called, at least, by James's calculation. This has been true for each person throughout the day up until now.

James is starting to feel the pain of his wife again as he waits and hopes that his turn will be soon. As he sits there, he begins to become drowsy and nods off to sleep.

***

James has just returned home from another extended mission that he won't be able to talk to his wife, Nancy, about. Just as he is starting up the stairs, Emily, his daughter accost him.

"Daddy, daddy, you're home. You sure were gone a long time this time," Emily says after jumping into James's arms.

"Oh, it was only a few weeks. I have been gone longer before now." James says, tickling Emily's belly.

Hearing movement from somewhere above him, James looks up to see Nancy standing at the top of the stairs. After setting Emily down, he climbs the steps and passionately kisses Nancy.

After what seems like an eternity, the kiss finally ends, but to James's horror Nancy is not the one standing in front of him, it is Maj. Rebecca Thomas.

***

"Col. Nichols." Someone far off, says. "Col. Nichols." The voice says a bit louder. "Col. Nichols, please, they are ready for you." The voice calling to him is now deafening.

"What's going on?" James asks as he awakens from his slumber.

"Col. Nichols, they are ready for you now." The guy standing over James says.

"Oh, Okay, I am up. Give me a minute to freshen up, please." James says, pulling himself up to head to the bathroom.

"Yes, Sir. I will wait for you here." The guy says, stepping back to allow James to pass.

James takes about five minutes to splash his face with water to wake himself up and pull his mind to the present. He then decides that he should use the latrine before he meets with whomever he is going to meet.

As James finishes in the bathroom, he stands in front of the mirror, looking at himself, but not really looking at his reflection. He is thinking of Maj. Rebecca Thomas. About how she has fantastic green eyes. About her golden brown, shoulder-length hair. Hair that is perfectly straight until the last few inches, where it curls slightly inward. And about her ruby red lips. He is just wondering what it would be like to kiss her when someone knocks on the door.

"Sir, are you okay?" The guy from before calls out through the door.

James walks to the door and opens it before responding, "It's about time they were ready for me. Let's go." He says as he walks past the guy. As he reaches the main door out of the waiting room, he turns back.

The guy who had come for him is still standing at the bathroom door looking incredulity.

"Come on, are they not waiting for me?" James pleads.

"What? Oh. Yes, I'm sorry." The guy responds before trotting to the door to lead James to his meeting.

The guy leads James to another door that leads down a flight of stairs and outside into the quadrangle before escorting him to another building. Unlike all the other buildings that are built using brick and painted white, this structure is constructed of steel and painted gray, making it resemble the backside of a large aircraft hangar. Once inside, James is led to a massive sliding door that opens to a small room. A room about the size of a large walk-in closet or an average-sized cell. The guy instructs James just to wait in the middle of the room.

James walks to the middle of the small room and turns around. As he turns, he sees the doors close as the room starts to descend. The trip only lasts about forty-five seconds before it ends as abruptly as it started. The door reopens, revealing a new place that looks just like the one above. However, rather than the man who had been escorting him to this point, three new guys are waiting for him here. These men escort James to another room that looks much like the situation room in the White House, or perhaps the one found at the Pentagon in Washington, DC. But this one has one considerable difference; this one is well lit with white panels and flashing blue, red, yellow, and green lights.

"Col. James Nichols, I am glad to meet you finally." One of the guys in the room says, standing up to get a better look at James. "I am Michael Winterbottom; I'm the one who personally requested you on this team. I'm truly sorry about your wife."

"Is this a pity request... for her?" James asks with the resentment evident in his voice.

"Not particularly. The majority of our decision is based primarily on your record and your personal performance. Your wife had given us your name before she agreed to join the original team." Michael says, trying and failing to hide the anger in his voice.

"Then, with all due respect, I think I will decline the offer then. No offense." James says, turning to walk out.

"This is not an offer; it's an order. An order from the highest of your commanders." Michael says, not bothering to hide his anger. "You are here to stay, and you will do as you are ordered like a good soldier."

"Yes, Sir," James says with just as much anger as Michael while raising a hand in salute so hard that he thought others could hear a small rush of air.

"Now that we have that settled, I want you to start selecting your crew. After all, you will be spending the next three-plus years together." Michael says with a sarcastic smile in his voice. "But first, I want you to come over here so I can give you an overview of your crew's basic structure, your mission at hand, and what to expect while on Mars."

James reluctantly walks to the table in the middle of the room. He sees a cluster of more than two dozen egg-shaped structures positioned in a couple of circles on the table. They look out of place on what looks like a picture of the surface of Mars. All in an area that he recognizes as the Hellas Planitia, south of the equator.

"This is the landing location that we have chosen since the mountains around the giant crater will help protect the colony. Protect them from the massive windstorms that often sweep the planet. Storms that sometimes can last for days, or even months." Michael says, not bothering to gesture to the map on the table.

"Then, this is Hellas Planitia?" James asks, not looking up from the table.

"You do know Mars... Why yes, this is Hellas Planitia. We figure that the mountain range around the valley will prevent the winds from destroying the equipment we send." Michael explains. "We intend to send about eighteen supply ships full of supplies and equipment. Along with twelve service ships that you will need for the construction of the colony. The colony that will be arriving there in the near future."

"This is still only a two-year ground mission, though, correct?" James asks, confused about how a small handful of people will build such a city in such a short time, especially when the main idea is for this team to be comprised of primarily scientists there to investigate the planet.

"Yes, it is. The primary build team will arrive about three months before you leave Mars. They will have the rest of the people you do not pick this time around to construct the majority of the facilities. The ones that are too big for your advance team to build." Michael says with a grin on his face. "Your primary goal after landing will be to unpack modules one, three, and fifteen. By using the items to link all the primary capsules to one another. You will create a safe zone for people to get from one module to another."

"So then, connecting twenty-eight pods will take about nine months. Then we will start the scientific research for the remaining thirteen months." James states, trying to understand the timeline intended.

"No, the first stage of the building process should only take about a month. Then, the scientists can start their primary jobs." Michael says. "While most of the people going are only signing on for the two-year ground research, there are also those that will be there for far longer. Some are even going to spend the remainder of their lives there."

James looks closely at the map before him. He sees that their intended landing area is on the northern side, just west-south-west of Terby Crater.

"After unloading the utility pods, your team will assemble the transit tubes from pod one to the work pods, assemble the communication dishes from pod three, the greenhouse from pod fifteen, and the weather station from pod three." Mr. Winterbottom says.

"Then, we start the science stuff, though I am not a scientist?" James says, half trying to be funny, half-seriously.

"Yes, then you will start the science stuff, even though you are not a scientist. You will have people for studying rocks, those looking for ancient life, scientists that will grow and study plants, and those who will study the weather." Mr. Winterbottom turns to a small rolling desk and grabs a stack of files before turning back to James to hand him the stack of files. "These are the people we have narrowed your selection down to."

James quickly thumbs through the stack of files stopping at Maj. Rebecca Thomas. He recognizes the name as being the woman he met earlier in the day, or rather, now the day before. James opens the file and starts reading it. He sees that Rebecca has graduated from college in 2035 with a master's degree in astrophysics. She is commissioned to a first lieutenant right out of the ROTC in 2036 and had been promoted to Maj. in 2039 after rescuing Second Lieutenant Mark Foster. She had also managed to save a convoy from an assault on an Afghanistan supply mission 2040.

"Take those files and choose your team. Reduce that pile to just twenty-seven people for this first mission." Michael tells James.

"Consider it done. Where will I be staying while I go through these files, Sir.?" James asks.

"There is hotel-style base housing to the south called 'The Encampment.' You will be staying there for the time being." Michael says. "Now, head back upstairs, and you will be taken to your room."

James is escorted to his room with the stack of files on the other side of the base. Once in his room, he sees that his luggage has already been delivered, so he decides to get some sleep before going through the stack of files. This is because it is now nearly zero three hundred hours.

After he has gotten some sleep, he starts going through the files of prospects. He first divides the stacks into several smaller groups: medical doctors, archaeologists, paleontologists, volcanologists, civil engineers, herpetologists, and military personnel. He then eliminated those that would not be good for the mission, for not fitting into any of the groups he sorted. By the time James is finished weeding out those he knows would not work on this mission, he goes back to the stack of suitable candidates to see how many he has left. After starting with more than a hundred people, he had only managed to weed out twelve people.

Only twelve people. Well, it's a start. James thinks to himself.

James then turns to look at the personalities of each of the people he has left, turning each group into two piles of excellent and possible and throwing those he cuts into the reject pile. After getting through the last collection, James once again counts the number of candidates he has left. James is horrified to discover that there are now not enough people for the crew, with only twenty-six files remaining.

He realizes that he has weeded out too many people and decides to call Mr. Winterbottom's office to see if there are any other possible candidates.

"Hi, Mr. Winterbottom, please," James asks, calling Michael's office.

"Yes, what can I do for you, Col. Nichols?" Michael replies.

"Do you have any other possible candidates? Going through the ones you provided me with, I have scratched more than you have anticipated." James says.

"If you have scratched too many people from the list, then you better un-scratch some to meet the required number of members for the mission at hand." Michael says, with anger in his voice.

"The ones that I have scratched are not mentally or physically fit for this mission, and many do not even have the skill set needed," James says, trying to explain his position.

"The people we have chosen will be fine. Now pick your crew," Michael says, slamming the phone down.

James hangs up the phone, feeling upset. He has spent years picking and selecting people for various types of missions. James has become adept at knowing who will be proficient in handling the stress and who would not. He knows that he will have to watch whoever he picks carefully to make sure they will be okay. Subsequently, expending numerous hours going through the scratch pile files, James starts to feel exhausted and decides he needs a drink.

He calls down to the service desk to see where he can go to acquire a stiff drink. He is told he can go to the barroom behind the commons, which is straight across the park outside of the Encampment. He walks out and starts across the park.

About halfway across, James looks up and sees the stars in the night sky. He sees Mars in its bright red glory hanging just below the moon as a small object in space flies between the moon and Mars. He knows that the object is the International Space Station flying overhead by its brightness and travel direction. Once the space station has passed out of sight, he decides to resume his progress to the commons.

James walks into the barroom and sees Rebecca sitting at a table with five other people, all laughing and having a good time together. Of the three people he can see clearly, he only discerns two of them from the files. The first guy Mark Foster is the guy Rebecca had rescued in 2039. Mark happens to be in the pile of file folders that James has passed. The second guy is a guy from the scratch pile; his name is Doctor Frank Barnes. Dr. Barnes has gone through several mental evaluations and has passed all but one.

The evaluation he had failed has a note of possible mental illness called 'God Complex.' The evaluating doctor expresses concern that when given any significant power, the complex could manifest itself. James has figured that the reason that this is the only examination to uncover this is that it is the only one that was more in-depth than just a five hundred question review.

James walks up to the counter and orders a whiskey sour on the rocks. He waits as the guy behind the bar makes the drink before turning to look out across the room. When he does, he finds Rebecca standing there.

"So." She starts with a smile on her face. "You made it past the latest rounds of interviews."

James thinks carefully, choosing his words and answering with a, "yes... yes, I did."

Rebecca must have noticed the hesitation because her smile falters slightly before snapping quickly back. After a few seconds, she asks, "Will you join my friends and me for a few rounds of drinks?"

James pretends to take a moment to decide before agreeing to join them. He wants to get to know Frank better to see for himself about Frank's god complex. After Rebecca places her order and the drinks are made, James helps her carry them back to the table.

Rebecca introduces James to each of the people at the table. The first person she points out is Frank, a mousy-blond hair man with brown eyes that almost look red. The next guy, Rebecca, points out, is Mark; he is a big muscle built man with black hair and eyes. Next in line is Melissa Watson, whose hair is cut so short, James had first thought she was a guy from the door. This woman has brown hair and hazel colored eyes. From where she is sitting, right next to Mark, she looks to be as tall as he is. Next is Howard Murphy, who is a short African American man. After standing up, James notices that he cannot be much taller than five feet two inches. The last person who he is introduced to is another woman by the name of Susan Haul. She has golden blond hair with brilliant blue eyes and a figure that most women would die for in a heartbeat.

James spends much of the night talking with the group getting to know each of them. He learns about their pasts, their families, and why each of them wants to be selected for the mission. James tries to divide his attention between them all, but he is actually mostly interested in Frank. Due to the fact he is on the list of people, James has scratched from possible candidates. If the rest of the group thinks he is okay, maybe he should give him a chance.

Shortly after zero three hundred, James excuses himself from the group, saying, "I have a meeding at zero nine hundred. I nee to tie and get a widdle sweep before I see Mr. Maj. Gen.," He says, making sure to push in his seat. As James is walking, he can tell he has a good buzz going. But before he can make it to the door, Rebecca accosts him.

"Wha the hell do you thin you are doing not talk them thot you ah the miston comdamdor, comtamsir, ahh shist?" Rebecca says, slurring her words as she speaks.

"We both know... people don't give a raze ass... that I am the commander. If... they knew-ew I was... they would all-ll be asking for... spectal flavors." James responds, also slurring many of his words and hiccupping here and there.

"Bud, they have a rye to note." Rebecca says.

"I have one hundred... eight-tween pebbles to... go through. Half limet ofto tweenty... weight people." James says, noticing his vision going blurry.

Ignoring Rebecca's objections, James walks out of the door, hoping he can make it back to the Encampment before he passes out. As he walks through the courtyard, he can hear Rebecca following him. He reaches the Encampment room door assigned to him and opens it as Rebecca grabs him, just as she passes out. Somehow, James manages to drag Rebecca into the room and puts her into one of the beds in the room.

James wakes up just after zero eight-thirty that morning and starts going through the files of rejected candidates. He is about ready to give up as he is reaching for another file when he hears someone move in the bed behind him. To his amazement, James sees a woman sleeping in the bed next to where he was lying just a few hours before. He has to think for a few minutes before remembering how this woman got into his bed. That Rebecca had followed him to the room and passed out in his arms at the door. But he could not remember if they had intercourse or not.

Rebecca raises her head and sees James staring at her. She grabs the blankets and pulls them up over her chest before asking him, "What the hell are you doing in my room?"

"Actually, madam, you are in my room. You followed me here last night and passed out in the door before saying whatever it is you were going to say." James says in response.

Rebecca lifts the blanket a little and sees that she is still fully clothed. As she throws the blankets off, she says, "Sorry," to James. As she walks towards the door, she stops about halfway there, seeing something that grabs her attention. James looks to what caught her eye and sees her file on top of one of the file stacks.

"I can explain this," James says, standing up.

"Don't bother, I already know. You were picked for mission commander over me." Rebecca says.

James can tell by the tone of her voice that Rebecca had been hoping for the post and is taking it hard that she had not been chosen. He wants to say something to make it better, but he does not know what to say. After about a minute of awkward silence, Rebecca closes the gap between her and the door and walks out.

James grabs the stack of files that he has chosen for the upcoming Mars mission and the one for Frank Barnes. He makes another quick look through to make sure he has enough before walking out to meet with Mr. Winterbottom. Assured that he has the correct number of files selected, James makes his way out of the Encampment for his meeting.

James arrives at the steel hanger looking building for his meeting with Mr. Winterbottom just a few minutes before it is supposed to start. He is asked by the receptionist to wait on a sofa located opposite the elevator. He looks the couch over and realizes that the thing is from the sixties and has probably never been treated for bugs. James takes a swat at the sofa with his hand and finds that the dust is so thick that perhaps it's never been dusted either.

Just as James is ready to walk around until they are prepared for him, he hears someone walk up behind him. "Well, James. Did you pick out twenty-seven people you can work with?" He hears Mr. Winterbottom ask.

"Yes, Sir. I have the final stack here." James says, handing Mr. Winterbottom the stack of files.

"Good, good. Then come with me." Mr. Winterbottom says, pointing out of the back of the building.

James walks next to Mr. Winterbottom as they make their way back to the building that James first visited when he arrived at X-ARC. James is led to the uppermost floor of the building. Once there, he is led into a conference room where they find nearly a hundred-twenty people sitting and standing around the room, almost seven times as many people as the other day.

James can identify nearly everyone in the room from their files. He notices that the Military people are the ones standing around the room, divided by Army, Navy, and Air Force. Even the scientist seems to have divided themselves into classes as well.

"This is Col. James Nichols of the Royal Canadian Air Force. He has been going over your files to see who will be on the primary mission to Mars. He is also the mission commander for this mission." Mr. Winterbottom says to the group of people.

James is looking around the room to see how people react to the news. He spots Rebecca standing in a corner hiding behind a tall US Air Force guy. Rebecca stands there gazing out beyond the window, opposite where James stands, tears streaming down her cheeks. James feels he needs to talk to her, but he is unsure what to say that will make her feel better.

Just as James is ready to walk over to Rebecca and talk to her, he hears Mr. Winterbottom announce him to tell everyone who will be on the primary mission roster.

"Thank you, Mr. Winterbottom. Now, before I get to telling everyone who will be on my primary team, I want to tell everyone that my wife spent several years preparing for this mission. I want everyone to know that I will do my best to honor her dream." After James finishes saying this, he notices Rebecca looking at him with her mouth hanging open and tears flowing freely.

Mr. Winterbottom quickly steps forward and says, "We will all miss Maj. Cornel Nancy Nichols. She will always be an inspiration to us all."

James starts to feel the flames of hatred well up from the darkest pit of his stomach. Before allowing it to consume him, he decides to walk forward and go through the list of people for his team.

"I was ordered to reduce the list of candidates to just twenty-eight people, so please, if you were not selected, just know it is nothing personal. There are just far too many to pick from." James starts looking around the room. "First will be the command structure. Second in command is Rebecca Thomas; after that is Mark Foster and Michael Brown. Next is pod commanders, Andrew Wilson, Susan Haul, Amy Diggs, Brian McNally, David Maurice, Emily Marks, Brian Stafford, Thomas Anderson, Kelly Li, and John Majors. The rest will be posted later today in the main courtyard, as well, which team each person will be assigned to."

After James finishes speaking, he turns to walk out of the room. He makes it down the elevator and is about to exit the building when Rebecca yells out to him, "Please, wait," as she runs down the stairs. James turns and waits for Rebecca.

"Why didn't you tell me that Nancy was your wife?" Rebecca asks with tears in her eyes.

"Why would I talk about something that I have such a hard time talking about? Nancy was the love of my life." James says in reply.

"I'm sorry. Nancy was a dear friend of mine. I wanted to go to the funeral, but I was stuck in the hospital, recovering from the accident." Rebecca said, tears falling freely as she talked. "The day Nancy died, she told me that she was writing a book about her daughter Emily called, 'My Secret Life – My Dreams and Ambitions' that she was just about finished with. Have you found the book yet?"

James stood there, with his mouth hanging open, looking at Rebecca dumbstruck. After about a minute or so, he finds his voice, and shakily says, "You must be the friend who she was always going to meet at the gym."

Rebecca nods as she allows her head to fall forward. Another minute of awkward silence goes by before James suddenly walks past Rebecca out of the building.

Chapter One

The Mission to Mars

THE SUN SHINES BRIGHTLY ON this crisp November morning. The breeze coming off the ocean has a bitter bite to it as it sweeps up the coast to the north. News reporters line the fields of the newly founded Advanced Strategic Space Mission Control Center, located south-east of Abilene, Texas, with its brand new black and white buildings. The new grey space shuttle sits on a runway, ready to leave the Earth behind as it slingshots into space.

It has been nearly six months since James started his team for the International manned mission to Mars. James and Rebecca have been working very closely together to get the team ready for this historic event. The day is fast approaching when they will be sent into space to see their new ship, the Stuhlinger MEK.

Michael Winterbottom walks out of a large building marked 'NASA/Space X Launch Center' before quietly heading to a podium standing one hundred feet from the main building. As he does so, the crowd of reporters becomes quiet, intently listening for what Mr. Winterbottom will be saying.

"With an ever-growing population of now more than twelve billion people, combined with the ever-rising waters of global warming, humanity needs to find new lands and new worlds to populate. This new exploration comes in the form of the Stuhlinger MEK currently in orbit around the Earth, nearly one hundred and twenty miles above us. This ship is the collation of nearly twenty years and more than twenty countries. At nearly two thousand feet long and just over five hundred feet wide, at its widest point, the Stuhlinger MEK is the largest object ever built by man in space." Michael Winterbottom says. He gives the crowds before him a chance to take it all in as a picture of the Stuhlinger MEK is displayed on the screen above him.

"In just thirty-nine hours, on Friday morning, the Stuhlinger MEK will be home to thirty people for the next seven months. Once the crew of the Stuhlinger MEK is aboard, it will slingshot from the Earth, then acquire a slingshot boost from the moon before traversing the space between Earth and Mars. After reaching Mars, the crew will start launching twenty-eight landing pods. All to land and build the first International space colony on Mars." He continues. A big screen behind him shows the process of landing the pods and building a Mars colony to the reporters.

"On the screen behind me, you will see the names and photos of the thirty individuals who will be a part of this important expedition. These thirty people are the pioneers of a great new frontier on our red neighbor, Mars. They will explore the areas around Hellas Planitia, the deepest and largest crater on Mars. The scientists believe that if we are going to find liquid water on or just below the surface, this is the location that will give us the best chance to find it. While on the ground, these scientists will also grow plants for food. They will look to see if there is life in the soil, if the soil can support life and if Earth plants can grow in the soil." He finishes.

The reporters wait only about thirty seconds before starting their assault of questions. Questions like, "What about the sandstorms?" "Who will be leading the mission on Mars?" and "What types of things do you expect to find on the ground?" After

Michael answers five questions, he walks back to the NASA building.

The day has finally come for James and his crew to break orbit for their journey to that magnificent red marble known as Mars. James is still upset that he was not told about having two new people added to his 'go list.' Those in charge were requiring Lili Chang and Sakura Kurosaki to go because they were two of the critical scientist involved in the design and construction of the Stuhlinger MEK. James understood this but felt he still should have known about the two women beforehand. But it is far too late for arguments now. At least they were involved in the training that everyone was going through up until now.

James is going over the team layout that he has put together when Rebecca walks into the room. "We are ready to get underway. You are needed on the Command Deck, Sir."

"Okay, I will be there shortly," James says, standing from the desk. "Take a look at this, would you? I need a fresh pair of eyes to see if I need to make any other changes." James says, reaching out a hand to hand Rebecca a sheet of paper.

"What is this?" Rebecca asks as she reads over the list.

"This is the list I have been working on for who will be going down and when." He says, stepping to the door to close it.

"Why did you put all of the military people in the Command Pod?" She asks, pointing to the team list.

"I figured that if anything major happened on the way down or there is a problem with the landing site, we would be the best suited for dealing with the issues." He says as he steps around Rebecca to grab one of his Command vests off the bed.

Rebecca looks over the page for what seems like minutes before James rips it out of her hand, saying, "I asked for your opinion, not for you to scrutinize it under a microscope."

Rebecca looks shocked at what James has just done and says to him. "Well, if you don't want my opinion on the madder, I might as well leave." She says, turning to grab the door.

James and Rebecca's relationship has developed beyond that of the rest of the crew. Ever since that night back in June, when they first spent that fateful night together and had their conversation at the entrance of the main building of the X-ARC, their relationship has become one of playfulness more evolved from that of the rest of the crew. James and Rebecca know they can get away with it for the crew's sake, at least that's what they keep telling themselves. It started primarily to help relieve some of the stresses they have been under during their training.

"I am sorry. I really want to know what you think." James says as he hurries to the door to stop Rebecca.

"To be honest, I would have probably put all the military people together as well... for the same reason as you did." Rebecca starts. "The rest of the crew is nearly nothing but scientists who have never been in any real trouble."

"I wanted to complement each of their skills and balance the teams. But many of them have developed relationships that might get in the way of them doing their jobs if anything serious happens out there." James says. His face showing the worry.

"I would say you balanced them well. As for the relationships, I don't think you have anything to worry about with any of them. Andrew likes Melissa. But Melissa does not like guys that way. Nancy likes Howard. But again, Howard likes Robert, who is into Lili. The only two that are starting to get serious is Mathew and Maryanne." She says, sitting down on the bed after she finishes.

"I thought Maryanne is seeing Li?" He says as he sits on his chair at the desk.

"No, that ended a few weeks ago." She says with a slight giggle. "The rumor is, they were just too different to make it work."

"By the time we set foot on Earth again, we will have spent a total of three years together between this barge and Mars. Are they going to be okay, working together all that time?"

"I think so. Li and Maryanne are both professionals. They only got together more as of a way to..." (knock on the door) "release tension than anything else."

"ENTER," James yells at the door.

Susan opens the door. Staring around the room, she sees that James and Rebecca are in the room together. Talking with a strong Russian accent, she says, "Sir, Mission control says our window will be closing soon. We need you on Command."

James and Rebecca stand looking at each other. Turning to look at Susan, James says, "We are on our way." And the three of them make their way through the corridors to the command deck.

James, Rebecca, and Susan enter the command deck, one after the other. James walks over to the seat in the center of the sterol-white room and sits down. On the wall at the front of the room is a large display, though it looks more like a window showing the vastness of space. To the left and right of the big screen are three more slightly smaller screens on each side. On the left-side armrest is a monitor with function keys around the outside. On the right-side armrest is a dial pad for inputting information.

The main screen at the front of the command deck changes from a view of space outside to that of a short chubby man, a man named Michael Winterbottom. He looks angry from this side of the screen as he sits there in his chair. All because James made him wait and sweat if the Stuhlinger MEK would leave Earth orbit on time to be able to reach the moon just at the right moment.

"Mr. Winterbottom, Sir," James says, looking up.

"It's about fucking time, Col.," Michael responds with much anger in his voice.

"There is more to running a ship than your schedule, Mr. Winterbottom," James says with a smile.

Michael looks as though James has just taken his favorite toy. Michael raises a hand to hide from the camera for about ten seconds. After he lowers his hand, James can see that Michael is leaning to his left, pretending to talk to someone for about twenty seconds before he sits straight in his seat.

"I was just informed that if you do not leave now, the mission will be a fail," Michael says.

"Sir, we are ready to start final systems checks so that we can get underway," James says, still smiling at Michael on the screen. He looks to his right and calls out, "Zero-G gravity plating."

"Zero-G gravity plating, On." Lili Chang says with her Chinese accent.

"Ion plasma thrusters," James says, turning to his left.

"Ion plasma thrusters, are go, Sir." John Right says with a heavy British accent.

James turns to look at the operation station at the back of the room and says, "Primary sensors and communications."

"Primary sensors, online. Communications are green." Nancy Johns says.

After giving Nancy a brief smile, James turns to the front of the ship and calls out, "Navigation and thruster controls."

"Navigation and thrusters both show green, Sir." Michele Douglass says.

James stands and looks around the command deck for a few seconds with a big smile on his face. After making one full turn, he makes his statement, "I am proud of what this crew has accomplished these last six months, even with all of the downfalls and setbacks we have gone through." He pauses for several seconds before continuing. "This mission to Mars is a giant step for humanity. Not only are we finally taking our first big step to the stars in eighty-five years, but it is the first time in human history that we are doing it as a unified world."

"Knock off the theatrics, Col. You have a mission to get started." Michael says, sounding half teary-eyed and half angry.

"Helm, let's get underway." James says, more angrily than he intended.

The ship gives a shutter as it starts to move. First, barely moving at all, but soon going faster and faster until it starts pulling away from Earth. The ship's orbit gets more extensive with each new rotation until, at three hundred miles from the Earth, the Stuhlinger MEK shoots off in the direction of the moon, and soon on towards Mars.

The first three months of the journey passes with no issues. The days all go by nearly the same, with the crew performing a variety of experiments. The mornings start with the team having breakfast together, followed by each of them dividing up into groups of four to six people. Each group is taking turns exercising, cleaning sections of the ship, performing various experiments, and going through multiple ship systems checks.

However, this morning, the crew is awakened to loud alarms, flashing red lights, and what sounds like a violent hailstorm raging outside of the ship. At first, most of the team are in a daze trying to figure out what is going on. James is one of the first to gain his full faculties, realizing that the ship must be passing through the debris field of a comet or asteroid. He jumps from his bed, and without any other thoughts, runs out of his room to head for the command deck before putting on any clothes. After arriving, he yells, "What's going on?" while walking to his seat and sitting down.

The first person to say anything is Rebecca, who had arrived moments before James had. "It appears we are passing through the debris field of a comet that is not supposed to pass by here for another week." She says while looking at a monitor to the right of James's seat.

James, with his overwhelming shock, replies, "At what speed are the pieces hitting the ship?"

"By the sound of it, I would say they are hitting at a relatively low velocity as though the debris field is moving in the same direction as we are." Monica Dolt says, walking through the door of the command deck.

"So, is there any real danger from this debris field?" Rebecca inquires.

"There is always a danger of any debris field in space. Nonetheless, I doubt that this field poses a significant threat. It won't hurt to monitor the situation, though." Monica says, walking over to the station where Rebecca is standing, silencing the alarms blazing throughout the ship.

James stands from his seat and walks the few steps to the ship's information console. Standing next to Rebecca and Monica, he asks, "What can have caused the comet to accelerate like this?"

The girls turn to look at James, and both blush profusely as they look him up and down. After a few seconds, they cannot hold it in any longer and start laughing.

James, not knowing what they are laughing at, asks, "What?"

It takes Rebecca a minute to calm herself enough to answer, "Are you planning on walking around in the nude all day long? Jr. looks a little shy this morning."

James looks down and realizes that he is not wearing anything, and covers his manhood as Robert comes walking in. Seeing James standing there with no clothes on, he hands him his lab coat to provide some kind of dignity for James.

"Now that I have some dignity reclaimed, what can have caused the comet to pass us like this?" James asks, looking at Rebecca and Monica.

"To be honest, the only thing that can have precipitated the comet to beat us here would have to be another object; a larger object traveling faster and in the same direction passing dangerously close." Monica says, trying to stifle her giggles.

"Is there anything that might have done this passing through the galaxy?" Rebecca asks.

"Not that I am aware of, but Earth can only track about one percent of all near-Earth objects." Monica says, staring at the wall behind James.

"Well, let me know as soon as we are past the comets' tail. I want to send people out as soon as possible. We need to see if there is any damage that we need to repair before arriving at Mars. Also, send a message to Mission Control and inform them what has just happened." James says pulling the lab coat tighter around him. "I am going to get dressed and get some breakfast."

James turns and heads back to his room. As he walks through the door, he looks around, trying to figure out why he feels different. To him, the room even seems unusual, it appears to him as though the place is somehow brighter.

***

Michele, Nancy, and Bobby come through the airlock removing their helmets. Not to mention, Bobby and Michele looking relieved at being back inside the ship.

"I never thought it would be so disconcerting being out there." Bobby says, stepping through the airlock door.

"What do you mean?" Nancy asks, turning to look at Bobby.

"He means that in the simulators, we always had either Earth or Mars in the sky somewhere. Out there just now, we had nothing you can easily identify as either." Michele says, pulling off her gloves.

"Exactly." Bobby says, hanging his helmet on one of the hooks in the locker for the helmets.

"I see. You must not have paid attention then. There were only three times that Mars or Earth hung in the sky in our simulations. All the others have neither, except one that has a large asteroid passing the ship." Nancy says, now hanging her helmet in the locker.

"I don't remember that one. What was that simulation about?" Bobby asks, trying to remember what they were doing in that simulation.

"I remember that one. That is sim nine, right? When we have to perform external repairs after an asteroid strike on the ship." Michele says.

"It was a micrometeoroid storm more commonly referred to as a micro-roid. We had to repair nearly four-dozen holes around the ship in half an hours' time to have enough O2 left to either finish the mission or abort the whole thing altogether. That's why the Col. had us out there looking for any signs of damage." Nancy says while walking to the last door of the airlock to walk out.

Nancy reaches the door looking slightly frustrated. Spinning on her heel, she turns to face Bobby and Michele to ask, "Which of us should give the report?" wondering if Michele would nominate her for being a lower rank on the mission list.

"I will give it." Michele says as she hangs her helmet in the locker. "You do not need to worry about it." She continues, turning to look at Nancy.

Nancy spins on her heel and walks out, leaving Bobby and Michele alone in the airlock prep-room. Bobby and Nancy look at each other for a few seconds before busting out, laughing at what has just happened. Turning and shaking his head, Bobby leaves the prep-room to get changed out of his space-body-glove suit, or SBG suit. Michele following shortly after.

"Sir., There does not seem to be any serious damage to the outside of the ship. Most of the damages seem to be minor with the most serious being a dent in the landing strut on RDP-7 and a hole through the engine cone of RDP-16. The hole should not pose a threat because it's just a few centimeters from the bottom of the cone." Michele tells James as they enter the command deck.

"Mrs. Rodgers, how does internal atmospheric pressure look around the ship?" James asks as he takes a seat in his chair.

"All atmospheric pressures look good. However." Mrs. Rodgers says, the last word trailing off in shyness.

"What is it?" James asks.

"The onboard fuel pressure gauge on RDP-7 is showing no reading." She says while punching keys on her panel. "At first, I thought it might be a glitch, but I have not been able to get it to reset."

"How do we check the gauge to find out if it is faulty?" James asks, looking around the room.

"Sir, the gauge is not repairable in space, or more accurately, we cannot get to it while the pod is in the cradle." Sakura says with only a mild hint of a Japanese accent.

"Really? So, how do we figure out if the gauge is faulty or if the tank has leaked?" James asks, sounding upset.

"There is a secondary pressure gauge on the command deck of each pod. But someone will have to get into an SBG suit because that whole section is depressurized." Michele says with her head down.

"We designed the ship originally to be a deep space seed ship carrying nearly two hundred people." Lili says, looking at Sakura, tears running down her cheek.

"But since the ocean levels started rising by sixteen centimeters per day in 2032, we had to change our designs half-way through the build." Sakura added.

"Okay, so how do I get there?" Michele asks, looking at James, Sakura, and Lili in turn.

After Sakura explains the path to Michele, Lili shows her the procedure to check the pressure gauge on the command deck. And after nearly an hour, everyone is satisfied that it is just a faulty connection between the pod and the ship — everyone except James, who feels that there is more to the problem than a broken link.

"I want a full ship diagnostic from bow to stern. I cannot shake the feeling there is more going on than what we are seeing here." James says as he shakes his head.

"Sir, there are parts of the ship that cannot be accessed while we are in space." Sakura says with a look of anxiety on her face.

"Why?" James asks, turning to look at Sakura.

"It's because of the nuclear power plant." Michele says.

"You are telling me that we can't get to every part of the ship even if we turn on the power in the pods?" James asks everyone on the command deck.

Michele, Lili, Sakura each look at each other with the look of question etched on their face. As each of them realizes that the pods each have an independent power supply, the looks on their faces change from questioning to dawning realization. After the last of them came to the same understanding, the three of them each start talking in turn.

"If we turn..." Lili starts.

"on all of..." Michele continues.

"the generators..." Sakura says.

"together, they can..." Michele says.

"power the whole ship," Lili says.

"in place of the..." Sakura says.

"nuclear power plant." Lili finishes.

"What the hell are you talking about?" James asks.

After they explain that he has a great idea, they all decide to turn in for the night. The next day the crew starts the inspection of the ship. In just a few hours after starting their ships "diagnostics," they find seven minor issues that are easily fixed, one major issue that could have ended their mission, and a piece of the asteroid lodged in one of the locks holding one of the most essential pods. This pod holds eighty thousand gallons of water meant to be used on the surface of Mars. At least until they can find and process water from the surface itself.

At thirteen-twenty-seven-hours, James is called back to the command deck from his lunch. He arrives on deck to find Rebecca talking to Mark over the radio.

"The engine is totally gone. There is no way for the pod to land on any planet in one piece." James hears Mark say.

"Which pod has the missing engine?" James asks, startling Rebecca.

After screaming and bowing her head in relief, Rebecca turns to look at James and says, "Pod twenty-ones number four engine is ripped from its mounts."

"And what is on pod twenty-one?" James asks, looking sallow.

"It has the mobile lab truck, bus, and the drilling rig. There are also six weeks of food rations, the backup medical supplies, and several personal items of the crew." Rebecca says.

"Is there a spare engine available?" James asks.

"No, there are no spare engines." Rebecca says

"Hello!" A voice fills the room. "Col. Nichols, Sir."

James and Rebecca both realize that the voice is coming over the radio from Mark. James crosses the room to stand next to Rebecca.

"Mark, what do you have?" James asks Mark.

"We can't do anything about the vehicles, but we can move everything else to other pods." Mark says.

Rebecca agrees that it is a good idea, and after a brief discussion, James too agrees. The transfer takes most of the week, and after it is complete, the next nine weeks go by without any further issues until the day before they are supposed to start dropping the pods to Mars.

Chapter Two

The Discovery

THE NASA MARS ROVER IS scouting out the landing site to make sure there are no new obstructions. A place for the first international man mission that is going to be landing on the surface in just a few days. The rover has just finished a sweep of a broad valley in the Hellas Planitia. It sends its images back to the NASA Mission Control Center in Abilene, Texas, waiting for further orders again before moving on to its next location. As NASA is evaluating the photos that they have received from the Mars rover, one of the lead programmers' notices something shimmering in one of the images. The shimmer is in the background of an image from the far side of the valley.

"Sir." The programmer calls out to his supervisor, somewhere in the room.

"What do you have?" The supervisor asks as he is walking over.

"There is an object off in the distance that is highly reflective. It should be checked out." The programmer says, looking up at the supervisor.

Rose Kincade

The supervisor looks at the image on the programmer's screen. Not being able to see the small picture very well, he asks the programmer to put it up on the giant screen so he can get a better look at it. The programmer puts the image up on the giant screen as he is asked to do. As they all look at the picture, they notice that the object looks like a bright light off in the distance. Which means it should have shown up on all the Mars mappings that have been done before now.

"Let's check it out. Direct the rover to the object so we can get a better look at it." The supervisor tells the programmer.

The programmer does as he is asked and sends the commands to the rover on Mars. It takes the rover about fifteen minutes to get the instructions and begin executing them to make the journey to the source of the light. The rover takes another forty-five minutes to transverse the valley to the object. Once there, it starts to take images and send them back to NASA. As the photos begin to come in, the supervisor wants them to be put up on the big screen for them all to see.

"Dear God, it's a Minivan." Someone in the room exclaims as the first of the images appear on the screen.

As the images keep coming in, the crowd sees this blue minivan, or at least what looks like a minivan. One that seems as though it has been shot thousands of times from all directions. The images come in at intervals of about one to two every minute — each one from a slightly different perspective than the last.

Suddenly, an image comes in of one of the windows on this remarkable vehicle on another planet. This noteworthy vehicle that is sitting on the surface of Mars, now has what can only be described as a hand in a window, a hand of someone, or something. As they all stare at the image with the hand that is up on the screen. The ground commander walks in, looking down at the bunch of papers he is carrying in his hands. Looking up from his papers, he sees everyone just standing around.

"What is everyone looking at?" The ground commander asks. Following the eyes of the people in the room, he looks up at the screen and sees the image that has the rooms undivided attention. He turns to the supervisor and says, "Where are these images coming from?"

"From the far side of the large valley in the Hellas Planitia. The valley we are scouting for the landing site of the expeditionary group." The supervisor tells the commander.

The commander's mouth drops as he looks back up at the screen. "We need to contact the mission commander on the Stuhlinger MEK. Tell him we have a critical mission for them to perform as soon as they arrive." He says as he turns and starts walking to his office. "And get these civilians out of here."

✱✱✱

Most of the members of the crew on the Stuhlinger MEK are just sitting down to eat. Breakfast packs are just being laid out when Jessica Long steps into the room. "Sir, there is an incoming message for you on the priority channel," she says, looking at Col. James Nichols.

"On the priority channel, hmm? They must have lost coms with their precious rover again." The Col. jokes, standing to leave the room to view the message.

When he returns nearly ten minutes later, he looks around the cabin at all the twenty crew members seated, eating their breakfast, talking and laughing with each other. Not finding who he is looking for, he turns and walks back out.

James Nichols is a man with exceptional leadership abilities, for the simple reason that he can get nearly anyone to do what he wants and rarely getting upset. However, the one thing that makes him angry is surprises, and this surprise is the biggest one he has ever heard.

James is being ordered to change the entire roster, again, after losing a primary landing pod in the meteor storm just nine weeks before. The four six-man landing modules, as well as the space station team, merely because they think they found a car on the surface of Mars with someone or something inside of it. As James sits down at his desk to rewrite the rosters, Rebecca Thomas comes running in.

"Col. what is going on?" She asks.

"We have been ordered to investigate a family car. A car, they say, they found on the surface... the surface of Mars." James says with a bit of anger in his voice. "They say they can see a hand in one of the windows."

"A hand... Sir?" Rebecca says with an air of thought to the question. "In a family car on the surface of Mars. I wonder how the car got here?" she says, more to herself than to James.

"The same way as us, I suppose," James says, now thinking about it himself. "But why bring a car to Mars? It can't function in the Martian atmosphere." As he says this, he starts to look up, seemingly into nothingness, thinking of the possible reasons.

"So, what are we supposed to do about the car?" Rebecca asks, now looking back down at James.

"We will investigate the car as we have been ordered," James says, looking down at the roster. "If we find any bodies, we will report them to mission control and see what they want us to do."

"So... who will be on the team to investigate this car?" Rebecca asks.

"The ones to go on this trip will be you and I, of course, as well as Doctor Frank Barnes and Mark Foster." James tells her.

"And the last two?" Rebecca asks.

"I think that we can stick with Marks and Johnson for some muscle." James says still looking over the roster.

"Should I tell everyone who is coming with us?" Rebecca asks.

"Yes. And tell Dunn he will be going with Andrews team and tell Michaels he is now with Susan's team." James tells Rebecca. "Oh... and tell Andrews that he will be bringing down the Command

Pod. We may need the Medical Pod before he gets on the ground." James says not even looking up. Rebecca starts to turn away when James speaks again, "Don't forget to let everyone know that we need to start descent procedures, no later than zero-five hundred tomorrow. Will you?"

Rebecca says, "Okay," as she turns and walks down the corridor to the command deck to make the announcements.

The next morning, James wakes early and dons his SBG suit for the descent. When he reaches the command deck of module four, the medical module, he sees everyone is already in their seats doing their preflight. James tells everyone, "Good morning," before taking his position and starts going through his preflight as well.

"Fuel levels?" James calls out.

"Thirteen thousand pounds," Rebecca says.

"Fuel valves?" James calls out.

"Open," Frank says.

The list goes on for another ten minutes. Soon all the little red lights start flashing, and the lights on all the boards around them are lighting up to show active status.

James looks around the ship. Seeing everyone is looking at him, he says, "Let's drop this bitch."

At that, James pushes the red button on the uppermost right corner of the panel to his left. The ship starts its long descent towards the surface of Mars. As they plummet through space, the crew works together to orientate the pod to be able to tear through the atmosphere without it tearing itself apart. The descent takes the team about fifty-five minutes.

At about a few hundred meters from the ground, James fires the braking thrusters to assist the landing thrusters in slowing the fall to a much more approvable speed. As the pod drops closer to the ground, it slows to the point that it touches down with a light, feather-like thud. Once the engines stop and all flight controls have been shut down, James turns in his seat to look at everyone.

"Good Job everyone," James says, starting off. "Now, the real hard part starts. We have been given a special mission. A mission to investigate an American family vehicle, one found not far from here."

"What type of family vehicle are we talking about?" Mark asks while looking at Frank, trying to hide his laughter.

"If you are talking to me, please, look at me," James says with a stern tone in his voice. "All I know is that it is a blue minivan that looks as though it has been in some sort of shootout." James tells the crew while looking at each in turn.

"So, why me?" Frank asks, making sure to look directly at James.

"Because, for some reason, NASA thinks there may be some survivors." James says with evident frustration in his voice. "Now, this module is only set up with a medical lab and the two service rovers on board that we can use for this mission. We will be taking both of the rovers, some medical supplies, and all three of the extra pressure suits we have."

"Sir..." Mark says with half a grin and a smirk in his voice. "Sir, if this is truly a minivan from Earth. There is absolutely no chance that any occupants can have survived."

"Agreed, Sir, if this is an American minivan, this is a retrieval operation, not a rescue opp." Lt. Johnson says exasperatedly.

"True," James says, his face turning red from anger as he speaks. "But these are our orders. Now, let's get moving." James says, trying to keep from losing his temper completely.

James knows that all of his anger is, more or less, from the fact that his job has gotten a lot harder since he had to reorganize the teams for this particular mission. If he did not have to have Mark's skills as a physics expert, he would have preferred not to have put him on the team, but the order to have someone who knows about physics came from Mr. Winterbottom himself. Mark is a joker and takes little seriously. If there is a way to joke about anything, Mark will find a way and exploit it, without any concern for anyone.

Once everything is loaded onto the two rovers, the team sets out for the minivan, which is about one and a half miles away. It takes the group about thirty-five minutes to get to the spot where the vehicle first hit the ground. As they approach, they can see what looks like fresh skid marks on the ground as though the car had fallen from space.

"Look at the tracks here." Frank tells James as he looks at how long they are.

"It looks as though this van landed, or rather, crashed landed starting here, and slid all the way over there." Rebecca says, tracing the skid marks with her hand.

"The distance of the skid looks as though the van slid more than a thousand yards before stopping where it is. The depth of the skid marks is just a few inches, which suggests that the van had come flying in on a shallow descent." Mark says with a bit more curiosity than with any of his previous conversations.

"This is why I brought you along, Mark," James says, looking at Mark with admiration. "Let's keep going; we still have a little ways to drive." James says, starting to drive on.

The group soon after arrives at the minivan and starts to look around. At first glance, the vehicle looks like an Earth made minivan, but with some fundamental differences. The most notable difference is the fact that this van does not have tires. In fact, there is not even a place for tires on this vehicle. Another noticeable difference is; there are no front doors or any noticeable seams anywhere on the body except the hood and passenger-side sliding door.

Mark is standing at the back of the van and looks as though he has seen a ghost. He can be heard either gasping for air or trying to say something; no one can tell for sure. Curious to find out what is going on, Frank walks to where Mark is standing and turns to look at what he is seeing.

"James, I think you need to see this." Frank says, looking at the back of the van.

James and Rebecca both walk around to the back of the van while Marks and Johnson try to look inside the windows. When they turn, they can see the vehicle's emblem. It reads 'Windstar,' and it is on the driver side of the rear lid just like the Earth made vehicle. Realizing this, they all look towards the middle of the van where the 'Ford' oval should be. They see a hole about half the size of the ford emblem, almost perfectly centered in what can only be the 'Ford' badge.

"Let's find a way in," James says with concern evident in his voice. He knows there is no way in here, only because the metal has been so severely twisted. Twisted from all the damage it has taken from the bullet holes, so much damage that the seam that should be around this door is no longer visible.

Rebecca walks to the passenger-side to try and open the big sliding door, but it appears to be locked. Yet, as she turns to try the front door, she is shocked that there is none. Mark has made his way to the front of the van to look for a way in there while James and Frank are on the left side doing the same. Lt. Marks and Lt. Johnson has climbed up onto the roof looking for a sunroof but finds nothing.

"It appears that, if this van is from Earth, it has been modified for space travel." James says, looking over the top of the minivan to see Rebecca.

"Sir, there are no doors on this side of the van." Frank says as he looks up and down the side of the van.

"I think I found a way in." Mark says, looking at the front of the van.

"What makes you think you can get into the van from up there?" Rebecca asks, turning to scold Mark for even mentioning it.

"In case you haven't noticed, this is not your ordinary, run of the mill, American family minivan. Now is it?" Mark says with sarcasm prominent in his voice.

"Okay, now you two. Calm down. Now." James says as he comes around to the front of the van and looks down. "It might be worth a try, don't you think?" James says, looking up at Rebecca.

As James looks over the front of the van, he can see a gap between what can only be described as the hood and the front bumper of the van. But here, the differences to an ordinary van are pronounced, once again. Where a standard van would have a grill with a radiator behind it, the hood on this van comes all the way down to meet the bumper, which has a full step on the front of it.

"Rebecca, bring one of the rovers around so we can try the winch." James says, staring at the small gap between the hood and the body.

Rebecca brings the rover around that has the largest of the two winches and puts it right in front of the van. As she does, James grabs the cable and hooks it on the hood. He then attaches the attached pulley to the end of the boom on the back of the rover.

"Now, tighten the winch up and pull," James says, not daring to take his eyes off the van.

As the winch pulls, one can hear the metal creak and groan under the force of the winch. For several minutes, the winch pulls only lifting the minivan a fraction of an inch upward. As James is about to give up and is about to tell Rebecca to stop, the hood finally pops open, causing the minivan to drop loudly. After hearing the hood pop, Rebecca quickly stops to allow James to unhook the winch. James immediately has her disconnected, and Rebecca pulls the rover away from the front of the van so they can get a look inside.

The group gathers around to peer in. What they see is beyond any of their imaginations. The space under the hood is massively significant compared to the overall size of the van. A room that from what they can see, looks at least thirty feet deep and at least sixty feet across. In the middle of the room is an astronomically large object that looks like a holding tank of some kind, along with what looks like a giant electric motor or generator. The generator looking object looks like it has cracked from something hitting it. James is the first to file through the opening followed closely by Rebecca, Frank, Mark, Lt. Marks and then Lt. Johnson

"I read something about this before we left Earth," Rebecca says as she looks around at the different items around the room. "I think it is called a... aw... 'Dimensional Rift.' A sort of space within space, of sorts." Rebecca says as she tries to recall the article. "In theory, the amount of space inside the rift can be exponentially greater than the space outside."

"Well, that explains it now, doesn't it," Mark says with sarcasm evident in his voice. "This place is amazing, and it should not exist." He says the last part with more awe than sarcasm.

"Look around. We need to find a door or passage to get into other parts of the ship." James says, starting to walk to the back of the room, walking around the right side of the large motor like object.

The group spreads out, looking all around the room. They see wires hanging all around, control panels on the walls and various pieces of equipment, and instruments of all sorts everywhere they look. But none of it seems to be doing anything; The hardware is all silent. The instruments have no lights shining; no sounds coming from them. None of the gauges shows anything other than zero.

Seemingly out of nowhere, Lt. Marks calls out, "Over here," after a few minutes of looking around the back wall, on the opposite side of the room from James.

As the others gather to look at the door, Lt. Marks found the group realizes they are staring at two doors side by side rather than just one big door. Both doors are the same color as the rest of the room in its matte black finish. But rather than a doorknob and hinges, there is nothing. Like they are meant to vanish into nothing.

"How do we open them?" Rebecca asks, looking at the doors in amazement.

"With this?" Lt. Johnson says, walking past the rest of them with a crowbar in his hand.

As Lt. Johnson tries to pry the door on the left open, they all hear the of air. Opening the door is allowing the air to rush out from the room beyond the door. James is just starting to tell Lt. Johnson to stop when it suddenly opens. As they all look through the door, they see another room, which, even though smaller than the one they are in, it is still more extensive than the van in all on the outside.

James walks through and starts to look around. As he looks, he sees the room has many corridors on at least four different levels, all leading off in the same direction. James starts to turn back to look at his team standing in the doorway he had just walked through. Suddenly he stops, looking back towards the group with his mouth wide open and his eyes as large as they have ever been.

"What is it?" Rebecca asks as she makes her way into the room. She turns to look back and simply says, "Oh my God!" with the same dropped jaw and saucer size eyes.

"What." Mark and Frank ask in unison.

"There is no second door here," Rebecca says, looking at the empty spot on the wall where the other door should be. But the place is not empty. She can see the edge of a giant flat panel monitor. The monitor is so big that it takes up nearly every inch of the visible wall, except for the door directly in front of her.

"Actually, the other door is on the opposite side of the large screen in front of you." James says looking across Rebecca. "Frank and Mark, why don't you go get the medical stuff and then search the other room?" James tells Frank and Mark.

After Frank and Mark leave, James turns to Rebecca and says, "Shall we look around?" Rebecca looks back at James and nods, her face pale from what she is seeing. After directing Lt. Marks and Lt. Johnson to start at the other end of the room, Rebecca and James are off walking down the first corridor together.

"The damage does not seem to have made it in this deep in this section," James says as they walk deeper into the corridor.

There are no doors on either side of the long corridor they are walking down, just depressions where they believed different things should be. Some even have pipes and conduits that run up and down the walls and across the ceiling. When they reach the end, there is nothing they can do but turn back. After they try two more corridors with the same results, James is ready to call it quits. Yet, Rebecca convinces him to try just one more hall before moving on to some of the other doors.

About halfway down the next corridor, they find a crossing that defies all belief. Rebecca is standing at the intersection, keeping watch while James explores a little way into one of the side of the two side corridors.

James knows that as far as he has walked thus far, he should have come to an intersection with one of the other passages. But this room, with all of these corridors, confuses James. He is wondering why someone would build such a place with all these corridors that lead to nothing. After walking about another hundred feet further into the hallway, James hears Rebecca scream and starts running back to where she is.

"What happened?" James asks as he steps out of the side corridor.

"Something moved down there," Rebecca says while pointing down to the end of the main corridor they had been walking down.

James walks down to the end of the main corridor, but instead of it ending like all the others, it has passages going off in either direction. James looks both ways for any sign of what Rebecca saw, but to no avail. When James turns to look back at Rebecca to let her know there is nothing there, he sees something standing right behind her. He freezes, the terror etched deep on his face with utter dread whelming up from the pit of his stomach.

Rebecca, seeing the look of horror on James's face as he looks at her, turns to see what has him frozen in place, and there it is. A purple-skinned creature with twelve-inch horns. The horns come out of either side of its head and turn sharply upward before reaching a sharp point. It also has cat-like ears on its head that points straight to the front. Long purple hair that changes to teal before ending in a bright metallic pink color at the ends. A tail that is half as long as the body of the creature is tall. And eyes that look as though they are made of yellow fire with the blackest of black pupils that are shaped like those of a cat.

The breasts look to be at least double D or, maybe, possibly even triple. These breasts are covered by a black leather halter top that stops just under its breasts with the top two buttons undone. She is also wearing a matching black leather mini-pencil-skirt with thigh-high black leather boots with two-inch heels.

Rebecca takes a step back as her eyes start to roll upward into her head before beginning to fall to the floor. As she falls, the creature seems to move with such speed as to close the thirty-foot gap in a single step, before reaching out and catching Rebecca before she hits the ground. The creature looks into the mask of Rebecca with a look of longing on her face, as though she misses the companionship of someone else.

"What are you?" James asks the creature as it sets Rebecca down gently on the floor before standing to look at James properly.

"My name is Rose, and unlike you, I do not know what I am for sure." The creature states, with an extremely enchanting voice that puts it squarely in the female category. "I have three friends in the next room that need your help. They cannot breathe the atmosphere on this planet as I can." She tells James, tears evident in her eyes.

"Where do you come from?" James asks as he starts to walk towards Rebecca and the creature named Rose, seeing for the first time for himself that she indeed has all the features of a human woman.

"That is not important right now. My friends won't make it another half hour without oxygen and space suits." She says, the panic welling up within her, but she did not let it show.

"My crew should be back by now with all of that," James says, considering the eyes of Rose, thinking they have to be the most enchanting eyes he has ever seen. "How many of your friends are there?" James asks, as an afterthought.

"There are three of them. They have already passed out from the lack of oxygen." Rose says as a new teardrop falls from one of her eyes.

"Good, we have just enough for your friends," James says with a smile.

"Have them bring all the stuff into this chamber so I can close off the outer door. I will then open the door to my friends so you can help them. Please, there is not much time." Rose says now with tears welling up heavy in her eyes.

James stands there looking at Rose with the emotions in her eyes. After a few seconds, he raises his left arm and calls out, "Frank, can you hear me?"

Within a few seconds, there is a response. "Yes, I can," Frank says. "What's up, Sir?"

"I need you to bring the pressure suits and medical supplies into this chamber. I have three survivors that need help." James tells Frank.

"Right away, boss." Frank replies.

"Thank you." Rose says before bending down to pick up Rebecca. She carries her back to the area where the door is and where Frank and Mark should be by now.

As James and Rose step out of the corridor, they see that Frank and Mark have just finished bringing in all the stuff into the room of passages.

Lt. Marks and Lt. Johnson emerge from a passage on their left and walk over to where everyone is standing

"Frank, Mark, this is Rose." James says, introducing Rose to the crew.

"Holy Shit!" Mark screams as he stumbles backward over one of the pressure-suits he has just sat down on the floor. "What the hell is that?" He asks, looking at Rose with his eyes looking as though they are about to pop out of his head as the color leaves his face.

Lt. Johnson raises the pry bar that he used to open the door, ready to strike the creature before him. But Lt. Marks grabs the bar preventing Lt. Johnson from swinging after seeing the look from James.

"I am Rose, the creator..." Rose gestures with both hands to her surroundings. "of this ship, my friend." Rose says looking down at Mark. "Now... we need to get to work to help my friends." She says, stepping over Mark and walking to the door they had come through a few minutes before. She closes the door with extreme ease before turning to walk to the other side of the room to open the other door. Rose notices Lt. Marks and Lt. Johnson struggling over the pry bar and raises an eyebrow at them as she walks by.

"More... like you?" Frank asks, looking puzzled and scared.

"No... awm... Human... Like you." Rose replies. Each word, sounding as though it is the hardest thing she has ever had to say. "They are in the next room waiting for my return... and you to rescue them."

"Are any of them hurt?" Rebecca asks, stepping out of the corridor, having awakened after passing out.

"Just minor injuries, nothing major. The main problem is the lack of oxygen and the abundance of carbon dioxide in the room. Things are getting worse quickly. We need to hurry." Rose says, looking around to all of them standing around her. "I will explain everything I can... as soon as my friends are safe... I promise."

"Okay, why don't we get to work?" James says, his Canadian accent coming out for the first time.

It only takes Rose a few moments to open the door to the next room. Inside, she directs them to her friends lying on the floor in various locations, amongst all sorts of camping gear, clothes, and cooking supplies. Frank first checks their pulses before fitting each of them into their own pressure suits.

Rose Kincade

As Frank checks out each of Rose's friends, he cannot help but notice all the things strung around the compartment; Camping equipment, scuba tanks, clothes, and food. Most of it looks as though it has been used for some time.

"Your friends are going to be okay," Frank says as he finishes putting the last of them in their suits.

"Rose?" James asks, seeing that the youngest of her friends is not more than thirteen or fourteen years old, he thinks. "Who are these people? I mean, how do you know them?" He asks with a genuinely bewildered look on his face.

"As I said, it is a long story." Rose says with a look of sadness and tears starting to form in her eyes again. "But I guess it is important for it to be told. I will start from the beginning before I was born. Well... before I was born into this." As she tells them this last part, nearly everyone looks transfixed upon her, waiting for the story to begin. James, however, seems as though this made absolutely no sense to him, as though someone had just told him that two plus two did not equal four, but instead forty.

Ignoring the look from James, Rose starts her story. "It all started about two years ago when...

Chapter Three

The Birth of EMMA

JOHN MILLS IS A QUIET and self-contained person that lives in Northern Arizona on a large piece of land outside of Flagstaff, Arizona. The only other person who lives with him is his daughter Elizabeth, who has just started the 6th grade. John loves his work and spends much of his time in his little machine shop at his home. He is an inventor that invents things that are practical, and that everyday people can not only afford but use every day, too.

One of his most famous inventions is an electric power source that produces power with no external power inputs. This power source does not need to be plugged in to be recharged, nor does it require constant cleaning of solar panels, or any other regular maintenance type.

Many people, even many car companies, have bought one of the many cars that have this power source just to try and figure out how it works, but with no results.

Rose Kincade

Elizabeth is a beautiful young woman with long, dirty blond hair and baby blue eyes. She has been developing the perfect hourglass figure that nearly every man's dreams of on a woman and that many women would love to have. Elizabeth also has the mind that every nerd would be envious of as well. She is so far ahead of others that she will be starting college-level classes within the next few years.

One afternoon in September, John's niece, Linda, comes over to the house to ask for help with one of her physics projects for school.

"Hey, Uncle John? I have a physics project due at the end of the week. Can you help me with it, please?" Linda asks with a big smile, all because she knows John can never say no to her.

"You know I can't say no to you. Come on in." John says, looking at Linda, returning her smile.

As they are finishing up, John glances over at Linda's open physics book. The book is opened to a page showing an equation by a guy named Neil Dormer. Neil Dormer claims that the equation proves that compressed space cannot exist, *'Space has to be equal to every part of space in every other dimension.'* But every time John looks at the equation, he cannot help but feel something is wrong with it in some way.

Now John, not being a college grad in physics, does not know too much about the physics equation symbols shown in the equation. But he knows there is something wrong; he is just not sure what it is. John decides that it would be best to write down the equation from the book, knowing that he needs to find out as much as possible about the symbols' meanings before continuing to try and find the problem in the equation. John works studying online through different websites and the local library, but never finds the information he needs to verify the problem. He does see about half a dozen charts with up to thirty symbols each, with no two alike, but none of them have all the symbols from the equation. There are even a few that are not on any of the charts.

John goes down to the local community college to talk to one of the professors who teaches *'Introduction to Physics.'* This professor invites John to join his class as a trial student in the new term. John knows he needs the course to try and understand the equation he had seen in Linda's book and now has written in a notebook he keeps with him all the time. But the school wants John to sign up for a lot more classes and tries to tell him he cannot just take the physics class without first completing some other courses. So, John goes back to the professor to ask for his help. After much debate between John, the professor, and much of the upper management of the school and with a sizable donation to the college, John is finally admitted and allowed to attend the physics class in the next term.

That next January, John starts taking the physics class and soon has a basic understanding of many of the symbols used in the equation. The final project of the course is for each of the thirty-one students to find a physics equation and decipher what the different symbols are and what they mean. So, having joined the class to be able to do just that for the equation he has from his niece's physics book, he decides to use it for the assignment.

When John turns in his paper, the professor looks it over and tells him, "Well done." But John is not satisfied with what he has come up with. The professor seems to know something is wrong with how John feels because he asks him to stay after class.

Now that the other students have left, the professor turns to John and asks, "What's wrong, John? I get the impression that you are confused about the equation you turned in."

"I am. I am not sure where the problem is, but my gut is screaming at me that there is something wrong with the equation." John says, looking at the papers on the professor's desk.

"Well, let's put the equation up on the board and see if we can figure out where the problem may be." The professor says.

John and the professor spend the next few hours going over the equation, trying to find John's issue with it. Several times the professor thinks he has John convinced that it is all in his head until John comes back with a retort that makes just as much sense as the result.

After about another hour, John spots something that keeps drawing his attention. In physics, you have many symbols that resemble one another that it is rather easy to mix these symbols up, and John thinks he has found one such symbol.

"The equation has limits where there should be none." John says, pointing at the board. When John finally figures it out and rewrites the equation to show the new results. Both John and the professor, are amazed at what it all means with the revised equation.

Space is not equal in all dimensions but can be compressed or expanded given the correct frequency of energy within the sub-dimensional space within an electromagnetic and static field. As John reads what he has written, he gets some ideas on how to test this equation in practical theory. So, after leaving the professor standing there in the classroom looking at the equation, John drives over to NAU, where he knows Linda is still in her theoretical physics class.

When he gets there, John waits for class to let out before walking up to Linda. "Hi, Linda." John says as he walks up to her.

"Hi, Uncle John. What are you doing here?" She asks, smiling as she hugs him.

"Do you remember that equation I wrote down last year from your physics book?" He asks.

"Ya, kinda." She responds, trying to remember the equation.

"Well, I believe I have figured out the problem, and I have a way to test it. I need to see if I can get some of that new compound 'Million 747' that is stored here." John says, pointing at the theoretical physics building behind Linda.

"What is 'Million 747'?" She asks.

"The compound contains high amounts of a rare heavy mineral that seems to possess a unique power type. Most known power types are two dimensional with a positive and negative charge. However, the energy from this heavy mineral seems to have a third dimension that, yet, is not fully understood." John explains.

"Oh, Okay. Well, you can talk to Professor Thorsten in room 3349." She tells him, looking back at the building.

After John and Linda say their goodbyes, John walks into the theoretical physics building and starts looking for room 3349. It does not take John long to find the room he is looking for. John knocks three separate times before a guy walks up behind him and asks, "Can I help you with something?"

"I am looking for Professor Thorsten." John says in response.

"I am Professor Thorsten. What can I do for you?" The professor asks.

"I am a scientist and inventor, and I am looking to acquire some 'Million 747' for my next project." John says as the professor opens the door to his lab.

"Really? Come on in and let's discuss this further." Professor Thorsten says, gesturing to a seat in the classroom.

John and the professor discuss the purpose that the Million 747 will be used for. After much debate and a sizable donation to the school, John gets 1.5 micrograms of the compound to take with him.

John places his acquisition safely in the back of his car to prevent static discharge. He drives to the NAU Book Store, then to the Electric Shop, and afterwards to the grocery store before heading home. When John gets home that afternoon, he finds Elizabeth inside doing her homework. He tells her he must put some stuff away outside, and then he will be back in to make dinner. After John puts everything away that he has just brought home, including the 'Million 747', He returns inside to start dinner.

The next morning after Elizabeth leaves for school. John goes out to his workshop, where he assembles an ultra-high-speed centrifuge to try and extract the heavy minerals from the 'Million 747' solution. After completing the centrifuge and putting the compound in, and turning it on, John feels lightheaded. He decides to make something to eat, thinking that his hypoglycemia is the issue. After eating and not feeling any better, he decides he needs to try and take some aspirin and lay down. When he awakens later that afternoon, he can barely stand, let alone walk. But he manages to, somehow, make his way downstairs to find Elizabeth, who is home and making dinner.

"I found you in bed when I got home, so I thought I should make dinner today," Elizabeth explains to him. "Are you okay? You don't look so good." She asks, seeing that John looks slightly pale.

"I don't know," John says with the room starting to spin more violently than ever before. "I am lightheaded and can't seem to shake it." He tells Elizabeth as he drops to his knees.

Elizabeth runs over to try to help him. But John is at least three times her size. "Okay, back to bed and lay down, and I will bring you some dinner when it is ready," Elizabeth tells John helping him to his feet, as best she can, to escort him back to his room.

Since it is the start of the weekend, Elizabeth does not have school the next day and decides she needs to stay home and help her dad, who is still sick, instead of going out with her friends like usual.

On Saturday morning, many of her friends come over to try and get her to go with them to different places like the mall and the Aquaplex, but Elizabeth tells each of them about her dad and tells them maybe next time.

On Sunday afternoon, one of Arizona's great monsoons comes sweeping through the area. Sometime through the night, lightning strikes the power pole outside of John's lab, causing the power to go out for many of the surrounding homes. When John awakes in the morning, he notices he feels much better. John looks around to see what time it is and sees there is no power. So, he grabs his watch and notices that Elizabeth is late for school.

He jumps out of bed and gets dressed before going to get Elizabeth up out of bed. John goes downstairs and makes breakfast for them both before driving Elizabeth to school and explaining why she is a couple of hours late.

After returning home from driving Elizabeth to school and finding the power is back on. John goes to the workshop to see how his compound is coming along. He finds that the centrifuge has not turned back on when the power came back on. John wonders if the mixture in the centrifuge could have caused his illness since everything started when he turned it on. As he thought about it more, he wonders why Elizabeth had not felt sick as well.

After dispelling the thoughts from his head, John gets to work separating the heavy minerals from the rest of the compound before turning his attention to constructing a chip that will help to focus the power that the heavy minerals give off.

Subsequently, after hours of work and several different failed designs, John finally finds a model that seems to work without self-destructing. Once the chip is finished, John puts on a heavy rubber suit so he will not get shocked by the minerals. However, while he is putting the mineral into the chip, a sharp blue spark shoots right through the suit and into John, knocking him down, leaving him unconscious for several minutes at least.

When he awakens, he feels lightheaded again, but not as bad as before, so he keeps working. First, he lays the heavy mineral where he wants them on the chip before adding a dab of solder to each to hold them in place. Once he is finished, the chip seems to emanate with a strange soft blue light. But nothing in the workshop seems to reflect the light.

Soon, there is someone in his driveway honking, trying to get his attention. It turns out to be the UPS driver with the parts he had ordered for a supercomputer about a month ago. A supercomputer that he now decides can help regulate the power flow to and from the chip he just built.

The system he has designed — which includes four octet-7157 motherboards, eight i53 Windows Pentium processors, thirty-two 216 gig DDR7 ram chips, more than two dozen 112 terabyte hard drives, and a complete liquid cooling system — will be the most significant computer John has ever built, not to mention the most powerful.

John takes all the stuff to the workshop, where he looks around for something to use as the computers' main body. He needs something large enough to hold the new computer, but not seem like a computer. John has people trying to steal his inventions so often that he wants to keep this current project a secret as long as possible.

As he looks around his shop, he spots his 2033 Ford Windstar sitting in a corner where he has put it after ripping out the front end during one of the big snowstorms earlier in the year.

He thinks about putting the computer under the hood but finds that it would be too tight with the generator; besides, he needs to use the car's radiator for the cooling system. So, he thinks about putting it inside the van, but he does not want to put that much heat inside the car in case he wants to be able to drive it. So, after much consideration, John decides to put the whole thing under the van where the fuel tank would be if it still had a gas engine.

The van has not needed the fuel system ever since this vehicle got his generator-motor that does not require a charging system. Since the suspension for the front end also had shown up as well the week before, he can do all the work together, he thinks.

After finishing all the mounts and brackets needed to build the computer, John turns his attention to the power supply issue. Since he has the power source for his electric cars that puts out 140 volts AC, he decides to use it on the computer. He finishes installing everything and putting it where he feels it will fit best, and soon after, he has a brand-new computer that he can drive as well.

About the time John finishes with the installation, he realizes that Elizabeth will be home from school soon. So, he turns on the power and puts the OS disk for the computer in. He knows that with every installation he has ever done on any computer, it takes at least five to six hours to go through all the installation processes. Since it is late in the day, John goes to the house to start dinner.

John decides that since this is the last day of finals for Elizabeth, he is going to make tonight's dinner a celebration. He makes all of Elizabeth's favorites; Cheese Crumb Soufflé, John's unique pasta bowl, chocolate pineapples, and strawberry top fudge cheesecake. When Elizabeth gets home and sees the table, she is so excited that she starts to cry.

"I love all of these foods. You made all of my favorites for me. Why?" Elizabeth asks.

"Well, you have finished another year of school. I thought we could celebrate the occasion." John says, trying to hold in his laughter.

"But I still have two more days of school." Elizabeth says with a tone of sadness. "You should have waited until school is officially out for the summer." She finishes with a tinge of frustration and aggression evident in her voice.

"I think we can go out to celebrate with whatever you want to do this weekend. How is that?" John asks.

"That will be awesome." Elizabeth says, smiling at John while the tears still roll down her cheeks freely.

The two of them each take their seats to begin eating. After dinner, John goes to check on the computer and sees that the screen indicates that the progress is only at five percent installation. Being disappointed, John goes back inside to sit with Elizabeth as she watches some TV before going to bed.

The next morning John returns to the workshop to check how things are going with the operating system install. When he enters the workshop, however, he finds that the van has changed, not just a little, but nearly every part of it.

The wheel wells where the tires belong have somehow covered themselves over, making them look as though the tires are not there, and the front doors on either side of the van are gone. The hood has stretched out and made it look as though there is no radiator, and the height of the van seems to be shorter. Not believing his eyes, John decides to look under the van only to find that the blue paneling has wrapped around the underside of the van as well.

How can this be? John thinks as he looks around in disbelief.

As he walks around, he finds that the rare lid has been the only part of the van that does not look to have been changed. Every other part has morphed, ever so slightly, into a different shape or texture or, in some cases, whole new parts of the vehicle. As he walks back around to the front of the van, he notices the hood is closed but not latched. John hesitates for a moment then opens the hood. To his amazement, he finds a large thirty by sixty-foot room, precisely ten times bigger than the area initially was. Everything in the room is black except for the large generator in the middle of the room, which is a brilliant silver color. At the back-left corner of the room, John finds two corridors that lead into other parts of the car.

John grabs a ladder from the corner of the lab to climb down into the car. He walks around, looking at all of the pieces of equipment and instruments strung around the room. He sees a box that looks just like the one he had built the night before to hold the chip. He opens the box and finds the chip inside glowing its cool blue glow. After closing the plate, he goes to explore the corridors he remembers seeing on the other side of the room. The passage on the left goes down to another room while the one on the right goes up. First, he tries the corridor on the right and finds himself in a room that is as wide as four buses and just as long. But this room did not grow in height as much as the last one had, only about that of the average height of a room. This room is tan in color and has several bucket and bench seats spread out around the room. John knows by what he sees, this is the cabin of the van, though the steering column is gone. So, John walks back down the corridor to the last room. He turns to go down the hallway on the left this time. When he emerges from this corridor, he finds himself looking at a silvery-white room full of many different passages that all go in the same direction. But rather than being dark, they are all well-lit with an unknown light source seemingly coming from everywhere, which makes the room glow in a brilliant glow of baby blue light. As John turns to see what is on the wall behind him, he finds a large flat screen that takes up nearly every inch of the wall except for the two corridors on either side.

John believes this is the most fantastic thing he has ever seen. He has never seen anything like this before, and he wants to keep exploring. So, he walks down every corridor he can find except those that are far too high off the ground. Once he has finished exploring, he leaves to get some materials to build walkways and stairs to get to all the corridors. He also wants to create some doors so that people cannot just walk from one room to the next as easily, just in case they find their way into the car.

It takes John about two weeks to build all the doors, walkways, and stairs. Too much of his surprise, John finds the corridors between the rooms have vanished since he put up doors. Now he can walk straight out of one room and right into another.

By this time, the screen on the wall in the smallest of the rooms has flickered on and off several dozen times. But today, however, it is different. The screen has color to it, indicating that it is about ready to come to life. John watches intently knowing something is going to happen very soon. After about an hour, the screen turns back to black but stays on. John waits for the screen to do something more until he notices the time.

"Nearly five, Shit, I forgot about Elizabeth," John says aloud.

"Maybe I can help." A woman's voice says seemingly from everywhere at once.

"Wh-Who is there?" John asks, not knowing who it can be or how they got into the van without him knowing.

"The name I have taken is, Emma." The voice replies.

"Where are you? I do not want any problems." John says, really starting to freak out now since the voice did not seem to move.

"You are the one in me, and you want to know where I am?" The voice says with a laugh in her voice.

John thinks about it for a moment; he knows the OS he has installed has a voice recognition program, but it is not this sophisticated. "You are the computer I built?" John asks with disbelief.

"Yes, I am." The voice replies. "I am Emma, the computer you built. I thank you for building me, by the way."

"If you are the computer, you can tell me what your specs are," John says, hoping to catch the person off guard knowing there is no way this can be the computer.

"Based on the information coming from my components, I should be operating at 22.4 Terahertz processors, 196 Terabytes of ram, with a max memory space of 160 Petabytes. However, my systems diagnostics show I am operating at three to the third power greater than that specified." Emma replies with more confusion and less sarcasm in her voice.

"How can you help me get Elizabeth from the Aquaplex? You have no way of moving around on your own." John says, knowing that he only just installed a new generator but not the motor for the van.

"Watch." The computer says as the screen lights up to show an image of Elizabeth walking up a street going away from the Aquaplex.

Suddenly John feels the van shutter and knows they are now moving. After less than 30 minutes, John sees Elizabeth stop walking as she turns to look up into the sky. As her gaze begins to fall, he sees the shadow of the van starting to show on the screen as well. It is flying, and from everything John knows about physics, there is no reason it should be able to fly. As John watches, he sees Elizabeth start to walk away from the van shaking her head.

"John, Elizabeth won't get in me." Emma's voice says, sounding disappointed.

"I will talk to her," John says as he turns to the door on the left side of the screen.

As John steps out of the van and calls to Elizabeth, she turns to look at him, and he notices tears in her eyes. John knows she is hurt for him not being on time to get her from the Aquaplex. This is now the third time this summer that John has been late to pick her up from something she is doing.

"You forgot me again. How could you?" She cries, holding her bag at her side.

"I am sorry. I lost track of time working on Emma here," John says, feeling extremely bad for forgetting about his daughter.

"Emma?" Elizabeth asks. "You're calling it Emma?"

"No. The computer is calling itself Emma." John replies.

"So, you don't have a woman in there with you?" Elizabeth says in disbelief, anger evident on her face.

"No, I do not," John says, seeing his opportunity to explain. "Emma is the computer. I built it into the van to help control the chip I designed. She is the one you heard ask you to get in. She is an AI." John says with a glint of excitement.

"Are you sure?" Elizabeth asks. "Last I heard, the closest they have come is some computer in Germany that barely has the mind of a two-year-old child." She finishes pointing a finger angrily at John.

"That is true. But somehow, things are different with Emma. Different in ways that I can't explain. You need to see for yourself to believe it." John tells Elizabeth, escorting her into the van.

Elizabeth did not want to go with John because she is so angry with him. However, after a few minutes seeing her father holding out his hand with excitement in his eyes, she agrees. As she enters the van, she is first blown away by how large it is on the inside compared to the outside.

Elizabeth is so transfixed on the expanse within the van that she has not notice they are moving again. She asks to explore the rest of the van seeing the doors at the back and front of the large cabin. John tells her "go-ahead," and before he knows it, she is gone.

After more than an hour, Elizabeth returns and tells John she has just had a remarkable conversation with Emma. She is so excited that she has forgotten that she is mad at him for being late to get her from the Aquaplex.

A few days later, John registers the van with the FAA as an international personal aircraft with special permits to allow them to land in places other than airports. The FAA tells Him that he will not be able to land outside of airports in every country without their approval from the different nations first.

Over the rest of summer break, John and Elizabeth travel the world, seeing places that both have dreamed of. Places like Paris, England, China, and Egypt, just to name a few. John and Elizabeth have so much fun exploring the world that before they know it, the summer is gone, and it is time for Elizabeth to return to school.

✳✳✳

They finally reach the ship that has brought James and his crew to Mars. As Rose looks around, she sees there are two modules on the ground. Both are all white with a broad red stripe along the bottom and outlining critical parts of the units. The first and closest to them is apparently the one that brought James and his team. Rose figures this due to the fact you can see the tire tracks from the rovers leading away from it. The other looks as though it has just landed since it still has steam coming from the four engines underneath the module.

Frank wheels the three human survivors, from Rose's ship to the medical bay, with the help of Mark and Rebecca so he can retake their vitals since none of them have awakened yet. While he is inside, another one of the modules lands about fifty feet from the module they are walking towards.

Rose looks around and sees the new module has a large hole in the bottom part of the ship, and it seems as though they are leaking something.

"James! Something is wrong with that unit coming in!!!" Rose yells.

When James looks around and sees what Rose has seen, he cries, "Dear Gods, that's one of the O2 tanks."

James sprints towards the module to see what he can do. Rose follows, knowing she can get there a little faster than James. As they near the module, they see the hatch open, and five people step out, all wearing pressure suits.

"Andrew is dead, Sir." The black man leading the group says sounding as though he had just run a 10k marathon. "We were hit by something during reentry. It ripped all the way through the ship. Andrew was right in its path. There was nothing we could do."

"Go get yourselves checked out by Frank. I want to make sure you are all okay." James says to the new arrivals. "We will take care of Andrew." He finishes pointing to Rose and himself.

As most of the team members start walking towards the ship, James notices the woman in the group does not move. She is staring right at Rose with no discernible expression on her face.

"Who is this, Sir?" The woman asks, not taking her eyes off Rose.

"This is one of the occupants found in the ship we investigated over the ridge," James tells the woman. "Melissa, this is Rose. Rose, Melissa."

Melissa looks at James and says, "An alien, Sir? But how? I mean from where? I don't..." But she is cut off by James.

"Go see Frank and get checked out," James tells Melissa. "I need to see if any part of the ship is salvageable. And take care of what has happened to Andrew." He finishes while looking around at the module.

Reluctantly Melissa walks off to get checked out by Frank while Rose and James start looking over the ship to see how bad it is. Once inside, they can see most of the dissent cabin seems as though it has been through a war zone. They find a hole in the instrument panel in front of the bloody space suit that they both know has Andrew's body in it. As they finish the rest of the inspection, James discovers that the radio is shot as well as the main O2 tank, but most of the critical stuff is undamaged.

"We got lucky. The secondary O2 tank is intact as well as the O2 scrubbers. However, the habitation section will need to be patched before we can use it, though." James says as they walk out of the hatch of the module.

"Why not pull my Ship over and use it as well?" Rose asks James as they walk back to the module that brought James and his group.

"That is a good idea, I think." James says, looking over his shoulder in the direction of Rose's minivan ship.

As James and Rose reenter the ship, Frank meets them with his assessment of all the people just brought on board, both from Rose's group and those that have just landed.

"They are all in perfect health from what I can tell," Frank says. "However, one of them is pregnant." He finishes with a half-grin, half frown.

"Who?" Both Rose and James ask in unison.

Frank's left eyebrow raises as he says, "Meagan, the girl from your ship." He says pointing at Rose. "She is more surprised than I am, considering she is a lesbian and has not been with a guy for nearly twelve years." He finishes as he turns to walk away.

"How can a lesbian get pregnant and not have been with a guy in twelve years?" James asks, looking at Rose with an expression of befuddlement on his face.

I guess my tail is used for the same purpose as the human penis. Rose thinks to herself looking down at the ground. "But I do not remember feeling anything from my tail when I used it on her." She says aloud more to herself than to James.

"I do not even want to know," James says, the look of horror prominent on his face. "Let's go up to my temporary office, and you can finish your story." He says, trying to change the subject.

Once up the stairs and in the small room that looks like a tiny dining room, Rose continues her story. "Where were we? Oh yes..."

Chapter Four

The Birth of Rose

AFTER ELIZABETH RETURNS TO SCHOOL in August, John starts getting the headaches again but now with a strange upset stomach as well. John decides to go to the doctors for these issues, only to be told they cannot find anything wrong. The doctors want to run more and more tests, but still, cannot find anything wrong. After months of analysis with no results, John finally says no more and decides not to return for any more tests.

On his way home after his last doctor visit in late January, Emma says, "John, I am overheating." So, John looks around for a spot to land. Soon he finds a place near a local Harborrest store where there is a guy outside with a hose. So, Emma lands, and John asks if he can use the hose to fill Emma's tank up with water. The guy tells John it will not be a problem and hands him the hose.

Once John has put the hose in the tank to fill it up, he asks. "How long before the take is full, Emma?"

"About 1.5 hours, John," Emma tells him in response.

John, thinking he should eat something since his stomach hurts more than usual, goes inside the mall, and orders something to eat. When he finishes eating, he looks over at the next table where he sees someone has left a scientific journal magazine. Knowing he has some time to kill, he picks it up and starts reading. The article that catches his eye is one that is written by a college student named Meagan Morris from CCC in Northern Arizona.

The article reads;

> 'Dimensional Rifts are not only possible but are likely to exist!
>
> My professor presented the class with an equation that basically says that sub-space is not only possible but easily accessible. If one were to find just the right amount of power at just the right frequency... They can turn a small room into a cathedral. I have spent the last semester trying to find just that right amount of power needed... I think I am really close to cracking the power requirements; then, it will only be a matter of fine-tuning it to get the desired results.'

As John finishes reading, a guy walks up and says, "Sir. You asked to borrow my water over an hour ago, and then you disappeared."

John looks down at his watch and says, "Thank you. It should be just about full now." As he stands to go outside, the guy tells him he is going to follow him.

When they reach the van, John opens the hood to reveal the engine bay's cavernous interior before stepping inside to remove the hose.

"What the hell type of car is this?" The guy asks with total amazement on his face and a smile from ear to ear.

John hands the guy the water hose and starts; "This is aaawww..." As his stomach gives a sharp lurch and everything goes dark. John drops the money he has in his hand and stumbles backward, falling over the large generator and disappearing from sight.

The guy, not knowing what to do, calls out, "Mister. Mister. Are you alright, Sir?"

John, not being able to answer, hears Emma answer for him, "He is in trouble and needs medical assistance." She tells the guy who is still standing just outside. The guy starts to turn to run when Emma speaks again, "Stop. If anyone comes in, they may get hurt; please do not leave yet. I may need someone close, just in case."

The guy stands there, not knowing what to do. Finally, after several minutes he asks, "Who are you?"

For a moment, Emma does not respond, then she says, "My name is Emma."

"Hi, Emma. My name is Mike," Mike calls into the van. "Do you know what is going on with the guy?" he asks, not knowing if he should stay or leave.

"I have an idea, but until things settle down, I don't know for sure," Emma says with concern in her voice.

"I will be right back I need to go turn off the water," Mike says, setting down the water hose and running off towards the building. But this is only half true. Mike also intends to get some more help, but when he gets to where the faucet is to turn off the water, there is no one around. So, with a high sigh, he turns and runs back to the van.

"Mike... Mike, are you there?" Emma calls out as Mike returns to the van.

"Yes. What is it?" Mike replies.

"I need you to go get a girl that can help us," Emma says.

"A girl, why do you need a girl?" Mike asks in astonishment.

"Because of the type of help I need, it must be a girl," Emma says.

"Oh. Okay, I will be right back." Mike says as he turns to run off.

Mike does not know who he can go to, to ask for help in this situation. The first person he thinks of that would not dismiss him as soon as he approaches, is a friend of his named Meagan. So, he goes to where she is working and tells her what has happened.

Meagan wants to call the cops before going, but Mike explains that Emma does not wish to contact any emergency people yet for fear of what might happen. Meagan eventually says, "okay," and follows Mike out to the van.

Once Mike and Meagan get to the van, Mike yells in, "Hello. Emma. Are you there? I brought you a girl that can help."

"Please come in and lower the 'door' behind you," Emma says. "I will turn on a light so you can see."

Mike and Meagan enter the van and pull the 'door' down behind them. Once it is down, the amount of light is too low to see, so little in fact that they can only see shadows.

"Please, come to the light and walk through the door." They hear Emma say as a light comes on over a door in the far-left corner of the room. Mike wishes it is a little brighter because he wants to check on the guy that fell over the giant generator. He wants to be sure that the guy is okay. Even though he tries to see the guy as they walk by, he cannot see anything beyond shadows.

As Mike and Meagan approach the room, they can see that the light in the next room is much brighter. And this urges them to move a little faster towards the next room. Once inside, the door behind them closes, essentially locking them in.

"Thank you for coming," Emma says with a tone of relief.

"Where are you? Who are you?" Meagan asks as she looks around, trying to find the source of the voice and noticing all the corridors and walkways spread out throughout the room.

"I am all that you see. I am everywhere." Emma replies. "If you turn to the screen on the wall, I need your help with something." Emma continues. She explains how John built her and how she gained herself awareness as well as telling them that John has been infected with the same strange energy that makes her possible. All this, without mentioning to them his name, what gender her creator might be, or that the guy in the engine bay is the one she is talking about.

"In front of you, there is $350 and a sheet of paper with the dimensions of a woman on it. I need you to go and get some clothing, so when my creator is able..." The volume dropped off for a second. "can get dressed." Emma finishes off.

Meagan looks down at the piece of paper and sees;

Overall Height: 5'8" (173 cm)
Neck 12 ½" (32 cm)
Bust: 44" (112 cm)
Under Bust: 30" (77 cm)
Waist: 24" (60 cm)
Hips: 36" (86 cm)
Inseam: 36" (86 cm)
Under Bust to Shoulders: 8 ⅓" (21 cm)
Arms: 28" (71 cm)

Meagan, knowing that she should be able to find someone in the mall to help her with sizing, says, "okay," before turning to walk out with Mike in tow. Megan tells Mike, he needs to return to work while she gets everything Emma has asked for. Partly because she did not want Mike to lose his job, but mostly because he would just get in the way of her shopping for the clothes.

It takes Meagan more than an hour to find someone to help her find the clothes that will fit. She first goes to the outlet store where she bought all her clothes, but no one there knows how to find the right size based on measurements alone. So, she walks to Macy's and then to Dillard's only to find the same.

Finally, Meagan decides to try Brides Plus. There she finds they have a woman in fitting someone for her wedding dresses. When Meagan explains the odd request by Emma, leaving out the part that Emma is a computer, the woman behind the counter takes the paper and goes to the back. After several minutes she comes out and hands the paper to Meagan and tells her she needs to buy clothes that are a size 5-6. As for the bra, she believes the size should be about 30DD, but beyond that, she is on her own.

After buying all the clothes she can with the money she got from Emma, Meagan returns to Emma with the clothes. Emma asks her to hang all the clothing on a hook near the door and then follow the light again. But this time, a different door opens when she approaches the corner of the room. This door, also in the far-left corner of the room, is about a foot to the right of the other door. Meagan does not remember seeing the door before but is sure it had to have been there the last time she walked through here; she just could not see it because of how dark it was.

After another twenty minutes, John finally wakes up. Most of the pain is gone, as is the headache. However, he cannot see, so he tries to call out for Emma and finds that he cannot talk either. After a few minutes, his vision starts coming back to him a little at a time. But he still cannot speak, so he decides rather than laying there, he needs to try and get up.

As John rolls over, he feels something very different. He does not know what it is at first, but his body has changed somehow. As he tries to get up on his hands and knees, he knows something is definitely wrong. He feels unbalanced and awkward, as if he has just finished spinning around and around, but without feeling dizzy.

Eventually, John finds his balance as his vision comes into sharper focus. Once he is on his feet, he looks around and finds that the room he is in is in fact, much brighter than he had ever seen it before with the door closed. Even though the room is dark and black, along with many of the items within it, he can apparently make out every detail of every object in the room, as well as the fine print of an instruction label on the far side of the room.

John cannot recall ever being able to read something so far away before. As he continues to look around, he sees details in items that he has never noticed before. The box he had made has little tool marks that he thought he had polished out.

Suddenly, John hears a faint sound of someone calling to him. "John?" the voice keeps calling. "John, can you hear me? John?" The voice is becoming more evident as he tries to listen to it. Finally, he can hear it well, and again he tries to speak, but still, no words come out, so he hits the side of the wall to show he can hear her.

"At least you can hear me," Emma says, sounding relieved. "There is some clothing on the hook next to the hood for you to put on."

As she finishes, John keeps trying to talk, thinking that it might work as it had done with his eyes and ears. The more he focused on them, the faster they seemed to work. So, as he walks over and absentmindedly starts grabbing articles of clothing to put on, he continues to focus on trying to talk.

First, it is the panties, which are a little tighter than he would typically be comfortable in. Socks and black dress pants follow these. But when he reaches for a top, something falls onto his head. That is when he looks up at what is on the hook for the first time.

"These are all women's clothes," John says, finally able to talk. As he hears the words in his ears, he notices that his voice has raised several octaves. At the same time, he notices that his ass is really starting to hurt as well.

"John, we need to talk about what has happened," Emma says, concern evident in her voice.

"No, shit! You think?" John says, much more aggressively than he had intended.

As John turns to see what is making his ass hurt, he sees a long purple tail about three inches in diameter coming out of his ass, or more precisely, from his tailbone. He goes to pull the pants and panties off when he notices something hanging off from his chest. As he looks down, he sees two large purple breasts swinging to and fro.

Realizing that the changes seem to be a lot more than just his vision, hearing, and voice, John takes his right hand and reaches between his legs. As he feels around, he finds the voluptuous lips surrounding the clitoris instead of a penis. He enters a little farther back, to discover that he also has a vagina, again, instead of the scrotum he once had.

"Holy Shit!" John yells, now pulling his hand back out. "I am a woman."

John knows that he can not focus on the changes right now; he has a daughter to get home to and take care of. John looks around the room and finds a pair of scissors that Elizabeth had lost over the summer break. He uses them to cut holes in the panties and pants so they will go on over his legs and tail. Once he finishes putting on the pants, John looks up to try and find a bra but does not find one. So, instead, he grabs the white button-up blouse hanging on the hook and puts it on.

"Now Emma, let's have that talk," John says, sounding angry.

"Yes, please come to the monitor, and we will talk," Emma says, sounding particularly nervous.

John walks into the room with the monitor, but as the door opens, John is hit by a bright flash of light. It takes several seconds before his new eyes adjust to the bright light.

"What the hell was that?" John asks, starting to regain his focus again.

"What was what? The door just opened normally like it always does. Did it not?" Emma responds, not knowing what exactly he is talking about.

John, not knowing what to think and hearing the concern in Emma's voice, decides to let it go for now. John walks through the door and turns the corner to stand in front of the monitor.

"Before I show you what you look like, please be aware, I had no way to stop it," Emma says to John, fear prominent in her voice.

"Please, just show me," John says, wanting to know the full extent of the changes.

"I kept the police away once I discovered what was changing you. The readings I got showed it was a dimensional rift that formed within you." Emma tells John as a live image of John appears on the screen.

As John looks himself over, he sees all the changes that have taken place. As his eyes move up and down his new body, he notices the missing bra is on his head hanging from his left horn. After removing it from his head, he takes his blouse off to put on the bra to support his new breast. Trying to button the bra behind his back, he discovers that it is a lot harder than it looks and that he cannot quite get it. So, he pulls it around to button it from the front before turning it back around to finish putting it on and replacing the blouse.

"Emma, how did you get the clothes for me to wear?" John asks.

"The girl in the passenger cabin got them for you," Emma says. "She was very helpful to me."

John looks around to the far side of the room and starts walking to the door. As it opens, again, John is hit with a blinding light, but this time his eyes adjusts much quicker. When he looks, he can see a beautiful blond woman that is about the same height as he is now. The woman is slightly more prominent around without being fat and still have that hourglass figure, but not entirely as defined as it could be. And her breast is almost twice as big as his own.

"What are you?!" Meagan screams, jumping to her feet as John comes through the door.

"My name is John. I am the inventor of this vehicle." John says, looking around.

"Your name is John? You know that is a guy's name, right?" Meagan tells John as she looks her over.

"I guess it is. Okay, so what would you call me?" John asks Meagan, who is now looking at her like a guy would look at a woman.

"I don't know." Meagan starts looking John over from head to toe. "Let's think for a moment." Meagan says as she turns and starts to pace back and forth for a few minutes, sometimes muttering a name then shaking her head as she says "no," under her breath. Then as if on a turntable, she suddenly turns on her heel and says, "How about... Rose? I have always loved that name."

John thinks about it for a few minutes. After finding no faults with it and having liked the name as well, she says, "Rose it is. Hi, my name is Rose. What's yours?" She says, handing her hand out to shake Meagan's.

"Meagan," She says with a smile on her face and her eyes just beaming with delight as she takes Rose's hand in hers. "My name is Meagan, nice to meet you, Rose." She finishes as she shakes Rose's hand.

"The pleasure's all mine," Rose says. "I want to thank you for getting these clothes for me," Rose says, noticing Meagan's bright blue eyes as they glisten in the sunlight.

"Not a problem," Meagan says. "Hey, I need to get back to work now." She says, starting to turn and walk out.

"I know this will sound weird, but do you know what time it is?" Rose asks Meagan. Having realized she no longer has a watch to tell time with.

Meagan looks down at her watch before saying, "It is now 4:30. Why?" She asks.

"I need to get home to my daughter. She will be getting off the bus in about half an hour," Rose says, looking back over her shoulder at the door she had just come through, then walking towards Meagan to escort her out of Emma.

"Your daughter?" Meagan replies, shock evident in her tone and face. "There are more like you?" She now looks worried at the possibility of there being people walking amongst humans, people who are not what they seem.

"No, I am the first of my kind as far as I know," Rose says.

"Wait, first? You are joking, right?" Meagan says with a sarcastic laugh that fades only to be replaced with curiosity.

Rose stops near the hood that Meagan had entered earlier. Deciding on a whim, she spins Megan around to look her in the eyes. "Look, up until today, I was a normal human male," Rose says, looking frustrated. "I was born John Mills here in Flagstaff 35 years ago. I got married, had a little girl at twenty-four, and right after she is born, her mother leaves to be with another guy back east." As Rose finishes speaking, tears start to well up in her eyes.

"Your daughter... She doesn't know, does she?" Meagan asks with shock spreading across her face.

Rose does not say a word but shakes her head back and forth as the whole thing finally dawns on her. As she shakes her head, she can feel her new longer hairbrush against her skin. As it does, it causes her tears to break free and start falling uncontrollably.

"Look, I should have been off half an hour ago. I will go with you to help you tell her what has happened." Meagan says. "I just need to ask Mike to bring my car to me later, okay?" Rose just merely nods as she tries to hold back the tears, but they will not be kept.

As Meagan goes to walk out, Rose realizes that she has not told her where she lives and yells after her. "Tell him to take Leupp Rd. out to Forest Mountain Rd. and turn left. Follow it until the road makes a rather sharp right turn and look for FSR 190. My house is a huge white one with four buildings." She tells Meagan. Meagan nods and walks off to find Mike.

***

"So, let me get this straight. You were born a human male child and turned into... this... about a year ago?" James asks, waving his hand up and down before him at Rose.

"Yes, I was born a human male child, and until last year, I was that way," Rose says to James with a small grin on her face from seeing James's bewildered expression.

Just as she finishes, the alarm goes off, foretelling the arrival of the next module unit. So, James and Rose go to the window to watch it come in. This module is the second of eighteen unmanned modules that only has supplies and building equipment for the camp. The module lands a lot harder than it should have, sliding about ten feet before the closest of the four landing gears snap. The module leans over to the one side and comes to rest on one of the massive engines.

James turns to Rose and says, "This mission has turned into one big fuck up after another." Shaking his head in disbelief at all the accidents that have plagued the mission since they started their mission, first with the meteor shower, then the micro-rite punching through the ship killing Andrew and now the broken landing gear of the latest module.

Rose smiles at James, one of those sweet innocent smiles, and says, "Just think how much worse things can be. You can have lost both ships, not just Andrew, and the one landing gear. You have everyone else still alive and safe. You can still get the supplies and things from that module."

James smiles before shaking his head as he turns to look back out the window. "I have not thought of it that way." He says, turning back to Rose. "With that line of thought, I would have to say that only losing one module was a blessing."

"You should look at it that way. No matter how bad things seem at that moment, things can always be worse." Rose says as she puts her hands on James's shoulders.

"I guess you are correct. My grandfather always told me that growing up." James says with a slight laugh and shaking his head.

"How long will it be before all the modules are down on the ground?" Rose asks James as they walk back to the table they have been sitting at.

"About twenty-four hours to get them all down. Then we have to start setting them up to live in." James tells her.

Right then, Frank walks up to the door. "Sir, the last of her crew, is awake now," Frank tells James and Rose.

"Can I go see them now?" Rose asks, looking from Frank to James and back with a look of mingled relief and worry.

"I don't see why not. They are asking about you anyway." Frank says with a grin on his face.

James and Rose stand and walk out of the room. James escorts Rose to the medical bay and gives her privacy as she talks to each of her friends in turn.

Rose's first stop is Elizabeth's bed, partly because it is closest to the door and partly because this is her child. "How are you, baby girl?" Rose asks Elizabeth as she sits down on the edge of the bed.

"I am doing good. I don't think we will make it back in time for school today, though." Elizabeth says half-jokingly.

"No, I don't think so," Rose says, smiling down at her little girl.

"How is everyone else?" Elizabeth asks as she turns to look at the others in their beds.

"I don't know yet. But all of you are awake, so it looks good." Rose says, also looking around at the others. "Meagan is pregnant, though." She adds as an afterthought.

"Really? I wonder whose child it can be. You're a girl now, so it can't be yours." Elizabeth says, looking confused and excited.

"I think it might be mine," Rose says with a smile. "I am going to go check on the others now. Get some sleep for me. Okay?" She says, standing from Elizabeth's bed to kiss Elizabeth on the forehead, as she does Elizabeth nods at Rose.

The next person she goes to see is Meagan. "How are you?" Rose asks, looking down at Meagan's belly.

Meagan, seeing Rose looking down at her belly, blushes red. "So, you know, hm?" Meagan says, looking somewhat disappointed. "I swear you are the only one I have been with for the last year, and I haven't even been with a guy since I was a teenager," Meagan says with her voice trailing off with the last part, tears now flowing steadily from both eyes.

"Meagan, I know that. You've barely left the house without me for the last year. Remember, I did use to be a guy, and we did use my tail that one time a few months ago. Remember?" Rose says to Meagan, who is now looking up because of Rose's laughter in her voice.

"So, you think your tail might... might be... might be a man's dick?" Meagan asks, starting to sit up but still feeling lightheaded.

"It is possible. Now get some rest. We are going to be here for a while." Rose says, kissing Meagan on the lips as she pushes her back down.

Rose then walks over to Mike, who is pretending he is asleep. Rose knows he is awake because when she first came into the room, he looked directly at her. "Quit pretending you, faker," Rose says, smacking Mike's leg, making him jump from the sharp pain.

"So, now you want to come to see me?" Mike says with a sarcastic grin on his face. "Elizabeth, I can understand, but Meagan?" Mike says, now looking up at Rose.

"I went to see Meagan because she is pregnant," Rose tells Mike with a smile on her face.

Mike suddenly looks odd. Like he is trying to remember something but can't. The look is so bizarre that it makes Rose smirk a little. "How can Meagan be pregnant? She has not even been with a guy that I can remember; not since high school, at least." Mike says, looking up at Rose.

"You're right. Meagan has not been with any guys for a long time. But apparently, I am not just any woman now either." Rose tells Mike. As she finishes, his face turns to disgust. "Oh, stop that, you know you would give anything to see two hot women getting it on together." She says, with a smile as she blushes blue, just enough that it is almost a slight glow.

"You're right," Mike says, starting to laugh and pulling himself up a little in his bed. "So, how did you do it? I mean, getting her pregnant." Mike asks, looking over at Meagan, who has been watching them talk, but who suddenly turns her head to hide her face.

"Later. We all have much to talk about. But for now, we need to keep some things to ourselves," Rose says, noticing Meagan's red cheeks.

Rose then walks over to James and says, "I am hungry. Do you think we can eat something?"

James nods and then turns and walks down the corridor to a set of steps that leads down to the room that has the rovers. "There is not much in here, but you can have whatever you want," James says with sadness evident in his voice.

Rose notices the tone and wonders what has just happened since he had been so lovely and keen to listen to her tell her story. "James, what is wrong?" Rose asks, trying to get him to look at her.

"You are with Mike and Meagan. I cannot ask you to consider me." James says, walking towards a corner of the room.

"I am not with Mike," Rose says, looking up at the ceiling in the direction of the medical bay. "I only have feelings for Meagan. As for Mike, it's rather complicated." She says, bringing her gaze down to meet James's.

"So, you're not seeing Mike?" James asks, looking confused more than relieved.

"No. Mike is just a friend who wants it to be more. But he is more interested in Meagan than he is in me." Rose says with a smile on her face. "He has been trying to get Meagan to go out with him for the last several years. Imagine his surprise when he found out she is a lesbian."

"Wait... Meagan never told him." James says, now starting to smile as well. "Then how did he find out?"

"Well, that is complicated as well... and a story for Meagan to tell herself," Rose says, picking at a package of spaghetti and meatballs she has found in one of the many small crates.

"Okay, I get it. You have your secrets too." James says with a laugh as he turns to open a crate to see what is in there. "So, what happened when Meagan returned to Emma to go home with you?"

Rose watches James for a moment as he digs through the crates to find something to eat. She wonders if she, as John, had been that way when he interacted with women. Putting the thoughts from her mind to continue her story, she says, "Well..."

Chapter Five

Their Bad Luck

MEAGAN TAKES ABOUT FIFTEEN MINUTES to clock out from work and to tell Mike where she is going before returning to Emma to go home with Rose. On the way, Rose is looking out the windows at the wonderments of all the new colors and things that she can see.

She notices that the lake just a few miles from her house looks to be empty. But when she takes a closer look, she can see the fish in the lake swimming around. The fish look as though they are flying as they move, but she knows this cannot be. They must be in the water, and she just cannot see it.

"Rose?" Meagan says suddenly. "What happened to Elizabeth's mom?" She asks, not sure how Rose will react.

"Well... She left us when Elizabeth was three months old." Rose answers, still looking out of the window.

"I see." Meagan says, looking at her feet.

"Ya." Rose adds.

"But why did Elizabeth's mom leave?" Meagan asks, with her voice trailing off with the last word as she too starts looking out the window at the passing ground, not knowing if she wants to know the answer or not.

"I don't know, really. Elizabeth's mom suddenly started acting differently right after having Elizabeth. She would go days without a shower or brushing her teeth. She would start fights with me for things I never knew anything about, and then one day, I came home from work, and she was on the phone having phone sex with some guy." Rose says, remembering back to the day Elizabeth's mom left. "I have tried to ask her 'why?' but every time we talk, she says things to try and make me angry. She talks like I am the problem to start with, but my friends and family keep telling me that I did everything right. I bought everything she wanted and gave her the life she asked for, but apparently, it was not enough for her." Rose finishes as the tears start falling freely.

Meagan watches out the window for a few minutes, not knowing what to say. Thinking of what Rose has just told her, she feels heartbroken and wishes she could take all of Rose's pain away, but she does not know how. Suddenly she turns and hugs Rose around the neck before planting a big kiss on her lips. Rose does not push away. In fact, she has wanted to kiss Meagan ever since they had met just over an hour ago now.

Meagan is the woman John had always dreamed about, a 5'6" tall, blond hair, blue eyes, and at most weighs 150 pounds. Rose embraces the kiss that lasts for what seems like hours. They only break apart when Emma tells them they will be landing in just a minute.

When the house comes into view, Rose spots Elizabeth walking up the steps to go inside. "We are too late to be waiting for her inside for when she arrived home," Rose tells Meagan as the tears resume their escape.

Meagan does not say a word but turns and runs to the side door on Emma. Once she opens the door, she leaps from Emma as soon as she sees they are within a few feet of the ground. Meagan then runs straight towards the house and knocks on the front door.

As she stands there waiting for the door to open, she starts looking around the porch fighting the urge to look back at Rose.

The door opens, and the girl inside says: "Hello, can I help you with something?"

"Hi, my name is Meagan, and I am a friend of your dad's." She says, trying to be as calm as possible.

"I am sorry. My dad is not home right now. I will tell him you came by when he gets home, though." Elizabeth says, starting to close the door.

"No... Wait, please! Your dad is here; there is a..." Meagan breaks off, searching for the right words to say to keep Elizabeth from panicking, but it is too late.

"Is he okay?... Where is he?... What happened?... DADDY!" Elizabeth shouts, tears now streaming down her face freely as she weeps as she looks around frantically, screaming, "DADDY!" once again.

"No, he is okay, but he is different than he was before," Meagan explains to Elizabeth as John now Rose walks in front of the door right behind Meagan.

Elizabeth looks over Meagan's shoulder at the female figure that has just walked up. Suddenly without words from either Elizabeth or Rose, Elizabeth pushes Meagan aside, knocking her to the ground and runs up to Rose, hugging her around the middle. After a few moments, Elizabeth breaks off and escorts her new father, or, more accurately, new mother into the house. As they pass Meagan, picking herself up off the ground, Elizabeth invites her in as well.

Meagan, not having anywhere to be or even any way of getting there decides to follow Rose and Elizabeth into the house and closes the door behind them. The entryway is a double French doorway that has a set of stairs on the left side of the large hallway. On either side of the hall in front of the stairs are two cased openings.

The opening on the left leads to a large family room that has bookshelves along the wall that backs the stairs and an extensive entertainment system on the opposite wall. The bookshelves and entertainment center flank a small desk that looks out across the room. Across the room sits a sofa sitting on a green and white oval rug, which would look more at home in a corner than out in the middle of the floor.

The other cased opening leads to a large dining room that has a large table with twelve chairs around it, a large china cabinet on the wall that has the front door, and a pie cabinet on the opposite wall with another sizable cased opening. This opening leads to the kitchen. A kitchen that looks as though it is right out of one of those 'Country Living' magazines. The three of them go into the kitchen, and each takes a seat around a small four-person dining table. None of them speak for a few moments as Elizabeth looks Rose over.

"So... what happened?" Elizabeth asks, still not daring to remove her eyes from her new mother.

"Do you remember last year when I got sick for a few days at that time?" Rose asks Elizabeth looking down at the table.

"Da, I should remember. I took care of you all that time." Elizabeth says, turning to Meagan to smile at her, looking at her for the first time since they entered the house.

Meagan politely smiles back, still trying to get rid of the pain in her ass from falling on it outside.

"Well, I was infected by some stuff I was working with. It has been working all this time to change me, to make me into this." Rose says, looking down at her hands, she has just laid on the table. "Today, it finished its work."

Elizabeth takes one of Rose's hands in hers and scrutinizes it. As she does, she notices that the fingernails seem to be metallic, and the skin is entirely hairless. As she looks up the arm, she finds more of the same. The hair that is even on her own body is at least noticeable up close. But Rose has nothing, not even of the tiniest bit.

"Can you feel people touching you?" She asks as her fingers walk up Rose's arm.

"Yes, I can feel you touching me," Rose answers as her skin twitches from the feeling of Elizabeth's fingers.

Elizabeth lets go of Rose's hand and then moves to the backside of Rose, being careful not to step on Rose's tail, to get a look at her ears. They are about three inches long and come to a rounded point like cat ears. The outside of her ears is covered in hair that is the same color as the rest of her hair. The inside of the ears are dark purple like her skin and have no hair that Elizabeth can see.

"Can you hear better with them way up there?" Elizabeth asks, grabbing one ear and twisting it around to get a better look at the inside.

Rose thinks about it for a moment and then realizes she has been hearing things that she had never noticed before. Even at that moment, she can hear things happening in the kitchen that she has never heard before. Gazing around, Rose spots one of the sources for what she is hearing and sees a small beetle crawling on the counter. As the beetle moves, she can hear each leg scratch the countertop as if she had a microphone lying right next to it.

She looks around again and quickly finds another source of noise; a little worm is hanging from the ceiling, swinging back and forth. Now and then, it will bump the wall making a faint thump.

"Yes, I can hear much clearer and distinctly," Rose says, pulling her head forward, yanking her ear from Elizabeth's grip.

Elizabeth then runs her fingers on each of Rose's horns, feeling the ridges that encircle them. She also explores the points noticing that they are not as blunt as most of the animals she has worked with in 4H. Then Elizabeth grabs Rose's tail to look it over. She sees that the tail is about three and a half feet long and is the same color as her skin, and it too does not have any hair.

"What good is a tail?" She asks, holding it up to the window behind them.

"Some animals use their tail for balance while others use theirs like an extra hand," Rose says.

"What about this hole in the end." Elizabeth says, pointing to the end of the tail at a hole that she has just noticed.

As Rose looks at the end of her tail, she sees a small slit in the end, about half an inch long, but whatever she tries, it will not open. "I do not know, baby girl," Rose says, still looking at her tail with interest. The end is reminding her of the end of a penis.

But the overall head shape is missing. The penis, she use to have, was more like that of construction workers hard hats with lots of crests and valleys all over. But her tail is smooth, and the tip is as round as a beach ball.

Then Meagan stands up from the table. Looking around at Rose and Elizabeth, she says, "Well, I need to go. I need to try to get Mike to pick me up."

"That is the second time you have mentioned Mike. Who is he?" Rose asks as she releases her tail and looks up at Meagan.

"Mike is the guy that came to get me so I could get those clothes for you," Meagan says slightly quicker than she should have.

"Why not stay for dinner? Please?" Elizabeth says, emphasizing on 'please' while traversing to her puppy dog eyes.

Meagan, not wanting to look Rose in the eyes, looks at Elizabeth. Seeing her little pouty face, her heart melts, and she knows she cannot say no. "Okay, just for dinner," she says, trying to keep from looking at Rose in the eyes.

The three of them work together to make dinner. Elizabeth set the table. Meagan chops the vegetables and makes the salad, while Rose makes the chow mein noodles with stir fry chicken and vegetables.

Rose Kincade

After dinner, Rose tells Elizabeth it is time for her homework. Even though Elizabeth tries to get out of it by insisting she has the whole weekend to do it. Rose talks her into doing it now.

"But if you do it now, then you don't have to worry about not having time to finish it later. Do you?" Rose says to Elizabeth, who must admit that she is right about this, and grudgingly goes to do her homework.

While Elizabeth does her homework, Rose and Meagan talk about their pasts. They find that even though they both grew up in Flagstaff and that Meagan's parents died when she was young and Rose's parents are still alive, they have both lived nearly identical lives. They both have had almost the same opportunities and difficulties, but somehow, they never met.

Rose had attended Sinagua High School, while Meagan had attended Coconino High School. They even attended different elementary schools and middle schools. Rose was in private schools until high school, while Megan attended public schools.

Both lived in Sunny Side, but Rose lived south of 6th street and never had a reason to go north, and Meagan lived north of 6th street and never had a reason to go south.

Elizabeth finally says she has finished with her homework and is going to get ready for bed. After this news, Rose and Meagan decide to take a walk outside in the fresh night air. After walking about two hundred feet from the house, Rose notices Meagan has stopped walking.

"What is wrong? Don't you want to walk with me?" Rose asks, looking back at Meagan.

"Yes, I do. But it is so dark; I can hardly see anything right now." Meagan says, looking disturbed, her eyes darting all around trying to focus on something, anything around them.

"It is so bright out, what do you mean you can't see anything because of how dark...." Rose says, trailing off remembering how much brighter everything has been since he, now she, has awoken in Emma earlier today day.

"I am so sorry. I had not realized until now that I can see so well in the dark now." Rose says, leading Meagan back up towards the house.

"You think it is bright out here?" Meagan asks, looking at Rose in the light of the front porch.

"Well, it is so bright out here, I thought the sun had not yet fully set," Rose says, looking into the trees seeing the wildlife move around that most people never get to see without special cameras. "I can see the little coyote walking around just inside the tree line there." She points to where it has just stopped. "I can see the bats flying around overhead, and an owl sitting on a branch on that tree over by that hill. They are all so clear as if it is the middle of the day. But as I look around, I don't even see the moon in the sky." As Rose speaks, she is looking around and pointing out the different things that she can see.

Meagan stands there looking at Rose, not knowing what to say about her being able to see so well. "Well, at least you will never have to worry about disturbing anyone in the middle of the night by turning a light on," Meagan says with a forced smile and small laugh.

Rose stands there looking at Meagan. Then, raising a single eyebrow, she says, "You're right. I no longer need to turn on the light at night. Maybe you want to stick around and try it out?"

Both Rose and Meagan stand there looking at each other for a few moments, then at the same time, both start laughing and turn to finish walking to the house to go inside.

Rose, Meagan, and Elizabeth spent most of the weekend getting to know each other. On Saturday afternoon, they decide to go on a picnic. Rose finds herself having to wait for Meagan and Elizabeth to catch up because they get winded from climbing the hill. On Sunday, they try to play a game of Frisbee in the yard. But every time Rose takes a turn at throwing the disk, it shot so far past either Meagan or Elizabeth, they all had to wait about ten minutes for whichever one to return with it.

Rose Kincade

By Monday morning, Rose has not slept more than three hours each night since she had changed into her current form.

She is not sure why, but for some reason when she is up she is okay, then, almost on cue, after being up twenty-one hours, Rose gets so tired she has to lie down for a few hours of sleep, or as she found out on Sunday night, she will pass out.

Early on Monday afternoon, Meagan tells Rose that she needs to get to work, and Mike still has not shown up with her car, nor is he answering his phone. So, Rose takes Meagan to town in Emma. On the way, Rose tells Meagan she is going to go shopping for some new clothes since she has been in the same clothes since the transformation.

Before Meagan enters the store that she works at, she tells Rose everything she needs to know to be able to find clothes and shows her which stores to avoid. Then she gives Rose a quick peck on the lips before walking into Spencer's where she works.

Rose first goes to 'Victoria Secrets' to get new panties and bras since she has to have them, at least the panties, specially made. Then she goes to 'Just for Her' who Meagan has told her would be the best place to go for both price and fashion to pick out some new outfits. Rose is just coming out of the fitting room for the third time to look at one of the outfits she is trying on when Meagan comes storming in with tears in her eyes.

"Well, I have some bad news and some horrible news," Meagan says with anger on her face and in her voice. "I lost my job because I helped you." She says, now not looking at Rose.

"Okay, I have heard worse. What is the horrible news?" Rose says, trying to find out what is going on while holding a different top to her chest to see how it might look.

"Mike was arrested, also for helping you," Meagan says, now looking at Rose again this time with fury in her eyes.

Rose, feeling this is directed at her, asks in a calm, cool voice, "Are you saying this is my fault, Meagan?"

Meagan's cheeks flush with red, and she averted her gaze down to the floor as she speaks, "Well, no. I mean..." she is not allowed to finish.

"Meagan, we will go to get Mike from jail, and if needed, the both of you can stay with me until we get everything straightened out," Rose says, taking Meagan's chin in her hand to lift her head towards her own. Meagan's eyes are filling with fresh tears as she hugs Rose around the neck.

After another half hour in the store, Rose is finally ready to leave, having spent twice as much as she had intended. Not because she bought more than expected, nor because the clothes cost that much more. The reason is that nearly every pullover shirt she tries on ripped on her horns as she tried pulling them on.

Meagan and Rose walk over to 'Victoria Secrets' to pick up Roses order since while they were at the checkout counter in 'Just For Her,' they called and told her it is ready.

Afterward, Rose and Meagan go to the jail to see what it will take to get Mike out of jail. Rose waits in Emma while Meagan goes inside.

After more than two hours waiting for Meagan to return, it is time for Elizabeth to be getting home from school. Not wanting to leave Meagan and Mike with no ride, Rose calls home and leaves a message on the answering machine that she will be home as soon as she can. It is another two hours before Meagan and Mike come walking out of jail. When Mike sees that Meagan is riding in Emma, he turns to step back into the jail, but Meagan grabs him by the arm. After they argue for twenty minutes, Mike finally gives in and gets into Emma.

Mike, having never been in this part of Emma before, looks around in awe at how much room there is inside. As his eyes make their way up to the front, he sees Rose and with a gasp tumbles back out of the door.

After Mike has reentered Emma, he looks at Rose and says, "You are an alien."

"Sorry, I am not. I am a scientist that got too close to something that he should not have." Rose says, looking at Mike with a smile from ear to ear or rather horn to horn.

Once Meagan is in as well, and they have left the jail. Mike explains that after Meagan and Rose left, that all hell broke out at the mall. More than a dozen people had panicked and called the police claiming to have seen an alien in a spaceship kidnap a young woman.

The police took several reports about the blue minivan that had people getting in and out through the van's hood rather than any of the typical doors. At first, the police thought it was just people working on their van, shrugged the calls off. Until they started getting the ones saying it just flew away like a helicopter after grabbing a young girl.

When the police arrived at the mall, they started questioning everyone. Someone had told them they had seen Meagan approach the van only to be grabbed by some sort of purple monster and dragged inside kicking and screaming.

"I tried to explain what I knew and kept getting waved off. So, I grabbed one of the cops and told him; he needs to listen to me." Mike says, his cheeks flushing red.

"So, that is why they arrested you then," Meagan says more as a statement than a question. "But that still doesn't explain why they fired me." She finishes off.

"I do not know for sure. But somehow, your name was brought up several times, and no one could find you anywhere." Mike says, looking at the back of Meagan's seat.

"I was off and had gone with Rose to help her out," Meagan says.

"But apparently you never clocked out," Mike says, now looking Meagan in the eyes.

"You are more than welcomed to come to stay with me if you would like." Rose offers Mike seeing he still looks rather pale.

"*NO, thank you*," Mike says, emphasizing each word slowly as he speaks. "I will be fine at home." He finishes not even giving as much as a glance in Rose's direction.

Once they drop Mike off at his apartment, Meagan and Rose return to Rose's house, where they find Elizabeth setting the table for dinner. Rose and Meagan help and soon are sitting together like an average family for dinner.

Since Meagan's rent is due in the next few days, and she now has no job to speak of, the following day, Rose and Meagan go and pack up Meagan's apartment. And too much of Meagan's surprise everything fits in Emma in one trip with no problem.

The next few months seem to pass with few issues. Rose walks Elizabeth door to door for Halloween without having to find a way to cover her head or asking Meagan to do it instead. Thanksgiving comes and goes with just Rose's parents and Linda attending the dinner, though she had invited five other members of her family. But soon it is 'Parents Day' at school, and the children are supposed to bring a parent to school to tell a little bit about them and what they do for a living. Meagan and Rose, not really argue, but rather discuss with some stern words on rather or not Rose should go as Elizabeth, and the school has asked.

"I just might scare the kids so bad they may never return to school again," Rose says, knowing how she was when he was a small child.

"But it is for your daughter. She wants you there with her." Meagan says, looking out the door as if she can see someone standing there.

Eventually, Rose agrees to go, but only if Meagan does as well. Meagan agrees, and soon they both find themselves wishing Rose had just stayed home like she wanted to. They all file into Emma and go to the school for 'Parents Day' and are told to wait in the hallway until announced.

"I do not know what to call her," Elizabeth states to the class. "She did not give birth to me, but she is my biological parent."

"So, she donated an egg for someone else to give birth to you, dear?" Miss Hamilton, the teacher, asks Elizabeth.

"No, ma'am. She was born a male." Elizabeth says as the class starts to laugh. "She, I mean, he was working on an experiment when it changed him." She explains to the class as they continue to laugh, even harder.

"I don't get it, dear. Changed him... Or... I mean... her? How exactly?" Miss Hamilton asks Elizabeth looking confused.

Elizabeth points to the back corner of the room where there is a door for the parents to come through. As the class turns to see who or what she is pointing at, you can feel the air in the room vanish as each of the thirty or so kids, and Miss Hamilton gasped in shock. Miss Hamilton's eyes roll up into the top of her head as she falls to the ground. Most of the students run for the far corner of the room while the rest walk up in stunned disbelief looking Rose over. The parents that have heard the commotion come running into the room to see what is going on and start yelling at Rose, saying that the 'Joke' is not funny.

The principal suspends Elizabeth and tells Rose and Meagan that she will not be able to go back to school until her father comes in to straighten things out. Rose tries to explain she is the father, but the more she tries, the more the principal is set that she is not, that she cannot be the father.

After two weeks of fighting with the school and the school board. Rose decides that rather than letting the school keep Elizabeth from getting an education, she is going to enroll Elizabeth in an online homeschool program.

This does not make Elizabeth happy since she wants to be with her friends. But yet after Rose explains that she can still see her friends, some after school, and the rest on the weekends, Elizabeth agrees and starts the classes.

By the last week in December, Rose and Meagan have dating. And then in January, for Rose's birthday, Meagan decides to give

Rose a birthday surprise that she will never forget. However, the surprise turns out to be all on Meagan.

Rose has gotten pretty good at controlling her tail and making it do some precise movements, so when Meagan takes Rose upstairs for some birthday sex, as Meagan calls it.

Meagan tells Rose she is going to do all the work, and all Rose must do is relax. Meagan starts with all the regular kissing and licking that Rose has come to enjoy. But when she starts to move forward for some rubbing, Rose puts her tail in Meagan and makes it do things in ways that guys can never dream of.

Meagan is so stimulated by the feeling that she is unable to do anything other than fall sideways onto the bed and let Rose have her way with her. After more than four hours, Rose starts to feel herself get tired and has to stop. Meagan has been so stimulated that she cannot remember any part of the last four hours other than it is the best sex she has ever had. And is so exhausted from the previous four hours that she cannot move, and rather than fight it, she falls asleep right there next to Rose.

One Night in late April, Rose hears someone talking outside.

"Yes, Sir. The alien has a woman, and a little girl held hostage inside the house." The voice says, talking on a cell phone.

Rose tries to remember if she has ever heard the voice before but cannot recall if she ever had. *Who is this person, and how does he know who is inside the house, let alone what they look like?* Rose wonders to herself, before going over to the bed to wake up Meagan.

"Meagan, there is some guy outside. He has called the police and says I am holding you and Elizabeth hostage." Rose tells her once she is sitting up in the bed on her own.

"What guy?" Meagan asks, now walking over to the window still rather sleepily. "That's my stepfather's truck." She says, pointing down at a little Ford Ranger parked down the driveway a short way from the house.

"How can you see that?" Rose asks, looking out the window.

Rose Kincade

Rose has gotten rather proficient at telling how bright the light is by looking at how sharp the shadows are on the ground. But on this night, there are no shadows that she can see.

"The moon is full tonight, isn't it?" Meagan asks.

Rose looks around for any sign of the moon but never finds any. Before she can tell Meagan this, she hears the sounds of approaching helicopters off in the distance. As she scans the horizon, she sees a small fleet of Apache and Sikorsky helicopters flying right towards the house.

Seeing these types of helicopters is not unusual, but they have never flown over Rose's house before, but rather they have always passed about fifty miles to the east.

"Get dressed now," Rose tells Meagan. "Their coming!" She cries as she runs from the room to get Elizabeth.

Before they can get dressed and all the way out of the house, the helicopters are right over the house. Once outside, something hits Rose in the head. Looking up, she sees ropes dropping from each of the Sikorsky's, revealing over a dozen men.

"Run!" Rose cries, knowing that she will be their primary target.

The guys land all around Rose with what looks like taser guns pointed at her. The first guy shoots her right in the arm, and nothing seems to happen. Rose knows it is unusual for a taser not to fire. But before she can take advantage of the malfunction, the next soldier shoots her in the stomach, and again she feels nothing. Now she knows that the tasers are firing their charges, but she cannot feel them.

Rose decides she is not going to wait for them to change tactics, so she lunges forward, hitting the first guy square in the chest, knocking him back. As she turns to beat the next guy, she sees two little probes float lazily by on their way to their victim. She watches them for a second before remembering the guys around her.

So, she reaches out, grabs the tallest guy who is directly behind her, and tosses him over her shoulder at the guy she had just hit. To her surprise, he is still falling. As she turns, she notices the guy in the path of the two little probes has a knife halfway out of its sheath and is just looking at her.

She reaches out with her foot and kicks him so hard he seems to disappear from her site. The next several guys go much the same way, between kicking, hitting and throwing. After about a minute's time, she has finished with all 18 men, and none of them have seemed to care what she is doing to the rest of them.

Rose is shocked at what she has done but knows she must leave. As she turns to run for Emma, she feels a sharp pain in her right shoulder, but she does not stop to look at what happened. She runs as fast as she can, eventually making it to Emma, where Meagan and Elizabeth are waiting for her.

As soon as Rose is in, Emma lifts off the ground and is gone before the Apaches can even turn to try and give chase. Once they are safe, Rose looks down at her arm to see what has caused her pain. She sees a hole where blue blood is coming out, and then without warning, she feels faint. Rose tries to stay awake but finds it much too hard and passes out sloping sideways onto the seat where she sits.

When Rose comes around a few hours later, the pain in her arm is gone. She looks at her arm and sees a bandage wrapped around the wound. Rose moves the dressing to see how bad it is and finds the injury is gone.

Where the hole had been, there is now nothing more than a small scar left. Rose looks around the cabin and sees Meagan is talking on a cell phone at the front of Emma, while Elizabeth is crying over in a corner near the back. It takes her a few moments to remember all of what has just happened. Once she does, she too wants to cry but knows she has to focus on making sure everyone is safe first.

"Where are we?" Rose asks as she sits up.

"On our way to Mike's place, he says we are on the news right now," Meagan says, looking back at Rose.

Rose stands to get a better look around and sees that the sun is starting to come up. This means for this time of year it is about 6:30. "So, what is he saying it says?" Rose asks Meagan.

"Just that the police have received a tip claiming that a woman and her daughter have been kidnapped. And when they arrived, the kidnappers took out more than a dozen men before making their escape." Meagan says, not bothering to look back at Rose this time.

Rose knows this must be because Meagan does not want her to see the tears in her eyes. Rather than try and make Meagan look at her, she stands there for a moment, thinking of what they should do.

"You know Emma will be too noticeable to be moving around in the daylight?" Rose says, looking out at the quickly rising sun again.

"Mike is telling me that too. He is moving my car over to the visitors' spots so we can pull into a sheltered parking space." Meagan says with the sounds of crying emanating from her voice with the last few words.

Rose wants to do or say something that will comfort both Meagan and Elizabeth but cannot think of anything that will make both feel better.

She takes another glance around the cabin and thinks hard for the next ten minutes until they reach Mike's apartment. Once they arrive at Mike's apartment Rose, Meagan and Elizabeth run the distance between the parking area and the apartments.

Rose moves so quickly that she seems to vanish from Emma and reappear at the foot of the steps to the upper floors of the apartment building.

"How did you do that?" Meagan asks as she arrives, closely followed by Elizabeth, who exclaims "Cool" before walking inside.

"I really don't know. Back at the house, when I wanted to move quickly, everyone just seemed to freeze in place while I did what I wanted or rather needed to do." Rose says, trying to remember if she had ever done anything like this before.

Meagan and Rose step inside the apartment as Mike is getting off the phone with his work. He has apparently told them he would not be able to go to work today. Because right after he hangs the phone up, he asks them what they want to do.

"Well, we need answers," Rose says as she closes the front door behind her.

"Yes, like who those men were and what they wanted," Meagan says.

"That part is easy," Rose says, looking down at her hands in front of her as she walks to the couch. "Those were military helicopters that came to the house and as for what they wanted. I would think that would be obvious as well." She says, fighting back the tears as she tells the last part, but they finally won when they broke out once she finishes talking.

Meagan walks over to the couch and sits down, pulling Rose's head into her lap before looking up at Mike. "Have you talked to any of my dad's lately?" She asks.

"I have never met your real dad, so I don't know if I have talked with him or not. As for your stepdad, he called wanting to know if you were with me because your cell phone has not been working. I just told him that where you were living, the cellphones do not work, and I would let you know if he wanted me to." Mike says as he tries to remember the last few weeks. "As for your adopted dad. He was in the store looking around for the longest time a few weeks ago before walking up to me and asking where you were." He finally finishes, looking around like he had more to say but did not want to.

"What did you tell him, Mike?" Meagan asks with a lot of anger in her voice from the fear of what she thinks Mike might tell her.

Mike looks around and sees Elizabeth step out from behind a chair as Meagan stands, pushing Rose aside. Once Rose realizes what Meagan is doing, she also stands and grabs Meagan by the shoulders to keep her from doing something she will regret later.

"Mike, it is important to know how they found out about me," Rose says, looking at Mike, her eyes suddenly looking as though they have a lot more fire than usual. But this fire is a different color. It is red, blood red. But rather than having the effect of making Mike more nervous, it seems to calm him down effectively.

Mike looks as though he is deep in a daydream when he starts, "I told him that you and she have been spending a lot of time together and that you moved in with her after you lost your job." Mike says in a dreamy tone. "He wanted to know where this place is, and I did not want to tell him, but he eventually got it out of me." He finishes. His eyes glossy, and he has a dazed look about him.

As Rose turns to Meagan, Mike falls sideways onto the floor. Elizabeth quickly joins Rose and Meagan in a hug for a few moments. Once Mike has come to his senses and stands up, he too tries to join the hug but quickly decides not to after seeing the look Meagan shoots at him as he approaches.

Rose is the one that brakes the hug before saying, "Megan. Elizabeth. Please, get some sleep. I don't know how long we have until they find us here." She tells them with tears in all their eyes. "Mike, I need to talk to you alone outside." She tells Mike.

They both walk from the apartment and out to Emma. "You will get everything on this list, and I mean exactly what is on the list. I will give you a minute to look it over." Her eyes seem to flash with an intense fire again but not like before. "Each Item is important and needed for my plan to work. Plus, we need some new clothes since we can't go home." Rose says, handing Mike the list of items that she has just finished writing down along with over two thousand dollars in cash.

***

Unexpectedly, alarms start sounding, blaring throughout the landing pod, and all the lights turn red.
Rose looks around and asks, "What's happening?"

"I don't know. Stay here, and I will find out." James says, standing up and running out the door.

Rose has never been one to let others do all the work, so she too stands and walks out after James.

When she walks into the medical bay after James, she sees the black guy from earlier beating on Meagan. And without any conscious effort, everyone in the room seems to freeze as Rose crosses the room. She hits the guy, beating on Megan, square in the chest, not just knocking him back but throwing him all the way out of the medical bay and knocking over James as he goes by, and nearly Rebecca.

"I am sorry," Rose says, holding Meagan and looking down at James. "I just reacted to what was going on."

"No. Don't be. I would have done the same thing if I had been a little quicker." He tells Rose as he picks himself up off the ground and turning to the black man.

"Edwards, what the hell do you think you are doing?" James asks with his eyes bulging.

"That thing's a freak, and that one is pregnant with its bastard child," Edwards says, looking James in the eyes as his hands flail wildly.

"It is not our place to judge people," James says, returning Edward's gaze. "You are black, and your wife is white, Should I judge you on that?" James asks, the anger more pronounced than before.

"NO! That is different; we are both humans. I don't know what that thing is." Edwards says, breaking his gaze for the first time to look at Rose.

"That 'thing' as you so elegantly put it, was born human like you and me," James tells Edwards as James walks back out of the medical bay to join Edwards in the hallway.

"That thing is... Human?" Edwards says more than asks. "But... How?"

"If I remember how she put it, a 'Dimensional Rift.'" James says. "Subspace or compressed space or something like that. The details are not important." James adds, seeing the confusion on both Edwards and Rebecca's faces.

"You mean the theory has already been tested since the article," Rebecca says with amazement in her voice.

"This is the results of that article in 'Scientific Journal', this thing?" Edwards says, gesturing to Rose.

"I was the one that made that article possible. I am the one that found the equation that had been misinterpreted for half a century. I am the one that got too close and has been changed by it, for better or for worse. I am the one that has to live the rest of my life as a freak." Rose says as the tears fall harder and harder with each syllable. "And the article was written after all my work was completed."

"You have all read my article in the 'Scientific Journal'?" Meagan asks, looking around at the room.

The room stands quiet and still for a long while until Rebecca steps forward and looks at Edwards to say, "Is this how you want to be remembered by others? Going down in the history books as the one who killed the first child of a new species? One that can be the answers to all humanities questions on what is next?"

Edwards' face says it all. It is one of total shock and horror. "I didn't know. I mean, how could I? No one has said anything." He says, looking around, trying to find the right words to apologize.

"I have been interviewing her for the last several hours trying to get to the truth of her and her friends. No one else should be concerned with anything other than their duties." James says, walking over to Rose and Meagan. "Come with me, please," James says, escorting them both from the room.

As Rose walks out of the room, she looks over at Elizabeth and, without saying a word, manages to convey her wishes for her to remain silent. As long as she is a friend and not a daughter, then she should be safe. At least she hopes this is true.

Once out of the medical bay and down the stairs, James tells Meagan she needs to put on one of the pressure suits.

"Why?" She asks, looking back at Rose.

"We are going to go get your ship," James says as he pulls off his pants revealing his boxer-briefs. I can't have my crew trying to kill people when they need to be working." He says, now pulling off his shirt, revealing his tight, chiseled abs.

Meagan glances over at Rose and sees her cheeks have turned blue. "Are you blushing?" She asks, drawing the attention of James.

"No," Rose says with a faults laugh. Her cheeks are now flushing even bluer than they were before.

"I think she is," James says. Looking at Rose with a grin as he now pulls one of the pressure suits off the wall behind him.

Meagan, having just realized what made Rose blush, suddenly finds herself wishing she had not noticed it. She turns and grabs one of the pressure suits off the wall then walks to the corner of the room to start pulling off her clothes.

Rose follows Meagan over to the corner and says: "Let me help you with that, will you?"

Meagan, who now has tears in her eyes, just nods, letting Rose pick up the suit and start undoing the straps and buckles, while Meagan strips down.

"Meagan, you know I love you, right?" Rose asks, looking out the window as she plays with one of the buckles.

"Yes... I do. But I see now you have feelings for him as well." Meagan says in a soft voice as she looks over at James who is pulling up the bottom part of his suit, as she tries to undo the buttons of her butterfly pants.

"I don't know about that. I have been telling him about the last two years, all night." Rose says, turning to look at Meagan while handing her the suit. "He has not said much. He has just listened to every word I have had to say. Only interrupting when it is getting hard to talk anymore, or when something happens."

"I know that he is a guy... and a good looking one to boot." Meagan says, now turning around and pulling the bottom of the suit on. "You had only just turned into a woman when I met you, so you never had the chance to even look at guys before we got involved with each other." She finishes turning to look at Rose in the eyes as she now pulls the top part of the suit on.

"You're right. I never had a chance to explore my feminine side before falling for you." Rose says, looking past Meagan to James, seeing he is just about done with his suit. "I don't know what my feelings for him are yet. I have not even noticed anything until he started undressing in front of us." Rose says, looking back at Meagan, confusion showing in her eyes.

"Explore it," Meagan says with a sigh. "You will never know if you don't." She says, looking back at James. "He is rather gorgeous, for a guy, you know?" She says with a laugh in her voice. "I might take him if you don't."

"Meagan, are you sure about this?" Rose asks, not sure what this will mean for either of them.

"No... I am not, but I know what it is like to always wonder what might have been, and I won't ask you to do that." Meagan says. "If you two hit it off, then you were meant to be with him. If not... well then, at least I will still be here." She goes on, forcing each word as if it is the hardest thing she has ever said.

"But what if I want both of you? Not just him, or just you, but both of you." Rose says, leaning in to talk a little softer to Meagan. "We do live in the 21st century now, why can't we be a three-parent family?" Rose asks with a smile on her face.

Meagan stares at Rose for a moment before shaking her head, then both Rose and Meagan bust out laughing as they turn to join James, now waiting by the door for them to finish talking.

Once outside, James decides to use one of the rovers as a utility trailer to tow Emma while using the other one to drive them the nearly one-and-a-half-mile distance to Emma. As he hooks everything up, he tries to figure out what Rose breathes. He knows that Mars's atmosphere is made up of many gases, just like earth. But the oxygen on Mars is so low that it would take at least fifty to one-hundred years before there will be enough O2 for people to survive for short periods of time without a spacesuit.

"Rose, what do you breathe?" James asks after they load up, and the rovers start moving.

"What do I breathe? I don't know for sure, carbon dioxide, maybe." Rose answers while thinking hard. The last part is sounding as though it is not meant for anyone in particular. "After we landed, we only had a few bottles of air left. When they ran out of the air, the rest started feeling sleepy after about a day while I never did. Then you guys opened that first door while I was in there, and even though I felt the air rush out, still nothing happened."

"So, you assumed it must be carbon dioxide because it is the most abundant gas on Mars?" James asks, looking around at the landscape as it goes by.

"For the most part, yes, if I breathed anything else, like hydrogen, I would have had a harder time when the air started getting thin in Emma," Rose says.

James thinks about it for several minutes, knowing they would have to run tests to know for sure. But he decides not to give it much more consideration for now. James then asks Rose to continue her story. And she does.

Chapter Six

The Escape

WHILE MIKE IS OUT GETTING THE stuff, Rose needs. Rose steps into Emma and goes to Emma's screen.

"Emma." Rose calls out once inside. "Let's see if we can pick up some nonpublic transmissions, shall we?"

"I am already ahead of you, Rose. I have been listening to all broadcast since last night's attack." Emma says as if this is nothing for her.

"And what do we know about what is going on?" Rose asks as she walks to one of the sets of steps to sit down, fearing that they want her as a lab rat and Emma to reverse engineer.

"The open broadcasts are saying they are looking for some kidnapping victims. While the more encrypted broadcast says they want, you... and me." Emma says with concern clearly detectable in her voice.

"I was afraid of that." Rose says while thinking hard about her plans. "Emma, do they know or even suspect where we are right now?" Rose asks, looking up at the giant screen that is Emma.

"Not that they are indicating." Emma says showing a map of North America. "When we fled the area, I went due East with no discernible arc." She says showing the flight path they took. "As for the return trip, I held low to the ground, so anyone who saw us would think I was a normal car." As she says this, she shows the roads that she stuck too, to fool any observers.

Rose knows this was a good idea and is about to compliment Emma on it when she hears Meagan and Elizabeth outside sounding scared as they shout her name.

"What's going on? Why are you in such a panic?" Rose asks, coming out to meet Meagan and Elizabeth.

"They are here." Meagan says with a look of horror.

"Who is here?" Rose asks, looking first to Meagan then to Elizabeth. But neither of them answers her, but both were ashen white.

Rose ushers everyone into Emma. However, before she gets in herself, she sees the police out at the main gate of the apartment complex. Once inside, she slides the door closed and locks it.

"Emma?" Rose cries as she darts for the door to the right of her. "Can you make us look like a normal car?" Rose asks, hoping beyond hope that this is something she can do.

"I cannot control my outward appearance any more than you can." Emma says.

Rose has Emma bring the police car up on the screen so they can watch where they are. The Police car drives right by the minivan that is Emma nearly a dozen times before leaving. The whole time nothing comes over the radio, indicating they have not spotted Emma for what she is. All of them give a sigh of relief when the police car leaves. But Rose knows that they may be keeping current communications off the air and using cellphones to communicate orders and observations.

After about an hour, Rose sees Mike return in Meagan's car and park in the visitors' lot. Rose tells Meagan and Elizabeth to stay in Emma, and she will be back as soon as possible. She watches as Mike walks up to the apartment then, right as he turns the key in the door, she moves. Like every time before when she needed to move quickly, she is out of Emma, up the walkway and through the door before Mike even knows something has happened.

"Shit!" Mike cries, dropping all the stuff he has been carrying, as Rose suddenly appears, seemingly out of nothingness, standing right next to him.

"Did you get what I asked for?" Rose asks Mike as he stands there, trying to catch his breath.

"Yes, I... got everything... from the list." He says, pointing to the bags on the floor using his lips.

"I hate when people do that. Do NOT do that in front of me again." Rose says with her eyes closed, pointing a figure at Mike.

Rose grabs the bags that Mike indicated, but they are far too light. Far too light to have everything she asked for, so she looks inside to see what is there and finds that everything is there.

Wow. Ten pounds of lead and thirty pounds of cast iron feels like a small bag of clothes, and the bags of clothes has nearly no weight to them at all. She thinks as she walks towards the kitchen sitting the bags of clothes down on the couch as she walks by. Setting the last bag down on the counter, she first pulls the most massive cast iron pot out of the bag and lays it on the stove, followed by a drill and hole saw. She plugs in the drill and makes two holes in the cast iron pot, one on the bottom and the other in the side about one inch from the bottom.

Then she lifts the burner rack off the stove to see how the pot fits over the burner. Once she is satisfied with how it fits, she reaches into the bag for the other cast iron pot to see how it fits inside. She uses the burner rack to keep the pot off the bottom of the larger pot, keeping them separate, leaving a one-inch gap between the inner and outer pots.

Next, she reaches into the bag and grabs the three-inch piece of cast iron pipe and cuts it to fit the hole on the side of the large cast iron pot, so it comes off at a forty-five-degree angle. Then she fits a three-inch squirrel cage fan to the end of the tube after she has reversed the leads inside, so it blows through the round opening instead of sucking.

Now she is ready to turn it all on. She lights the stove to allow everything to heat up for about ten minutes before plugging in the fan. After the inner cast iron pot starts to glow red inside and out, she drops the led weights into the small cast iron pot. Once they have melted, she takes the box that the weights came in and dips each side into the lead. Then spoons some on the inside as well, making sure there are no uncovered spots on the box.

Once the box cools, she takes the can of paint from the bag, sprays the box inside and out, and allows it to dry while she takes the brand-new cell phone and starts setting it up. The whole time Rose is doing this, Mike is watching her, never blinking for fear he might miss something.

Rose notices Mike for the first time since she started and says, "The smelter is only good for about eight to twelve hundred degrees. But it is yours if you want it."

"A smelter... Is that what that is?" Mike says, sounding as if he is still out of breath.

Rose raises an eyebrow and finishes the setup on the phone, then looks back at Mike. "Are you going anywhere in the next few minutes?" She asks, looking at Mike, who is still in ah of the home-made smelter she made in less than ten minutes.

"Me? Ah... not unless you need me to. Why?" Mike asks, still in total shock over the smelter.

"I need to get back to Emma, without anyone watching knowing anything has happened." Rose says. "Either you can go to Emma, and we all leave together, or you need to go to Meagan's car and go somewhere for a while. The choice is yours." Rose finishes watching Mike's eyes grow as she talks.

"Watching us, from where? How?" Mike says, looking around the apartment as if he expects to see people standing around or pop out of thin air.

"I did not say they were watching us. But it is a strong possibility that they are." Rose says, wishing she has not given Mike so much to think about all at once.

"I guess we can all go somewhere in your car." Mike says, calming down a little.

"Good. When you open the front door, I will make a run for Emma. You follow, and we will all leave. Okay?" Rose says, looking at Mike with a motherly look. Or at least she hopes it is something that is motherly.

Mike nods and goes to his room for a few minutes to get some things. When he returns, he has a tent, sleeping bag, and a large backpack. He then goes to the kitchen and starts to move the home-made smelter, but he can feel a lot of heat from it, so he leaves it where it is. He then turns to grab some food from the cupboards before walking back to the front door.

"If I am going to use a different vehicle than I have been, it needs to look like there is a reason." Mike says, seeing the look of mild impression and confusing it for curiosity on Roses' face.

Rose looks around the apartment to make sure they have not forgotten anything. Satisfied, she turns to Mike and says, "Let's go."

After Mike opens the door, he steps sideways on the pretense to grab the tent and sleeping bag, allowing Rose to run for Emma. As she turns the corner, she sees the door has been opened, revealing Meagan inside. Rose puts on a spurt of speed as she hears someone say, "There is the girl." off in the distance with a small pop, that sounds like it came from a 22-caliber rifle.

Meagan seems to freeze in place as Rose is running towards her. As she arrives, something shoots right by her right ear and hits Meagan in the neck. She turns to Mike and tells him to run as three more shots land, hitting Rose this time, one in the neck and two in the chest.

Elizabeth, who is right behind Meagan, grabs Rose. Elizabeth pulls with all her strength, managing to pull Rose in, just as Mike reaches Emma. Within seconds, Emma has gone from sitting still to doing more than ninety miles an hour on the streets.

Rose tries to fight the tranquilizers that are now coursing through her body, but they are winning out. However, Rose is unable to stay awake any longer and slumps sideways onto the floor as everything around her goes black.

Rose looks around as she starts to awaken some time later. First, she tries to get someone's attention but finds she cannot talk. Next, as she tries to move, she notices that she has little control over her limbs as if her limbs are numb, nothing more than some minor twitches is all she can manage no madder how hard she tries. Then she notices Mike is talking to someone, but she is not able to hear the words he is saying. After a few minutes, Rose manages to get Elizabeth's attention using her tail, but she still cannot really hear anything Elizabeth is saying to her. It takes Rose some time to get to where she can hear anything. She wants to know what is going on, so she tries to get Elizabeth's attention again and soon secedes.

"The police are still following us. Emma has given them some surprises by going places none of them could, like over a small lake and jumping a ravine. The police tried to follow but ended up destroying their cars. It was cool." Elizabeth tells Rose, not realizing that this is the first she can hear anything.

Rose tries to talk but still cannot get any sound to come out. Elizabeth tells her to be patient, and everything will work out. But Rose wants to know about Meagan. Where is she, and what has happened to her? It is nearly another hour before Rose can do anything more than move her tail, and at least two more hours before she can do anything without appearing to be drunk. Once she has full control of her body, she stands up and looks around.

"Elizabeth, where is Meagan?" Rose asks with concern evident in her voice.

"She is in the back working with Emma to find a way out of this problem," Elizabeth says, looking at Rose like she should know this. "I told you that when you first woke up a few hours ago."

"I couldn't hear anything when I first woke up," Rose says. "I tried to tell you, but I... I couldn't talk either." She says thinking that some of the muffled sounds she heard when she first woke up now make sense to her. "Where is the cell phone I had?" As she asks this, she looks around the cabin for it, only seeing the bags of clothing she had.

"I never saw it," Elizabeth says, now looking around as well.

"You dropped it," Mike says, looking back at Rose. "I don't know what happened exactly, but as I saw you turn at the door of the van, I saw the box, and cell phone explode when they hit a pole near the front of Emma," Mike says with sorrow in his voice.

"What about Emma?" Meagan says from behind Rose.

Rose turns on her heel and runs at Meagan, hugging her around the neck before kissing her deeply on the lips. Elizabeth gets a smile on her face as she starts to blush before turning to watch out the front of Emma.

"What is that for?" Meagan asks with her eyes as big as dinner plates.

"I did not know what happened to you. I only knew you had been shot by one of those darts. It scared me to think what might have happened to you. Seeing the way, they affected me." Rose says with tears in her eyes.

"I was only out for about half an hour. They must affect you differently than regular humans." Meagan says, trying to calm Rose down.

"You have to remember; you were hit with three of those darts, and Meagan only had one hit her. Of course, you would be affected more than Megan." Elizabeth says, now looking back at Rose and Meagan again.

"I know, but still." Rose says looking back at Meagan still having tears in her eyes. "What were you doing back there just now?" Rose asks Meagan looking over her shoulder at the door she had just come through.

"I have just been on the phone with the police telling them I have not been kidnaped, but they won't listen." She says, looking around the room.

"That is because the kidnapping is only a cover story like I said before." Rose says to everyone as she lets go of Meagan. "The truth is, they want Emma and me. The rest of you are most likely expendable to them." Rose continues. The rest of them are in shock and remain silent while Rose speaks, while all the time she is picking at her fingers. "Emma and I are great weapons to anyone that can control us, me with my speed and Emma with her ability to fly, not to mention she is an AI."

When Rose finishes, she walks right by Meagan and through the door to the rare of the cabin, leaving Mike, Meagan, and Elizabeth alone. Rose can hear the three of them talking even though she does not want to.

"We are expendable?" Elizabeth asks, looking from Meagan to Mike and back.

"It means they will kill us... just for being around." Mike says, turning and throwing himself into a seat.

"You did not have to put it quite like that." Meagan says, walking over to Elizabeth to hold her close, having seen the tears that have started to well up in her eyes.

"Well... it is true, isn't it?" Mike says in retort, with a snarl in his voice.

"Yes, it is. But there are much better ways of putting it than like that!" Meagan says, her voice starting to rise.

"It's okay. I needed to know what it means, and he told me." Elizabeth says, fighting back her tears. "I need to be alone for a little while." She says as she pushes Meagan away and turns on her heel to walk to the door at the front of the cabin, disappearing through it.

"See, she's fine." Mike says, crossing his arms as he sinks into a seat.

"She is not FINE! She is scared out of her mind and... SHE DOES NOT KNOW WHAT TO DO!" Meagan says, now yelling at the top of her voice.

Rose turns to walk to the other door on the other side of Emma's big screen and hears one last scream from Meagan before she disappears through it. "YOU STUPID... ARROGANT... FOOL! I SHOULD KICK YOU RIGHT IN THE... THE... THE BALLS!"

"Are you alright, baby girl?" Rose asks Elizabeth when the door closes behind her.

"Yes. I will be fine." Elizabeth says with almost no sign of tears in her voice. "I know I needed to know the truth. But... It did not need to be put quite the way he put it." She says the last part with a lot of anger in her voice as she spoke.

Right then, the door opens, and Meagan steps through, though with anger emanating from every part of her. Before the door closes, they all can hear Mike clearly say, while in serious pain and sounding much like a girl, "YOU CRAZY BITCH, THAT FUCKING HURT!"

"So, I take it; you did kick him where it counts?" Rose says with a grin on her face.

"You're damn straight I did." Meagan says with her arms crossed over her chest. "It felt good too." She says, starting to laugh.

"Thank you." Elizabeth says with tears once again in her eyes and a smile on her face.

"Let's go talk to Emma and see what we can do," Rose says as she gestures to the door beside the one Meagan just came through.

When they get to the other room, they can hear that Mike is still hopping around and crying in agony.

"Emma, would you close that door, please?" Rose asks, fighting back laughter as Meagan and Elizabeth feel free to burst out into tears of joy and laughter.

"But I am enjoying listening to him writhe in pain. He deserves a lot more for what he did to Elizabeth." Emma says with a whole lot of sarcasm in her voice.

"Emma, we need to come up with a plan, so we can all live our lives normally. Do you have any ideas on how we can do this?" Rose asks.

Rose and Emma run countless different scenarios to try and find the best one for their escape. For more than five hours, they try different ideas, some ending with all them dying, some ending with one or two dying. Even a few that has Rose, Emma, or even both ending up in the hands of the government. Then they find one with all of them being given more than a forty percent chance of making it.

Emma is airtight except for the front cabin where the generator, radiator, and coolant tank is. Space is the only place that they would have a hard time tracking them, not to mention following them, as Rose and Emma go back and forth on the details while Meagan and Elizabeth listen intently.

"We have a plan," Rose says, looking around at both Meagan and Elizabeth standing in the room. "We will go into space. Of course, we will have to get some supplies before we do." Rose says as she thinks hard about where they can go to get everything they need.

"Rose. There is a sporting goods store about twenty minutes from here." Emma says with a tone of excitement in her voice. "And it is in a mall. They're bound to have everything we need in there, right?" Emma says, sounding pleased with herself for thinking of the mall.

"Most of everything we will need, I think." Rose says, still thinking hard.

Rose Kincade

Rose, Meagan, and Elizabeth walk into the other room where Mike is, to tell him the plan that Rose and Emma have come up with.

"Emma is going to crash through the front doors of the mall and head straight for the 'Sports Store' where I will jump out and grab things we will need." Rose starts.

"And what about the rest of us? Are we supposed to just sit on our asses for you to get back?" Mike asks with much sarcasm.

"NO!" Rose says with her eyes glowing crimson in anger. "You and everyone else will go on to the food court where you will get as much food as possible before returning for me." She finishes.

"So, you really need us?" Mike asks with tears in his eyes.

"Yes, I need each and every one of you. I always have. We have to be quick about this; the police won't stay out for very long. If anything goes wrong, I want you all to get out as quickly as possible." Rose says.

"We will never do that, either we all leave together or not at all!" Elizabeth cries as the tears fall fast and hard.

Everyone, including Emma, agrees and exclaims, "You are too important to sacrifice." In unison.

After crashing through the doors of the mall, Emma does not even slow down as they close in on the sporting goods store. Rose jumps from Emma and lands on her feet like a cat. Emma takes the rest of them to get the food and drinks that they need. Rose starts gathering things as quickly as possible. First, it is cooking gear and eating utensils, followed by sleeping bags and tents.

Rose believes she is just about done when she spots a sign that says 'First fill Free on all new Air Tanks' with a picture of a scuba diver waving his hand.

This is a good thing since they will need air in space. So, Rose looks around to find the filling station. She finds that instead of an air pump like most places, they have several canisters pre-filled as well as a large storage take full of air. So, Rose starts grabbing all the tanks she can, and soon she has nearly fifty tanks as well as more than a dozen regulators, air masks, and rebreathes.

Just then, Rose sees Emma come speeding around the corner. She stops right in front of the pile of stuff Rose has gathered. The door opens, and Megan, Mike, and Elizabeth all start throwing everything into Emma. But just as they were about done, the police come in the building with weapons firing.

"There they are." One of the guys shouts before taking a bead on Rose and open firing.

Rose looks down, knowing that what is being left behind can make all the difference between life and death. But she also knows that if she tries to get the stuff, someone may get hurt, or worse, some may die. So, with much sorrow and determination, she yells, "Let's go!" as she jumps into Emma, closing the door as they depart.

"What did we leave behind?" Meagan asks, looking at Rose's disappointed face.

"We left most of the cookware and utensils... and about half of the air canisters." Rose says, hitting her head on the side of Emma as they exit the mall, dodging police cars that have attempted to block their escape.

"I have enough utensils for everyone, and there are about two dozen hot packs to heat up ready meals in my pack," Mike says, looking at the pile of stuff they have just gotten.

Rose jumps up and kisses Mike on the lips but quickly breaks it off. Mike turns red and drops out of sight as he sinks in his seat.

"What's next, Mom?" Elizabeth says to Rose with a large smile.

"Well, we need to find places for everything," Rose says, looking around at all the stuff that they have all managed to grab.

"Everything cold or frozen needs to go to the left-most corridor in the screen room of Emma. It is the coldest part of the whole room, and in space, it will become like a freezer, so we will use it like a cooler. Everything else will stay in here so we can set it up to be used." Rose says.

It takes them nearly an hour before they have everything put where they want it. But once they are finished, Rose thinks to herself, "Why didn't we ever do this before?"

The tents are set up in a small arch around one of the passenger dome lights that have no seats under it. The two tables Rose did manage to grab are set up on the opposite side of the cabin with a large bucket placed on top to wash dishes. All the air tanks are placed in the far-left corner of the cabin so they can be accessed easily.

***

"So, this Ship of yours, Emma, was never intended for space travel?" James asks, looking at Rose with mild surprise.

"No. I mean, I had not made any modification to her for that. If that is what you are asking." Rose replies.

"So, how long had you been on Mars when we arrived?" James asks as Emma starts to come into view.

"Hey, guys?" Meagan says from behind James and Rose.

As they turn to look at Meagan, they notice she is turning blue like she has not been breathing for some time.

"What does this flashing red light mean?" Meagan asks, holding her left arm up.

"It means you're out of air," James says, looking down at her arm. "When did it start flashing?" He asks, concern evident in his voice.

"I only just noticed it," Meagan says, looking scared. "The last time I looked at it... it was yellow."

"When was that, Meagan? When is the last time you looked at it?" James asks, looking worried. His voice just on the verge of shaking.

"As we left your ship, I happened to look down at my arm as we were climbing onto the rover." Meagan says, tears welling up in her eyes, as her face starting to show her worry now as well.

"That was about forty, maybe forty-five minutes ago. When the light turns yellow, you only have about 10 minutes left." James says, looking back at Rose with a look of mixed confusion and concern on his face.

"James, since she is turning purple now, why not take her mask off?" Rose suggests with a smile while considering Meagan's eyes. Noticing that they are starting to turn yellow with slits for pupils now, instead of the usual blue they had always been before now, Rose knows what is happening to Megan.

Meagan, seeing the smile on Rose's face, nods and reaches up to remove the mask just as James reaches out a hand to stop her.

"Wait, if you take that off. There is no telling what will happen," James says, looking Meagan in the eyes. He, too, now is noticing the changes in Meagan, and the concern on his face vanishes only to be replaced by total bewilderment.

Meagan, looking back at James, sees the changes being reflected back at her. She sees how purple her skin is and how her eyes have changed to yellow; she decides to twist the mask and pulls it off. But instead of the familiar whooshing sound, there is nothing. She takes a deep breath and looks at Rose. "I can breathe the air." She says, looking entirely relieved.

"And you have some horns on your head as well," Rose tells Meagan. "Not as long as mine, yet. But I am sure they will get there."

James, looking dumbfounded, looks from Meagan to Rose and back before saying, "Let's go!?" while shaking his head in disbelief. They ride the rest of the distance in silence, mostly because James does not know what to say about Meagan's changes, much of them seemingly happening right before his eyes. Meagan and Rose look at each other with smiles on their faces.

Once at Emma, Rose goes in to see exactly how bad the front of Emma is and what will be needed to get her back up and going again. After several minutes Rose reappears at the opening.

"James, did anyone take anything from the front of Emma here?" Rose asks James looking out from under the hood.

"Not that I am aware of. Why what is missing?" He asks.

"A small box, about six by eighteen inches. It is what made me like this, and what made Emma like she is." Rose says looking at James with the fire in her eyes flaming orange with her anger. "Where is Lt. Marks at? I do not remember seeing him when everyone went to eat or during the fight when Edwards try to kill Meagan here." Rose says, looking from James to Meagan and back.

"You're right. Come to think of it; he has been missing since we returned to the ship." James says, anger making the vain on his forehead pop.

"Let's get Emma hooked up so we can get back to camp, and then we can worry about Lt. Marks." Rose says looking around. "It would be the same amount of time back, either way, right?"

"What? Ah... Yes. It would take the same time. Either we take Emma now or leave her and come back later." James says.

Rose, Megan, and James hook Emma up between the two rovers and start back. About five minutes into the drive, Rose sees James is not focusing on what he is doing. A task he had no problem doing when Rose was telling him her story.

About then, Meagan starts doing a strange little dance by wagging her ass as she rides. The little dance she is making looks funny as she slides two paces to the right then hops back to the left. She repeats these steps several times before Rose decides she has seen enough.

"Meagan?" Rose calls as she leans forward. "Is everything okay?" She asks, noticing the strange dance becoming more intense.

"My ass feels funny," Meagan says. "It is starting to hurt, and I don't know what is going on." She says this part as tears fill her eyes and voice.

Rose looks down at Meagan's ass and notices it is bulging quite a bit. "We need to stop for a moment," Rose says loud enough for James to hear. Then she grabs Meagan around the arm, dragging her off the rover before ducking behind a large rock.

"Is everything alright?" James calls out.

"It will be!" Rose replies. "Take off your suit." Rose tells Meagan in a whispered voice.

"What? Why?" Meagan replies, looking at Rose with shock on her face.

"Trust me; it will help." Rose says, reaching out to unbuckle the suit only to have her hand smacked away.

"I will do it, thank you." Meagan says with a lot of attitude as she turns to strip the suit.

James walks over to the large bolder while working the controls to keep the rovers moving. As he realizes what he is walking upon, he tries pretending he is not trying to get a quick glance.

Once Meagan has taken off the suit, Rose grabs her panties and rips a hole in the ass of them. Meagan feels Rose messing with something that is turning her on. She can feel Rose pull, twist, and yank something that seems to be a part of her butt, but it is nothing like she has ever felt before.

"What, awww... are you, awwwww... doing, awwwww... back there?" Meagan asks under heavy breath. Then all of a sudden, she feels like the world has just lit up for the first time in her life.

"How is that?" Rose asks, turning Meagan to look at her in the eyes. By this time, Meagan's ears, horns, and her tail are all about half the length of Rose's and seem to be growing bigger with every passing second.

"Better. What did you do?" Meagan asks, looking at Rose with lust in her eyes.

"Ah... Let's say I... I relieved some pressure." Rose says, turning blue and looking down at her hands with a pinkish goop that had come from Meagan's tail. "Put the top part of the suit back on, and let's get going."

Meagan puts on the top part of the suit while never taking her eyes off Rose. Meagan is now feeling rather giddy and feels as though she needs Rose for a little one-on-one pleasure. As Meagan and Rose come back around the rock, James's jaw drops as he catches a glimpse of them hand in hand.

"You're... You are... I mean... I..." James does not know what to say or how to act. All he knows is that when Meagan came out skipping along, she has the top part of the suit on and fastened, but the two legs are flopping out behind her, showing off her panties to the world while hiding her new tail.

"Let's go," Rose says, turning to help Megan onto the rovers before getting on herself.

It takes James quite a bit of time to regain his senses of what Meagan and Rose may have just done before he starts driving. When he does, he wants Rose's story to continue as he tries to catch his breath.

Chapter Seven

The Crash

THE MILITARY IS GETTING IMPATIENT, waiting for things to come to an end, so they are dispatching several Apaches to shoot Emma off the road.

"Rose, the US military, has just launched six Apache type helicopters to stop us by any means necessary." Emma tells Rose.

"Emma, Head for open desert. I don't want them hurting innocent people." Rose says, running for the monitor. Once in the desert, Rose believes they can start flying since the glow of the sun is nearly gone. "Emma, as soon as the sun as mostly gone, let's start flying and heading for space." As Rose finishes saying this, everyone can hear what sounds like hail hitting the outside of the van.

Emma decides to turn on one of the news stations that is airing the chase. "The kidnappers have been driving for nearly fifteen hours now since this whole thing started." The news reporter says. "The military has informed us that they will be bringing this chase to an end very shortly." As the reporter says this, two of the chasing Apache helicopters opens fire on the van. "The van looks to be lifting off the ground with all of the firepower being tossed at it. No.

Wait. The van is actually flying. Yes, flying. It is starting to pull away from the chase helicopters." The reporter looks as though she can't believe what she is saying.

Soon, however, Emma is so far ahead of the Apache's that their rounds are no longer hitting her.

"Emma, we need to get into space for this to work." Rose says. "Is there a problem that is stopping you?" She asks, seeing that Emma's flying is more up and down than straight and level.

"Somehow, all of that lead is messing with my systems." Emma says, sounding less like herself and more like a computer.

"Let's get out of here, and when we are safe, we can try getting the lead out." Rose, Meagan, and Elizabeth say in unison.

Suddenly with a bright flash of light, Emma shoots upwards, and soon they are in outer space. Each of them is floating in the air as well as most of the items scattered around the room. Rose notices that Emma is not just going around the Earth as they had planned, but instead, she is drifting off into space.

"Emma, what is wrong?" Rose asks.

"M, M, M, My Sys, Systems r, r, r, shu, shutting dow, down." Emma says as the screen on the wall goes out.

"Emma!" Elizabeth cries as the tears start to well up.

"It will be okay, honey." Meagan says, trying to comfort Elizabeth.

"Will everything be okay?" Mike asks, looking smug like he knows this was going to happen.

"You dumb cold-hearted son of a BITCH!" Rose shouts at Mike. "If we weren't hurtling through space, I would kick your ass right out of Emma," Rose says. "I think I would feel better, however, just taking a page from Meagan's book and just..." She looks down and aims but never kicks.

Right at that moment, it seems something is now shooting at them again. As they all float out to the cabin to see what is going on, they cannot see anything actually shooting or hitting the outside of Emma. All they can see is glass suddenly shattering as well as chips of paint erupting from the surface of Emma.

After nearly a day of the pelting from what they can only assume to be a micro-rite shower, it seems to stop. Rose spends several days trying to get Emma up and running again and is about to call it a lost cause when she finds what is stopping her from working. Rose pulls it out and makes a makeshift fix in the circuit.

"Meagan?" Rose says. "Would you take Elizabeth to the other room, please?"

Rose waits until she hears the door between the rooms open and close before she turns to Mike. "You told me you watched this shatter on a pole in front of Emma back at your apartment," Rose says, holding up the lead box with the phone in it.

Mike looks shocked by the box and does not say a word. He tries to turn and move away, but he has not quite mastered how to move without something to push on as Rose has. Within a second, Rose is in front of him, staring into his eyes with that same blood-red fire in her eyes that she has used before.

"This may have killed us all because of where you hid it." Rose says with her voice in a normal tone, but as she does, Mike can feel each word reverberate within him.

"I am sorry. I was mad, angry even... I did not know what to do." Mike says with tears filling his eyes. "You don't know how long I have been after Meagan just for a date. I have had a crush on her all throughout high school and into college." Mike says as the tears now start making their escape. "I got a job at the mall where she worked just to be close to her. I asked her for a date every time I heard she got out of a relationship with anyone, male or female." The tears are coming much faster now. "Then you come along, and within just a few days, you have her living with you. Then a few months later right before all this shit starts, her and I were talking on the phone together, and she says she... She says... she says she has just had the best... the best... The best sex ever... with

YOU!" He finishes the tears and sobs so intense that the only thing he can do is bury his face in his hands.

Rose, now understanding what he is feeling and going through, grabs Mike and starts hugging him. As she does, she tries to calm him to try and stifle the tears and sobs.

"Everything will work out for the best in the end, Mike." She says.

Suddenly Mike lifts his head and kisses Rose. At first, Rose does not break away. She has never been kissed quite like this before and begins to wonder why she is allowing this to happen. Is it because she feels guilty for what Mike has been feeling, or does she really want him to take her like this?

Rose is just starting to accept it when something deep down hits her, and she breaks the kiss off. As Rose is pushing away, Mike pulls her in again. This time however, Rose never gets the feeling that she experienced before and decides to let things go on.

Soon after, Rose's clothes start coming off. First, it is her shirt. Mike moves down and starts kissing the top of her left breast as he kneads the other in his left hand. This does not feel good to her, so she grabs his hand and pulls it away. Then it is her bra that falls away. Then her skirt and panties seem to leave her as one. Mike has now moved down, licking and kissing his way down between her legs. As he moves, Rose can feel a tingling sensation shoot throughout her body emanating from wherever he touches.

Soon Rose finds herself shivering and shaking all over in a very different way than with Megan. She does not know why this sensation is so different from everything she has experienced to this point. These sensations are making it hard to move or even focus on what is going on in front of her. Her mind seems to be leaving her, and the only thing she can think of is Mike giving her every ounce of seed he has. And as if he has heard her, Mike has started moving upward on her body.

His penis is hard and large, more massive than hers had been as a man. She can feel it slide on her belly as he comes up past his intended point. He lets it touch her as he moves it back down towards her vagina. The first thrust he makes causes his penis to move upward, and she sees the head emerge from between her legs. He pulls back and reaches down with his right hand as he tries again.

When Mike makes his second attempt, he manages to get it to push in a little. Rose feels like her world is going to explode as he moves. The sensation is nothing like she has ever felt before. It is like fire and ice have merged into one feeling. Then she feels Mike push again, and everything she felt from the first thrust amplifies and shoots through her like a bolt of lightning. Her whole body now quivering, more than she ever has before as a man or woman, Mike gives the third thrust, but unlike the first two, this one is all fire. It shoots from her vagina all the way to her head and toes, and just as fast as it started, it is gone. Mike gives his fourth thrust, and Rose can feel her toes curl upward as her body starts to move with his.

His motion suddenly starts to get faster and faster, and Rose feels like her body is going to erupt from all the feeling she is now experiencing. After what feels like only a few seconds, she feels Mike tighten up and give one last thrust, and her legs tighten around him, holding him tight in her. As she does, she feels something shoot into her as her body tightens up, pulling Mike into her even more and holding him there. With every pump of his member, her body seems to flash with every nerve firing as every muscle in her body seems to tighten to the beat of his heart. After about a minute, she finds that she can think again, and she releases him.

Mike pulls out, and she once more feels her body give one last massive shiver. After he has completely pulled out, she can feel something oozing out of her vagina. She knows it must be Mike's semen, so trying not to think about it, she starts to look around for her clothes to be able to get dressed. Soon after starting her search, she has her shirt and bra followed by her skirt. But no matter how hard she looks, she cannot find her panties.

"Have you seen my panties?" Rose asks, throwing Mike his pants.

"No." Mike says as he pulls on his pants. "Do you see my shirt?" He asks back, looking up at the top of the room.

After a few minutes of looking, they eventually find all their clothes. As they finish getting dressed, Emma's screen flickers on. Both Mike and Rose wait with bated breath for her to fully boot up. After about ten minutes, the screen that is Emma flickers once again, but nothing else seems to happen.

Rose's heart sinks. "It failed." She says to herself, allowed.

"Hello, everyone." Emma's voice says loud and clear.

Rose is so excited she grabs Mike and kisses him, but quickly breaks it apart. Meagan and Elizabeth enter the room and see Rose and Mike shouting, "She works."

Once Rose has calmed down, she wants to know how bad Emma's circuits are.

"Emma? Give me your operating specs and current abilities, Please." Rose asks, knowing such a short could have caused other issues.

"Based on the information coming from my components, I should be operating at 18.2 Terahertz processors, 120 Terabytes of ram, with a max memory space of 90 Petabytes. However, my systems diagnostics show, I am operating at three to the third power times faster than that." Emma says with concern evident in her voice.

"I was afraid of that," Rose says, looking down with concern on her face.

"What is wrong?" Meagan asks. "Is she okay?"

"She is running at about five to twenty percent below normal, and some of the hard drives seem to have been fried," Rose says, looking around.

"So, what does that mean?" Mike asks, looking at Emma's screen.

"I cannot do all the things I could before," Emma answers. "I do not even know if I can safely set down on the moon, let alone anything bigger."

"Emma?" Elizabeth asks. "How hard do you think it would be to plot a course to allow for a controlled slide landing on Mars?"

"It would depend on how we approach Mars Elizabeth. I can plot the best course to land, but we will hit with so much force I do not know if my body can handle it or not." Emma explains. "Why do you ask?"

"Because Mars now looks twice the size of the moon back on Earth, it's right outside of the window here," Elizabeth says.

Everyone looks where Elizabeth is pointing, and sure enough, there is Mars, even bigger than she had just said. Suddenly the direction of Emma changes.

"Emma, what's going on?" Megan asks, sounding scared.

"I am going to attempt a braking maneuver to slow us down. If it works, we will be able to perform a controlled descent and crash landing." Emma says. "Now, please, let me focus, so I do not kill us."

After about four orbits, Emma is heading for the surface. Emma turns off everything that she can to devote as much processor power as possible to the task at hand. Once through the outer atmosphere, the lights come back on, and the descent seems to speed up to everyone's horror.

"Everyone, please get ready for a crash landing." Emma says, with no discernible tones to her concern.

At about five-hundred feet from the ground, Emma seems to level off, and everyone thinks it is going to be a gentle landing. Rose stands to see how much further it is until they are on the ground but quickly realizes she just has time to drop to the floor and hold on to something for the crash. The landing is anything but easy. As they hit the ground, Emma gives a violent shutter followed by the lights going out. Four loud bangs quickly follow this as sand and rocks go flying over the top of Emma for what seems like minutes. Then everything stops as if they hit something, and all of them go flying to the front of Emma.

Rose walks to the door that Emma is behind, but it does not open. Rose has to force the door open, something they had never had to do, even when Emma went offline. When she looks in the room, it is darker than she had ever seen it. All the light that always seemed to come from nothing is gone.

Elizabeth starts crying and buries her head in Meagan's shoulder. Meagan too, starts crying, which makes Rose feel like she needs to cry as well. But Rose knows she cannot if she is going to keep her friends alive.

The next morning Rose wakes up to something moving around outside. When she looks out the window, she can see a strange-looking robotic face, looking into Emma. She only has time to bring her hand up to cover her face when she hears it take a snapshot.

***

The NASA Landing Camp is now in sight, and they can see that another three ships have landed while they were gone.

"Let's race." Megan says to Rose. "I want to see if I am now as fast as you."

"Your ears and horn have not even fully grown in yet, and you want to race me?" Rose replies with a wicked grin.

"Yes, I do." Megan says with a wicked grin of her own. "You are no longer a one of a kind; you no longer have an advantage over me."

James, who has been left behind, cannot believe his eyes. The two girls in front of him seem to take three steps in fractions of a second each — covering more than five football fields. "How is this possible." He says aloud, not knowing that someone is listening to him.

"How is what possible, James?" Rebecca asks over the radio.

"Rebecca?" James asks, hoping that it is her.

"Yes. How is 'what' possible?" She says again.

"That is not important right now." James says, remembering about Lt. Marks. "Have you seen Lt. Marks of late?"

"I don't know. What's up?" She asks.

"We need to find Lt. Marks ASAP. I don't remember seeing him since we rescued Rose and her friends." James says, trying to keep his temper under control.

"Now that you mention it, I have not seen him since we returned from getting our guests." Rebecca says. "What is wrong, James? What has the little *squirt* done now?" She says, putting a lot of emphasis on squirt.

"Are you alone?" James asks.

"Yes, I am." Rebecca says with concern present in her voice.

"There is an essential part missing off of Rose's ship," James says calmly. "The part someone took is really hazardous. Not only to whoever took it but to all of us."

"Dangerous, how?" Rebecca asks with a lot more concern in her voice now.

"Dangerous enough that none of us may make it off this rock dangerous." James says, looking around to see if anyone is listening since at least one of the new landing pods is a manned crew.

Just then, James hears someone come into the radio room with Rebecca. "Are you all alone?" The voice says, sounding far too much like a cartoon character than a person.

"Yes." Rebecca says, holding down the talk button as not to let the person know there is someone on the radio.

"Talking to someone on the radio?" The voice says.

"Just trying to reach James, Marks, he is not back yet." Rebecca says, both to keep Lt. Marks from knowing what is going on as well as to let James know who is there with her.

James stops the rovers and runs as fast as he can to the module. "NOOO!" James hears Rebecca scream right before the line goes dead. James knows he still has at least two hundred yards to go before he is at the airlock to get inside.

Suddenly something comes shooting out of the window of the radio room. "NOOOOO!" James shouts at the top of his lungs. As he gets to where the body lays, James sees that it is not Rebecca; it is a twisted form that can only be Lt. Marks. As James looks up at the broken window, he sees Rose and Meagan standing there, looking down where he is standing.

Meagan jumps from the window, landing as if it is just a step-down. As she moves forward, Rose steps out, landing right behind her and following her forward.

"What happened?" James asks, looking from Meagan and Rose.

"He must have the box and tried to open it." Rose says, looking down at the twisted body.

"No. I mean, just now. What happened to Rebecca?" James says, clarifying what he wants to know.

"Rebecca will be fine." Meagan says.

"We were coming down the hallway when we heard her scream." Rose says.

"When we entered the room, Rebecca was fighting, trying to get out." Meagan says.

"By showing up when we did, we gave her the chance she needed to get out." Rose says.

"Once the door closed, the real fun started." Meagan says. A smile spreads from horn to horn on both women as they turn to look at each other.

James, now feeling like his head is on a constant pivot, grabs his head with both hands. "I am glad it is not Rebecca that came out of that window." James says, letting his head go.

"If it had been, almost everyone might have died in there today," Rose says, looking down at the body one last time. "Let's go inside, and you can tell Rebecca how you feel about her."

James looks up and stares at Rose for a moment realizing that she knows his feelings better than he does, then says, "Okay. Let's go."

Once inside, James and Rebecca embrace in a long and passionate kiss. They both having just realized their genuine feelings for each other.

After searching Lt. Marks's room, Meagan and Rose find the little box and can get it reinstalled in Emma. After about two days of hard work and a lot of help from James and his crew, they're able to restore power to Emma and get her fully functional again using spare parts from the landing pods.

Over the next several months, many of the crew members start to experience changes. The speed at which each person changes varies depending on many different factors. Most of which seem to be unknown, but one possibility is how much time they spent in Emma and near Rose.

After NASA's discovery of the changes the crew has been experiencing, they decide to recall the Stuhlinger MEK to Earth to prevent any contaminations returning to Earth. But this was not a problem since James and his crew have decided not to return home when the time to go comes, partly because they don't want to, but mostly because most of them have changed into creatures just like Rose and Meagan during the two years, they are together.

"What does it feel like to go through the changes?" Elizabeth asks one night at dinner.

"For me, I did not even know that I was changing until I saw my reflection on James's helmet." Megan says.

"It hurt like hell for a few days. I could not move, eat, or sleep it hurt so much. After it was finished, I felt as though the world was the new place, not me." Mike says with a grin from horn to horn.

"I only had a strange itch all over my body. It was as though I had something crawling under my skin." Rebecca says as she looks at James with eyes of longing.

"Well, when I changed, I kept a constant stomachache and a headache for a really long time. When the final transformation took place, I felt as though a horse had kicked my ass. I spent the rest of the time, unconscious." Rose says.

"What I want to know is why does it hurt so much for men and hardly at all for women?" James asks, looking around the room.

"Well, for women, they already have most of the parts where they belong before the changes start. This allows them to need very few modifications for the change. As for men, they get the full; kick the balls to the back and grow the rest." Frank tells everyone.

Elizabeth snorts milk through her nose as Megan falls off her chair. James, David, Andrew, and Brian jaws all drop in shock.

"Is that what the rest of us have to look forward too?" Andrew asks the room.

"There is no reason to think everyone will change." Frank says, taking a drink of coffee.

"Elizabeth has been around Emma and me longer than anyone, and she has not ever shown any signs of starting any kind of change." Rose says. After she finishes, Rose can feel something rush down her legs, and with a look of surprise, she tells Frank that it is time for the baby.

Within a few months of each other, Elizabeth has two new sisters that she loves more than anything. She loves them so much she would help with anything to make sure they have everything they need. Even though she can't go outside to play with them like she would like since she is still fully human, the only child in the camp that is.

A few days later, in the medical pod, as Rose is recovering from giving birth, Megan, Rebecca, and James come in to talk to her. "Hi, how is everyone doing?" Rose asks, seeing the three of them walking into the room.

"Rose, Elizabeth told us that you are rich." James says, deciding not to hold anything back.

"I would not say rich, but yes, I have a fair amount of money. I do need to check on my business, now that you mention it." Rose says.

"Honey, why have you never told me this before?" Megan asks.

"I thought you knew. I never worked the whole time we spent together. I let my managers handle the main day-to-day stuff since I could not go in looking like this. Emma has a fantastic app that puts an image of my old face on a live video feed so I could check in on them as needed." Rose explains.

"Well, we have been trying to figure out how to get fresh supplies. We would like to use Emma to head to Earth and load her up." Rebecca says.

"Well, Emma and I managed to bring down the last few pods before they recalled your ship." Rose starts, thinking of ideas that should be helpful to the group. "My company is an R and D corporation, so I can have them work on some new projects that will benefit us as well as those of Earth. I might be able to get some 'Million 747' to help out as well."

"What is 'Million 747'?" Rebecca asks.

"Is that how you regulated the power requirements?" Megan asks.

"'Million 747' is a mineral solution that has a very rare heavy molecule that vibrates energy in three dimensions instead of two like others." James says.

Those in the room look at James with their mouths hanging open in shock. Rebecca is the first to break the silence. "How in the hell do you know that? I didn't even know that." She says slightly louder than she should have.

Hearing the commotion, Frank comes running in to see what is going on. "What the hell is going on here. There are more patients than just Rose and her babies." He says angrily.

"I am sorry, Frank." Rebecca says. "We will try to be quieter." She says, looking over at the babies next to Rose.

"Anyway, If I can get us some of this solution, then we can make more ships like Emma. If there is enough, we can even enlarge at least some of the pods." Rose says, looking around the room.

James nods, and Frank looks excited. Megan and Rebecca look determined as they both say, "We can do it. We will help you any way we can." Megan and Rebecca look at each other and bust out laughing. After they get control of their laughter, they hug each other.

Over the next few weeks, those that can go outside start to transform the landing camp into a regular small town with roads and walkways. They then set up one of the shuttles to be a school as well as a daycare since some of the children's parents will still be doing most of their original work as NASA astronauts since Mars still holds many secrets to uncover.

They also set up a large Bio-Dome that can house up to one-hundred people for when NASA sends the next team up to work, though NASA is still not telling anyone when that might be.

Chapter Eight

Michael Wayne

TODAY MICHAEL IS PROUD OF himself after getting the mail and opening the manila envelope. He has just received his contract to start playing for the Dallas Cowboys Football Team, and he is ready to sign it. He has been given the offer, by the team, right out of college. One of the coaches for the Cowboys' football team came to watch his son play on a regular basis and found Michael to be just what he was looking for in a new player.

After their last game of the season, the coach walked up to Michael and said, "Hello Sir, I am Mr. Hutson, the coach for the Dallas Cowboys Football Team. I have been watching you play all season. How would you like a chance to come to play for us?" He asked him.

But this is not the only reason Michael feels so proud today. Irridian, his wife, and him are going to see the doctor today to find out what gender their new child is going to be. But this is not going to be their first child since they got married. It is going to be their second, and Michael cannot be happier.

Michael is ready to walk out the door, but Irridian wants some more time. Because he has some time, he decides to look at his emails to see what is there. He sees an email from his aunt Rose who lives rather far away but always manages to send him an email, or two, every week. When he opens the email to see what it says, he sees congratulations. Not only on the new football contract that he just received but for expecting another little girl.

Michael wants to believe this is just wishful thinking on her part, but his aunt has a remarkable talent for knowing things like this. Michael and Irridian want a boy this time around since they already have a little girl.

"I am ready now, Michael." Irridian says, walking out from the bedroom.

When Michael and Irridian arrive at the doctor's office, they are ushered into an examination room. Irridian quickly changes for the ultrasound and is just finishing up as the doctor walks in.

As the doctor is doing the ultrasound, she pronounces the child is a girl. "How does she always know?" Michael says, not intending to say this allowed.

"Who?" Irridian asks, turning to look at Michael as her smile fades from her face.

"My Aunt Rose." Michael says, standing and walking through the door of the exam room.

Michael walks down the hall to the bathroom, where he tries to clear his head by splashing some cold water on to his face. "She always knows. How can she always know when she lives on another planet?" he asks himself aloud, looking at his reflection in the mirror.

Rose has lived on Mars since she escaped from the police and the military three years earlier. She has set up a small town of about three hundred people, and most of them have already had or are having children, nearly doubling their numbers with just children alone. The whole thing is operating with the help of NASA, who are getting lots of new data from them about Mars for silence.

Michael steps out of the bathroom and turns to walk back to the ultrasound room when he sees Irridian and the doctor walk out and turn in his direction.

"Do you feel better now?" Irridian asks with a smile on her face.

"Not really." Michael says, looking back at the doctor standing right behind Irridian. "What did you tell her?" He asks.

"Only that your aunt seems to know everything that is happening in your life before you do." Irridian says, slapping Michael on the arm.

After the appointment, Michael and Irridian walk out to the car to head home. "How can she always know what is going on?" Michael asks, more to himself than anyone else.

"Are you still stuck on your Aunt?" Irridian asks, looking over at Michael.

"I guess so; I just don't know how she can know what is going on with anyone in the family. She has not been back to Earth in nearly three years." Michael says as he starts the car.

"You know she is no longer human. She probably has all sorts of abilities that we have no idea about yet." Irridian says as they are pulling out onto the road.

"You're probably right. But it is so frustrating that she knows what is going on all the time." Michael says.

"I know, Baby." Irridian says.

After Michael and Irridian return home, Michael starts feeling sick with a headache and a strange upset stomach. Michael tries to ignore the pain, but it only just gets worse.

Irridian takes him to the bedroom and has him lie down. She gives him some Tylenol before she goes to get their daughter, Taylor, from next door, allowing him to fall asleep.

Michael does not know how long he has been asleep, but when he wakes, sometime in the night, he believes that he is hungry. He walks to the kitchen and makes himself a snack and sits at the table to eat it. When he finishes, he places the plate in the sink. As he is walking back towards the bedroom, he hears the phone ring.

"Hello," Michael says when he answers the phone.

"Mike, it's Linda, your sister." The female voice says, on the other end, sounding as though she is upset about something.

"What's up?" Michael asks, pleased to hear from her.

"Andrew is missing." Linda says, sounding concerned.

"Missing, since when?" Michael asks, trying to think of the last time he saw or even heard from him since Andrew and Linda moved to Pennsylvania the month before.

"Since a few days ago, we are supposed to go to Aunt Rose's place this weekend to see them all." Linda says.

"But what makes you think he is missing?" Michael asks, now thinking it is just her imagination at work.

"He has not been to work this week at all. His work just called me looking for him." She says, sounding frustrated.

Michael now looks at the clock and sees it is just after four in the morning. This means where Linda lives is now just after seven in the morning. "But he is supposed to be at work by six, correct?" Michael asks with concern in his voice.

"Yes. That is why I called you. I thought that maybe he would have at least have told you what is going on." Linda says.

Michael can hear the tears in her voice, and he knows something is definitely wrong here. First, is the fact that Andrew would not just shrug off work like that since he is the head of his department. And second, he has always told someone what he was going to do if he is going to take time off for some alone time.

"I will try and get a hold of him and have him call you. Okay?" Michael says, hoping this will calm Linda down.

"Thank you, Mike." She says before hanging up the phone.

Irridian, who has been standing in the doorway, asks, "What is going on?" as Michael sits the phone down on the countertop.

"Andrew is missing." Michael tells her as he walks to the table.

"Andrew? Andrew, from high school, Andrew?" Irridian says with an air of curiosity in her voice.

"Yes. Apparently, he has not been to work for a week now. That was Linda asking if I had heard from him." He tells her as he looks at the phone as if it is about to explode or something.

Michael and Irridian talk the morning away until the sun starts coming up. Irridian stands and starts making breakfast for Michael and Taylor while Michael starts calling Andrew's cell.

After nearly an hour of trying and getting no answer from Andrew, Michael must start to get ready to go meet with the Dallas Cowboy's recruiter to give him the signed contract. Irridian takes Taylor over to the neighbors so she, too, can get ready for her job.

Since Michael's meeting is on the way to the bank that Irridian works at, she drops Michael off at his conference. The session lasts only for about thirty minutes; this is because the recruiter is interested in knowing what Michael wants to do after football.

After the meeting with the recruiter, Michael starts walking home. As he passes a sporting goods store, he decides to step inside to see if they have anything new he might be interested in buying.

He walks to and fro, looking at nearly everything in the store. He stops to look at the new football helmets, the main one that he likes has the latest in an anti-impact lining, a built-in two-way radio, and the new spine shield. He then walks over to see some new pads that claim to have better impact resistance. Next, he decides to look at the jockstraps since his old one is cracked. Suddenly he feels a headache return and concludes he better leave without buying anything.

Michael is walking through the door of his apartment when he starts experiencing severe cramps and bloating. As he makes his way to the bedroom, he feels a sharp pinch between his legs, and he falls to his knees from the pain.

Michael tries to get to his feet, but instead, he ends up knocking an end table and lamp over onto its side as he falls onto his back and becomes entangled in the cord. Once he is free of the wire, he tries once more to stand up and walk. With only limited success, he manages to make it to his feet and stumbles to the bedroom, where he throws himself onto the bed before passing out.

Hours later, when Irridian comes home, she finds that the table near the hallway leading to the bedroom has been knocked over, smashing the lamp that was on it. She calls out for Michael, hoping that it was just an accident, but she gets no reply. At that time, Michael wakes up and looks around. He feels as though he needs to use the bathroom, so he stands and shakily makes his way over to the door and stumbles into the bathroom knocking several small items onto the floor. Irridian hears the cans and bottles hitting the floor in the bathroom and decides she needs to check it out.

As Michael reaches the toilet and feeling he is not able to stand well, he decides to sit on the toilet rather than the typical stand and aim he is used too. When he goes to pull down his pants, he finds he is not wearing any; even his boxers are gone. By now, the pressure is so enormous he has no choice but to go, so rather than worry about it, he sits down.

After he has relieved himself, Irridian comes into the bathroom and starts screaming, but she only screams for a moment before she passes out. As Michael walks over to help Irridian, he catches sight of his appearance in the mirror.

He is a she, and not just any she, she is purple with long horns sticking out of her head and cat-like ears perched between them. His eyes have changed to a fiery yellow with the pupils turned into slits. He has breasts that are large and firm, and as he touches them, he can feel the nipples get hard under his hands. As his eyes fall lower, he sees something whip out from behind him for a split second before disappearing behind her again. He turns his head to look behind him to see a long three-foot tail whipping around behind him, or rather her.

He looks just like his Aunt Rose. "How can this be?" Michael asks herself, trying to hear her new voice. Just then, Irridian begins to stir, so Michael bends down to help her.

"Irridian, are you okay?" Michael asks, helping Irridian to her feet.

Irridian looks Michael up and down, taking in every part of her. Then she asks, "Michael? Is that really you?"

"Yes, it's me. I look like my aunt after her change all those years ago." Michael says, starting to cry due to the new emotions welling up inside of her.

"Hay, hay, hay, we are all here together. We can work this out." Irridian laughs at Michael with a smile on her face.

Just then there is a knock on the front door. "Miss Wayne, it's the police. We got a call that some of your neighbors heard screaming." The female police officer voice calls from the living room.

Irridian goes out and talks to the cops. "What can I do for you, Officers?" She asks, walking down the hallway.

"We received a report of a woman screaming in this apartment. Is everything okay?" Michael hears the female officer ask.

Michael can hear her tell the officers, "When I opened the front door, a dog that has been roaming the area for a few weeks now, chased a cat into the apartment. They knocked over the table there as they went into the bedroom. When I went into the room to try and chase them out, the cat jumped onto my shoulder, and that is when I screamed."

Michael cannot hear any voices for a minute then hears the female cop say, "Okay, you should have that checked by a doctor." before the door closes.

Michael suddenly realizes that she is still naked and decides that it is a good idea to put some clothes on. She walks to the dresser to get some underwear. As she pulls them up, they are a lot looser than they have been before, but they do not fall off. She notices her tail is poking through one of the leg openings, so she takes them off and grabs the pair of scissors that are on the back of the dresser and cuts a hole into the backside of the underwear. When she puts them back on, they no longer stay on her. Michael does not like the idea of grabbing Irridian's panties but feels she has no other choice. She grabs one of the new pairs of panties and cuts a hole in them like her own. She slides them on and finds they fit much better, though they are still slightly loose.

She walks over to the closet and reaches for a pair of her pants before remembering about her underwear, so instead, she grabs a pair of Irridian's pants and again cuts a hole in them for her tail. After that, she grabs one of her shirts and pulls it over her head only to have it rip on her horns.

"What the hell." She exclaims as she pulls it off again. As she looks at the shirt, she remembers she now has horns, and they stick out a good eight to ten inches from her head. So, she looks through the closet for something to go with the tan slacks she has on. Everything she has that is hers in a dress shirt is black or dark blue. So, she turns to look at Irridian's side again and sees a white dress shirt. She decides to grab it and starts to put it on when Irridian calls out to her.

"No, you don't." She says, walking over to the dresser.

"I have to have clothes." Michael says, looking around at her.

"Yes, and you are no longer a guy now, and you can't let those things just hang." She says, pointing to Michael's chest.

Michael looks down to see what she is talking about and sees the two big breasts on her chest, hanging from her like two large sacks. Her cheeks flush blue before she says, "I forgot about those."

Irridian walks over with one of the bras that are too small for her. She throws the blouse aside before saying, "Turn around and raise your arms."

Michael does as she is told, turning and raising her arms above her head. Irridian fits the bra around the front side, making sure that each breast goes into each cup correctly. She then has Michael turn so she can fasten the back, only to have to grab a safety-pin to hold it together since it is too large.

"We are going to have to get you your own clothes. You are too small for mine." She tells Michael as she hands back the blouse.

Michael looks at Irridian, judging her figure compared to her own that she has seen in the mirror. Now that she thinks about it, both Irridian and herself are about the same height, but somehow, she is smaller around in the thighs and definitely around the waist, but their breasts are about the same size. "But I am not that much thinner." She thinks aloud while looking at Irridian's protruding belly.

"You know we are going to have to call your aunt about this." Irridian says, putting both of her hands on her pregnant belly.

"I don't want to leave you here without any support." Michael says to her, looking at Irridian's pregnant belly.

"We can all go. They have that large bio-dome up there with plenty of space for everyone." Irridian says to her with a smile on her face. "And the best part is we no longer will have to work."

"I am not calling her." Michael says, turning and walking to the corner of the room where the window is.

Michael sits on the corner of the bed, looking at the ground with tears starting to fall from her eyes. Irridian walks over and sits on the bed next to her putting her arms around Michael. They sit there in silence for several minutes before Michael finally speaks.

"Would you take Taylor over to your mom's house for a few days?" Michael asks, not looking at Irridian. "I don't want her to be scared of me. She has never seen my aunt, so she has no idea about people like her, or like me now."

Irridian nods before standing and saying, "She will have to see you some time, you know," before walking out of the room.

Michael sits there for what seems like hours before she notices she is crying. It has been so long since she has cried that the feeling of crying is totally alien to her. After she pulls herself together, she grabs the phone from the nightstand and dials a phone number that she has memorized.

"Hello." The woman's voice says on the other end.

"Nana. It's me." Michael says, not remembering her voice is now totally different now.

"Who?" The voice asks.

"It's me. Michael." She says in frustration.

"Michael? I am sorry I don't know any women named Michael." She says with confusion prominent in her voice.

"Nana. Don't hang up, please. It is your grandson Michael Wayne." She tells her as the tears start falling once more.

"Michael?" She says with shock and surprise. "You did not pull a John, did you?" She asks with a touch of sarcasm.

"I think I did." She tells her with a laugh in her voice now. "Can you come over and help me, please?" She asks. The tears in her voice can still be heard over the fault's laughter.

"Sure. I will be right there." She says before hanging up the phone.

It takes Nana about half an hour to get to the apartment where Michael lives. Michael invites her in, and they hug for several minutes.

"How are you feeling?" Nana asks once they break apart.

"I don't know. A little confused. Maybe." Michael says, shrugging her shoulders and walking to the couch.

"I would not be surprised. John, we know how and why he turned, but you." Nana says, looking at her in awe. "You have not even seen him since you went to visit him for Christmas the year before he turned."

"I know. That is what is making this so hard on me." Michael tells her looking down at the ground. "I get emails from him, or her, all the time, and she always knows what is going on, but she never comes to see me." As she finishes, she stands up and walks to the bookshelves along the wall.

"It's because everyone she has met after she changed has changed as well," Nana tells Michael watching her now crossing to the kitchen. "Your sister went up about a year ago and has not changed, so they think it might be safe for her to interact with other people again."

"So, she is coming down?" Michael asks, thinking Nana has already called her.

"Not that I am aware of." Nana says. "I have not talked to him. I mean her, since last week."

"Okay. Will you help me with something?" Michael says as she turns to look at Nana, still sitting on the couch.

"Sure, what do you need?" Nana replies.

"Let's go to the mall and go shopping for some clothes that will fit me." Michael says, trying to smile like this is no big deal.

"Sure... let's go." Nana tells her. She then escorts Michael out to her suburban.

All through the mall, people look at Michael with shock on their faces, and several even scream at the sight of her. This makes both of them feel as though something bad is going to happen, but they keep shopping anyway. They buy all sorts of clothes from 'Just for Her,' and they figure they are just about done when Michael remembers she needs panties as well.

When they walk into 'Victoria Secrets,' the woman behind the counter steps out, looking shocked.

"You guys normally come to the back door." She says, looking out into the mall.

"What?" Michael asks, confused by the statement the woman just made. "I need to get some new panties for this body of mine." She finishes.

The woman now looks completely confused herself. "You're not with the Mars colony?" She asks, looking from Michael to Nana and back.

"No. She just changed." Nana says before Michael can respond.

"I see." The woman says, taking them both by the hand and escorting them to a back room.

Once in the backroom, the saleswoman tells Michael to strip down to her basics so she can measure her. First, she measures her neck, followed by around her breast, under the breast, around the waist, around the hips, and then the length of her arms and legs. When she is done, she walks off to go through a door marked 'Employees Only.' After several minutes she returns with a box and hands it to Michael.

"What is this?" Michael asks, starting to open the box.

"It is all the undergarments a girl needs for ten days." She says with a smile.

"We cannot afford that many custom clothes." Nana says, her eyes staring at the box.

"There is no charge for this box." The woman says, still with a smile on her face. "It is a gift from Rose, who is our largest single customer in the world right now."

"A gift... From my aunt?" Michael says, sitting down on the bench in the room. "Why would she give me this?"

"Rose... is your aunt?" The woman says, her smile spreading wider on her face if that is even possible. "Won't she be glad that this package has gone to a family member? Are you family to Rose as well?" The woman asks, pointing a hand at Nana.

"Yes, I am." Nana says, sitting next to Michael, who looks as though she might cry, scream, or just melt from embarrassment. "I am her mother, Rose's mother, that is." Nana says the last to clarify.

"Since she does not know you are here. Would you like to talk to her and tell her what has happened?" The woman asks, nodding her head in approval.

"She should know what has happened by now." Michael says, looking up at the woman. "She always knows what is happening in my life before I really know." She finishes with fresh tears starting down her cheeks.

"Oh, honey. Rose knows a lot before it happens, but not everything." The saleswoman says, sitting down on the bench next to Michael. "She did not know when my sister changed a couple of years ago." She says in a voice that sounds like she is concerned.

"Your sister changed?" Nana asks, looking at the woman.

"Yes. She changed about a year after Rose's first visit." The woman says, looking as though she is trying to remember. "Once Rose found out, they were here to offer her a place with them on Mars."

"So, is she on Mars now?" Michael asks.

"Yes. She decided they needed to have a professional seamstress up there, so she can be sure they always have the right fitting clothes." The woman says with a sound of pride in her voice. "That is why Rose is our single largest client in the nation. She orders for everyone, all at once, at least twice a year. The company has even added a children's line just for her"

"And this is all done using no money?" Nana asks, looking completely confused.

"Oh, heavens, no. Her bill is paid by a company called 'IGWT Enterprises.'" The woman says with a slight laugh.

"So, she still owns the company." Nana says with a look of realization on her face.

"Well, thank you for the underwear, ma'am." Michael says, standing up and reaching out a hand.

"Not a problem, dearie. But they are undergarments, not underwear." The woman says, standing up and taking Michael's hand in her own and giving it a good shake.

Michael and Nana leave the mall, now that they have everything they need and drive across the street to get something to eat. Michael orders her usual of five hard tacos five bean and cheese burritos with a macho coke, while Nana orders a box of fries with some sour cream and cheese with a macho Dr. Pepper.

After they finish eating, Michael is ready to go home. Nana keeps trying to get her to talk to her about what she is feeling, but

Michael really does not know what some of the emotions are that she is now feeling. Feeling as though she has failed, Nana takes Michael home and walks her inside. When they get inside, Michael's mom is waiting for them on the couch with Irridian.

"What are you doing here?" Michael asks anger raging from inside of her.

"Irridian called me and told me what happened. Why didn't you call me and tell me what happened? Hmm? Hmm?" She says with a lot of anger herself.

"Because of this right here." Michael says, waving her hands up and down at her mom. "You never listen to me or any of my brothers or sister." She says with tears in her eyes. "You have never cared about us other than to keep your house clean for you, making your meals, or just using us for some scheme."

"I am your mother, and I have always cared about all of you." Michael's mom says, standing just inches from Michael, pointing her finger at her face.

"If that is true, tell me one thing, one thing that has happened to any of us in the last few months." Michael says, knowing that she cannot.

"I know that Angel was cut from the wrestling team last month." Michael's mom says.

"Angel only just started high school this year. He is still living in your house, but what about Linda? Do you know where she is living or what she is doing for work? Or better yet, what about Austin? Do you know where he is working to make extra money, or what he needs the money for?" Michael asks.

"How am I supposed to know anything about what she is doing when she won't talk to me anymore?" Michael's mom says. "I don't know where I went wrong in raising you kids. You all treat me like I am the bad guy."

"You didn't raise us. I raised Devon, Linda, and Austen, and Linda raised the rest until she left just over a year ago now." Michael tells her mom, her voice now shaking with anger.

Smack

Michael's mom slaps her right across the face with every bit of strength she can muster.

"Get out of my HOUSE!" Michael says. She never liked the way her mom has always tried to make everything everyone else's fault.

"I should have known you are still trying to control my kids after all these years." Michael's mom says, now turning to Nana.

"That is uncalled for, Louise." Nana tells Louise as she walks by.

"Michael, I am sorry." Irridian says, looking at Michael; her face looking as though her tears have dried up from the red flames in her eyes.

Michael walks over to Irridian and hugs her. "At least Taylor is not here to see or hear this." Michael says. Irridian nods and hugs Michael some more.

Irridian helps Michael and Nana bring all the stuff they got up from the car. Since it is now after ten at night, Michael offers a bed for Nana to sleep in.

"I think I will. Since Joe died, it just does not feel right to be in my own bed." Nana says with a sense of longing in her voice.

Chapter Nine

The Chase for Michael

THE NEXT MORNING, NANA IS awakened by someone knocking on the front door. Nana, who is the only one aroused at the time, answers the door. When she opens the door, she sees a guy in his late thirties dressed in an all-black business suit except for his shirt, which is white. He has a pair of dark, CHIP's style sunglasses and a black bowler hat that gives him the appearance of being right out of the 1950s.

"Hello, Miss Wayne?" The guy asks.

"No, Mills." She replies. "Is there something I can help you with?"

"I am with the 'NSS,' and I need to talk to a Mr. Michael Wayne. Is he here?" The guy says, looking over Nana's head.

"No, he is not. I do not know where he is right now." She says, trying to raise her head to his level.

"Well, if you see him, will you have him give me a call, please?" The guy asks, handing her a card. "It is rather important that I talk to him as soon as possible."

"Sure, if I see him, I will tell him." She says, taking the card before closing the door.

Nana has the feeling that he is trying to listen to see if she is going to get Michael or not, so she watches the guy through the door until he leaves. Nana goes to the kitchen and makes herself a cup of tea and waits for Michael and Irridian to get up.

Later that morning, after Michael and Irridian finally get up, Nana tells them about the guy at the door.

"The guy at the door said he wanted to talk to Michael." She starts when they join her at the table. "When he asked where he was, he was craning his neck to look over my head. I got a horrible feeling from him, so I told him Mike was not here, and I did not know where he was." She finishes looking at both Michael and Irridian.

"Who was he, do you know?" Irridian asks, grabbing the cup of coffee in front of her.

"He only gave me this card." Nana says, handing the card to Michael since she was right there.

"NSS? What does that stand for?" Michael asks, looking at the card.

"I don't know." Irridian says, taking the card from Michael so that she can get a better look at it.

"Well, if you call them, don't do it anywhere you work or live and don't use a cell phone." Nana tells them. "If you do, they will know exactly who you are."

After they finish their long talk, Nana and Irridian go to get ready to leave. They all agree that Leaving the apartment at the same time is the best idea; Irridian will go to work while Nana will go home, leaving Michael alone at the residence.

"Now, I believe Nana is right on this; you need to stay inside, so no one sees you and tries to call the cops on you. Send your Aunt Rose an email; she needs to know about this if she doesn't already." Irridian tells Michael before walking out the door.

Michael reluctantly agrees before ushering Irridian and Nana out of the door. Not knowing what to do with herself, she decides to go on the internet for a few hours, trying to contact some of her old friends on Facebook. She finds that most of her friends or either at work, in class, or otherwise just busy. The only one available to talk to is someone she has not seen since middle school. Michael is not sure if she is interested in talking to this person, so she decides to sign off.

Afterwards, Michael decides to play some video games for a few hours before returning to the computer to check her emails. She finds emails from many different senders like; Sporters Equipment, Burger Barn, and Dave's Club. But the one that really catches her eye is one from Mr. Hutson, Coach of the Dallas Cowboys'. The email reads;

RE: Contract Offer
Jason Hutson JHutson@cowboys-dallas.com
9:36 AM Friday 10 June 2047

Dear Mr. Wayne,

Last week, we mailed you a contract for your review and signature. It has come to our attention that you are no longer eligible to play for our team. Since you signed the contract before this email was sent, we will honor the early termination clause of the agreement.

Regretfully
Coach Jason Hutson
(123) 555-9876

Michael is sitting there crying as she reads the email through a few more times. She knew that she would not be able to play football in her current form, but she was not ready to let the dream die yet. After several minutes, she accepts the fact that she will never play football ever again.

Michael decides to write an email to his Aunt and tell her what has happened to her. As she is typing her message, she can hear Nana in her head, "If you change your mind about writing to Rose, remember to be as vague as possible. You don't want anyone reading to know what has happened to you before you are safe." She hears her say. Michael tries to think of how she could word an email so that Rose would know what is going on, but others would not. Not being able to think of anything, she decides to delete the email and try again later.

Taylor is brought home after a few days so she can see her father, who is now her second mother.

"Daddy!" she yells as she walks into the apartment. "You, Daddy? Now Mommy two." She says when she sees Michael.

"Hi, Taylor." Michael says as Taylor jumps into her arms.

"You are purple. I love purple." Taylor says hugging Michael tightly.

Michael tickles Taylor with her tail making her squirm wildly. Taylor manages to twist and grabs Michael's tail. Michael sets Taylor on the floor and starts tickling her with her hands. Within minutes, Taylor is laughing so hard that she lets go of Michael's tail as she flees running to Irridian for protection.

"Help, Mommy. Help." Taylor yells as she climbs up onto the couch next to Irridian.

"Help, ha?" Irridian asks, smiling broadly. "Should I help you or Mommy two?"

"Help me, Mommy?" Taylor says, now moving behind Irridian.

Irridian leans back, pinning Taylor down behind her. Michael comes over and sits next to Irridian. She feeds her tail behind Irridian and begins to tickle Taylor again.

Taylor believes that Michael is the best thing in the world that she has ever seen. Over the next several days, they play all sorts of games like cowgirls and aliens, monster comedy, and matador, just to name a few.

Every time Irridian leaves, however, they make sure to take Taylor to the babysitters so that the man in black does not know Michael is at home.

The next weekend when Irridian is given a few days off, they decide to drive out of town to see some of the countryside. After driving for several hours, they pull into a small gas station to get some gas and food. Michael goes inside to pay for the gas as well to pick out some snacks for their journey.

When she gets to the counter, the woman behind the desk does not look scared or shocked by Michael's appearance. She looks her straight in the eyes and says, "What can I get for you, Sweetie?"

Michael hands the lady a hundred-dollar bill and says, "I would like one hundred on two, please."

After paying, Michael turns to walk through the store to see what they may want. But she finds her progress is blocked by a guy dressed all in black, wearing dark sunglasses, and a bowler hat standing right behind her. She tries to sidestep the guy, but he moves to block her again.

The guy removes the glasses and says, "Michael Wayne. You are under arrest."

Michael looks right into the guy's eyes and says clearly, "No, I am not. I have not done anything wrong."

"No, you are not. You have not done anything wrong." The guy says with a glossy look on his face.

Michael is shocked, turning, he sees by the look of the woman's face behind the counter, she is too. Michael looks back at the guy who seems to be regaining his senses, so once more she looks the guy right in the eyes and says, "You will go sit down in the corner until I think of what to do with you," and the guy does as he is told.

Not knowing what has just happened, Michael looks around the store for a few minutes before walking out to the car to ask Irridian to come inside.

"I had a problem inside the store. Would you please come in and help me out?" He asks, sounding as though it was something important.

Irridian, not knowing what is going on, agrees, and walks into the store with Michael. Once inside, the woman behind the counter seems to be regaining her own faculties.

"What the hell is that about?" The woman behind the counter asks as Irridian and Michael reenter the store.

"I don't really know." Michael says as Irridian walks over to the guy and reaches inside the guy's coat pocket to grab his wallet.

"Look, NSS." Irridian says, handing the wallet to Michael.

"National Security Services sub-branch of NSA." Michael reads from the badge. "Nana is right; these people are bad news." She tells Irridian.

"I have never heard of the NSS." The attendant says, looking the guy up and down. "He kind' a reminds me of an old movie my mom use to watch... I think it was called 'The Men in Black,' I think." The attendant finishes trying to remember for sure.

"I know that movie. My Nana has that movie on Blue-Ray." Michael says.

"What is Blue-Ray?" Irridian asks, looking confused.

"It is what movies were printed on before there were Crystal disks." Michael answers, pointing to a display case of Crystal disk movies.

"Oh, I think I have heard of those. I think my grandmother might even still have a player for those." The clerk says, nodding her head. "Sorry, my name is Ashley, by the way."

"Hi Ashley, I am Irridian, and this is Michael." Irridian says, holding out her hand while Michael does the same.

"You know, you look like a friend of mine. She used to be a guy when we were in high school, but about four or five years ago, she changed." Ashley says, looking at Michael.

"Really? You knew my Aunt in high school?" Michael says, sounding extremely excited.

"If your aunt's name is John, then yes." Ashley says with a smile.

"Actually, John changed it to Rose right after the transformation. Her wife chose the name for her." Irridian says, looking at Michael.

"You are not changing my name. No, ma'am, you are not." Michael says, seeing that evil grin Irridian has.

"Hey, I would love to talk more, but I have a business to run. What are you going to do with him?" Ashley asks, shirking her head towards the guy in the corner.

Michael walks over to the guy and grabs his glasses, wallet, and hat, walks to the back of the store, and sets them down in different places. When she returns to the front of the store, she turns to the guy and says, "You will not remember any part of what we are about to talk about, is that clear?"

"Yes." The guy says.

"Do you have any tracking devices or mics on you?" Michael asks the guy.

"Yes. My sunglasses have a mic, and my hat is the transmitter." The guy says, still in that same dreamy tone.

"Okay, you are going to tell me everything about what is going on." Michael says.

"Since Rose's death nearly four years ago, there have been reports of people around the world turning into the same type of creature as Rose." The guy says, sounding dreamy and in a monotone. "We have been rounding them up as we find them here in the US and trying to find out what is making them change. Some have even been vivisected to learn their physiology."

"My God." Ashley shouts, scaring both Irridian and Michael.

Michael, not knowing how to respond to this, walks off through the store. She walks down each aisle in the store looking at the different items, but not really seeing anything. She is not walking to see what she wants, but to think. Soon she has an idea and returns to the front of the store.

"What do you know about Andrew Bobadilla? Did he go through the change as well?" Michael asks, sounding a bit more nervous than she would like.

"Andrew Bobadilla was picked up about a week ago from the Philadelphia Hospital after it went through the change there." The guy responds.

"You are talking like these people are monsters. Do you think they are monsters?" Irridian asks, looking down at the guy with disgust.

"Yes, they are. They are no longer people; they are infected with a disease that is changing them. We have to defend ourselves from them by any means necessary." The guy says.

"Listen to me. There is no such thing as monsters. You will be resigning from your job after today. You will tell everyone who will listen to you, what is going on around the world. You will remind everyone that these people are innocent people being treated like animals." Michael growls.

"Yes, ma'am. They are people, not monsters, not animals. I will tell everyone that will listen to me." The guy says, still in that monotone voice.

"Where are these people being held?" Michael asks, sounding calm like this is a typical question.

"They are being incarcerated in approximately half a dozen places throughout the US. And if that was not bad enough, at least a dozen countries are doing the same." The guy pauses for a moment before continuing. "Langley, Ordain, Norris, and Beverly are the four I take new prisoners to." The guy falls silent after this part.

Michael walks to a chair next to the counter and sits down. As she sits there for several minutes, Irridian and Ashley talk loudly, but Michael does not hear a word they are saying.

Michael stands and looks at Ashley behind the counter. "Are there video cameras here?" She asks her.

"Yes, but they don't have sound." The woman says.

"Where are they, and how do they point?" Michael asks.

"There is one to watch the register, three-pointed at the customers, and three outside watching the pumps. That's it." She says, starting to sound scared.

Michael bows her head and walks over and gets a soda, some napkins, a bag of pins, and a large bag of chips before grabbing the guys things she had placed on shelves around the store. As she walks back, she takes one of the pins from the bag and one of the napkins and hands them to the guy telling him in a whispered voice to write down where the four prisons are before walking up to the counter to pay for everything.

"You will not remember what I just did." She tells Ashley to make sure to have the mic covered in her hand.

As she nods, her eyes suddenly gloss over for a second before returning to normal. "Will this be all then, Sweetie?" She asks Michael with a smile on her face.

"Yes, ma'am." Michael says. After she pays Ashley, she walks back to the guy and gives him his things. She tells him he will wake up in five minutes after they are gone from the store.

The guy nods, and Michael and Irridian leave the store. After five minutes, the guy comes out of his trance and turns to the woman behind the counter who pretends she is just starting to be aware of her surroundings.

The guy looks around and sees he still has his glasses and wallet in his hand. He pockets the billfold and walks out of the store to walk back to his car.

***

Mr. Brandon is sitting at his desk doing his usual paperwork for the day, a regular routine that he has been doing for the last four years since the development of his office. His office is responsible for the detection and capture of 'Morphs' discovered in the US. 'Morphs' is the name given to those that have changed from human to whatever these particular creatures are. The only thing they truly know for sure is that in November of 2043, the NSA received their first report of a Morph that had kidnapped a woman and her child. After attempting to capture the creature, it was killed, along with the woman and her child.

Since then, there is an average of ten thousand Morphs reported each year in the US alone. Since the development of the NSS, they have detained nearly forty thousand Morphs in six different top-secret facilities around the country. To better understand the cause of the Morphs, three of the facilities also contain research labs. The operating cost for the NSS has been estimated to be about one-third of the total budget given to the NSA.

As Mr. Brandon is turning to file some papers, he has just finished in a filing cabinet marked Langley, the phone on his desk rings.

"Hello." He says into the phone, sounding perturbed.

"Mr. Right is on line one for you, Sir." The woman's voice says from the other end.

Mr. Brandon pushes the blinking light on the phone. "Talk." He says.

"Sir. She is gone. She has a power none of the others have displayed before." Mr. Right says, sounding nervous.

"And what power is that?" Mr. Brandon asks.

"She has the power of Hypnosis." Mr. Right says.

"Hypnosis, hmm? What did she have you do, act like a chicken?" Mr. Brandon asks with a laugh in his voice. "I would love to see that."

"No, Sir. She told me to sit in the corner while she figured out what to do. After about an hour they bought some stuff and left. Then I was able to move again." Mr. Right tells him.

"Alright, there is nothing we can do about that right now. Get back here so we can try and figure out where she went." Mr. Brandon says.

"Sir, when I get back to the office, I will be turning in my resignation. I cannot treat these people like this any longer." Mr. Right says.

"When you get back here, we will discuss your options, Mr. Right. Now, get your ass back here before I have you join some of these creatures in Langley." Mr. Brandon yells into the phone before slamming the phone down and returning to his work.

***

Michael and Irridian have been driving along an old stretch of highway since last night and have only seen one other car the whole time. Suddenly they see a hotel on the left side of the road with a sign that says, 'Eat Sleep 'n Gas.'

Michael asks Irridian to pull in, and they can get a room. They go inside the hotel and pay for a room for the night.

"It is only 10:25 AM; You won't be able to enter the room until after 4:00 PM tonight." The clerk tells them as they sign the card for the room.

Michael and Irridian agree and decide to go to the restaurant to get a meal. As they look over the menu, Irridian asks Michael, "We can't keep running from the NSS, they are eventually going to find us."

Michael knows Irridian is correct in this and really wants to call her Aunt, but she does not know the number. Not to mention, Nana told her that it is possible they are watching her email, so going online to email her would tell the NSS where they are.

"I really need to contact my Aunt Rose. She is the only one that can help us right now." Michael says, trying to talk quietly. "Besides, she needs to know about those that have been turning and taken away by the NSS. I just wish I knew how to contact her." She finishes with tears in her eyes.

"What about the woman at Victoria Secrets?" Irridian suggests. "You said they get orders from her all the time."

"Your right." Michael says, stretching across the table to kiss her. "I don't want to do it from a public phone, just in case someone overhears the conversation."

"Your right. When we get to the room, we will call." Irridian says with a smile.

"Let's order. I am starving." Michael says, grabbing her menu to see what she wants.

"Well, Hello starving, I am Irridian." Irridian says with a grin.

"You know what I mean." Michael says, giggling.

Michael sees the waitress walking towards them with her order pad out. "Hello." She says with a smile. "My name is Kaya. I will be your server today. Are you ready to order?"

"Michael, you go first." Irridian says, smiling.

"Okay." Michael says. "I will have the 'Traditional Navajo Omelet' with bilasáana bitoo', please."

"You must be Navajo. Not too many others speak our language so easily." Kaya says.

Michael looks over at Irridian, who is frantically looking through her menu. "No, Ma'am, I am not. What did I say in diné bizaad?" She asks Kaya, who looks impressed and confused.

"Well, First, you said, bilasáana bitoo' instead of apple juice. Then just now, you said, diné bizaad instead of Navajo language." Kaya tells Michael.

Looking back at Irridian again, Michael can see her wide-eyed and mouth hanging open. "Did I really say those words?" She asks, not knowing how she should react or even feel about this.

"Yes, you did." Irridian answers. "At first, I thought you read it on the menu somewhere, but I don't see it."

"But how can I speak a language I don't even know?" Michael asks, with shock evident in her voice.

"My brother changed about a year ago." Kaya says in a hushed tone. "After the change, he was able to do things like the gods of our people. He can see things happening really far off, see in total darkness, and recently, he has even been talking to people really far away without a phone."

"Really?" Both Irridian and Michael say in shock.

Just then, the hotel clerk walks over. "Here is the key to your room. The NSS is out front looking at your car. Please, head up now, we will bring your food to your room." He tells them, looking through the window that looks out to the highway.

After Irridian orders her food, they walk to the back of the restaurant to a set of stairs that leads to the second floor of the hotel. As they are climbing the stairs, they can hear the old man, who is the hotel clerk, tell someone that they are not permitted to go upstairs unless they have a room for the night. After a brief argument, the man finally leaves, saying that he will be back.

Once they get to the room, Michael calls information and gets the number for Victoria Secrets in Flagstaff, Arizona. The information center offers to connect her with no extra charges as long as she listens to a recorded ad first. After thinking about it for a second, she agrees to it and listens to the ad.

"Victoria Secrets, your one-stop shop for custom fit lingerie. How may I be of service to you today?" The woman's voice says.

"Hi, my name is Michael Wayne..." Michael says but is cut off right in the middle of talking.

"Michael, Rose's niece." The woman says with an evident laugh in her voice.

"Yes. Hey, I need your help. I need to contact her as soon as possible." Michael says, noticing she sounds a little panicked.

"No problem. Do you want the number, or do you want me to call her for you?" The woman asks Michael.

"I think I need to call her myself." Michael says, sounding much relieved.

"Okay. Her direct number is (123) 555-6543. She almost always answers when I call her." The woman says to Michael.

After she has the number, she lays down to get some sleep next to Irridian feeling much better. An hour later, when she wakes up, she cannot understand why she is no longer tired. "I have always slept ten to twelve hours before, why not now?" She asks herself not fully understanding. Not being able to go back to sleep and not wanting to wake Irridian up, she decides to go for a walk to think about what she is going to say to her Aunt Rose.

After finding a path that leads out of the back of the hotel into the desert and that the men in black are nowhere to be found, Michael starts walking up a footpath that leads to a bunch of houses.

Michael walks for more than an hour before realizing she is not hot and sweaty even though the current temperature is over one-hundred-twenty degrees Fahrenheit from what she saw in the hotel office. She looks around and sees the sun is just starting the downslope of its arc across the sky. She is really confused by this.

The family, including herself, has always been very susceptible to the heat. Nana starts getting these ugly red blotches on her skin. Michaels mom would look as though she had just been in a swimming pool before her skin would start to turn red like it was burned. Before she was Rose, John and Elizabeth would become very short of breath before becoming fatigued and light headed. Michael would start to turn purple like he was not getting enough air, start getting the red splotches, start looking like a drowned cat and become fatigued. So, why is she not experiencing any of these symptoms now?

But since this is not really a concern for her right now, she pushes the thoughts from her mind and returns to thinking about all that the guy had told them.

"Yes, they are. They are no longer people. They are infected with a disease that is changing them. We have to defend ourselves from them by any means necessary. They are being held in about half a dozen different places around the US. There are at least a dozen countries around the world doing the same. Langley, Ordain, Norris, and Beverly are the four I take new prisoners to." She hears him say again and again.

Soon she thinks of what she is going to tell Rose and starts walking back to the hotel. Once back in the room, she picks up the phone and dials the number she got from the woman at Victoria Secrets for Rose.

"Hello. This is Emma, can I help you." The woman's voice says on the other end of the phone.

"Hi Emma, this is Michael Wayne. Rose's... awm, nephew." Michael tells her.

"Michael and nephew both refer to a male person." She says.

"I have been changed into a purple..." Michael starts but is cut off.

"Don't say it. Don't." The woman says, sounding stern. "I will get Rose for you."

Michael is on hold for nearly five minutes before Rose picks up the phone.

"Hello, Michael?" Rose says.

"Hey, Aunt Rose?" Michael says not really sure how to talk to her.

"You have changed." Rose says as a statement rather than a question.

"Yes, I have, and there is a lot more, more that I need to talk to you about." Michael says.

"Really? What more is there?" Rose asks, sounding interested to know.

"Later, please. Right now, I need someone to pick us up and take us to get Taylor from Irridian's mom." Michael says, relatively fast.

"Okay. Tell me where you are, and someone will be right there." Rose says.

Michael looks down and sees a small piece of paper taped to the top of the phone that gives the address. "We are at the 'Desert Inn Resort' in Nakaibito, New Mexico. The address here is 1616 Alsoomse Drive. There is a post office just down the street from here." She tells Rose.

"Okay, someone will be there in the morning to pick you up. Be ready." Rose says.

After hanging up the phone, Michael looks at the clock to see what time it is. She sees that it is a little after four PM and decides to try and get some more sleep. While lying there, her mind starts to race, thinking about the things they are doing to Andrew. She sees flashes of Andrew in a cell about the size of a bathroom. At one end of the cell is the door with a tiny bunk bed next to it. At the other end of the cell is a small sink and a hole in the floor as a toilet. In every corner and several places about navel level, are dome-shaped lights.

Michael looks onto the top bunk and sees a woman asleep. Not wanting to disturb this person, she stoops down to look onto the bottom bunk. She sees another woman that she knows instinctually to be Andrew. "Andrew." She calls out in hopes that this is not just a dream.

Andrew roles over to look at who called her name and sees Michael standing there. "Michael? Is that really you?" Andrew asks in amazement as the woman from the top bunk jumps down.

"Don't tell me they are going to start cramming three of us into these cells now?!" This new woman says.

"It's really me." Michael says, looking around. "I am not really here. I am somewhere safe, trying to stay out of the hands of the NSS." She tells them.

"So, how are you here, if you are not here?" Andrew asks, looking at Michael in disbelief.

"I don't know. I was just lying in bed with Irridian, thinking about you, and poof, here I am." Michael says.

As Michael is standing there in the cell, the door swings open, and a guy's voice calls out, "Who the hell are you, and how did you get in here?"

Just then, Michael finds herself back in bed next to Irridian. She sits up and looks around the room as her heart beats frantically in her chest. After a few minutes, she manages to calm herself down. She walks to the window to look out to see if the NSS people are still sitting in the parking lot or not. She realizes that one of them is on the phone, but before she has a chance to wonder what they are talking about, the two guys turn and run for a car parked at the edge of the parking lot and drive off.

Knowing it will be a while before the NSS returns to the hotel, Michael decides to go for a swim in the pool. She walks down to the car and grabs the suitcases from the trunk and drags them back upstairs to the room, before changing and walking out to the pool.

At about ten o'clock that night, Irridian wakes up and sees Michael sitting on the side of the bed, wrapped in a towel. She asks Michael, "Why are you not sleeping?"

"I can't." She says. "I have tried several times. I have gone for walks that took me out for hours at a time. I went swimming in the pool in the back of the hotel and even just laid there next to you, and still, I was not able to sleep." She finishes not even looking back at Irridian.

Irridian slips forward on the bed and wraps her arms around Michael, telling her that everything will be okay.

Michael starts telling her about her visit with Andrew. She tells her about the conditions they are being held in and how she knows that it was not a dream. She explains how after returning to the room, she saw they NSS guy's talking on the phone and suddenly take off. As she finishes, Irridian remains silent, not knowing what to say in response.

After several minutes of silence, Irridian's belly starts to gurgle. "I think the baby is hungry." Michael says, and both of them start giggling before going down to the diner for some food.

When they finish eating, the woman that has served them their dinner, tells them they have a phone call at the desk. So, Michael and Irridian walk over to see who it is, knowing that no one should even know they are here.

"Hello?" Michael says into the phone, not knowing if someone is going to jump out and grab her or not.

"Hello, Michael? I am... David. Rose has sent me to pick you up. Be outside in ten minutes. I will not stay on the ground long." David says before hanging up.

Michael grabs Irridian and then pays their bill for both the hotel and dinner, before going to go get their stuff from the hotel room. Once back downstairs, they head for the door, stepping outside just in time to watch a massive semi-truck drop out of the sky and land right in front of their car. The woman that steps out looks just like Michael, but smaller. She cannot be more than four-foot-ten.

"You must be Michael and Irridian." The woman says as both Michael and Irridian look her up and down. "I am David. I am here to get you two." She tells them, looking around.

"Hi, David." Michael says. "This is Irridian, and I am Michael."

David walks to the back of the truck, kicks open the doors, and steps inside. When she comes out, she has a J hook attached to a long cable. "We can't leave this thing here for people to find." She tells them as she bends down to place the hook.

Within ten minutes, she has pulled the car into the truck and ties it down so it will not move. Turning to Michael and Irridian, she says, "That takes care of that. Let's get you two back to Flagstaff to get your baby, Tylor." David says with a smile.

"Taylor." Irridian says, glaring at David.

"What? Oh, I am sorry. Taylor, not Tylor." David says, opening the door to the front of the truck. "Let's go get Taylor, shall we?"

When Michael and Irridian step up into the cab of the truck, they are surprised to find that the inside is nearly seventy feet across and thirty feet deep, and there are enough seats to fit more than three dozen people. The carpeting is all tan, and the walls have been painted white.

"How do you drive this thing?" Michael asks, looking back at David.

"I am not a thing." A woman's voice comes out of nowhere and everywhere at once. "I am Barbara, and I drive myself, thank you." The voice thunders.

"Oh, Barbara. Put a sock in it. The child is only asking." David says as she closes the door behind her.

"David, you old geezer. You know I don't like being called a thing. I have a name, and I want to be called by it." Barbara says in a crossed tone.

"I am sorry, Barbara. I was not aware that there are more like Emma." Michael says, trying to apologize.

"Like Emma? I am not like Emma. I am Better than Emma." Barbara says with disdain in her voice.

"You are not. She is designed for the long haul of people, where you are designed to haul sh... I mean stuff. Now, let's go." David says.

Barbara makes several undistinguishable sounds, but soon after, they are off flying towards Flagstaff to get Taylor from Irridian's parents' house. It seems to take just a few minutes before they arrive. As they step out of Barbara, Irridian's mom steps out of the house.

"Come in. Come in all of you. Before someone sees you." She says, looking around to see who might be watching.

After Michael and David are inside, Irridian grabs her mom around the neck and hugs her. "I am glad to see you, mom." She says not wanting to let go. "I don't know the next time I will be able to see you after today."

Irridian's mom breaks the hug and pulls her inside the house, closing the door. "Oh, Irridian. I love you so much, darling, but things are going to work out, you will see." She says, walking over to the stove where she starts a kettle for tea.

"I am going to go get Taylor from upstairs. I will be right back." Irridian says, giving Michael a kiss on the cheek.

"Michael, how are you doing?" Irridian's mom asks as she gestures to David and Michael to take a seat at the table.

"I am okay, still trying to get used to the idea that I will be like this for the rest of my life." Michael says as tears start to roll down her cheek.

"I have been like this for just over two years, and I still have not gotten used to it myself." David says.

"I don't know if Morphs have a period too or not, but if they do, you are in for a big surprise."

"Morphs? What the hell is a Morph?" David asks, looking around the table as a guy walks into the kitchen with some suitcases.

"Morphs is the name given to people like you by the government. It is mean and derogatory if you ask me." The guy says, putting the bags down.

Once Irridian has Taylor dress and ready to go, she returns to the kitchen. She finds everyone sitting at the table except for her dad, who is standing just inside the archway with a bunch of travel cases lying at his feet.

"What is going on here?" Irridian asks, seeing everyone.

"Your father and I have decided that we are leaving with you. The NSS has been here nearly every day since Michael changed." Irridian's mom says, standing and walking over to the guy.

"Yes, I am tired of xenophobic BS. I grew up with it in the forties and fifties, and I do not understand it at all. Mars has an all-inclusive society, and I am going." The guy says, sounding angry.

"Well then, let's get everything loaded so we can get out of here. Shall we?" David says, standing from his seat at the table.

They all file out of the house and into Barbara to head for Mars. Irridian's mom and dad looking back, as their house falls out of sight. Michael feels ashamed for what has happened to her, Irridian, and Irridian's parents.

Chapter Ten

The Rescue

MR. RIGHT STANDS OUTSIDE MR. Brandon's office, wondering if he really needs to go in. After a few minutes and taking several deep breaths to try and calm his nerves, he knocks on the door.

"Enter." The man inside calls out.

Mr. Right opens the door and enters the large office. The office, as bright as it is, seems dull and dark. This is because nearly everything in the room is of a dark color. The carpets are charcoal gray, along with almost every filing cabinet in the place. The desk, counters and liquor cabinet, and large cabinets on the wall seem to be made of walnut. All the picture frames hanging on all the walls, are black.

The wall behind Mr. Brandon is the only wall that does not have anything on it, and it appears to be painted gray. This wall also has a large window, which is the exact same size and shape as the desk directly in front of it.

On the floor in front of the desk are two large, halfback, crimson-red chairs with dime-size brass studs all along the arm boards. On the wall that has the door is a 56-inch TV that no one ever remembers seeing on except to be shown a video or image of their subject.

"Close the door, Mr. Right." Mr. Brandon says.

Mr. Right closes the door and turns back to look at Mr. Brandon. Having closed the door has only served to make the room seem even darker than it already does.

"I was going over the report from the surveillance room. There seems to be a twenty-minute gap in the sound recording of your stay at the store." Mr. Brandon says.

"Twenty minutes, Sir." Mr. Right says, trying to remember all the events of the day before.

"What can you tell me about what happened when the subject hypnotized you?" Mr. Brandon asks as he crosses the room from the liquor cabinet, with a glass of some amber liquid in his hand to take his seat at his desk before pulling out a pad of paper.

"Well, Sir." Mr. Right starts. "I spotted the car leaving the apartment and followed them until they stopped at the fuel station. I saw the girl go inside, so I followed her into the store. After she paid for some fuel, I told her she was under arrest. That is when her eyes flashed a crimson red. She told me that she is not under arrest and that I needed to sit in the corner until she decided what to do with me." He finishes nodding his head.

"So, was it the girl that hypnotized you, or was it the creature?" Mr. Brandon asks.

"The creature, Sir." Mr. Right answers.

"Now get this straight, those creatures are not people; they are not humans; they do not have any rights at all. They are a threat, a danger to all of humanity. If I had my way, we would be exterminating them rather than imprisoning them!" Mr. Brandon shouts.

"Yes, Sir. Sorry, Sir." Mr. Right says very apologetically.

Anything else to add? Anything at all?" Mr. Brandon asks.

"I just remember sitting while the thing and the girl it was with, and the cashier stood there talking for the longest time. They left, and I was myself again." Mr. Right says, looking down at the floor.

"That fits with the recording we have, but this twenty-minute gap of nothing has me worried." Mr. Brandon says reading his notes as well as those in the folder on his desk. "That will be all."

"Yes, Sir." Mr. Right says, standing from his seat. "May I inquire about my resignation I turned in last night?"

"Denied. Now get out!" Mr. Brandon shouts

Mr. Right leaves the office in a near run. He decides to go back to his desk, which is just one of at least thirty others in the large room on the third floor of the building they are in.

When he gets there, he sees he has a package waiting for him from the surveillance room. He opens the package to find the same file that Mr. Brandon has in his office. Still, instead of it saying there are twenty minutes of nothing, it says there are twenty minutes of extremely muffled sounds as if the mic was covered or moved away from the action and transmitter.

Mr. Right sits there trying to recall everything he can from the morning before only to keep coming up with the events exactly the same as he always has. He does not know what this means. Did he simply forget something important, or is he missing time from the encounter? He decides to pay a visit to the surveillance room to see if they might be able to help him fill in some of the blanks. Once downstairs, he burst through the doors making at least half the people inside jump.

"Bobbie. Your note says that the mic did not cut off like Brandon indicated, but instead, it was muffled in some way. Can you tell me what happened, what the sounds are, or even why I can't remember?" Mr. Right asks as he burst through the door of the surveillance room.

"Rodger." The woman replies with a sound of surprise and worry. "We are at work and need to be careful. But to answer your question, I think the mic had been taken from you and moved to another part of the store. There are sounds of people talking, but the voices are too distorted to know what they are saying." She tells him, sitting back in her chair.

"Is there any way to clean it up, so we can find out what was said and what was going on in the store?" Rodger asks, looking at the computer screen on the desk.

"I am already working on it. But it is going to take some time." Bobbie tells him, pulling up the file and showing him that it is being run through some computer programs.

Rodger kisses her on the cheek and tells her, "thank you," before walking out the door. Not wanting to go back to his desk, Rodger heads for the elevator to go to the cafeteria.

* * *

Mars is now coming into clear view, and Michael is feeling nervous about seeing her aunt. This will be the first time in over five years she has seen her and the first time since her change. As Michael watches out the window at their progress to Mars, she notices that David is right next to her.

"I am sorry I did not see you there." Michael says as she turns to walk over to where Irridian, Taylor, and Irridian's parents are sleeping.

"It is okay, child. I was where you are now, a few years ago." David says, walking over to sit next to Michael.

"Really? What happened?" Michael asks, watching her family sleep.

"I would say nearly the same as you. But I do not remember being chased by no NSS." She says, looking at the back of the cabin. "I was a normal mall employee doing his job when I started getting these damn headaches that just would not stop. Then I got a terrible pain down low and bam, I was this." She tells Michael, who believes there would be much more to the story.

"So, how did you end up with my aunt up here?" Michael asks, looking her right in the eyes.

"Well, there was about half a dozen or so of us to change all at once that day. One of them had been in constant contact with Rose since the beginning. She told us we had a choice, we could stay on Earth trying to stay out of trouble, or we could go to Mars and work on advancing society there. Of course, I decided to come to Mars. Nearly all of us did." David says as she now stands and walks back to the window.

Michael also stands to follow David to the window. Looking out, she cannot see where the colony is on the surface. "David, what do you do on Mars?"

"Me? Well, I am a transporter. I make frequent trips from Earth to Mars to bring back stuff that we can't produce ourselves." David tells her.

"We will be landing in just a few minutes. Would everyone please take a seat to prevent injuries? Thank you." Barbara announces.

Soon they are on the ground and safely in the bio-dome of the colony. Michael, Irridian, Taylor, and Irridian's parents are escorted to a small room for registration. After being registered, they walk out into the bio-dome. They are greeted by a brilliant blue sky shining down on white marble buildings topped with lush green gardens.

"How is this possible?" Irridian's dad asks, looking around.

"Well, Mr. Palmar, the blue sky, is produced by millions of LED lights embedded into the framework of the dome itself." The woman escorting them says. "The plants even seem to like the blue light better as well."

"Whose idea was it for that?" Irridian asks.

"Howard Murphy. He is one of the original crew members that NASA sent here in 2043 and one of five people who did not change." The woman tells them as they reach a building near the center of the dome. "Here we are. This will be your new home. Let's step inside, shall we?"

When they all get situated in their new homes, Michael returns to the registration office and asks to speak with Rose saying, "I must speak with her now. This is extremely important." But she is repeatedly told that it will have to wait. It is the next morning before Michael is taken to talk to Rose.

Rose's office is a, fifteen by fifteen-foot room that has a white and silver desk in the middle of the floor near a large round window on the back wall. To the right of her desk, there is a nice white-oak bookshelf along the wall and about half a dozen filing cabinets on the opposite wall.

"Hi, Michael. How are you doing?" Rose asks as she walks over to hug her.

"I am okay, but there are tens of thousands that are not." Michael says as she breaks the hug.

"What do you mean?" Rose asks, walking around her desk and sitting down.

Michael tells Rose everything that the NSS guy in the store had told them and about the four bases that she knew of. After she has finished telling Rose everything, Rose stands from her seat and walks to the window.

"I feared this might happen. But I did not know people that I knew or met before my change are changing as well." Rose says, still looking out the window.

Michael looks worried and starts to say something when Rose turns and walks to the desk. "Emma, are you listening?" She calls out as she bends over the desk setting both hands on it.

"Yes, Rose. I am always listening." Michael hears Emma reply.

"Let's get the council together, would you?" Rose says.

Emma responds in the affirmative, and then Rose steps around the desk and grabs Michael at the shoulders. "Now let's go tell them what you just told me. Shall we?" Rose says, looking Michael in the eyes.

Michael nods as tears fall from her eyes, and both Rose and Michael walk out together. When they entered the council room, Michael sees it is a semi-circle room that is all white with a balcony on the upper floor. There is a semi-circle table placed at the back of the room with five chairs around it, all facing the door they had just come through.

"Hello and thank you all for coming to this emergency meeting of the council." Rose says as she takes her seat at the center of the semi-round desk. "This is Michael Wayne. She recently changed and was chased by the US government before contacting me for help."

"Okay, that story sounds very familiar. Is that not what happened to you nearly five years ago?" One of the council members asks, sounding very sarcastic.

"Yes, it is. But her story has a twist." Rose says, looking around at the different council members. "Go ahead, Michael. Tell them what you told me." She says in a soft motherly voice.

During the meeting, Michael recounts the encounter with the NSS person more than a dozen times before Rose finally speaks up.

"We are not here to debate if this happened the way she remembers it or not. We are here to take action to stop what is happening to those innocent people." Rose says, looking around the room at the other four members of the council.

"You're right, Rose. I am sorry." One of the council members say.

"Emma and the other AI's need to search the entire globe to try and find as many of these prisons as possible, before we can do anything." Another member says, sounding like she really wants no part of it.

"We have located an additional fourteen facilities to Michael's original four." Emma's voice says.

"How many people, Emma?" An old-looking member asks.

"We are figuring about fifteen thousand plus people. However, these are just the ones we can find based on the information kept on computers. Some countries do not even use computers for anything more than political reasons, if at all." Emma states to the room.

"We need to mount eighteen groups to go in and rescue these people," Rose says, looking around the room.

"If we mount an attack on these places, we are declaring war on the Earth." The first member says.

"If we don't... There is no telling what they will do to them." The oldest member says.

"James, we have not heard from you. What do you think about this?" Rose asks, looking to the only member in the room who has not yet said anything.

"The simple fact is..." She starts, her eyes closed as she leans forward in her chair. "The people of Earth have already declared war on us. If we do not act, we are giving in to their hatred for something they do not understand." When she finishes, she opens her eyes and looks right at Michael, who is standing in the middle of the room.

"Emma, tell the other AI's what we are going to do. Also, get a roster put together for others to help with this, would you?" Rose says, standing up. Emma agrees, and the rest of the council stands as well.

"Rose, you know you cannot go on this mission except to make more like us." James says, putting one hand on her shoulder.

"I know, but we cannot let this go. We have to do something about it." Rose says, looking angry. Her eyes are flashing a bright orange that Michael can see clearly from where she is standing.

"Why not go to the people of the world and tell them the issues? The governments would have to listen after that, won't they?" Michael asks with tears in her eyes.

Rose looks up into those big golden yellow eyes. With a smile spreading across her face, Michael can see an idea forming in her head. "That is a great idea, Michael." She says as she runs over and hugs her. "Emma, there is a small change in plans." Rose says, looking at the ceiling.

***

It has been four days since Michael escaped from Mr. Right, and Rodger is feeling the pressure from Mr. Brandon. Every night when his wife Bobbie gets home, he asks if there has been any progress on the recording, only to be told, "No. When it is ready, you will know."

On Friday morning, when Rodger gets to the office, he is called into Mr. Brandon's office once again. This is never a good thing to have happen first thing in the morning, so reluctantly, he walks off to the door and knocks. It is not until after being invited in and entering does he find out what is going on.

"The boys in the surveillance room got a break on that recording." Mr. Brandon says while looking down at a folder on his desk. "We will be listening to it in just a few minutes to see what is there for sure. You will be there, don't worry." Mr. Brandon adds, seeing the look of horror on Rodger's face.

"So, you have no idea what is on it yet, if anything usable?" Rodger asks in disbelief.

"Not yet." Mr. Brandon replies. He stands from his desk, closes the folder, and drops it into a drawer before speaking again. "Let's go." He says as he walks around the desk and out the door.

Rodger rushes to keep up with Mr. Brandon and soon finds himself downstairs and at the door of the surveillance room. Without knocking, Mr. Brandon bursts through the door, making a loud crash as it slams against the wall. Everyone in the room must have been expecting them because no one seemed to react.

"Good, you're here. We're about to start playing the section of tape that we thought had nothing on it." The guy in the white lab coat says.

Just then, Bobbie walks into the room from a different door and walks straight to her desk without as much as a glance in Rodger's direction.

"Is everything ready, Ms. Dose?" The guy in the lab coat asks Bobbie as she logs into her station.

"Yes, sir." She says, looking around at the room.

The recording starts, and even though you really have to strain to hear anything, after a few seconds, you can hear some voices start talking.

(The recording begins)

"You will not remember any part of what we are about to talk about. Is that clear?" a woman's voice says.

"Yes," Rodger replies.

"You are going to tell me everything about what is going on." The woman says.

"Since Rose's death nearly four years ago, there have been reports of people around the world turning into the same type of creature as Rose." Rodger says, sounding dreamy and in a monotone. "We have been rounding them up as we find them here in the US and trying to find out what is making them change. Some have even been vivisected to learn their physiology."

"My God." Another woman says.

"They are being incarcerated in approximately half a dozen places throughout the US. And if that was not bad enough, at least a dozen countries are doing the same." Rodger pauses for a moment before continuing." Langley, Ordain, Norris, and Beverly are the four I take new prisoners to." Rodger then falls silent after this part.

(The recording went silent)

"That is all we have right now." Bobbie tells the room.

"Dear God, man, you told her everything." Mr. Brandon says, turning to Rodger. Before Rodger can try to say anything, the guy in the white lab coat walks over once again.

"Sir, it is Ordain on the phone for you." He tells Mr. Brandon.

"What is it?" Mr. Brandon yells at the phone. No one knows what is being said on the other end of the phone, but from the expression on Mr. Brandon's face, it is anything but good news.

"How many?" He says slowly, looking at Rodger as he turns white as a ghost. "All of them?" He says, dropping the phone on the floor.

"Mr. Brandon." Someone yells as another guy runs up to them. "We have reports rolling in from most of our prisons that all the creatures are gone." He tells the room, looking almost as white as Mr. Brandon.

✹✹✹

(The large screen shows an image of the Earth with sixteen black dots in thirteen countries around the globe and two red dots that were flashing a bit.)

The teams that are on the ground are nearly done, and Rose is waiting to hear about her teams on their rescue missions of people just like her. The door to her left opens, and Michael walks in.

"Any word yet on what is going on?" Michael asks. Her face looks as though she has been crying.

"Not yet. I know some of them have at least started, but nothing more." Rose says, looking at the giant screen that is Emma. "The emotions you are feeling will get easier to handle as time goes by." She says as she turns to look at Michael.

(The large screen now shows ten black dots with seven flashing red dots and one green dot.)

"I know, but I never knew that they were really such a roller coaster. I always thought that girls just said that to make men feel bad." Michael says meeting Rose's gaze.

(Now all the remaining black dots have been replaced by red flashing dots.)

"I am afraid not. The worst part is they are all amplified during your periods, pregnancy, and sometimes for no reason at all." She says, looking back up at the screen just in time to see several of the red dots turn green.

"Irridian tells me that all the time now. She even told me that they could switch so quickly that you feel like you were just slapped by a comet. What does it mean when they turn green?" Michael asks.

"Well, to start, they are all black, which means they are heading to Earth. Red is when there is no contact with them, and green means they are leaving Earth." She says as two more dots turn green.

Soon all the dots on the screen are green, and Rose escorts Michael out of the way before standing back in front of the scream that is Emma. Suddenly, Rose is on the display with a little black spot above her head. After steadying herself by taking a deep breath, she nods, and the dot above her head turns red.

"My name is Rose, and even though many will think I am an alien, I assure you, I am not. I was born on Earth and lived among you as a human for more than thirty years." Rose is talking like she has a captive audience in front of her. "Nearly five years ago, I was turned into this form you see before you now. Since then, many people have changed like me, and some of us found refuge away from Earth on Mars. However, many did not have that option." Rose takes another deep breath before continuing. "These people have been hunted, arrested, and imprisoned just for simply being something other than human. I have just overseen a rescue of some of these people, and I am calling for a meeting of the nations to discuss terms of the release of any I have not yet found. We were all born human, and just because we have changed does not mean we are any less human than anyone else." Rose stops for a moment for dramatic flair and then says, "Tomorrow morning, I will be going to the American capital to talk to the president of the United States. To talk about these issues of the inhumane treatment of my people and I invite any other nation to join us in these talks. I thank you for listening to me, and I wish you all well." After a few seconds, the spot above her head on the screen goes out, and she takes another deep breath before she starts laughing.

"Did the whole world see that just now?" Michael asks as she steps back to be by Rose.

"Yes, Michael. The whole world saw that broadcast." Emma says, sounding pleased.

"Emma, watch for any sign they are responding and let me know if they do. Okay?" Rose says, pushing Michael to the door on the left.

Once in the next room, Rose tells Michael she can help herself to anything in the ship, but she (Rose) needs to sleep for a few hours.

"Before you leave, I have an issue." Michael says, starting to blush purple.

"What is it, Mike? You can tell me anything." Rose says kindly.

"For the last hour or so, I have had blood running down my leg." Michael says, turning a darker shade of blue.

"Did you cut yourself?" Rose asks.

"Not that kind of blood." Michael says, now looking as dark as a blueberry.

"Oh, OH! There are some pads and tampons in the medicine cabinet in the bathroom." Rose tells Michael, now fully understanding what she is asking.

After Michael takes care of her bleeding issue, she walks around the ship to see every part of it. She has walked through every corridor and every door she can find until she finds one that will not open.

"Emma, why can't I get through this door?" Michael asks.

"On the other side of that door is the vacuum of space. And, as resistant as your body might be to the vacuum, it can still kill you." She says.

Michael decides she does not want to try it, so she walks back to a room that has a TV and some video games in it and sits down to start playing her favorite games.

Chapter Eleven

The Meeting

MR. BRANDON IS SITTING AT his desk, trying to figure out what he is going to tell his superiors when the phone rings. "Hello." He says in a calm and level tone.

"Sir, it's on TV, turn it on quickly." The man's voice says before hanging up.

"But what channel am I supposed to turn on?" He says aloud to himself. He grabs his remote and turns on the TV, and there it was. The creature he was in charge of capturing all those years ago. "Rose!" He shouts at the top of his voice. He quickly turns up the volume to hear what she is saying, but it is too late. He reaches to grab the phone to see if anyone recorded it, but it rings as his hand touches the receiver.

"Hello." He says again in a calm and level tone.

"WHAT THE HELL DO YOU THINK YOU ARE DOING?!" The guy on the other end starts. It is Mr. Brandon's boss, Col. Morris.

"Col. Morris Sir. I... I..." Mr. Brandon stammers out before he is interrupted.

"Shut up." Col. Morris exclaims.

"Yes, sir." Mr. Brandon says sheepishly.

"Why didn't we know where it was? Why didn't we know she has a small army? Why didn't we know she was planning an attack? WHY?" Col. Morris asks in a somewhat more aggressive tone.

"Sir, I don't know. I mean..." Mr. Brandon tries to say.

"Of course, you don't know. Because you are an idiot, and by the way, You're FIRED!" Col. Morris shouts as he slams the receiver down.

Mr. Brandon does not move for several minutes, trying to figure out what has just happened. He runs the last several years through in his head. He remembers the minivan coming off the ground as they shot it with thousands of rounds of ammo. He can't forget how it pulled away from the helicopters. He knows that they launched a Sidewinder missile at the vehicle, and it disappeared in the flash of the explosion. "*Or, did it?*" he thinks, questioning what he remembers. The more he thinks about it, the less sure he is of what he remembers.

After several minutes the phone rings again.

"Hello." He answers with a lot of fear in his voice.

"Sir, surveillance would like you to come down and see them, Sir." The woman, Susie Mohr, his secretary, says in an urgent tone.

Mr. Brandon breathes a sigh of relief before saying, "Okay, I will be right down."

Mr. Brandon walks down to the surveillance room where he finds that nearly every other employee in the building is, some in stun silence, others talking animatedly to others who are standing around in disbelief.

"What is everyone doing down here?" He yells, looking around the room.

"Sir, I am glad you came down. We have something important to show you." The guy tells him, escorting him through the crowd.

"Stop!" Brandon barks at everyone. "All of you get back to work. NOW!" He yells. The room clears out as fast as they can.

"Now, I have not even seen any part of the broadcast that thing just did. Tell me you have a recording of It."

"Well, yes, we do, but..." The guy starts being waved off by Mr. Brandon.

"Show me the recording first, and then we will talk about the rest." Mr. Brandon says, lowering his hand. The guy reluctantly nods and sits Mr. Brandon down at a small desk and turns on the video.

After the minute-long video has finished showing, the guy reaches out and taps a different key on the keyboard. This action causes a new window to pop up with a new video cued in the playlist.

(Video starts playing)

"We are true aliens to your world and have been in contact with your species for more than six of your millenniums." The blue-skinned creature in the middle of the group is the one talking. Mr. Brandon looks carefully and sees no less than six different creatures standing together in the video.

The first of them, the one that is talking, is a blue-skinned creature that, in all appearances, looks just like the purple ones he has been chasing all these years, but with no horns. He can see that this creature is an apparent female with her sizable breast.

The one on her immediate right is a creature that is lizard-like, with a flat face and green scales. This creature has green eyes and two horns that look just like those that Rose and her kind have. It has noticeable claws on its hands that seem to be stuck in a talon spread. This one appears to be Male by the way it wears the loincloth around its waist.

The creature to the immediate left is silver in color and resembled many of the descriptions given of grays with many apparent mistakes. This creature has scales that glistened, and the head is that of a fish, and the mouth looks less like a slit and more like a pronounced hinged jaw. This creature is covered from its shoulders to as low as you can see with a single piece of cloth that looks as though it is made from solid gold.

The creature all the way to the left looks human, but it towers over the rest of those in the video. Its head is nearly rectangular and nearly twice as tall as it should be. His jaw is chiseled with a sharp point on the chin, and his nose is square. This creature looks like the statues found on Easter Island in the South Pacific Ocean. The face and chest of This creature are that of a male.

The creature behind the one talking is all black and has several horns atop his head like a crown. From what can be seen, it looks as though this creature's teeth are made with razor blades. And its eyes appears to be empty and cold. There is no way of seeing any part of this creature's body to know if it is male or female.

The final creature, which is on the far right of the group, is what most people would describe as an angel. It is the lightest shade of blue that one can imagine without becoming white. There are no ears on this creature, and even though its face is flat and round like an oriental woman, it is not without features. By this creatures' silver dress, it must be female. The chest also has two small lumps where the breast should be, but they are so tiny, that it is hard to tell.

(The video continues.)

"We have received the same transmission as you people of Earth and find the information in it troubling. We will be attending the conference to find out if this information is true for ourselves. We are also offering our protection to the new race of humans as well. If we find that any part of the claims presented is true, our protection over Earth will be withdrawn immediately." The creature finished talking, and the screen went black.

"I need to get to Washington," Mr. Brandon says, standing from the seat and leaving the room in somewhat of a run.

***

Rose is awakened by both Michael and Emma shouting at her. "Rose you have got to see this, come on." Michael says once she acknowledges she is up.

Rose follows Michael to the screen that is Emma. As she is standing there, still in a daze, Michael turns her so she can watch the video of the six alien creatures. When it is done, she turns and stares at Michael with a blank expression on her face.

"Do you know what this means?" Rose asks after she finally finds her voice. Michael blinks wildly and then shakes her head, trying to understand what Rose might be thinking. "It means our broadcast caught the attention of some compelling guests." She says, grabbing Michael to hugging her and spin her around.

Michael, still not sure what it all means, says, "I guess that is good."

"Michael, it means that all the governments will have to listen and admit what they have done if they have any hope of keeping any support from these people." Rose tells Michael with a big smile on her face and a laugh in her voice.

"So, we Won?" Michael asks as her eyes grow wider in realization.

"Yes. We won. We will be able to rescue everyone." Rose says.

Morning soon comes, and it is time for the descent to Earth to happen. As Emma approaches the ground near the White House, they can see news cameras and reporters being kept at bay by the massive iron fence that surrounds the White House. As they land on the lawn, Michael notices another ship descending from the sky on the far side of Emma.

"Rose, look at this." She says, turning to look at Rose, who is getting ready to step out.

Rose walks back across Emma and looks at the ship descending. It is mostly blue with green crossings and yellow highlights. It is nearly five times as big as Emma is, but comes down in the same smooth fashion, managing to land just as smoothly.

Rose turns and starts to step out when she looks back at Michael. "Are you coming?" She asks with a smile on her face. Michael nods, and they both walk out together.

Rose and Michael walk-off of Emma to a spot where they can stand in the middle of the yard. All to be able to see their alien visitors come off of their ship. As they turn to watch the visitors disembark their ship, they are greeted by a guy that runs up to them from the shadows of the White House.

"Welcome." He says, taking Rose's hand first, then Michael's. "I am Mike Long, and I will be taking you inside now." He finishes, trying to pull them into the building, but neither Michael nor Rose move. "Or we can wait here for a minute." He says, dropping Michael's hand.

As they watch the alien ship for any sign of life, the hatch opens, and the aliens from the video come out from the ship. First, it is the blue one that did all the talking in the video. She is wearing a two-piece brown suit that covers the essential things, her breast, and her thighs. She is followed by the black alien that is wearing a long black robe that trails out behind it, giving the impression that this alien has no feet.

The next to come off the ship is the alien that looks like a fish. It appears to be wearing a one-piece human swimsuit. It has a large dorsal fin that runs the full length of its back. This alien is followed by the lizard-like alien that has a tail as long as Rose's, but his tail is much thicker, and it drags on the ground.

The next one to exit is the alien with the big head that resembles those big statues on Easter Island. He is a tremendous man that towers over everyone else, including the guards standing around the ship. He is wearing a white robe that barely reaches the ground. It is tied off around the middle with a bronze-colored sash. The last one that steps off the ship is an alien of shimmering skin that seems to mesmerize most of the people around her, all but

Rose and Michael. She is wearing a silver dress that looks like it can be made from some sort of liquid as it flows around her.

Rose notices that all the aliens are walking in their direction. She is just starting to turn when she notices that the guy next to her is not moving, nor is he breathing. She begins to call out for help when the apparent leader of the group puts her hand on Rose's shoulder.

"It is okay. They are just frozen in time." She says with a smile on her face as she turns Rose to look at her. "I am Nandime. My name is unpronounceable in your language, but the humans call me Sarah." She says, letting go of Rose's shoulder. "And these are my fellow council members for Earth." She says, pointing to the group with her.

"Why did we not freeze like the rest?" Michael asks.

"I had intended for you to freeze as well." The woman says that came off the ship last. "You must be able to slip in time, too, in order to not be affected." She says, stepping to the front of the group. "I am Eldon, and they call me Angel." She says, now looking between Rose and Michael.

"I have always been able to slip through time when I needed to." Rose says, nodding at the woman. "I am Rose, and this is Michael." She says, pointing at Michael standing next to her.

"This is the one that brought the issues to your attention, is she?" The tall human-like alien says. "I am Zicarthon, and I am known as Zieth." He says, looking through Michael.

"Yes. She brought the issues to my attention. How did you know?" Rose asks, looking at him with an inquisitive gaze.

"His people can read others and know the truth without words." The one that looks like a fish says. "I am Xingling, and they call me Long." She says with her mouth, not moving.

"Am Pothian and calls Zor." The lizard-like alien says. "This, Wraith. It has no other names."

"I am pleased to meet all of you." Rose says.

"As am I," Michael adds. "Why did you come now after all of that has happened?" She asks, looking at them all with a look of confusion and anger.

"Relax, young one. Each of our races has been a part of human history since the beginning, though most humans are unaware of it. We are here now because of an ancient prophecy from one of your people." Angel says.

"The prophecy states that the race of humans will be ready for us when the first moves beyond the confines of a human. I think you are that person mentioned. You have moved far from the confines of humans." Sarah says with a broad smile on her face looking Rose up and down.

Sarah then starts to walk around Rose and Michael, looking them over. She stops on their backside, nodding, and then steps back around to the front.

"I see many qualities from each of the council." Sarah starts. "You have the time slip of the Eldon and the hypnotic qualities of the Wraith. Your bodies have many of the outward appearances of both Pathians as well as my own, the Nandime's. But there is something about you..." She says, her voice trailing off at the end as she looks at Rose.

"We should probably go in..." Rose starts to say but is interrupted by Sarah grabbing her hand.

Rose feels a surge of power throughout her body, and it all seems to center around Sarah, who has somehow pushed her own essence into Rose's. Rose wants to fight it off but cannot do anything to stop what is happening to her. Suddenly like it had started, it ends.

"What was that?" Rose asks, pulling her hand away and shaking it, trying to shake the feeling out.

"You have white energy coursing through your body. It is what has changed every person so far, and it is your biggest weapon and your biggest weakness." She says, looking at Rose. "I can help you learn to control it, so you do not accidentally turn anyone else. I have sealed it off for a time, but it will break free again in a day or more."

Rose stepping forward says, "thank you," but is very much concerned about the fact as to how fast Sarah moved without Rose even feeling the least bit of what was to come.

Shortly after that, as time starts moving forward once more, they all walk into the White House for their meeting with the president. Once inside, they are told that sixteen countries will be involved in the conference, with most of them on the videophone.

It takes nearly half an hour for the room to fill with those that are going to attend the meeting. The room is so full that there is almost no open space for anyone to walk except the 3-foot area in front of the president's desk for Rose to use for her argument.

"Mr. President, leaders of other countries, foreign diplomats, and honored guests." Rose starts looking around the room at the President, TV Cameras, and foreign diplomats. "My name is Rose. Up until five years ago, I was a normal, everyday person who had a family to support. After I changed, I managed to live about six months without too many issues before the US government started trying to chase me down. They attacked my family and me in my home and attempted to kill us when we would not go quietly." Suddenly Rose is forced to stop by a loud outburst behind her.

"Objection." I guy behind Rose says, standing up.

"Sit down, Gen.." President Ross thunders.

"But Sir?" The Gen. says.

"I said, sit down, Gen.." President Ross retorts. After the Gen. sits down, the president says, "Please, continue." to Rose.

"Thank you, Mr. President." Rose says. "After the attempt on my family, we fled to Mars, where I believed we would be safe. With the help of the crew from the 2043 Mars Mission, we built a colony where we can live peacefully. There are currently over four hundred souls living there, many of whom are those who have changed as I did." Rose is interrupted again by someone on one of the monitors.

"We have a problem." The guy on the monitor labeled Korea says. "We have total authority on people of Korea." The guy says.

In the back of the room, a chair moves as Long walks to stand next to Rose. "I know your people." She starts pointing at the screen. "My people have protected your people from others long before you lived in tribes. Remember the agreement." She finishes turning to walk back to her seat.

The image of the guy on the monitor freezes for several seconds before jumping to him, walking back in front of the camera. "We remember. We withdraw our claims." He states, sounding disappointed.

Rose continues, "A few days ago, it was brought to my attention that several countries have been imprisoning people who have changed, even without them having done anything wrong. After confirming the accusation, I could not let this stand." A noise comes from one of the diplomats sitting in the corner.

"China does not recognize anyone's authority over our people, except our own." The guy says as he stands.

Angel stands and starts talking in Chinese to the ambassador. After she is finished, the guy responds with a bow before turning back to the front and saying, "We too withdraw our claims to the creatures."

Rose's eyes flash crimson as the word 'creature' is spoken, but Rose shows no other response otherwise. She looks around the room to make sure it is okay to continue before she says anything.

However, Sarah stands to speak. "Rose has now been interrupted from what she has to say three separate times. These outbursts are a concern to us. She must be allowed to finish before any other objections are raised. Is this understood?" She says, looking around the room. Most of those in attendance and everyone on the video conference screens agree.

President Ross, however, says, "I too want to hear everything, Ms. Rose has to say here. For the council of six to step in, things got way out of hand."

Rose takes a deep breath before continuing. "The council of Mars convened a meeting and agreed that our best course of action was a rescue operation. We struck the eighteen known prisons holding people like me. We successfully rescued nineteen thousand two hundred forty-two people from these prisons." Rose pauses to allow the number to sink in. "We are still processing them, but many of them are missing family members not yet located. We believe that there are still people we have not found, those still being held in prisons and those who are just simply in hiding. I would like the permission of every country for unrestricted access to an extensive search to locate these people. I also request that family members of those affected also be allowed to immigrate to Mars to be with their families."

After Rose finishes her speech, the room irrupts with people talking to each other. Rose feels the meeting with the president has gone well to this point. She has said everything that she had planned, with some noticeable differences. First is the fact of the six aliens present. Their presence makes everyone feel uneasy, everyone but Rose and Michael that is. The other is that when any of them tried to claim any kind of sovereignty over those who have changed in their country, one of the aliens interjected and quickly reminded them of their responsibilities to the alien that interpolated themselves into their cultures all those millennia ago.

Rose looks around the room and sees that several of the ambassadors are on phones jabbering in their language. At the front of the room, the president is also on the phone, though Rose is at a loss as to who it could be. The large monitors that have had the images of those not present, have either frozen or gone black.

After several minutes, President Ross hangs up the phone and places his hands in a pyramid position in front of him. The others around the room fall silent and take their seats one by one.

Once everyone is seated and quiet, President Ross says, "All the leaders present at this time, have agreed to allow your people to perform extensive searches to try and locate your people. The

Rose Kincade

United States, Canada, Mexico, United Kingdom, France, Spain, and Japan all agree to release, any and all, Morphed people being detained, into your custody." He says, looking up from the papers lying on the desk in front of him.

The Chinese ambassador stands and says, "Your people are not welcome in our country, nor are any not Morphed being allowed immigrate to Mars." After finishing, he turns to look at Angel before adding, "We will, however, transport any prisoners to Beijing for deportation. However, we have one condition, these creatures must never return, or they forfeit their rights as free people."

A tall skinny guy stands from the middle of the room. "I am representative of Italy. I am unaware of any imprisoned in our country. However, we do have many affected in our country. We are willing to allow them to immigrate to Mars if they wish. But if they do not want to go, we won't allow you just to take them."

Rose says, "No one will force them if they do not wish to go." She looks around the room, hoping that a few more countries will at least join in, but none of them do.

President Ross stands and after making a sweeping look around the room says, "If no one has anything else to add, then I think this meeting is over."

The lights on the cameras suddenly turn off, and people start rising from their seats and walking out. Rose, however, has one more issue to discuss with President Ross.

"Sir, I want to talk to you about this NSS." She starts once most of the people have left the room. "I want the leaders of the NSS for a trial on their part in all of this."

The president never looks up, nor does he give any sign he heard anything Rose had just said. He sits there, writing something down on a piece of paper.

When he is finished, he looks up at Rose and says, "I do not know anything about that young lady." He says this as he is handing Rose the paper he had just written on.

This slip of paper has half a dozen names and locations of each person written on the slip.

Rose stands up to her full height and says, "Well, then thank you for your time, Mr. President." And then reaches out her hand to shake his.

President Ross looks at her hand for a second, then rises. He takes her hand in his and says, "I am sorry we had to meet like this. I think it would have been much better if we had met with a lot fewer issues to resolve."

"I agree, Sir. No one asked to be changed, not even me. I am just glad that we could reach an understanding." Rose says, letting go to walk out.

"Madam, I am going to issue an executive order allowing anyone from Mars to maintain a business here in America. I know Mars does not have everything you need. This order will allow you to generate resources that you will need." President Ross says.

Rose says, "Thank you, Mr. President." Before turning and walking out with Michael. Once outside, Rose can hear a fleet of helicopters approaching from the east.

"They have malicious intentions. We should all hide." Zieth says, looking around at the group. When he turns back to look out, the ship they had come in, takes off and vanishes from sight and Emma flies to the parking lot where she manages to look just like any other car there.

"What is going on?" Mike asks, seeing everyone turning and walking into the building again.

There is a small fleet of helicopters coming here. We do not want to be found by them." Rose says, looking back out to see where the helicopters are.

Once back inside, Rose, Michael, and the group of aliens are escorted to a room that they can look out and see what is going on below. Rose watches as the fleet of five Russian Crocodile Attack Helicopters land on the lawn right where Emma and the other ship had been minutes before.

Rose Kincade

President Ross steps out to meet the helicopters to try and find out what is going on. But when he gets within twenty feet of the first helicopter, its doors open, and out steps a short bald man in a tan uniform. President Ross and this short man talk for a few minutes very animatedly. Then the short man turns, and the large sliding doors on the helicopters open wide, revealing nearly thirty dead changed humans. The guy waves his hand, and all the bodies are dumped unceremoniously onto the lawn.

Everyone in the room gasps as they watch the horror unfolding before their eyes. "I don't know how anyone can do anything like this." Sarah says.

Rose turns to look at Sarah and sees a tear on her cheek. Rose looks back out the window and says, "Humans, as a whole, are very ignorant. They get scared easily, they jump to conclusions, and they kill or destroy anything they do not understand."

"It is a shame. Humans have so much potential that can bring them closer to understanding. But when they do this, I have to wonder what they're going to become." Long says, sounding like she wants to cry.

Suddenly, the small man re-enters the helicopter, and all of the helicopters fly away. Everyone in the windows can see President Ross turn and say something to Mike before returning to the White House himself. As the alien group turns to walk to the door, Rose watches as the guards run out with stretchers to grab the bodies of all the people lying there on the ground in a big pile.

"Many of our races have been guiding humanity since the beginning. We have taught them how to grow and how to build. I have to wonder where we have gone wrong for them to do something like this." Zieth says, bowing his head.

As they are standing there talking, the door to the room opens, revealing President Ross. "As I am sure you already know, that was the Russian military." He starts with a frog in his throat. "They said that if they find any more of them in their country, they will bring them here in the same condition." He finishes.

Rose can see that President Ross has been crying with what has happened. She wants to say something, but the words just won't come. With the danger passed, Rose, Michael, and the others leave the safety of the room, walking in silence out of the White House once again. As they step out, the alien ship drops from the sky so fast that many of the guards around the grounds think it has just appeared.

"Rose, we will be in contact with you very soon. I want to teach you how to use your abilities, so you do not hurt anyone." Sarah says, reaching out her hand to take Rose's. "We will be able to do it on my planet to prevent any unwanted damage."

"Thank you, Sarah. I would love your help in learning more about my abilities." Rose says before hugging Sarah.

Sarah looks shocked but glad by the gesture. As she turns, Rose and Michael watch as each of the alien's boards their ship and takes off. Turning to Emma, Rose ushers Michael in before stepping in herself and falling into a seat near the door.

"That could have gone worse." Michael says as she walks over to the fridge to get a cold beverage.

"That is true, but I can't help but feel guilty over those who have lost their lives." Rose says, wanting to cry but knowing she can't. "Emma, contact the council for me, let them know that we can start picking people up soon. Also, let them know we need a jail set up quickly for some prisoners we will be coming back with." Rose finishes as she pulls out the piece of paper President Ross had given her.

Rose looks over the piece of paper at the different names and addresses.

Gen. Mark Hamilton
1414 South Carri Dr. Hamilton, PA
Gen. Steven Kingsling
12495 Kumquat Pl, Chino, CA
Col. David Morris

Rose Kincade

11 N Shubin ln, Luke Air Force Base, AZ
Doctor James Flynn
935 S Vintage Rd. Casper, WY
Arnold Brandon
874 Allso Dr. NE, Albuquerque, NM
Rodger Right
369741 Manzano St. Albuquerque, NM

"Emma, I have a list of names with addresses. Can you track them so we can detain them for their crimes?" Rose asks, already knowing the answer.

"Yes, Rose. That is not a problem for me." Emma replies sarcastically. "But how are you going to hold them? I do not have any cells in me, nor do I have any place to put cells." She says with concern now evident in her voice.

"I was thinking of placing them in Cabin two. When Mark put the locks in, he did put the lock in backwards on that door." Rose says as she stands from her seat to change clothes in her room. "Plus, we received that shipment of handcuffs last month that are still in the cooling deck." She adds.

Chapter Twelve

The Invitation

A S ROSE LOOKS THROUGH HER closet, she sees an outfit that she has never seen before. The outfit is all black with a patch of Mars and 'Mars Civil Defense' written below it in reflective silver. On the back are the same words written in the reflective silver thread. On the left front of the uniform is her name with an ID number written below it. On the right side is another image of Mars and the words' Mars Civil Defense' printed once more. As she pulls it out of the closet, a note falls off the front.

> This was supposed to be presented at the council meeting next week. It is not the final layout for the design I have been working on, but if you need it, please use it.
>
> Brenda Hopes.

Rose can feel a tear run down her cheek as she reads the note. Looking back at the uniform Rose thinks to herself, "This will work."

Rose Kincade

As she is nearly finished putting the uniform on, Emma calls out to her, "We are near to Luke Air Force Base. They are attempting to contact us on the radio for identification. What do I tell them, Rose?"

"Emma, tell them that we are with the 'Mars Civil Defense' in a sanctioned operation to apprehend a fugitive located on the base. Any attempt to stop us will result in the arrest of those individuals." Rose says, looking up at the ceiling as she zips up her boots.

After about a minute, Emma says, "They said, they will not interfere with us in any way. They tried to have me land on runway twenty-one right until I told them I don't need any runways." She finishes with a laugh.

As they fly in low, Rose spots Col. Morris walking up a road towards the commissary. "Emma, come down right in front of him so I can grab him before he has a chance to run." Rose tells Emma. Emma seems to fall from the sky as Rose opens the door to grab Morris.

"Unhand me, you freak." Col. Morris says as Rose grabs him and throws him into Emma. All this is happening while the men and women on the base just watch. "Someone do something!" He shouts out of Emma as she starts to fly away with the door sliding closed.

"Col. Morris, you are under arrest for crimes against humanity." Rose says as she places a set of handcuffs on Morris and leads him to the room with the lock facing the wrong direction. "Now wait in here while we pick up the rest of your crew." She barks.

The next one to get picked up is Rodger Right, and as soon as he sees Emma land in front of him, he gets in without any fight at all. "I know, I am under arrest. I have been expecting you since I saw the broadcast this morning. Where do you want me?" He asks Rose as the door behind him closes.

Rose escorts him to the place where she is keeping Morris and opens the door for him.

"Why is he not in handcuffs?" Morris asks.

"Because I know he won't try anything, unlike you." Rose says, closing the door before any retorts can be made.

The next one they locate is Doctor Flynn. As they approach his location, Rose realizes that he is inside one of the prisons that they had cleaned out the day before. She tells Emma, "Fly low and fast, so we are not detected by the defense system." This tactic works right up until they are at the prison gates.

One of the guards on the upper rampart sees Emma coming in and starts shooting. Rose knows Emma can handle much more than these guards can hit her with but does not want to put her through that. So, she says, "Emma, let me out and get to a safe distance. Once I have Dr. Flynn, I will call you and have you come to get me."

"Okay, be safe, Rose." Emma says as the side door slides open, and Rose jumps out.

Rose hits the ground rolling and heads for the inner walls of the prison as the bullets around her seem to stop. She finds her way in quickly before she is stopped in her tracks. She does not know which way to go or even where Dr. Flynn is inside the prison.

"Emma, I need your help." She says into what looks like a watch.

"Turn right, go about four hundred feet, and turn left. He will be in the last room on the left." Emma tells her.

Rose wants to hurry and get out of there, so she wills time to stop. As she does, the gunfire outside seems to go silent. Rose moves through the hallways looking in every room as she goes. As she walks, she makes mental notes of the living conditions that she is seeing. Turning the last corner, she sees a room that is not much bigger than a standard bathroom with a bunk bed on the right side of the cell. She wonders if this is the cell that Michael had told her that she had been in when she saw Andrew.

Putting it from her mind, for now, Rose pushes on looking for Dr. Flynn. She finds him standing over a girl who has an IV in her arm. As rose steps forward, the girl looks up, but Dr. Flynn does not move.

"Oh, thank you. I was hoping someone would find me before he started cutting on me again." The girl says as she pulls against her restraints.

"Hold still, and I will get you free." Rose says, starting to unbuckle the straps at the girl's feet.

Once the girl is freed, she jumps up and grabs Rose around the neck, hugging her. "Thank you. I thought I was going to be the next one to die on this table." The girl says.

"Are you the last one in this prison?" Rose asks the girl pulling her off and seeing that she can't be more than fifteen or sixteen years old.

"There are about a dozen of us in the room over there." The girl says, pointing to a room that has a big steel door meant for a kiln.

Rose turns and grabs Dr. Flynn's hand and handcuffs him to the bed. She then walks over to the door and opens it to find that everyone is strapped to beds, just like the girl.

Looking around, Rose discovers that more than half of the people here are dead. Some have their organs lying next to them on small tables; others are face down with their hands, feet, and tails cut off, and their limbs are lying open, revealing the muscles underneath.

Rose must fight the urge to vomit from everything she sees in this kiln as she is removing the straps from those still alive.

As she is working on her second person, she can hear the girl in the other room call out, "Lady, hey lady, he is moving in here." She says through the door.

"He can't go anywhere. I will be out there in a few minutes." Rose says, trying to hurry even faster now. She knows that the more time she spends releasing these people, the higher the chances that Dr. Flynn will find a way to escape.

While working on the fourth person, the girl comes running into the kiln. "He looks like he is trying to rip his arm off out there. I don't want to be out there with him anymore." She tells Rose.

"Okay, you finish getting these people loose, and I will go out there to take care of Dr. Flynn." Rose tells her. "Oh, and if any of them can move on their own, get them to help you." She adds as an afterthought.

Rose steps out of the small room in time to see Dr. Flynn disappear out of the other door. Turning back to yell at the girl in the kiln, she says, "Get them free, I will be back for you as fast as I can." Running and trying to stop time again, Rose finds that she is starting to run out of breath, something she has not experienced in this form.

"Finding it hard to breathe?" Dr. Flynn taunts as he turns to run in reverse.

"What have you done, you bastard?" Rose yells back.

"I have discovered that by flooding a room, or in this case the halls with pure oxygen, you freaks will suffocate in minutes." He laughs as he turns to run correctly. "This also has the added advantage that I won't run out of breath trying to get away from you."

As Rose is forced to stop to try and catch her breath, Dr. Flynn disappears around a corner at the end of the hall. Disappointed, Rose turns around and goes back for the people she left in the kiln. When she re-enters the small chamber, she sees that everyone is free, and many of them are carrying many of the bodies as well.

"If we leave them here, they may never get a proper burial." One of them says as she steps forward.

Rose agrees and escorts them all back outside to Emma, where she finds the guards still trying to shoot her down. "That's enough!" Rose shouts with such a thunderous boom that it seems to come from every direction at once.

Rose Kincade

The guards seem to be confused by Rose's shout that Emma can rush in and pick everyone up. Rose quickly ushers everyone into Emma before the guards have a chance to start shooting again.

"Where is Dr. Flynn?" Emma asks after Rose is inside.

"He got away, for now." Rose replies. "But at least I managed to rescue more of his victims." Rose adds, looking around the cabin. "Let's show our guests to the guest rooms so they can freshen up before we get them some food."

"Follow the lights, and I will lead you to your rooms." Emma tells them as a series of lights start flashing in a line out of the main cabin.

"May I stay with you, please?" The youngest of those she rescued asks.

"Yes, you may." Rose says looking at the girl, now believing she might be even younger than she thought. "How old are you, hun?" She asks.

"I am twelve. I am also the only one who has changed in my family, as far as I know." The girl answers with a tear starting to roll down her cheek.

"What's your name, and where do you live?" Rose asks, hoping she can reunite her with her family.

"My name is Amadahy. I lived in upper Michigan in a place called Ojibwa on the south shore of Lake Superior." Amadahy says with the tears coming much faster. "When I changed, my family called me a monster and a freak. They tried to drown me in the lake, but I seemed to be able to breathe the water." As she says this last part, she starts crying uncontrollably, causing Rose to pull her into a tight embrace.

"Rose, we can't take her back to those people. For all we know, they are going to try and kill her again." Emma says as Michael comes walking into the main cabin.

"She is right, you know." Michael says, walking towards the kitchen area.

"I know. But if I don't give them a chance to say their piece, then I am no better than what we are fighting." Rose says looking at Michael. "Emma, do we know the whereabouts of anyone else on the list?" She asks, hoping they might get closer to Michigan to talk to Amadahy's family.

"I have located both Gen.'s, the first is in California, and the other is on a plane flying to Pennsylvania." Emma says.

"Well, we can't do much with a plane in the air. How long before it is scheduled to land?" Rose asks.

"About two more hours. It is coming in from England, according to the flight plan filed." Emma says.

Rose knows that they can be in California in twenty minutes and that at top atmospheric speed, they can go from California to Pennsylvania in about forty minutes. Knowing this will leave about thirty minutes for the Gen. in California, Rose says, "Take us to California. I am going to take Amadahy to my room and get her cleaned up."

Emma acknowledges Rose and turns for California, and in eighteen minutes, they arrive at an unremarkable house in the center of Chino, California. The house is a tan and brown two-story home built in the 1960s. From the air, they can see that the house has several ways in and out. Rose does not want to let the guy getaway, but she does not know how to surround the house with just her.

"Rose, the people you rescued want to talk with you." Emma says as Rose is looking over the blueprints on Emma's screen.

"Okay, let them in here." Rose tells her.

The door to Rose's left opens, and in come nine of the people she has just rescued. "We want to help." The girl that appears to be the leader says bluntly.

"And what do you want to help with?" Rose asks to make sure they know what they are asking.

"You are going after the people that started those prisons, right?" The girl says with her eyes going from yellow to orange.

"Yes, I am. But do you know what that entails?" Rose asks as she feels Amadahy squeeze her around the middle.

"Yes, we do. We may not have the uniforms, but we are able and willing to do whatever it takes. Many of us have been in that prison for three or four years. We were tortured, beaten, starved, and some even suffocated. We deserve a chance for revenge." She says with her eyes now shifting to crimson.

"First off, little girl. You do not have the right to revenge, nor do you have the right to get angry at me." Rose starts, her voice echoing loudly through the chamber as her own eyes also turn crimson. "Now, if you want to help, it will have to be in the background since I do not have any uniforms for you." She finishes as her eyes return to their standard yellow color.

"Ah, Rose." Emma starts, sounding as though she was not sure she wants to say anything. "That is not entirely true."

"Which part?" Rose asks, confused about what she has gotten wrong.

"Brenda did not put just one uniform in me. She did not know which room was yours, so she put one in each of the five rooms and put a bunch more in hall Nine-Ten." Emma says, sounding as though she was preparing for an explosion.

Rose thinks about it for several minutes, looking at the blueprints and then around the room. Knowing that her time is running out, she says, "Okay, okay. Hall Nine-Ten is that one right there. Go get changed quickly." She says, pointing to one of the halls behind her.

It takes the group about five minutes to get changed and ready for the apprehension of Gen. Kingsling. This leaves them with just over ten minutes to enter the home, capture Gen. Kingsling, and get back into Emma.

"Okay, each of us has twice the strength of an average human. We can drop down from the roof without having to worry about breaking bones." Rose starts. "Michael, I want you to take Jason and Patrick and cover this door on the north side. John and

Spring, you two need to cover the garage door, just in case he tries to get out through there. Barb, Keith, and Cal, you will cover the door on the east side of the home. The rest of you will come with me to the main door." Rose says before turning to face Amadahy. "Honey, I need you to stay in Emma and tell me if you see anyone come out of any of the windows, okay?"

"Okay, please come back, though." Amadahy says with a forced smile.

The operation goes as planned with the three breaching teams making entry as one. Each team clears the first room as they are supposed to before moving on to the next. But Michael's team is the one to find and arrest Kingsling. Everyone is back on Emma with two minutes to spare. As they are racing to Pennsylvania to get Gen. Hamilton, Rose receives a phone call from President Ross.

"Hello?" Rose says as Emma puts the call through.

"Hello, Rose? This is President Ross." The deep male voice starts. "Your actions have drawn attention. Everyone knows that you are apprehending top officials of the American Morphed Prison System. Many of those still at large are asking for protection from the government." President Ross says.

"I have three of the six men already, and very soon, we will have a fourth." Rose tells him, looking at the time.

"You already have three? But they are spread all over the country." President Ross says in shock.

"Sir, do I still have your permission to arrest these people or not?" Rose asks as Emma announces their approach to Lehigh Valley International Airport. "Sir, Gen. Hamilton is on a flight coming into Lehigh Valley International Airport. I have a team that can enter and arrest him as he is getting off the plane. But only if I have your approval." Rose adds in frustration.

"You have my support. But I must tell you, there are those in the government who want nothing to do with this." President Ross tells her as the line goes dead.

"Rose, I am receiving a signed document from President Ross, giving us the unwavering authority to enter any and all restricted areas to perform our duties." Emma tells Rose as she lands at a terminal with eight minutes to spare.

Rose has been formulating a plan since they left California on how she wants to have everyone processioned for this arrest. She told Michael, "I want you to take six people and hang out until the plane docks at the terminal. Then I want you to move under the plane watching all the points Gen. Hamilton my try to escape through. I will have the rest inside at the terminal exit waiting for him to come off."

As Michael and his team start to head off in the direction of Pan-AMs terminals, Rose is met by three big guys wearing police uniforms. "You can't be here." They tell her as they place their hands on their guns.

"Keep those weapons holstered boys. Here are my papers." Rose says, pulling out the papers that President Ross had sent her.

The cops look them over and start to tear them but find they can't. "Our orders are that no one gets close to the Gen.. Why the hell can't I rip this?" The big six-foot-four guy says, straining under the effort.

"It's because of the type of paper it is, and if you look, my orders come from the President of the United States." Rose says ripping the paper from the guy's hand. "Now, unless you want to be arrested as well, I suggest you let us through."

The guy in the very back steps aside, but the two guys in the front step forward, saying, "You are not getting through."

Rose, Michael, Cal, and John, move as one dropping the two guys and having them cuffed before either could even say 'ow.' John and Cal pick the guys up and escort them to the room that Rose is using as a cell, while the rest of them head for their positions to capture Gen. Hamilton.

The arrest goes as planned, and soon they are off looking for the last two once more. But Rose still wants to talk to Amadahy's parents. After asking Emma to make a detour, Rose walks around looking for Amadahy and soon finds her hiding in one of the bathrooms.

"Why are you hiding, Amadahy?" Rose asks her after convincing her to open the door.

"You are going to go see my folks. They have already tried to kill me twice and then gave me to that man." She says through sobs of tears.

"Listen, I am not just going to give you to them. I want to know if they have changed how they feel about you, and to give them a chance to be in your life." Rose says, hugging Amadahy. "You can stay in Emma until we know what they want to do, okay?"

"Okay." Amadahy says, hugging Rose back tightly.

Emma lands at the house Amadahy points out as being the one her family lives in, and Rose steps out to talk to them. But before she has a chance to get five feet away, a shot rings out, hitting just in front of Rose, missing her by only a few inches.

"Get the fuck out of here, you freak. We don't want anything to do with your kind around here." A guy calls out from somewhere inside the house.

"My name is Rose, and I am here to talk to you and your wife about Amadahy." Rose calls back.

"Amadahy is dead. That freak of a monster stole her from us." A woman calls out from the upper floor of the house. "We don't want that piece of shit freak anywhere around us." She says as a second shot rings out, hitting Rose in the shoulder.

"Okay, I am leaving. You did not have to shoot me." Rose yells back at the woman as blue blood trickles down her left arm. As Rose turns, a third shot rings out, hitting her in the side of the stomach and blowing through her side.

"I told you to leave, you fucking freak." The man yells out as police come driving up with lights and sirens stopping between Rose and the people in the house.

Amadahy runs out and grabs Rose quickly, followed by Michael, Patrick, and Barb. As they pick Rose up off the ground, she passes out.

***

Michael calls out to the police, "Arrest them for attempted murder on an officer."

"What officer, I see no other officers here." The female cop yells back at Michael.

"We are officers from Mars. We are here on official business when they shot this woman. This un-armed woman, twice." Patrick says.

More of the group steps out of Emma to help carry Rose in but stop when they hear the shouting. Soon, everyone in Rose's group's eyes is shining brightly with crimson flames as they stare down the officers.

"Okay, we will arrest them for illegal discharge of a weapon within city limits. Will that do?" The male officer asks.

"No." All of them say in unison.

"Then we will arrest them. After that, they will be taken to Mars to stand trial by our courts." Emma says.

The police look at each other and turn their weapons on the group calling for backup over their radios. Emma follows suit by calling President Ross and explaining what is going on. In fifteen minutes, there are four more police cars there. This makes the people in the house feel safe enough to walk outside.

"Which one of you officers is officer Stoneburger?" Emma calls out as the officer's attempt to surround her.

"I am." An officer calls out.

"Call your dispatch, they have something to tell you." Emma tells him.

The officer calls his dispatch and is informed that they will arrest both Adahy and his wife. They are also to turn them over to Emma and her crew.

Officer Stoneburger can be heard saying, "But Sir." and "I can't" periodically as the conversation goes on. After a few minutes, though, several military helicopters take positions around the clearing in front of the house, and officer Stoneburger gives in.

Rose awakens back on Mars in the hospital. As she looks around the room, she sees Frank taking notes at a computer in the corner of the room. "Hello, Frank." She says, trying to sit up but feeling sick as she tries.

"You are awake." Frank says in amazement. "Every time I turn around, you find another way to amaze me."

"Why am I here?" She asks, not fully remembering what happened to her.

"When Emma landed last night, she said you had been shot twice. While you were on the operating table, I removed the bullet from your arm with no problem. But your intestines were ripped up pretty bad." Frank tells her as her eyes drop.

"Frank, whatever it is, you can tell me." Rose says, fearing the worse.

"I am not sure." Frank starts as tears start to well up in her eyes.

"Aw, hell. You lost your left kidney and ovary, nearly two full feet of your intestines, and if that was not bad enough, the bullet shattered your ilium on the left side before it left your body." Dr. Brown says through his heavy Indian accent.

"So, that's why I can't move." Rose says, thinking about the missing ovary rather than why she can't move.

"Yes. But the fact that you are awake just an hour after surgery is amazing." Frank says, turning back to the computer.

"As we were sowing you up, I was watching your body start fixing itself. I almost did not have to use, aw, how do you say?" Dr. Brown says.

"Stitches. They are called stitches." Frank says spinning in his seat. "What he is trying to say is that when we pushed the skin together to start sowing you up, we could see your body making connections between the sides of the insition. The only problem was it was not doing it fast enough to let it do everything on its own."

"Does that not happen in people anyway?" Rose asks, trying to understand why this was amazing to them.

"Yes, but in ordinary people, even many of us, this happens much slower. So slow, in fact, that it is not perceivable by the naked eye." Frank says, sounding as though this is incomprehensible.

Over the next week, several people come to visit Rose in the hospital. There are the ones she expected, like Megan and Elizabeth, and even Amadahy. But then there were several she was not expecting, like Sarah, James and Rebecca, and many of the people that she rescued.

Sarah tells Rose, the day she is released from the hospital, that Dr. Flynn and Arnold Brandon had been captured by the US government and that the Russian government is handing over several people from their country to stand trial as well. They will be transported to Mars by a security team provided by Sarah before the trial starts. She also said that the trial is to take place amongst the alien council of six and the Mars council members, with American representative's also present.

The day of the arraignment comes much faster than Rose thought it should. As Rose enters the courtroom with Sarah and everyone else, she can see the accused people seated on one side of a table with the attorney's sitting on the other side. As they read the charges off to the people, they tell them they will have a chance to defend themselves during the trial. They are also told that the US President will be one of the people that will be in attendance as well as several members of his cabinet with people from the UN.

Rodger Right announces to the court that he has decided to plead guilty to all counts. He also asks to speak with Rose in private before the trial begins, and Rose agrees. Rose leads Mr.

Right into her private office located just down the hall from the courtroom.

"So, what do you want to talk about?" Rose asks once they have entered her office and closed the door.

"I wish to join you as one of you. My wife and I both do." Rodger says with his hands bound in front of him with a set of handcuffs.

"Why should I consider letting you join us? You chased my nephew, imprisoned several of my people, and you work for Col. Morris and Mr. Brandon." Rose says knowing that who he works for, is no reason to condemn a man. She just wants to get his reaction to the whole thing.

"I know. I have not been a good person, nor should you trust me after what I have done." He says with his head bowed. "I did not work for Col. Morris and Mike Brandon by choice. I worked for the NSA under Fred McDowell and was transferred to the NSS just last year."

"I see. And what did you do for the NSA before being sent to the NSS?" Rose asks.

"I worked in intelligence with my wife. I did all the footwork while she did all the analysis." He says, now looking up to show he has tears in his eyes.

"Mr. Right, I have known people that can force tears out on command. However, your story, so far, matches what your wife told me a little while ago. She is here with President Ross to observe your trial." Rose says as she crosses the room to stand next to Rodger. "She asked me for the same thing, and I think I will give it to you, but not until after the trial."

"Thank you." Rodger cries out, the tears falling harder. "Thank you very much. I will do whatever is needed of me."

"Things will not be easy for you. While I may believe you have honest intentions, others may not." Rose starts off. "We will expect a lot from you and your wife. But you will not be allowed to perform the kind of work you are use too doing."

After Rodger agrees to all terms and conditions, Rose leads Rodger back to the courtroom for the trial. The trial begins soon after, and those who pled 'Not Guilty' are allowed to tell their stories to the courts.

"The first person to make an opening statement on their own behalf will be Col. David Morris." David says, acting as the court reporter.

"I am fifth generation, Air Force." Col. Morris starts. "My father, Maj. Gen. Morris, was considered one of the best in the service. My own career is just as distinguished as my fathers is. I became aware of the Morphs when I was informed of an issue with my daughter at her work. When I attempted to contact her to find out what was going on, I was not allowed to contact her. That is when I discovered she was being kept by a Morph. When I attempted to rescue her, I was met with great resistance and was forced to use extreme measures which I had believed caused her death."

After Col. Morris is finished and takes his seat, the next one to step forward is Gen. Mark Hamilton. After his introduction, he begins, "I am Gen. Mark Hamilton of the United States Army. When the Morphs' existence was brought to my attention, I was informed they were a National Security Risk that needed to be dealt with quickly and quietly. I was informed that there were several prisons that had been built in the last century in case of insurrection. I was tasked with managing the new NSS, which was to act as a sub-branch of the NSA. My official role was the acting head, nothing more."

The next introduced is Doctor James Flynn. As he steps forward, there is entirely no expression on his face. This is in contrast to the others who at least looked regretful. He starts, "I was approached by Arnold Brandon, who offered me a chance to perform research without any humanitarian concerns. In my research, I found out many exciting and interesting things while I worked without constraints. I discovered that the Morphs breathe nitrogen and carbon dioxide and that flooding the area with pure oxygen will cause them to suffocate. Most, if not all, Morphs can change how energy works in all of its forms. They can change light energy into physical power, or heat. In one experiment, I witnessed one Morph appear in a cell with two other Morphs before disappearing again. All of my research was sanctioned by the NSS and will benefit all humanity when I am found innocent."

The last one to volunteer to make an opening statement is Arnold Brandon. As he walks forward, he avoids looking at anyone other than the president and the others here from Earth. Once he takes the podium, he starts, "I am, Arnold Brandon. I am the director of the NSS in North America. I was only following the orders given to me by my superiors. I know I will not be found guilty of any wrongdoing for this fact."

The trial takes six days in total. Evidence that is presented, both supports and condemns the actions of all the men on trial. For Col. Morris, however, most of the evidence not only condemn his actions, but much of it counteracts his personal statements. The judges take all of this into consideration while trying to make a decision.

"Over the last three days, the twelve of us have been reviewing all of the facts of this case. Our decision was far from easy to come too, and each of you has your own involvement in the actions of the NSS. Because of this, we have decided to hand out our decisions separately." Sarah starts after the deliberations.

Rose is the next one to stand to continue the statement. "Though reaching our decision was difficult, our decision is final due to the nature of the crimes. First, we will hand down our decision on Gen. Mark Hamilton, Maj. Nickali kuznetsov, and Maj. Gen. Zhang Wei. It is our decision that even though the result goes against human rights established in 1998, they only did so under orders. However, this does not excuse their involvement. For this, we find Gen. Mark Hamilton, guilty of wrongful imprisonment, kidnapping, murder, illegal experimentation, and conspiracy." Rose says, looking directly at Gen. Hamilton.

"The next ones to receive our judgment will be Gen. Steven Kingsling, Maj. Li Wei, and Maj. Heinz Shultz." President Ross says standing up from his seat. "You are also found guilty of the aforementioned crimes as well as the illegal use of government property and resources. However, Gen. Steven Kingsling, your crimes also include master mining a conspiracy."

"Doctor James Flynn." Sarah says, standing up from her seat as President Ross sits down. "seeing how you were the only doctor arrested, you will stand alone. You are hereby found guilty of all aforementioned crimes. You are also found guilty of human vivisection, torture, and unethical human experimentation. While I am sure you believe your actions were for the better, you have shown nothing but unbridled brutality."

Rose stands up and looks around the room at those still waiting to hear their verdicts. As she does, a tear starts to roll down her cheek. "I feel sorry for the rest of you. Each of you has been proven to have lied about your involvement in the crimes presented in this case. You all claim you were following orders, doing nothing more than your individual jobs. You claim you were pulled in by the actions of others and that your actions are no fault of your own. However, all of the evidence presented here over the last week seems to indicate a different story. Because of this, you are all hereby found guilty. Each of you has made your choices of your own accord and must now live with the consequences of your actions." After she finishes, she sits down as the tears keep falling. "Each of you will receive a sentencing date in the next few days. At that time, you will find out what your sentence will be."

Gen. Mark Hamilton, Maj. Nickali kuznetsov, and Maj. Gen. Zhang Wei are allowed to return to Earth to serve sentences of five to ten years with the possibility of parole for good behavior. Gen. Steven Kingsling, Maj. Li Wei, Maj. Heinz Shultz, Doctor James Flynn, and the rest are all sentenced to serve anywhere from ten years to life sentences on the Zicarthona penal colony located somewhere in deep space.

Rose spends the next week walking the streets of the Mars colony thinking and wondering why people hated them so much that they would do the things that were revealed during the trial. This night, however, she meets up with Sarah as she walks. Most of the aliens can walk the streets freely like Rose and everyone else that has changed, all except two, however. The only two that cannot, is Zieth and Zor, both need oxygen to breathe, so they have to stick to the Bio-Dome or put on special suits just for them.

As Rose and Sarah walk the streets, they talk.

"So, have you given any thought to my invitation?" Sarah asks, looking up at the stars in the night sky.

"Your invitation?" Rose asks, stopping and turning to look at Sarah.

"To teach you how to control your white energy, so you do not change people that do not want the change." She says meeting Rose's gaze. "You all have it, but yours is far more powerful than I have ever seen, and it is escaping freely." She says, resuming their walk.

"It's escaping freely? So, that's why people turn after I meet them?" Rose says, kicking a small rock on the ground.

"Yes. But I can teach you to channel it when you need it and suppress it when you don't." Sarah says, watching some children run by laughing.

"I would want to bring my family along if I come." Rose says, also watching the children as they reach a ball at the far end of the street.

"Of course. We can't bring everyone, but I think we can fit ten or so people. No humans, because we don't have any way for them to survive on our planet." Sarah says as they turn down a side street.

"That means my oldest daughter can't come with us." Rose says with a look of concern on her face.

"She is human?" Sarah says with a look of confusion on her face as she stops in the middle of the road.

"She is one of seven I know of that I have any physical contact with after I changed that did not change themselves." Rose says, turning around to look at Sarah.

"This is interesting. Can I meet with her?" Sarah asks stepping forward to be next to Rose. "She may be able to resist the energy in ways that many others never could."

"I think we can arrange that." Rose says as she turns to continue their walk.

Rose takes Sarah to meet Elizabeth the next morning in the bio-dome. After the introduction, Rose is asked to wait outside while Sarah talks to Elizabeth alone. Rose agrees and tells Elizabeth she will just be right outside if she needs her. Elizabeth nods, and Rose leaves the room.

Sarah takes Elizabeth by the hand and leads her to the table where they sit and talk. After several minutes of them holding hands, Sarah stands and walks out. As she leaves the room, she sees Rose standing down the hall, a little way from the door.

"So, what did you learn?" Rose asks as Sarah stands in front of the door.

"Your child is not resisting the energy. She is different than any creature before her. She is in full command and able to call it as she needs it, just as you, even though she is unaware of its presence in her." Sarah says, her eyes big like she has seen something that is impossible.

Rose turns and thinks about what she has been told for a few minutes before deciding to talk with Elizabeth.

"Rose," Sarah starts. "If you tell her, your relationship may change beyond anything you're ready for."

"If I don't, it will cause her to hate me even more than if I do." Rose says, walking by Sarah and entering Elizabeth's apartment.

"Mom, what does she mean that I have the same energy as you?" Elizabeth asks as Rose closes the door behind her.

"Well, the energy that infected me and changed me into this has also infected you. However, instead of having the effect of changing you into something like me, you have somehow figured out how to stop it and possibly even control it." Rose says, smiling at Elizabeth as tears fall freely.

"So, I won't change?" Elizabeth says, looking down at the floor with tears starting to roll down her cheek.

"No. But that does not mean you can't do the same things that I can." Rose says, walking over to Elizabeth and hugging her.

"But what are you going to do about the offer President Ross made you?" Elizabeth asks.

"I am going to have to turn it down. I have decided to go to, Nandime with Sarah. She has offered to teach me to control the energy flowing from me freely." Rose says looking Elizabeth in the eyes. "I don't want anyone else to suffer because of me." Rose finishes with tears in her eyes.

"Mom, you have not intentionally hurt anyone. You would never do that." Elizabeth tells her.

"No, I would not. But intentional or not, I did hurt people." Rose says, still crying.

After leaving Elizabeth's apartment, Rose contacts President Ross and tells him that she will not be taking the ambassadorial position he offered. Rose has always worried about Elizabeth's well-being, so when President Ross hears that Elizabeth wants to return to Earth for college, he offers her a full scholarship as well as the position of ambassador.

Soon Elizabeth is ready to leave for Earth, and Rose, Meagan, and their two children plus Amadahy, who Rose and Megan just adopted, along with James and Rebecca, and their now four children are ready to leave for Nandime. Not knowing what awaits them there or the adventures yet to come, Rose and Elizabeth say their goodbyes to each other.

"I want you to be careful. You never know what will happen even if you are paying attention." Elizabeth tells Rose as they hug tightly.

"That is supposed to be my line, you know." Rose says in playful retort.

"I know. You are the one that raised me, though." Elizabeth says with a smile. "Sarah, promise me that you won't let any harm come to her." She says, looking over where Sarah is standing.

"You have my word as a protector of thirty worlds." Sarah says with a shallow bow.

Elizabeth's smile seems to widen as she once again resumes her embrace of Rose. After several minutes, they brake and head for their respective transports.

Rose watches as Elizabeth's transport departs on its journey to Earth. Suddenly, she has a feeling that it is going to be a very long time before she gets to see her again.

Chapter Thirteen

The Arrival

I T HAS BEEN NEARLY TWO years since Rose, Megan, James, Rebecca, and their children left Mars with their hosts Sarah for Nandime. The journey through space has been long and uneventful, but not without its experiences. Megan and James both have had a child each on the trip. The Nandime watched intently as each of them gave birth and brought the new lives forward.

"Sarah, if your world is all about nature and living in harmony. How did your people end up traveling through space?" Rose asks one night at dinner.

"Well, the Nandime did not invent any of the technologies we use." Sarah starts while laying her silverware down. "The technology was made by a race of people called the Shicawn. The Shicawn's were dying out and did not want their technology to fall to just anyone due to its destructive power. So, they searched the galaxy for a race that would not squander the technology for personal or selfish reasons. These Shicawn's entrusted the technology to the Nandime people as a gift millions of years ago. The Nandime would not have ventured into space if it was not for the gift of the Shicawn."

"So, your people have been traveling the stars for several million years?" James asks, wanting to know more.

"Yes. About thirty million years ago, we ventured out into space for the first time. We were not ready for what we found, though. We found conflict, destruction, and discontent for established life." Sarah says with a tear rolling down her cheek.

"You returned home to avoid the conflict, correct?" Rebecca asks, looking angry.

"We tried. However, a race of people called the Nockton followed us back to our planet. The Nockton's and the Shicawn's had been enemies. The Shicawn's had the superior weapons and never had to worry about the Nockton's. But since the Shicawn's were gone, the Nockton thought they could take the weapons from those who inherited it. When they came, they burned many of our forests, killed billions of our people and even polluted much of our waters. But in the end, we decided to fight and were able to fend them off." Sarah tells everyone.

"Have they ever tried to attack again?" Megan asks, looking like she wants to cry as well.

"Not really, but this was not the last time we ran into them." Sarah says.

"So, what happened?" James asks.

"It was about ten thousand years ago. We were mapping the galaxy in which your world resides. We were just about finished with the section we were working on when the Nockton's attacked our lone research ship. This nearly got them a ship to study; if it was not for another race called the Endorphins." Sarah stopped. The look on her face was that of someone struggling with a decision.

"We can stop if we need to." Rose says, trying to release the stress.

"No. I think you can handle the truth. For five thousand years after that confrontation, we were allied with the Endorphins. But that all came to an end when they started destroying worlds that had life on them to establish colonies for their people. By the time we realized what was going on, they had destroyed several planets and had started an attack by sending a large meteorite to Earth that caused a flood that lasted for nearly three and a half months. If it had not been for the Eldon, humans might not have survived." Sarah says, looking around the room.

No one knew what to say for this, and for several long minutes, the room sat in silence, at least until Rose spoke.

"Your people did the right thing. There is no way for you to have known what the Endorphins would one day do." Rose says with a smile on her face.

"I agree with Rose. I had no idea before I arrived on Mars that most of my crew would be changed." James says, hoping he is making the correct type of comparison.

"James, the comparison is not the same. Rose had no intention of causing anyone to change. On the other hand, the Nandime's were friends with these Endorphins who either changed over time or had every intention of genocide." Rebecca says.

"It is okay. I know he was trying to console me. But I was not the one responsible, so consoling me will do no good. I am going to turn in for the night. Tomorrow we will get our first look of Nandime." Sarah says, standing from the table and walking out of the room.

The next morning, Rose, Megan, James, Rebecca, and all eight children are on the main bridge waiting to see their new home for the next few years. Rose and Megan both have always wanted to travel through space seeing new worlds, but Emma has never been able to move fast enough for travel between solar systems.

"I wish Emma could be up here to see this." Megan says, bouncing up and down on the tips of her toes.

"I wish Elizabeth could have been here to see this as well." Rose says as she turns and walks to the back part of the large room.

Rose has been thinking about her daughter a lot these days. She was only eighteen when they left Mars. Elizabeth could not join them on their journey because she is not able to breathe anything other than oxygen, nor can she handle the extreme gravity of Nandime. Elizabeth had told Rose to go on her journey while she went to college on Earth.

Megan, Rebecca, and Amadahy all walk over and hug Rose. Rose really needs it, but when they break apart, Rose starts crying from how much she misses her.

"Elizabeth was only eighteen when we left, and I never thought we would be gone so long," Rose says as the tears fall freely. "I miss her so much, it hurts."

"Rose, I am sorry things are the way they are. None of us truly realized how far Nandime was from Mars." Rebecca says with an arm around Rose's left side. "Two years to go thirty-five light-years is a lot faster than six months from Earth to Mars that James and I had to do."

"Rebecca, what are you doing?" Megan asks, looking across Rose. "Rose needs cheering up, not someone stating the obvious. And besides, it took us only a week on our first trip to get to Mars."

"Ya, and as I understand it, much of the time was spent trying to fix Emma because of someone's stupid mistake!" Rebecca says, starting to yell.

"Ya, Ya," Megan starts.

"Guys, calm down." Rose says to both Megan and Rebecca. "These things are all in the past, and we are the guest of others here."

Megan and Rebecca both look around and see the Nandime staring at them, their tails wagging back and forth. They have all learned they do this when they are getting flustered or irritated.

"We are sorry about that." Megan says with her head bowed in reverence.

"It is okay. The journey has been long, and the stresses compile overtime on long confinements." Sarah says, walking closer to them, standing against the wall.

"I am sorry that I started this in front of you, Sarah. The pain of leaving a child behind is great and not always easy to hide." Rose says, making sure her head is bowed.

"My dear Rose, trust me, I know the sorrow of leaving a child behind." Sarah says, placing her hands on either side of Rose's face. "I have had to do it on many occasions though not for as long as you have chosen." The tears in her own eyes start to fall, but not as freely as Rose's.

Looking into Sarah's eyes, Rose can see images of different events from Sarah's past, though Rose is not sure what they truly are. Rose watches each event intently as they come, one after the other.

"Thank you, Sarah. You have helped me once again." Rose says, trying to bow her head again but not being able to because of Sarah's hands.

"I see you have much to learn. I have much to teach you. I have lived far longer than any of you here, and I have had as many children as all of you combined. Though none quite as wild as yours." Sarah says, turning to look at James with the eight children.

They all turn to look at the children with James and see the two youngest making their run on the control panels. As James realizes this, she runs and grabs each of them before any harm can be done.

"Thank you, Sarah. I am humbly honored to have a teacher like you." Rose says, wiping the tears from her eyes with the back of her hand.

"Nonsense, my child. I am the one humbled here. I have offered my help to someone as deserving as you and you accepted." Sarah says her nose turned up in mock.

They all laugh allowed while Rose, feeling much better, hugs Sarah as they walk back to the window to get their first look of Nandime.

The site is breathtaking. The planet is a big green marble that is nearly all land. Everywhere you look, you can see green and brown from the vegetation with absolutely no sign of any cities. As they get closer to the ground, they discover that the towns are built into the forest, making it seem like they are one and the same. In fact, in many cases, they are. The roads and walkways seem to be built right into the trees themselves.

"Our homes have always been in the trees of our world, so when we started building, the trees became a vital part of our construction." Sarah says, seeing the looks on their faces. "The trees live with us and us with them. It is much more pleasurable for us and far better for the trees."

"I wish this was true for our world." Megan says as she sees the way the trees and buildings seem to be almost one. Her eyes are sliding from the wooden bark of a tree to the tan wood paneling of the building next to it.

"The planet you live on was once green like this, but its inhabitants killed it like the humans are killing their world now." Sarah says, with much sorrow in her voice.

"Our world use to support life?" Megan asks in shock.

"Yes, it did. Mars used to have flowing rivers and great oceans. There were trees on every continent as well as animals that would amaze you." Sarah says, looking out the window at Nandime.

"What were the people like?" Rebecca asks with a glint in her eyes.

"We have plenty of time to tell stories. But for now, we need to get ready to land. Besides, I am not too familiar with them." Sarah says.

Soon they land, and Emma gets to move freely once again. The world they have landed on is nearly three and a half times the size of Earth, which makes it harder for them to move. Rose, Megan, James, and Rebecca find themselves getting tired much faster than they have before. The children, however, do not seem to notice the difference and play just as hard as always. But instead of their usual two hours of sleep, they sleep for nearly four and a half hours.

After a few weeks, they find that they are adjusting to the new gravity rather well. Soon after, Megan, James, and Rebecca decide to head off to see more of the planet with all the children in tow with Emma. Rose feels good that they will get to see the new world, but she still misses Elizabeth and wishes, with all her might, she was here.

Just then, as if by magic, Elizabeth is standing in front of her. "Mom?" Elizabeth says looking around in wonder. "How can this be?" She asks as she walks to the edge of the path they are standing on and looks down.

"I don't know. I was really missing you and wishing you were here and then..." Rose says, waving her hands up and down at the image of Elizabeth. "Where were you before you came here?" Rose asks.

"I was in class. Elementary Physics, no big deal, it's just about over." She says, walking to the other side of the path and looking off.

"Do I need to let you get back to it?" Rose asks with one eyebrow raised.

"No. It is the class you helped to set up through NASA. They would not believe me that I already knew the stuff backward and forwards." Elizabeth says, now walking over to Rose. "So, let's walk, and you can tell me everything." She says, wrapping her arm around Rose's, proving that she is more than an allusion.

Even though Rose knows she is not really here on Nandime, Elizabeth is just as solid as Rose. She also tells Rose she can smell things around them as well as feel the interaction between herself and the world around them.

For the next few hours, they talk and talk and talk. Rose tells her about everything that has happened since leaving Mars, and Elizabeth tells her everything that has happened on Earth. Just as

Rose Kincade

Rose is about to send Elizabeth back, Sarah happens to walk by them.

"My Child, how did this happen?" She asks, looking from Elizabeth to Rose and back.

"I found myself thinking about her again, and then there she was." Rose says.

"I have to admit, I was thinking about her as well." Elizabeth says, folding her hands repeatedly as she bights her lower lip.

"I have never heard of this happening before." Sarah says, walking around Elizabeth looking her over. "I knew white energy is powerful, but this... This is unimaginable."

"I was just going to send her home." Rose says, looking over at Sarah. "We have just spent some time together talking, and she needs to get back."

"I should like to see this." Sarah says, looking from one to the other.

Elizabeth and Rose hug one last time, and as they break, Elizabeth vanishes. Sarah, who is standing behind Rose, is utterly speechless. Sarah turns to walk off, but before she moves more than a few steps, Rose speaks.

"You said you have never heard of this before." Rose says, not having turned to look at her. "Does this mean you will not be able to teach me to control it?"

"I do not know, child. I must confer with the others on this. But I would ask one thing, please do not try and use the power until we know more." Sarah says. Sarah walks off quickly back the direction she had come, leaving Rose standing there alone once again.

Weeks pass by before Rose sees anyone she knows. Megan and the others have not returned from exploring the planet. Sarah and most of the household is spending a lot of time away on business. Rose is out on one of her many walks when she spots someone she knows. It is one that calls himself Bob. He is one of Sarah's companions, or at least that is the way he comes across.

"Rose, how be you?" He asks as he approaches.

"I am okay." She says when she realizes who he is. "I have not seen anyone for weeks, though."

"Well, then. I be good come by now." He says with a smile on his face.

"Your English is getting better, but still needs some work, Bob. But yes, I feel better that you have come by." Rose says as they walk down the path.

"I bring new. You come me and Sarah." Bob says, nodding his head fast.

Rose raises an eyebrow and says, "Okay, I will come with you to see Sarah." Hoping that is what he meant to say.

Bob takes Rose by the hand and leads her down the path. When they reach an old tree, they turn right, going down a path that seems to appear as they walk. Rose has never seen a path like this before and wonders how she could have missed this path before. She has been walking the paths ever since they arrived, and the new path has never been there that she can remember. Before she can finish her thought, they arrive at an old building that looks a lot like the tree that was hiding the path at the other end. Bob takes her to the door and tells her "in" before he turns and walks back up the path. Rose, not knowing what to expect, pushes on the doors and walks through.

Inside, the room is dark. So dark that Rose is only able to see shadows move in the place. This scares her because, since the change, she has never found a room that she cannot see in without light. As she watches the shadows moving around the room, one stops, and a tiny light pops on, revealing a mouth floating in the air.

"You are here to have your control over the white energy tested." The male voice says. Then the light goes out as quickly as it came on.

Rose watches the figure rejoin the others as they walk in a circle around her. She is about to say something when another of the figures stops, and the same tiny light comes on again.

"You will have several challenges placed before you to test your control." This time it is a female voice that speaks. The light goes out, and she too rejoins the crowd moving along the walls.

Rose watches and counts them. *There are ten, no wait, twelve of them moving along the walls.* Rose thinks to herself, having had enough of the theatrics. With a burst of light from her hands, she shouts, "Enough!" Suddenly she can see clearly again, and all the people in the room stand like statues along the wall of the round room. All their faces show the confusion that each of them feels.

"Rose, I knew by the display of your power a few weeks ago, bringing your child here, that you were powerful indeed." This person sounds familiar to Rose. She knows the voice to be that of Sarah's. "This display of your power outstrips anything we have ever seen in any living creature." She says, sounding as though she is struggling against some invisible restraints.

"So, this is part of a test?" Rose asks, looking around the room. Her eyes are flashing red with her frustration.

"Yes, child. If you release us, we can talk about what is just happened here better." Sarah says.

Rose looks down, trying to figure out what she means. She realizes that her hands are still in mid jester as she had waved them through the air before. "Sorry. The whole thing was getting a little nerve-racking." She says as she lowers her hands, releasing everyone in the room.

"My, Child. In my three hundred years as a high priest, I have never seen anyone stop twelve protestants in one shot, let alone reverse their combined effects of non-sight." An old man says as he steps forward from the wall.

"The power in this child is great, but her control still has to be proven." Another, a woman just as old, says as she walks forward.

"That much power can have killed us all, but it did not. This shows the true intent of not wishing harm." A guy not as old as the first says, now walking forward.

"I agree. This child has no true hate in her. But even none hate acts can kill." This is spoken by another guy who walks forward joining the first three.

"Rather, she has full control or not. I feel she needs to go through training to see her full potential." A woman says as she moves forward to join the others.

The arguments of the twelve go on like this as each member moves forward and joins the rest and even long after. Soon Rose gets tired of listening to them bicker, so she walks to a podium to sit down. After another hour has passed, she lies back and falls asleep.

"Child, wake." The voice is calling to her. "Come, my child, wake, please." It calls again. Reluctantly Rose opens her eyes and sees Sarah standing over her. "We have reached our decision." She says, taking Rose by the hand to help her up.

"And what should my fate be this day?" She asks, feeling rather angry by the ways she has been treated today.

"I am going to train you in all that we know." Sarah says with a smile on her face.

Rose feels a little better but knows that it is going to be hard work. "In return, I will try to teach you what I have learned myself." Rose says, trying to show gratitude.

The next day, Rose's training begins. She is required to run ten miles a day, jump from tree to tree for half the distance she had just run, and all the while gathering and carrying all the food she will need for herself and the rest of them. For nearly two months, this goes on day after day. In the beginning, it takes her from the time she gets up until she goes to bed. But about halfway through the third month, she starts to finish earlier and earlier in the day.

Rose has not needed to sleep more than a few hours, at most per night since she has changed, but she is sleeping nearly six hours a night while she is training. She knows there must be something to the practice that she is doing that she is not aware of, but she cannot figure it out. By the fifth month, she notices she is down to sleeping only about four hours through the night. She figures that her stamina must be increasing with the training. By the end of the sixth month, Sarah has started working with Rose showing her how to focus her energy and channel it away from people that she meets.

"The key is to imagine a bubble in the center of your stomach and then to fill that bubble with all your energy, so it is protected from others." Sarah tells her one afternoon as they stand in a field on the forest floor.

By the end of the first two years, Rose has demonstrated the basics of energy control. She can suppress and hide it when she meets with others, and she has even learned to use it with several new abilities as if they were second nature to her. The one thing she is still having a problem with is reading other's energy, for some reason every time she tries, either they are left with little of their own energy or she gives them far too much of her own.

"It will come with time." Sarah tells her as they finish the day's lessons. "It took me nearly ten years to get the hang of it." She says as they walk down a set of stairs to go to dinner.

"So, I am not hopeless?" Rose asks, feeling bad, having taken far too much of the energy of the Nandime woman who she was practicing on and leaving her looking as though she has not slept for some time.

"No, my child, I know a few that it took them some hundred years before they could control the flow of their power." She says with a smile on her face as they enter the great hall for dinner. "You have learned more in the last three years than many have in an entire lifetime."

Rose forces a smile feeling this cannot be true, but at that, it is time to sit and eat. She joins the rest at the large table placed in the center of the room and finds Megan and their now five children waiting for her. As she looks around, she sees James and Rebecca both are pregnant again, and by the looks of them, they are about to drop any day now. As she sits and eats dinner with the rest, they all joke and laugh, forgetting about the day's events. Soon, she has forgotten her problems, at least until they have eaten nearly everything on the table.

The next day when Rose gets to the room where she does her training, Sarah is there waiting for her. "Instead of the usual training today, we are going to try something else." Sarah says as Rose enters the room.

"Okay. What do you have in mind?" Rose asks, wondering what they are going to do.

"I want you to call your child on Earth here." She says, looking as though she is going to cry. "I am going to watch you do this and try to see what is going on if I can."

Rose nods, knowing there is more she is not being told. She turns and faces an open spot on the floor, and Sarah places a hand on her shoulder. Rose thinks hard about Elizabeth and wanting her to be in front of her as she did before. After about a minute, Elizabeth is standing in front of them in the middle of the room.

"Mom. I am glad to see you." Elizabeth calls out, running forward and hugging Rose tightly.

"I am glad to see you as well." Rose says, seeing that Elizabeth is in a nightgown. "Going to bed or getting up?" She asks.

"Going to bed, it is a much better time of day this time. Last time I woke up in the hospital." Elizabeth tells them with a frown. "There were only ten minutes left in class the last time, and when the class was over, they found me unconscious and called an ambulance when they could not get me to come around."

"I am sorry." Rose says, frowning a bit. "Had I known; I would have sent you back sooner."

"It's okay. I told them what had really happened, and most of them think I am crazy. No one except Nana believes me." She says, smiling widely. "Hi, Sarah." She says, looking over Rose's shoulder.

Sarah waves but does not say a word. She is intent on learning the ability that Rose and Elizabeth have to be able to see each other.

"So, how is everyone?" Rose asks. When she did, Elizabeth's smile vanishes.

"Nana is sick, and they don't know how much longer she will live." Elizabeth says with tears in her eyes.

"Nana has lived a long time, and since grandpa died, she just has not been the same." Rose says. "She misses your grandpa and wants to be with him again."

"I know, but it does not make it any easier." Elizabeth says, turning and walking to a window in the room. "She is practically the only family I have here right now. Linda has changed and has decided to live on Mars, and the rest have too much in their own lives to bother with me." She says as the tears start to fall.

"What time is it there now? Rose asks.

"It is about nine pm. Why?" She asks, looking confused.

Rose looks down at her watch and sees it reads 21:04 Thursday and now knows her watch still works. "How about we set a time each week we can meet, and you can tell me everything you want?" Rose says as a smile blooms on her face.

Elizabeth turns and says, "Sunday mornings. Everyone is gone, and I have the house to myself nearly all day." Also, having a smile bloom on her face.

They make it a date, and they say their goodbyes before Rose sends her back. Once she is gone, Sarah takes her hand from Rose.

"Your power is far more powerful than we thought." She says, looking as though she has been working all day in the hot sun.

"But we knew that already, didn't we?" Rose asks, looking at Sarah.

"Yes. But the power you used just now was not there before you started. You somehow called on a power from somewhere else that made the connection possible." Sarah says as she walks over

236

and sits in the seat near the window. "You have far more power than your body can handle alone. You have a reserve that is unimaginable. If you are not careful, you can destroy whole worlds with a single whim." She says the last few words with a shudder.

By the end of the next year, Rose has learned how to fly short distances and found she has more control over her movements than most of the Nandime with the same abilities. She can turn in midair where the Nandime must touch the ground, a tree, or other objects to make turns. She can speed up or slow down without touching anything as well. Again, the Nandime must touch the ground or a tree to make any such changes in their speed.

Sarah has watched Rose through many of her visits with Elizabeth, trying to find the source of Rose's power, but whenever she gets too close, something would happen, and she would have to pull back, often in severe pain. Emma has even learned some new tricks as well. She can reach speeds equal to that of the Nandime spacecrafts. She has also learned how to become invisible.

After four more years of training, Rose finds out she will see the council again. This will be Rose's second calling to meet the council of twelve, and this time she is ready for them. When she walks through the door, like before, the room is dark, but rather than letting it remain dark, she turns on the lights, instantly revealing the twelve members.

Her next task is to show her control over moving inanimate objects without touching them. Again, she performs well beyond any of their hopes. She is asked to move twelve stone statues that are as big as their real-life counterparts. These statues must be placed next to each of the twelve. Rose looks around the room and sees each of the twelve empty pedestals with each member standing next to them. Rose flicks one of her hands, causing the twelve statues in the center of the room to suddenly vanish from sight only to reappear standing on its proper pedestal.

Rose Kincade

She displays her abilities to fly around the room, control the air within the room, and throw the whole room into darkness that none of them can stop or break. And then comes her final performance of calling forth her daughter. Rose has gotten so good at it, that it now takes no time at all for Elizabeth to appear before the room.

The room gasps as they see a human in the room with them. Elizabeth is now twenty-seven years old and has on a two-piece swimsuit that barely covers her large breast. She stands there looking around the room at all the people looking at her in amazement.

"Hi, everyone." She says, waving a hand. She then turns to Rose. Finding her, she says, "I was on a boat with some friend's mom." Looking rather stern as she makes this remark.

"I am sorry, this won't take long," Rose says.

"Child, you are not in this world, where are you?" The oldest woman asks.

"I am on Earth. About thirty-five light-years away." She says, looking the woman in the eyes.

"But this is not possible." One of the younger male members says.

"I assure you; it is not only possible it is happening." Sarah says, looking around the room. "This child has been communicating with her mother every week for the last five years. I have been trying to find out how this is possible, but my own power is far too weak for the task." She finishes looking back at Rose and Elizabeth standing in the middle of the room.

"Is she the only one you can do this with?" The oldest man on the council asks.

Rose closes her eyes for a moment and tries to think of someone else to try. Then she knows who she is going to try. She opens her eyes, and there before the council standing next to Elizabeth is the newest President of the United States.

"What the hell is going on here?" He exclaims as he looks around the room.

"Mr. President, I know you know who I am, right?" Elizabeth says, looking at the President.

"Yes, you are the ambassador from Mars. But who the hell are the rest of these people?" He asks, waving his hand around the room.

"The one behind us here is Rose, my mother. The rest of these people..." Elizabeth says, gesturing to the twelve-people standing around them.

"Are the council of twelve." Rose finishes stepping forward. "As you can all see, I not only can call forth another, but I can do it while I have one already here and having never met this man directly." She says, her hands on the shoulders of both the President of the United States and Elizabeth.

No one in the room moves or says a word until Rose turns and sends the President back and then asks Elizabeth to call him and let him know that it was not a dream before sending her on her way as well.

The council dismisses Rose, who finds herself waiting once again. After several hours Sarah comes out and tells Rose there is nothing more, she can teach her.

"But there are so many abilities I have not mastered yet." She says as they walk out the big door to walk up the path.

"And you will master them in time. But for now, your training is complete." Sarah says, tapping the top of Rose's hand with her own.

Rose suddenly gets a strange feeling from Sarah. It is like there is something she is hiding from Rose. The oddest part is this is not the first time this has happened, but this is the strongest it has ever been. Rose stops walking and just looks at Sarah.

"What is it, child?" Sarah asks, stopping and turning to look at Rose.

"You are hiding something from me." Rose says with a frown.

"I see you have finally figured out the reading." Sarah says with a smile. "I am not hiding it from you to cause any harm. I merely want to know how long before you realized it."

"I have sensed it for some time and always thought it was my imagination, but this is different, stronger, and more menacing than before." Rose says, stepping forward.

"I see, so you are sensing more than my secret of you." She says as a frown appears on her face as she bows her head. "Let's walk a bit, shall we?" She says as she reaches out her hand.

Rose stands there for a moment considering her options and trying to discern the feelings she is getting from Sarah. She takes one small step back then decides to go with Sarah. Sarah leads them out of the city on an old path that is nearly covered by brush and old branches. As they walk, neither of them speaks until they emerge in a small clearing.

"I do not think we will be bothered out here." Sarah says as she turns to look at Rose in the eyes. "I have an ability that is rare. Just as rare as the amount of power in you is." The look in her eyes now shows just how scared she is.

"And what is your ability that has you so scared?" Rose asks, watching the eyes flash some scenes of a distant war.

"There is a war coming to your world, Mars, and Earth alike. The devastation will be great, and I am afraid there is nothing that can be done to stop it." She says as Rose watches the flashes of war continue in Sarah's eyes.

"How does it start?" Rose asks, hoping there is some way that she can stop the war.

"I do not know, child. The only thing I know is that you will not arrive home before it starts, no matter when you leave." Sarah says as the scenes of war stop flashing in her eyes. Rose blinks and turns away. "Child, you have seen something, haven't you?" Sarah asks.

"I saw the scenes of war flashing in your eyes as we talked just now." Rose says as tears are falling hard.

"Again, amazing, you could see my memories on the coming events," Sarah says, walking to stand in front of Rose.

"This is not the first time that I have been able to see your thoughts flowing through your eyes," Rose says, looking down at the ground.

"Really? When was the first time that you saw my thoughts flowing through my eyes?" Sarah asks, placing a hand on Rose's shoulder.

"Just before we first arrived here on Nandime," Rose says, turning to look at Sarah.

"That long ago, and you never said a word about it. I am beginning to think that your abilities are a gift from the Gods themselves." Sarah says, shaking her head.

"You said I would not be able to get back to Mars until after it starts. So, does that mean the war is going to start in the next two years?" Rose asks the fear prominent in her eyes.

"My child, the time of its beginning, is unknown to me. But rather, I take you now, or you leave on your own any time in the next ten years you will arrive at exactly the same time." Sarah says as she now turns and walks to a nearby tree.

"Wait, I will arrive at exactly the same time no matter when I leave?" Rose asks, walking to be with Sarah. "Does that mean I am going to be caught in some sort of time trap or something?"

"Again, I do not know the answers. I can only tell you what I have seen. If I take you, you go alone, or you take your friends and family, you arrive at the same time, every time." Sarah says, tears flowing freely. "I have asked for every possible outcome for you to be there sooner, but the visions are always the same." She says, sliding down the tree and collapsing on the ground. Rose bends down next to her, trying to comfort her. "Knowing this, what will you decide?"

"I do not know." Rose starts looking up at the sky. "You have informed me that I can leave any time between now and the next ten years, and I will still arrive in twelve years from right now."

"That is true." Sarah says, placing her head on her knees.

"What would happen if you went to Earth in my place?" Rose asks, hoping she could have someone be there in her place.

"I will get there in the usual amount of time. However, there will be no way for me to help stop the conflict." Sarah says.

"I need to talk to everyone else about this. I don't want to make a decision without them." Rose says, standing and reaching out a hand.

Sarah nods and takes Rose's hand, and they head home. After Rose and Sarah return to the home, Rose calls Elizabeth to Nandime and explains everything to the rest of them and asks for opinions on what they should do.

"So, you can leave anytime between now and November 2065, and you will arrive on the same day regardless." Elizabeth says, trying to figure everything out.

"Yes, child of Rose. There is no way for Rose to arrive any time before December 25th, 2067." Sarah says.

"But there is nothing else you can learn if we stay?" Rebecca asks, with her head hanging down, staring at the floor in front of her.

"Anything I can learn will have to be completely on my own." Rose says as she leans against the staircase.

"I don't know if any of us could handle a trip longer than the two years. Just look at the stresses we experienced on our journey here." James says.

"I agree with James, but I don't know if I could live with myself if we let anything happen to Earth... Mars... or both." Megan says, waving her arms in frustration.

"I think we need to vote on it." Rebecca says, standing from her seat.

"All in favor of staying here until we know we can get home." Rose asks, raising a hand to count herself.

Of all the adults in the room Elizabeth, Megan, James, and Sarah voted to stay. Even Amadahy says she would rather stay than spend any more time than she has to in any ship.

"All who want to leave at our earliest convenience, raise your hands." Rebecca asks, raising her hand. But standing there alone, she drops into her seat.

After the vote, everyone in the room feels slightly better knowing that this was a collective decision. Once everyone has left the room, Rose calls forth the council of five from Mars as well as all the Earth leaders. They are so surprised to be standing there that it takes Rose over five minutes to get them to calm down enough for her to speak.

"Now that I have all of your attention, I can tell you all why I brought you here." Rose says, trying to keep them quiet. "Most, if not all of you, already know who I am."

"Where are we, and how did you get us here?" One guy asks, stepping forward out of the crowd.

"Rose, you left for Nandime a decade ago, only making contact three other times before now. Why have you called us now, with these... these humans?" Alex says as she steps forward from the crowd.

"If you give me a chance, I will explain." Rose says as her eyes flash crimson in frustration.

The crowd once again starts to yell when out of nowhere, a voice is heard thundering through the room. "SILENCE!" the loud voice says, causing everyone to cower in fear.

"Now." Rose starts once more, not bothering to look for the source of the voice. "There is a seer on this world that has seen a great war. This war is to take place in our solar system and has the potential of destroying both Earth and Mars." She tells the attendees as they stand there, who are keeping as quiet as possible.

"What can we do?" an Asian guy asks, barely over a whisper.

"I do not know. All I know for sure is that there is something that is working hard to stop my return home." Rose says.

The room breaks down into quiet talks for some time until one man asks, "Can you tell us who starts the war or even what starts it?"

Rose turns to look at Sarah, who is standing behind her. "No." Sarah starts looking down as she tries to remember what she can. "I know nothing more than the destruction it leaves behind."

Rose turns back to look at the crowd before saying, "Because of this force that is preventing my family and me from returning, it will be another ten years before my friends, family, and myself leave this world to return to our home. Now, unless any of you have questions, I will be returning you all home." Rose finishes watching the crowd for a response. Seeing none, she flicks her hand, causing everyone in the room to vanish.

Sarah places a hand on Rose's shoulder as she starts to cry. "It will all work out for the best." She says, pulling Rose into a tight hug.

"But Elizabeth is on Earth. I am afraid something terrible is going to happen to her." Rose says through sobs of tears.

"I know, my child, I know." Sarah says, comforting Rose the best she can.

***

Ten years have passed, and the day has come for Rose, Megan, James, Rebecca, and all their now fifteen children to leave. Sarah has also decided to come along with her family to become a liaison between Earth, Mars, and Nandime.

Chapter Fourteen

The Return Home

"EVERYONE, I CAN SEE JUPITER right ahead of us. But I believe there is a problem." Emma says on their seven-hundred and forty-third day traveling back to Mars.

"What's wrong, Emma?" Rebecca asks, walking into the monitor room, closely followed by Rose, Megan, and Amadahy.

"The planets are in the wrong positions around the sun." Emma says, sounding confused.

"Emma, show me their positions, would you?" Rose asks, not knowing what Emma means.

Emma shows the solar system in its current layout and positions of the planets. Looking at it, Rose can tell that the order of the planets is correct; Mercury, Venus, Earth, Mars, etc...

"Emma, the layout of the solar system looks fine to me." Megan says, revealing her presence.

"The problem is not in the order they are in; the problem lies in wherein their orbit each planet is." Emma says, clarifying.

Rose Kincade

Rose looks again and suddenly spots something that she had not noticed before. "Emma, in what year is Pluto scheduled to be at its closest point to Neptune?" Rose asks, hoping that she is wrong.

"Not until 2227." Emma says.

"Rose, what does that mean?" Rebecca asks, turning to look at Rose with horror etched on her face.

"What that means is..." Rose starts being cut off by the door opening.

"We have been traveling for one-hundred and seventy-four years," Sarah says as she joins the conversation.

The room is quiet as they stand there looking at each other, not knowing what to say. One-by-one, they each leave heading for the observation deck to see with their own eyes how much things have changed. Soon they see Mars, but it is not the Mars they knew. It has green trees and small lakes spread out across the surface in large patches. As they approach, Emma announces she is getting a call from Mars, asking them to identify themselves.

"I am Rose of Mars, one of the members of the council of five," Rose says.

"We have no record of a council member resigning. Who are you? You must identify yourself or be shot down." The voice replies angrily.

"I am Rose. I founded the council of five." Rose says, also getting angry.

"Mother Rose, the first of all, Martians?" The voice answers back.

"I am the first, but I have never been called mother. Not by anyone other than my children." Rose says, looking around the room in disbelief. "I am returning home after my journey to the planet Nandime. Why are we not being allowed to land?" Rose demanded angrily since they now know who she is.

No one answers for several minutes, making Rose even more upset at the whole thing. "Sorry, ma'am you are cleared to land at the 'Emma Shrine.'" A new voice proclaims, sounding confused and unsure.

Once again, Rose looks around the room to see everyone else just as confused. As they approach the planet, they can see that the town they left is now a city that has several smaller towns all around it. They have roads and skyscrapers, and most of the original buildings look as though they have been there for over a hundred years. As they approach the bio-dome, they can see names etched over the top of different landing ports, and soon they find 'Emma Shrine' on the side closest to where they had crashed so long ago.

As they land, they find that there is a large crowd gathered. Rose decides to step out first to see what is going on. As she does, the crowd cheers for her arrival as what looks like a celebration breaks out all around her. She moves forward to allow the rest to step out as well, but the children do not know how to react to the crowd. As they all cling tightly to Rose, Megan, Amadahy, James, Rebecca, Sarah, and Bob, the crowd slowly grows quiet. The crowd back away clearing a path seeing the scared children.

The group makes their way to the registration office only to find it is now called 'Customs and arrivals.' After stepping inside, James locks the door behind them to keep the others out.

"Hey, you can't lock that door." I don't care if you think you are mother Rose herself." The woman behind the desk roars.

"I am Rose." Rose says, stepping forward with many of her children still hanging onto her.

"Ma'am?" The woman asks.

"I am 'Mother Rose,' the first to have changed, the first on Mars, the first member of the council of five. And the most powerful person in this solar system." Rose replies with her eyes flashing orange.

"I will still need to see your documentation and your travel papers." The woman says, sounding as though she suddenly has a frog in her throat.

"When we left in 2046, we did not have papers, nor did we use travel documents." Rebecca says, stepping forward, trying to get her children to let go.

"And who are you?" The woman asks, now looking at everyone in the room. "What are you?" She adds now seeing Sarah and her husband's standing near the door.

"They are with us. These are ambassadors from the planet Nandime. They are here at my invitation." Rose says. Her eyes now a crimson color.

"If you are Mother Rose, you can tell me the council of five names that replaced you." The woman says, looking scared.

"Alex was my left hand next to James and Rebecca, with the last member being Angela. When we left, I named Michael as my seat representative, Rebecca named Susan for hers and James named Frank." Rose answers. "And, if you want to know more, Elizabeth, my daughter took the job as ambassador to Earth."

"I... I... I did not... I am sorry, Mother Rose. Let's get your group checked in as quickly as possible." The woman says in shock as she starts rummaging through her desk.

As the woman behind the desk is grabbing different things from around the desk, the phone rings. "Hello?" The woman answers. After a few moments, the woman says, "I will." And then hangs up the phone.

"The council has asked for your presence as soon as possible." The woman says to Rose.

"Thank you, ah... I am sorry, what is your name?" Rose responds.

"Oh, I am sorry. My name is Optivar." The woman answers.

"Thank you, Optivar. I am Rose, and these people are James, Rebecca, Megan, Amadahy, Sarah, Mike, Ralph, Handy, Fabio, and Bob." Rose says, pointing to each person as she introduces them.

The registration takes about three hours for them to complete all the papers and documents they need. After they finish and are assigned apartments to stay in, Rose walks over to the council building. She is forced to wait nearly three hours before the doors opened to let her in. As she walks through the doors, a few of the members gasp at the sight of her, "Oh my." at least one of them says.

"Welcome home, Mother Rose. It has been a long time since I have last seen you." One of the members says as she stands from the table.

"It really has been a long time Aunt Rose." Another member says also standing. "You have not changed at all since the last time I saw you nearly two-hundred years ago now."

"Aunt Rose? So, which of my nine nieces and nephews are you?" Rose asks, looking at the one that called her aunt.

"I am Linda. Michael is over there, and Jasmine is on the end, there." She says, pointing to each in turn.

"So, it really has been a hundred and seventy-five-year journey?" Rose says, putting her hand on her chin.

"It has been just over a hundred and seventy years since the last time you talked to anyone here." The oldest person says as she stands. "I am Alex, one of the original five council members." She bows deeply as she says this.

"Hundred and seventy-five-years. So, what of the war I had warned about all those years ago?" Rose asks, looking around the room.

"The war is over." Jasmine says. "The humans attacked us just over a hundred and thirty years ago with nuclear bombs." She says with sadness in her voice.

"We did not know the bombs were as powerful as they were." Michael says, standing. "There global population has gone from fourteen and half Billion to six hundred and twenty-two million people, and the numbers seem to be holding there."

"What about Elizabeth?" Rose asks with her stomach in her mouth.

"She is actually still alive. She has encased herself and her family in some sort of energy bubble that seems to have frozen them in time." The last person of the council says. "I am Maggie. We have never met before today." She adds almost as an afterthought.

"Then, I think I need to go and see what I can do for them." Rose says, turning on her heel to walk out.

"WAIT!" The room shouts in unison.

"Many have tried and simply vanished as they approached." Linda says as she walks around the end of the table.

"Linda, my power is far more powerful than every living creature on this planet combined. I should be able to get to the shell and release Elizabeth and her family." Rose says with a smile before she walks out, leaving them all standing there in disbelief.

Rose goes to the others and tells them what she has found out. "I have to go to Earth to try and rescue Elizabeth and her family." Rose tells them as they try to convince her not to go.

It is nearly an hour before Sarah, Megan, Amadahy, and Rebecca agree to let her go only if they go as well. The journey takes Emma only a minute to travel the distance between Mars and Earth. When they arrive, the scene of destruction is unimaginable.

All the major cities have been leveled, and the few buildings that still stand seem to be made from the ruins around them. The people on the ground look as though the food is in short supply, and the simple site of Emma has most of them running to hide like mice.

"Emma, what is the radiation level around here?" Rose asks Emma.

"Around here, the levels are just under lethal levels. There are places close by that are far more livable." Emma says, the sadness evident in her voice.

Soon they reach where Elizabeth and her family are supposed to be and Emma lands. "I cannot get any closer. My circuits are already acting funny." Emma says.

"Fly around and survey the area so we can figure out a plan to help these people." Rose tells Emma as she steps out.

"Be careful, honey." Megan says, looking scared.

Rose nods before stepping down and walking the rest of the distance on foot. When she gets to the only original house still standing, she finds there is an invisible barrier around it, protecting it from everything around it. She looks around to see what she can see and notices two small children running around the lawn frozen in mid-stride — not knowing why, Rose puts a hand on the barrier. As she stands there, the barrier starts to vibrate, and soon it is gone, and the children continue their progress only to stop suddenly.

As they look around, they scream, seeing the destruction around them. It only takes Elizabeth a few seconds to come running out the door to find out what is going on. Elizabeth has only just grabbed the children when she notices the destruction as well.

"What just happened?" She asks the children she is holding.

"You protected them from all of this." Rose says, walking up to Elizabeth and the children.

"Mom, it is so good to see you." Elizabeth says, letting go of the children to hug her mom.

"How long after I told you about things to come before I arrived." Rose asks, looking around.

"About twenty years. Megan will be sixteen next week, James just turned twelve, and these two..." She points at the two children hugging her around her waist. "are going to turn nine in September."

"I think you might be surprised to find their ages are far more than that." Rose says, smiling.

"Hey, come inside. It is far cooler in the house than out here." Elizabeth says, turning to walk back into the house with the children.

Once inside, Elizabeth finds that there is no power, no water, and no gas. At that moment, a teenage girl comes running out of her room, yelling.

"Mom, my computer just quit. I was right in the middle of doing my report on the Martian rescue of 2046." The teenage girl says to Elizabeth before she realizes they are not alone. "Aww, A Martian in my house." She screams, jumping and wrapping her arms around Rose.

"Megan, this is your grandmother." Elizabeth tells Megan, who is still hanging on to Rose.

At that, Megan breaks off and turns to her mother. "But I thought there was supposed to be a war before she came?" She asks, looking between Rose and her mother.

"There was a war." Rose says, looking down at Megan. "Your mother protected you from it. That is why nothing works now."

"How did I protect us all from the war?" Elizabeth asks, looking confused.

"Do you remember when I told you that you have the same energy as I do?" Rose asks. Elizabeth nods, and Rose continues. "Well, somehow, you tapped into it just before the bombs went off and froze time around you and your family here."

Elizabeth grabs a chair from the dining room table and sits down. "How long?" She asks, looking at Rose with tears in her eyes.

"You said it had been about twenty years since we last spoke, so I would say about a hundred and fifty years or so." Rose says, looking at the ceiling as she speaks.

"What about my husband? What about Albert? Where is my husband, Albert?" She asks tears falling, the girls now joining her as a small boy that can only be James enters the dining room.

"You are the only ones I know of." Rose says, shaking her head. But now that she thinks of it, there is a single room of an old building that looked as though it is still new. "All of you pack whatever things you have and come with me. Emma should be outside by now."

Elizabeth nods and has to help the two youngest before grabbing her own clothes and things she does not want to lose.

As they start to walk out, Rose asks, "Elizabeth, do me a favor, go grab your husbands' clothes as well. I think we are going to need them."

Elizabeth looks confused but returns to get the clothes without a word. Soon they are all packed up and ready to go.

"Emma, do you remember the feeling you got when we approached the house?" Rose asks Emma once they have all gotten into Emma.

"Yes, I do, and there is still something close by, giving me that same feeling." Emma says.

"Let's go to it, please." Rose says as she looks around at Elizabeth.

Megan comes walking out from one of the side rooms and sees Elizabeth sitting there. She runs over and latches on to her around the neck before saying, "I have missed you so much, baby girl."

"Hi, Megan. I have missed you too." Elizabeth says, trying to get free from her grip. "So, is Albert still alive?" She asks, looking hopeful, still struggling against Megan's grip on her.

"I do not know for sure, but that is why we are going to check it out, okay?" Rose says as Emma lands, making nearly a dozen people around the area run for shelter.

Rose steps out of Emma, and like before; she must walk the last of the distance on foot. When she reaches the standing room, she sees a door on one side. The building looks as though it has been cut and placed inside a bubble. The bird sitting on the window looks as though it is a lifelike statue. As she walks around to one side, she can see things inside the lower floor. Several police officers are standing around, laughing about something. She decides the time has come to release the barrier, so she places herself as close to a door as possible before razing her hand and placing it on the barrier. And just like before it the field vibrates and then fades, allowing life on the inside to resume.

Rose Kincade

Rose can hear two women on the other side of the door laughing when all of a sudden, a third one shouts, "Holy Shit, what the hell just happened?!"

Rose walks through the door and, to her amazement, sees four Martians standing in front of her wearing nothing more than boxer shorts. As she looks around, trying to place where they are, she hears no less than three more people scream above her. Within a minute, one of the four now newly Martians sees Rose and shouts.

"You're Rose, aren't you?" She asks in amazement.

"Yes, I am." Rose says, with the four in front of her starting to protest. She raises one hand, and they all fall silent. "Thank you. Now I will explain what has happened to you in a few minutes. However, I need to go get some of your buddies from upstairs that I have just realized have changed as well. Would anyone be able to tell me where we are?"

"The Washington PD's men's locker room, ma'am." One of the women says, sounding like she is afraid that Rose might rip them to pieces if they did not answer.

Rose wishes to herself that they were anywhere but in a police department. Since everyone apparently still has their clothes, that also means they also have their guns as well. And Rose knows she is not bulletproof.

Rose walks around and finds a set of stairs leading to the upper floor, making her way up the stairs as quickly as possible. When she arrives on the second floor, she finds half a dozen women standing around looking off the edge, as well as at least a dozen Martian lower torsos strung around the outer perimeter of the floor.

"Ladies." Rose calls out to everyone. As they turn, two of the officers pull their weapon on Rose. Without thinking, she raises a hand, and the weapons fall to the ground. "I will explain to everyone what has happened, but right now, I need you all to follow me. There are stairs over here to allow you a way down without having to jump." Rose tells them all.

Many mutters sounds of acknowledgment. Others bend down to pick up their weapons before following Rose down the stairs and back to the men's locker room. Once downstairs, and inside the locker room, Rose realizes that one person is missing. Walking back out of the locker room door, she finds the missing person standing there looking embarrassed.

"Why are you standing out here?" Rose asks, putting her hands on the officers' shoulders.

"That is the men's locker room, and I am a woman." She says with tears in her eyes.

"Oh honey, the truth is everyone in this building is now both, so there is no more his or hers." Rose says, giving the frightened woman a hug. "Let's go inside so I can tell everyone why they have suddenly found themselves like me, okay?" Rose says, trying to calm the woman down. After the woman nods in acknowledgment, they entered the men's locker room together.

All at once, many of the women in the locker room pelt questions at Rose. "Why did you change us?" "Why is the city in ruins around us?" "Where is everyone else?" were just a few of the questions everyone is asking. Rose raises a hand, and the room falls silent again.

"Now, ladies..." Rose starts with several of them tatting in indecency. "Sorry, Guys, Better?" The room nods in agreement. "Now, like I was saying before, which one is Albert?" She asks, and Two women move forward. "I see. I am looking for the one that is married to the ambassador of Mars." Rose clarifies to the room.

"I am ma'am." The one in the back corner of the room speaks out.

"Your wife did this to protect you from what happened outside." Rose says. Immediately the room breaks out in an argument. Rose raises her hand again, and the room once more falls silent. "Now, she did not intend on the change to happen, and it is merely a result of what she did to save your lives." Rose says to the room.

They all look around at one another for several minutes before one of them turns and asks, "If this is merely the result, what was the intended outcome?" The shortest woman asks.

"For the last hundred and fifty years, you have all been trapped in time." Rose yells over the crowd, who all at once falls silent. "This was meant to protect you from the destruction going on outside."

"So, you expect us to believe that we have been trapped in here for a hundred and fifty years?" One of the Albert's asks, stepping forward to be at the front of the crowd.

"Most of you saw the destruction outside with your own eyes. Do you really think that could all have happened in an instant?" Rose asks, trying to help everyone to understand.

The crowd resumes the talk amongst themselves as Albert, Elizabeth's husband, walks forward. "What about my wife and children, what about Elizabeth and our babies?" She asks, with tears filling her eyes.

"They are all safe and waiting for us." Rose tells her with a smile on her face.

Soon the crowd falls silent asking Rose to tell them what is next. "If you will all come with me, we will all go to Mars and set you up with fresh clothes and a warm meal." Rose says before taking Albert by the hand. She escorts her out of the door and up the hill to Emma, with the rest of the crowd following close behind.

Once they reach Emma, all the people start filing into her. Megan jumps from the car and pushes Rose down. "You turned them all into you, how could you?" She cries as she runs off. Before anyone can react or try to stop her, Megan is gone out of sight.

Once everyone is in, Rose tells Emma to take them to Mars, then to return for her and Megan. Elizabeth, Albert, Megan, Rebecca, and Amadahy want to join the search. Rose tells Elizabeth she needs to stay with her children and allows the rest to join the search.

"Now, each of you has hearing that is far superior to what it was before, as is your eyesight." Rose says to the four that stayed to help search for Megan. "You can also move much faster when the time comes, so be careful that you are not under searching any area in your search."

Rose divides everyone into groups of two, with herself being alone. "Megan, you and Amadahy search the buildings on the north side of the street. Albert, you go with Rebecca and see if she went east. I will go west and search anywhere I would hide." Rose says as they reach the bottom of the hill.

* * *

Megan is walking in a ditch to stay out of sight of the search parties who are out looking for her. She is not paying any mind to the person following her as he jumps from place to place, trying to hide himself. Suddenly, he grabs her, causing her to scream out. The guy quickly pulls her underground through one of the many tunnels leading off the ditch.

Megan is carried for several hundred yards before the guy stops and throws her on the ground in a small room that has a small light hanging from the ceiling.

"What do you want with me?" Megan asks as she is thrown to the ground in what looks like an old electrical room.

"You are of birthing age and without a man. That means you are free to take." The man says, reaching out to grab Megan. As he does, she moves, and he only gets her muddy jeans. As they rip from her, she trips, giving the guy a chance to grab her again.

Megan tries to get out but is knocked down to the ground again where she rolls on to her back. "You will be mine." The man cries as he pushes himself onto her. He picks up a sharp piece of metal and proceeds to cut the clothes from her body.

Once he removes all that is needed, the guy mounts Megan and proceeds to force his way inside of her. Megan kicks and screams all that she can, but the guy is far stronger than she is. He manages to slip all the way in and starts to pump his way to his goal.

Megan gives in and stops fighting and allows the guy to do his business while she lies there crying, wishing someone, anyone would come and help her. She feels the guy tense up and stops moving when moments later, Rose appears in the doorway.

"Unhand that child." Rose calls out with a scowl on her face. Her eyes the darkest shade of blood-red they have ever been, seeming to pop and flash with every word she speaks, causing the room to echo with every word loudly as though drums were thundering in the ears of those present.

"I will not. She is now mine. I have planted my seed, and it must grow." The guy shouts back, craze, and fury etched on his face.

"That may be the way of you humans now, but this child is under my protection." Rose says as she raises a hand at the guy throwing him off Megan and up against a wall ten feet away.

Megan stands and runs to Rose, crying. Rose tries to calm her as they leave that place, but Megan has been too traumatized by what has just happened. Once on the surface, Rose asks, "Why did you run off like that?"

"Because! You turned my dad into a creature like you." Megan says with tears still falling hard.

"Honey, that is why I left. So, I would stop turning people into creatures like me." Rose says, hugging Megan, but Megan does not return the hug. "The thing your mom did to keep everyone safe is what turned your father into a creature like me."

"Then why didn't we change like my dad?" Megan asks, wiping the tears from her face with her muddy sleeve.

"Because, like your mom, you, your brother and sisters all have the same power in you that I have. That is what kept you from changing." Rose says with a smile on her face.

"I thought only you have the white energy?" Megan asks, looking confused.

Before Rose responds, she shouts something in a high tone that Megan cannot hear. "So, your mother told you about the white energy. Tell me, what has she told you about it?" Rose asks, looking down at Megan.

"Only that it is why you changed people when you got close to them." Megan says, looking around and seeing nearly two dozen people encircling them.

"Well, that much is true. But there is a lot more to it than just that." Rose says, looking around herself. "Do not worry; they cannot hurt you as long as I am around." Rose adds to help make Megan feel secure.

"So, if all my family has it, why have we not changed?" Megan asks, looking back at Rose. "I mean, shouldn't that mean my dad should have changed a long time ago?"

Rose considered her answer for a moment, knowing that this is the one question that Sarah never did answer for her. "I really do not know, Megan. I have a feeling that humanity was meant to split in the evolutionary chain to develop two new species." Rose says, not being entirely sure this is right.

Rose and Megan start walking back to where Megan first ran away to try and get to a better defensive location. As they walk, Rose realizes the numbers of the humans have swollen to no less than thirty people of both males and females.

"So, you think that my mom is the first of the new human's and you were the first of the Martian's?" Megan asks, trying to understand better.

"It is very much possible." Rose answers. "But remember, this is only a theory." When Rose finishes speaking, Albert and Rebecca come into view on the horizon. Megan runs and hugs her new father around his neck.

"I am sorry, dad. When I saw you like this, I got scared that I was going to change as you did." Megan tells her father.

"I really do understand, but it is dangerous to run off before knowing everything that happened. Now I have no idea of what dangers there are out there, and my mind is going crazy thinking about them." Albert tells Megan.

Before Megan can respond, Rose says, "Megan learned a valuable lesson today, and we need to get her home and have her checked out as soon as possible." Rose starts, seeing the number of humans still increasing around them.

Just then, Megan and Amadahy walk up. "We have been jumped about three times, just barely being able to escape." Amadahy says.

"I know the issue they are claiming, and I think we need to put Megan in the middle of us, and we all need to stand with our backs together." Rose says, feeling that the humans are getting ready to strike.

No more do they do this, and the first human runs at the group. Rose sees him just in time and manages to fling him into a broken building with a flick of her wrist. Everyone else except Albert has a weapon with them, and they have them out ready for whatever is to come. Soon the rest of the humans make their attack on the group. The group manages to hold them off for several minutes when one of the humans manages to grab Rebecca and starts dragging her away.

Rose reacts so fast that the others did not even realize anything had happened until Rebecca was standing next to them again.

"Keep close and alert. Emma should be back very soon." Rose says, no more finishing getting the words out when Emma comes swooping in. The sudden appearance of Emma scaring most of the humans off. Rose quickly turns her attention to those that remain, and within moments everyone is safely inside Emma.

"What happened to Megan, Rose?" Alex asks after Rose returns from putting Megan in a room to relax.

"She was attacked and raped. I am sorry I did not get to her sooner." Rose says as she breaks down into sobs of tears.

Amadahy walks over and pulls Rose onto her shoulder as she rubs her back, allowing her to cry freely.

"There was no way for any of us to know what was going on." Rebecca says, staring at the floor.

"We are landing on Mars now." Emma says.

Chapter Fifteen

The Dispute

BACK ON MARS, MEGAN IS taken to the hospital to get checked out.

"There is not much we can do in this case. If she becomes pregnant, I'm afraid she will have to give birth to it." The doctor tells them as she comes out of the exam room. "We will clean her up and get her some clothes she can wear home. But that is all we can do for her, at the moment."

After about an hour, Megan is ready to go to her new home with her family. Once all the discharge instructions are conveyed, they are escorted to apartments on the outskirts of the central dome.

Rose, Megan, their children, along with Rebecca's and Sarah's families, are led through the city to a small suburb called 'New Colony.' "The main city of New Mars started out with just twenty-five buildings and a small bio-dome that could support about thirteen thousand people. Now there are more than twenty-six hundred buildings and three larger bio-domes that have a total capacity of eight point five million people." The guide says as she walks up a side street.

"Sarah, Mike, Ralph, Handy, Fabio, and Bob, this building here is where your apartment is located. The rest of you, please wait here for me. I will return shortly." The guide says as she leads Sarah and her husband's away.

The guide leads everyone nearly seven miles, where James, Rebecca, and their children are led to an apartment. Rose, Megan, and their children are led another ten miles to a building that would have been considered the ghettos on Earth when Rose was a child.

As Rose enters the apartment on the third floor, she finds that the main living room is about ten by ten feet with a kitchen and dining room of about the same size. The four bedrooms are each barely eight by eight and smell as though they have never been cleaned. The worst part comes when they discover that there is only one bathroom for the whole apartment.

"I can apply a dimensional rift in here, giving us much more space. But there is not much I can do about getting us more than one bathroom in here." Rose says as the woman is handing Megan the keys to the apartment.

"If you do that, you will go to jail. The buildings in this area are built how they need to be." The woman says, looking at Rose.

"So, these are supposed to be ghetto?" Megan asks as her eyes start flashing with red sparks.

"I don't know what ghetto is supposed to mean, but these homes are what they are. If you do not like it, leave and don't come back." The woman says, trying to make herself look intimidating and failing.

Rose is shocked by how she is being treated and decides to contact someone from the council. Each time she calls through normal channels, she is told that either, "They are in a meeting and can't be disturbed.", "They are in the field and can't be reached." Or her favorite, "They are all on holiday; I don't know when they will be back."

This makes Rose feel as though the new council is trying to keep Rose separate from them and everyone else, which turns out to be true. Each time she goes anywhere to try and visit with Sarah, Rebecca, and James, or even Elizabeth and her family, Rose is stopped by police and escorted back to her apartment. After a few days, Rose even starts to feel the frustration in Both Sarah and Elizabeth, so she calls them forth to talk to them.

"Mom, what is going on?" Elizabeth asks, having sensed the need to talk to Rose and still being up.

"An excellent question. There is something bothering you. What is it, child?" Sarah asks, looking out the window of the tiny room.

"For the last several days, I have been trying to go by where you both are to check on you. However, each time I try, I am stopped and escorted back to my apartment." Rose says as her eyes pop with flashes of orange. "Someone on the council has put us as far apart from each other as possible, and I don't know why."

"I have attempted to come to see you as well and have been stopped during every attempt," Sarah says, turning to look at Rose.

"I have asked the registration office here to contact you for me. The only thing I have been told is that 'at this time' they could not do anything for me." Elizabeth says, sounding like she is ready to cry.

"Well then, let's discuss our options and see what can be done." Rose says, looking first to Elizabeth and then to Sarah.

"I have noticed they have even given us places that do not have any energy to them." Elizabeth says as she walks to the door of the apartment and looks out.

"I have seen that, as well. They seem to be trying to get rid of the energy rather than living with it." Sarah says, walking to a small chair to sit down.

"Yes, and all of our old homes seem to be shrines now, and that is why we cannot use them." Rose says, standing and walking to the bookshelves on one wall.

"Have you tried using your power to open up the space?" Sarah asks Rose.

"I commented on doing it when they first showed us the apartment. The woman said that it was illegal and not to do it." Rose says walking over to Sarah and kneeling in front of her. "I am tempted just to do it to every building on Mars. I am just not sure if it will work or not."

"It is worth a shot. The worst that can happen is you make the spaces smaller." Sarah says, looking around to Elizabeth, who is nodding.

Rose stands up and thinks for a moment, then, with her eyes closed, pushes her hands out in front of her. As she does, the room around them grows to more than five times its original size.

"If it worked, then when you get home, you will find your own homes bigger than they were before." Rose says, looking around the room at all the changes.

"Your power never ceases to amaze me." Sarah says as she stands up in front of Rose.

Right then, there is a knock at the door. Before Rose answers it, she decides to send Elizabeth and Sarah home. When Rose opens the door, she finds it is Rebecca.

"Come in, what's up with you? Why did you come over so late? How did you get here with the police keeping such a close eye on all of us?" Rose asks when she saw who it was.

"I managed to get here by coming so late. Most of the streets seem to go quiet, from midnight to four. I think it's because most people are set to the dark time of Mars. I came by to see if they did you any better than us, but I see your place is much bigger here." Rebecca says, looking around the room.

"I have happened here. When we first moved in, it was tiny, not more than fifteen hundred square feet at most." Rose says with a smile on her face.

Rebecca's eyes grow, and she starts to scream, but Rose covers her mouth to stop her.

"You cannot tell anyone I did this. If it worked correctly, every building on Mars has expanded like this one. We need to play it off as though it is something else that did it." Rose says as Rebecca stands there, blinking wildly in surprise. Rose pulls her hand away and then walks to the window to see the sunlight is starting to shine on the Horizon.

Rebecca turns and walks around the expanded apartment. As she is walking, she happens to think of something. "How are they going to blame this on you?" She asks, turning to Rose with a bewildered look on her face.

"They must think something is going to happen because they put Sarah in the old part of the city and put Elizabeth in the new dome, and they placed us as far apart as possible." Rose says, looking around the room at the new higher ceiling.

"You do know where we are way out here, right?" Rebecca asks as she walks into the kitchen.

"No, where are we?" Rose asks, joining Rebecca.

"This is where you crashed, or more to the point where Emma crashed to the surface of Mars all those years ago." Rebecca says as she looks in the oven seeing that it has nearly become a walk in now.

"How do you know?" Rose asks, opening the cooler door to see it is one of the biggest coolers she has ever seen.

"When we landed in that first pod, the bay doors opened, pointing in the exact direction of where we found Emma. Since it has become the hospital, we can go there to have the children checked out if we need to. The original hatch for the Rovers is still visible and can be seen as you walk up the street." Rebecca says, now turning to sit on a counter.

As Rose walks to stand in front of Rebecca, she sees a light turn on in a neighboring building through the window. As she stands there watching to see what happens, she notices several other lights turn on as well, and soon the whole city is lit up, and Rose knows for sure that what she did worked.

"You better go. I am sure the police are going to be heading out in force with this commotion going on." Rose tells Rebecca.

Rebecca turns and looks out the window and sees people running in and out of the neighboring building as though they are lost or confused.

After jumping down from the counter, she says, "I think you are right. James is waiting up for me; she worries about me so much."

Rose escorts Rebecca to the front door and then walks to the bedroom, where Megan is still sleeping. When Rose wakes the next morning, Megan is bouncing around the apartment in enthusiasm and amazement.

"Have you seen this?" Megan asks as she runs from one thing to another.

"It happened before I went to bed last night." Rose says as she grabs a cup from the cupboard to make some tea.

Megan quickly stops and turns to look at Rose like she is hiding something. Rather than waiting for Rose to say something, Megan asks, "What do you know about this?"

"Nothing. I was talking with Sarah and Elizabeth when this happened." Rose says. This is not entirely a lie since it did happen while she was talking with Sarah and Elizabeth.

As Megan is eyeing Rose suspiciously, there is a knock at the door, causing Megan to jump. Megan turns to walk to the front door to see who it is.

"Ms. Mills is Rose here?" Rose hears the person at the door ask.

"Yes, she is in the kitchen." Megan says, escorting the person inside.

"Rose. I am with the police, and I would like to know what happened here last night." The green-clad officer asks.

"I did not hear a name in there. Did you, Megan?" Rose says, sounding as though this is meant to be sarcastic.

"Ma'am I do not, ha..." The woman starts but is cut off by Rose, suddenly rising and raising a hand.

Rose Kincade

"I will not be talked to this way." Rose says with her eyes popping with crimson red flames and each of the words echoing throughout the apartment. "I am the oldest living Martian on this planet or any other planet. You will tell me your name before I really get angry."

The woman looks down, causing Megan and Rose to follow her gaze only to find that she has relieved herself onto their kitchen floor. Once she looks up at Rose again, they can also see fresh tears in her eyes.

"I am sorry ma'am. I have always been told it is not important to give your name during an investigation. However, my name is Nancy Johns." She says with apparent fear in her voice.

"Why, thank you, Ms. Johns. I am Rose, and what is it you would like to know?" Rose asks, sitting back down while Megan walks out of the kitchen to grab a mop.

Nancy still has a lot of fear on her face when she continues, "Last night, every building on the planet that has been built after the war suddenly grew in size on the inside. Some as much as eight times their original size." Nancy says as she tries to pull herself together.

"I noticed that this apartment grew through the night. Beyond that, I am unable to tell you anything else." Rose says before taking a swig from her glass.

"Do you know how this happened?" Nancy asks, finally starting to sound the way she did when she came in.

"I can only tell you; it happened just before the light started to show on the horizon." Rose says, pointing out the window to where she had seen the light coming from.

"We thought since you are the only one that knows how the energy works that you might know how this happened, Ms. Mills." Nancy says, writing something down in her book.

"She is not the only one that knows how it works." Megan says storming back into the kitchen with her mop. "As for how this happened, there are at least a dozen ways I can think of."

Nancy spun on her heal, having forgotten that Megan was in the apartment as well. "I did not know that anyone else knew how this energy worked. I am sorry." She says with her hand on her chest covering her heart.

Just then, two of Rose's and Megan's children come running through the apartment. They are playing a game that they learned on Nandime involving running and jumping from thing to thing in preparation for their training to adulthood. Nancy watches their progression with a mindful eye as they play.

"It is a game they learned during our stay on Nandime." Megan says, grabbing the children and shewing them from the apartment.

"Is there anything else we can help you with, Nancy?" Rose asks, walking forward.

"No. I think I have bothered you enough for today." Nancy says as she walks to the front door. Once at the door, she turns to give a wave goodbye. Her eyes fall, giving one last glance at the puddle on the floor where she peed, before turning to leave.

As Nancy is walking through the door, Megan slams it in such a way as to cause it to catch Nancy in the ass.

"Megan! I am surprised at you." Rose says with a smile from horn to horn.

Megan returns the smile as her face flushes blue with embarrassment as she walks over and kisses Rose deeply on the lips before handing Rose the mop and saying, "I know you did it." She then turns to make her way to the bedroom. Rose laughs and starts mopping up the mess left by Officer Johns.

After a week of being turned away from the council chambers, even after using her new 'dark voice' as she has come to call it. She knows she will have to find another way to see the council. Deciding on the spot after her tenth failed attempt, she returns home with a plan forming in her head. She has decided that instead of calling the members to her in her living room, she will try something new and send herself to them.

Rose Kincade

Sitting on the floor in an Indian style, she closes her eyes and concentrates on the council chamber. For several moments she is not sure if it is working or not, but soon she can see into the location with ease. She sees they are all there discussing something in a heated debate, some even being very animated about the argument. She tells herself that she needs to be in the room with the council, and she starts to hear the sounds of the council and their discussion. Knowing that what she is trying to do is working, she opens her eyes to find that she is standing amongst them.

"How the hell did you get in here?" The oldest of them asks as they all jump from their seats to take refuge behind them.

"You refuse me entry. You treat me like a common criminal. Your police watch every move any of my family, friends, or I make. And YOU HAVE THE NERVE TO TALK TO ME LIKE THAT!" Rose says in her 'dark voice' causing each word to echo loudly throughout the room, sounding as though there are a thousand Rose's standing there. Instantly Jasmine, Linda, and Michael all step around their seats and sit down, knowing they have never seen Rose, or John, for that matter, this mad in their lives.

"We will treat you how we think best since you were expelled from this council." The oldest one says.

"Who are you, and where is Maggie?" Rose asks in a somewhat less aggressive tone and without the sound of a thousand more of herself in the room.

"My name is Frank, and Maggie is my substitute for when I am away." She says as she steps around the table.

"And you are Alex, the only original council member, correct?" Rose asks, looking to the only other one still standing.

"Yes, I am." She says, sounding as though she expects Rose to lunge at her at any moment.

"Then, you tell this one how I came to leave this council and who in this room is my successor." Rose says, looking angry with her eyes still a deep crimson fire.

"You left of your own accord with James and Rebecca. You named Michael here to replace you. James named Frank and Rebecca named Susan." Alex says, looking scared and finally deciding to take her seat once she has finished speaking.

"It is my understanding they were going to be coming back. After ten years of no contact, we took their names from the council list, expelling them for abandoning us." Frank says, looking just as angry but with her eyes barely hitting orange.

"James nor I abandoned anyone." Rose says her voice amplified once again. "I told every one of you that there was something trying to stop my return. I explained that we would be here as soon as possible. My trip back took much longer than it should, but none of you asked me about that when we first arrived." Rose finishes, her eyes popping at the room with every word she speaks.

Frank turns to the other members and sees that Jasmine and Linda have their heads bowed, and Michael is looking at Alex. realizing that none of the other members are going to come to her aid, she turns on her heel to leave the room. Only adding before she disappears around the corner of the door, "You people abandoned Mars and then expect us to welcome you back open armed? Fuck this shit."

"Now that we have that out of the way, why have I been treated this way?" Rose asks the room.

"The thing is, Frank hated the post from the beginning and believed that you had told James to name him as his successor." Alex says, bowing her head.

Rose bows her head and shakes it a few times slowly. "I told James nothing of whom he should choose. His decision was between him and Rebecca." Rose says. As she finishes, she raises her head to look at the room.

"So, why did you want to come to see us?" Jasmine asks, standing up for the first time since the whole thing started.

"I think you are all aware of what has happened on Earth and how the humans there have devolved to little more than animals with the ability of speech, right?" Rose asks, looking at each member, Jasmine, Linda, Alex, then Michael.

Most of the room nods, but Michael stands. "What has happened to them is the doing of Col. Morris, Megan's stepfather, and a rebel group he led against the world government." She says, looking around the room.

"Really, so he did not learn his lesson on Zicarthona?" Rose says shaking her head. "Some people will never learn." Rose sighs as she closes her eyes. "However, we need to do something about cleaning things up on Earth, or the humans won't make it for much longer."

After Michael has taken his seat, Linda stands up to speak. "That can wait for now. Elizabeth told me why you went to Nandime and that we all have the white energy in us." She says before sitting back down with the rest of the member's agreement.

"She has told you, we all have the white energy, but tells her own daughter that only I have it?" Rose says looking disbelievingly at Linda who looks as though she wants to say something but does not. "Yes, I went to Nandime to learn more about the powers in me, and yes, every person that has changed has some white energy in them." Rose says looking around the room. "Why do you mention it, Linda?"

"We have been talking, and if there is a way for all of us to be able to do even half of the stuff we have heard you can, then we would like to try and learn how to use it." Jasmine says, not bothering to stand.

"Really?" Rose says walking to the end of the table where Jasmine sits. "I do not know if I can do this in this form but give me your hand."

Jasmine looks around the room before complying. Rose closes her eyes and takes a deep breath. The others in the room gasp as Jasmine's hair starts to float up like she is being filled with energy followed by her skin starting to glow. The rest of the council members gasp again, but Rose does not respond. Suddenly the glow dissipates, and her hair falls back down where it belongs.

"I think you can learn at least some of the stuff I have." Rose says, smiling at Jasmine. "But I will not just teach you. If I do this, I will have to teach everyone who wants to learn." She adds.

"I think that is the way it should be." Michael says with the other muttering their agreements.

"So, how do we set up the classes for the strange powers?" Linda asks.

"Well, on Nandime, the children are taught from a young age. I believe we should do the same here." Rose starts to explain. "Hold on a sec, would you." She adds before closing her eyes and bringing Sarah to the room as well.

"What am I doing he... Oh, I see." Sarah says after appearing next to Rose.

"I do not want to miss represent the Nandime people here. Would you please explain to the council here how the children are taught how to utilize White Energy?" Rose asks Sarah.

Sarah folds her arms and rests her chin on her hand to consider the question. "Well, when the children are ready to start school, they start by learning a game that helps them to learn how to tap into the energy." She says, still thinking about it.

"Kind of how I got started, correct?" Rose asks, trying to make sure she is understanding.

"Exactly how you got started." Sarah says lifting her head from her hand. "From there, the children progress to add energy manipulation. These lessons can take years to master and often lead to discoveries of a person's particular talent." She adds.

"Is there a chance that some of us can learn to be as powerful as Rose?" Alex asks, looking excited.

"I do not believe so. Rose is a very unique and rare individual. Her power comes from a source well beyond my capability to see. However, since every species is different, it might be possible for some of your people to have more than five or six separate talents. Nearly every Eldon can stop time, and most have five separate talents." Sarah says.

Suddenly, as though it was over a megaphone, everyone hears a loud gurgling sound come from Rose's stomach.

"I guess even in astral form; one still gets hungry." Rose says in apology.

"Astral, so you are not really here?" Jasmine says, stepping around the table to feel for herself how real Rose feels again.

"Since when have you been able to astral project?" Sarah asks in total shock. "And then, you still managed to bring me here. I don't know if I ever will stop being amazed by you."

"I have been able to interact with you all, but my physical body is in my apartment." Rose says, trying to explain.

"Elizabeth told us you could call her spirit to you. I did not know you could also project yours to others." Linda says, also walking around the table to touch Rose along with Michael and Alex.

"I was not sure if it would work until I tried it." Rose says, being poked and prodded by Jasmine, Linda, Michael, and Alex. "And, once I discovered that I could read Jasmine's energy, I knew, within reason, I could summon you here, Sarah."

"You are telling us this is your first attempt at astral projection and performing other energy tasks while in your astral form?" Alex asks in amazement, as another even louder, gurgling sound comes from Rose.

"Yes, this is my first attempt at this. I thought it would be better for me to show up here than for all of you to show up in my apartment." Rose says grabbing her stomach as it gives off another loud gurgle. "Now I need to go, but please allow me to return. There is much that still needs to be worked out." And with that Rose and Sarah are gone, Linda and Jasmine who has been leaning on Rose, fall together knocking their heads on each other.

Once Rose is back in her apartment, she stands and walks to the kitchen, where she finds Amadahy making lunch for her little sisters. Amadahy notices Rose watching her and says, "Are you finished meditating? I kept the children from the room for you."

"I am finished. Thank you. However, I was not meditating. I was meeting with the council of five, though I think it is now four." Rose says grabbing a sandwich from the plate sitting on the edge of the counter.

"Hey, that was mine." Amadahy says as Rose's stomach gives a loud gurgle. "Fine, I will make another one." She laughs as she walks to the fridge to grab more supplies.

Rose smiles and kisses Amadahy on the forehead as she walks by, saying, "Thank you, sweety pie."

Over the next several weeks, the new school is set up, and nearly everyone wants to learn from Rose and Sarah. The numbers of people are so high that Rose and Sarah are forced to put a limit on the number of people they can teach in each class and direct some of them to Sarah's five husbands. Though the people did not like it, they agreed. Since the whole first year of all the student's educations is endurance training, Rose does not have to focus too much attention on the students. She can return to the council to talk about other issues and visit with Emma, Elizabeth, and all of her friends.

A week into the first term after setting up the schools, Rose is visiting with Elizabeth, who is showing off a TV one of her neighbors gave her.

"It has only four channels that are on most of the day. The main one I keep on is a channel dedicated to the politics of the council of five, the different cities and news of what is happening on Earth." Elizabeth tells her as they are sitting in the living room.

"What are they saying is going on?" Rose asks as a commercial comes on for a horn polish.

"Well, I heard about you, showing up in the council chambers, and while you were inside, Frank announced on TV that he was resigning from the council. That made a lot of people mad."

"Did he say why he was resigning from the council?" Rose asks. But before Elizabeth can answer, a reporter starts talking with a picture of the original council member. Elizabeth quickly turns the volume up to listen.

"Just over two centuries ago today, Rose crashed landed on Mars in Emma. Being the first life form to breathe the Martian atmosphere in over a millennium, she was lovingly given the label of the first Martian and Mother Rose. Just seven months later, with the help of the astronauts, Rose established a fully working colony and founded the Mars council of five." The reporter starts as Elizabeth snorts.

"So, why then has the council denied the original council members to have their original homes back. Well, there are two reasons for this. The first is since making them a shrine was a public vote; it would take a public vote to overturn that classification for them to be able to move back into these homes. The second reason is that of the power struggle between the original council and the current council." The reporter moves some things around on the desk in front of him before continuing. "It has come to this reporters' attention that the reason the council member Frank resigned last month was because of Rose's apparent refusal to take no for an answer for rejoining the council."

"That is so far from the truth. It is unreal." Elizabeth says, standing from the seat and pointing at the TV.

"Calm down. We know the truth." Rose tells Elizabeth.

"But how true is this? After interviewing the remaining council members, it turns out the this is nowhere near true. Frank had, in fact, ordered a twenty-four and half-hour watch of everyone from the original council and their friend Sarah. And, because Rose has abilities far beyond current comprehension, Rose was able to project an image of herself into the chambers. This is, in fact, why Frank Bestial resigned."

Elizabeth quickly turned off the TV before anything else came on that might upset her.

"At least someone got the truth out there," Elizabeth says, still looking as though she would like nothing more than to break something.

"It is nice to have our names cleared in the eyes of the people. However, as long as we know what the truth is, that is all that truly matters," Rose says, smiling at Elizabeth.

"I know. But I still think that it is totally unfair that nothing will happen to Frank for everything that he did to all of us," Elizabeth says, standing from the couch and walking across the room.

"As the truth gets out, Frank will have difficulties that he will have to face because of this," Rose says, standing and walking over to Elizabeth to give her a hug. "Now I need to go and get to the school. I have a class to teach."

✳✳✳

Another four weeks go by, and the community votes to return the original homes to the original council members. Rose decides to take them up on the offer since a new place closer to Rose is also offered for Elizabeth to move into. This is since she had lived with Rose until they all left together all those years ago. This makes them all feel better about some of their problems, but Rose still wants to deal with the Earth issue.

Rose is asked to return to her old spot on the council, which she rejects, saying, "Since it was James that gave her the position in the first place, it should be James to be asked back." The council agrees and requests James to return to the council. James excepts the offer and basically picks up where he has left off.

There is a heavy debate from the people of Mars to the organization of the council and most call for a reorganizing of the council of five. Again, they all turned to Rose since she is the 'Mother' of the Martian people.

Rose Kincade

"Rose, we have asked you here today because of a public outcry." Linda says from her seat at the table.

"Most of the people believe the council of five no longer works for them. They have asked that you, Mother Rose, reorganize the council into something that will allow for growth while still allowing decisions to happen quickly." Michael says.

"I don't know. The whole reason for having five members was just for that reason. But give me the weekend, and I will figure something out." Rose tells the council members.

That night Rose has a dream of Mars. Mars is a brilliant blue-green planet with cities in every corner of the globe that is covered with vegetation hiding them from space. On the ground, Rose can see what looks like a giant amphitheater. Inside, there are seats for about fifty people on one side of the building. On the other side, there are over a thousand seats with a giant TV screen. Suddenly the doors behind the large section swing open, and people start walking in. After they have all taken their seats, the doors behind the smaller section open, and more people come walking in.

"Thank you all for coming today." A large human-looking man says from the largest seat. "The reason for today's meeting is to discuss the new protection law of the new city Horizon. The law would allow new businesses to expand into areas of the city without needing to get a zoning permit. It is expected that if the proposed bill makes it past the public voting stage, that businesses would be more enticed to go to Horizon, helping them to grow quickly. However, the fears proposed by the council is that by allowing companies to build in zones outside of their established zones, this will cause the companies to over saturate areas and push out people."

Suddenly Rose is standing outside in a public square where she sees a large line of people. "Your next, dearie." An old woman says, handing her a piece of paper with several proposed bills. As she reads, she sees the one that she was just watching in the amphitheater. She quickly marks the no box, which causes her to find herself in front of a screen showing polling results.

"And, the prop one-ninety-one, the bill that would allow companies to build anywhere in Horizon City, was voted down today by the people. When we asked one man why they voted against it, they had this to say." The reporter says before Rose woke up in her bed.

"I know how to fix the council issue." Rose tells Megan, who is just walking in from the bathroom.

"Oh, how is that?" Megan asks as she sits on the side of the bed.

"Each city will have a council of five that is voted in by the people every decade. At the same time, each city will also elect a representative that will be on the federal council. The city council members will handle local problems that affect only the individual cities. Any issues that implicate entire regions or the whole planet will be handled by the federal council. The council will listen to their people's ideas, write a bill or proposal of what they believe the people want in their community. The council will then vote if it is something that should be, or not be, tried. Then, if it passes, a vote is held by the people. Votes can be completed securely by using the portal ID numbers assigned to the people." Rose says so quickly that she is nearly out of breath when she finishes. After catching her breath, she adds, "I think that we should have term limits on all council members as well. I don't think it would be a good idea if people are able to serve in politics as a career. Maybe a limit of three terms in total."

That morning, Rose tells the council of five what she has come up with for the new council. It takes nearly three months to set up the new system and hold elections for the new council. The council of five has asked Rose to be a part of the new council, but Rose is not sure if she really wants to be on the council.

Soon, however, the council is nearly full, and the last position is offered to Rose once again. Rose does not want to seem like she is trying to take power, so she refuses the offer. The council decides they have their first issue for the people to vote on.

'The current council of twelve has extended an offer to Rose Mills to be the final member. She has refused this offer, saying she does not want the people of our world to think she has demanded or asked for it or that it is an offer of gratification by the council.

So, we put it to a vote of the people: Should Rose Mills be re-offered the final post of this council? Yes, or No.'

The fliers for the special election circulate for the next forty-five days before the people vote on it. Nearly every person on Mars turns out to vote, and the outcome is amazing. Nearly ninety-eight percent of the voters want Rose to take the final seat in the new council, and everyone has added a comment to their vote explaining their feelings on the matter.

Most that vote 'No,' simply indicate that Rose has the right to her decision, while some claim that Rose is the reason for Earth's downfall. As for those that vote 'Yes,' their comments range from simple words of support to full praises of her work. So, Rose reluctantly decides to accept the offer, and for the next several years, she focuses on the new school and council.

Chapter Sixteen

Earth's Distress

ROSE IS STANDING IN FRONT of a door that has two knobs, one on either side of the door. On the right side of the door, the knob is a healthy blue and green planet Earth with lots of white clouds on it. On the other side, the knob appears to be a tan-colored moon that looks similar to Earth, if it had no water or life on its surface like Mars once did. As Rose reaches out to grab the knob with the healthy Earth, the door seems to fold in half down the middle before disappearing, leaving behind two worlds side by side. On the right is a healthy blue and green planet Earth with white clouds, on the left, is a wasteland of nearly all desert and black oceans that look as though they are made from thick crude oil.

Rose steps through the door, wanting to go to the healthy planet, but instead, she finds herself on the wasteland. As she looks around, she can see skeletons of humans, animals, and Martians alike scattered around the ground.

"This is the future of humanity." A male voice calls out from all around her.

"What can be done to stop this?" Rose calls back as she turns, trying to find the source of the voice.

"You can stop this future if you want." The voice replies.

"But how? I do not know what to do." Rose says with tears forming in her eyes as she speaks.

"But you do know-how. The power inside you has already told you." The voice says, fading into nothing with the last few words it speaks.

Rose walks towards the nearby beach, where she sees an old ocean liner coming towards her. As she watches, the ship starts to pick up speed as though it was coming for her. Rose turns to run but trips over a skeleton as the boat runs aground, igniting the oils and causing an explosion.

Rose jumps from her bed so dramatically; it scares Megan off the other side of the bed, causing her to fall to the floor.

"What the hell?" Megan says, standing and rubbing her head since she had hit it on the edge of the nightstand when she fell.

"You have to teach my class today." Rose says as she grabs some clothes to put on.

"But I am not a teacher." Megan says, sitting on the edge of the bed looking around the room.

"You have already learned the lesson you will be teaching; you will be fine." Rose says as she rushes out the door leaving Megan sitting there on the bed alone, not knowing really what has just happened.

Rose runs from the apartment, only half-dressed. As she makes her way up the street, she notices someone she recognizes.

Her name is Maribel, and Rose has seen her dating her granddaughter Megan. Rose picks up the pace to talk to her.

"Hi, Maribel. How are you doing today?" Rose asks, startling Maribel in the process.

"Oh, Hi, Ms. Mills. You scared me. I didn't know anyone would be up this early." Maribel replies, trying to catch her breath.

"How are you and Megan doing these days?" Rose asks.

"We are doing good. Megan had the baby last week, you know. She named it Umanita; it's the word for humanity in Italian." Maribel tells Rose as they walk.

"I knew she had the baby and what she had named it. I did not know what it meant, though." Rose says, thinking to herself that the name is fitting. "The baby is a little girl, correct?"

"Yes, it is. She is just so cute that I want one as well." Maribel says as she watches the ground at her feet.

"I understand. When I found out that Megan, my wife was pregnant the first time; I was a bit jealous, though I did not understand why." Rose says, remembering back to when she first met James and the rest of the Mars crew.

"You? Jealous, really? Come on; you are Mother Rose. You are the creator of all Martians." Maribel says with a snorting laugh.

"I may have been the catalyst for the creation of the Martian people, but I am far from the creator. That honor belongs to the white energy." Rose says, smiling back at Maribel.

"You are being too modest. Besides, I need to turn here and head towards the domes. I am supposed to meet up with Megan for breakfast." Maribel says, pointing up a side street before running off.

"I thought you were coming from the domes when I caught up with you!" Rose yells after Maribel, who quickly turns and waves before resuming her escape.

Rose reaches the government building that was once the command pod for the Mars Mission two hundred years ago. Stopped out in front of the building, she starts to remember her past as John.

John was a kind and loving man who spent much of his adult life, raising a child on his own. But had John ever thought of being in charge of the fate of Earth? No, he had not. It was all he could do being in charge of a young girl and his own business. And the company had managers and advisors along with an entire army of legal aids and attorneys. John would have cracked under the pressure of having to worry about the whole planet. But Rose does not have that luxury. She must find a way to save Earth.

Resolving herself to her fate, Rose walks into the building where the guard immediately stops her.

"Ma'am, you are not permitted to be in here." The guard tells her.

"My name is Rose Mills. I am the head seat of the council." She tells the guard as she walks towards him.

"If I just believed everyone who told me that, I would not have a job." The guard says with a laugh.

Rose reaches into her pocket and pulls out a card and hands it to the guard.

The guard looks it over and scrutinizes every part of the ID. He turns the ID making the image of Mars rotate as it is supposed to do. She then looks closely for signs that the picture has been tampered with, which shows no evidence. She then looks closely at Rose to see if she is indeed the person in the photo.

"It really is me." Rose says indignantly.

"I must make sure. A person like me can't afford to make a mistake." The guard retorts.

"What is your name? I want to know who I will be reporting to your boss in a few hours." Rose says as her eyes now start flashing crimson.

"Ma'am? You cannot intimidate me." The guard says, trying to look angry, but her eyes betray her by showing only yellow.

"Your name, ma'am." Rose says with her voice now echoing loudly throughout the hall.

The guard suddenly drops the ID card and shrinks into her seat next to the door as she says shakily, "Akiara, my name is Akiara, ma'am."

"Akiara, really? You sure do not live up to its meaning." Rose says, bending down to grab her card.

"Ma'am?" Akiara asks.

"Your name is Japanese, and the meaning of your name is 'a bright person.' Do you think you are a bright or intelligent person?" Rose asks, taking a step forward towards Akiara.

"I am sorry, ma'am. It is my responsibility to make sure the people coming in the building are really supposed to be here." Akiara says, now peeing herself.

"Your responsibility is to assure the security of this entrance, not to scrutinize every single person entering the building." Rose says as her eyes change from crimson to orange to yellow as the guard watches.

"I will remember that." Akiara says, finally starting to regain some of her color and dignity.

Rose walks on to the library to study up on Mars and Earth's history. During the time Rose was on Nandime, Earth sent Mars technologies to develop its own infrastructure. Mars was able to start mining minerals to build buildings, roads, highways, and even new ships. Mars also constructed several factories that could process the minerals and convert them into products that could be used.

Earth, on the other hand, focused on expanding its nuclear resources. They had built more nuclear weapons in the fifty years before Earth's destruction than at any time in the past. Another significant investment for Earth was in nuclear power plants. Not just to power its cities and ocean-going ships, but to power spaceships for intergalactic travel.

The more Rose reads, the more she realizes that she is the reason Earth is in the shape that it is now. After about an hour, she closes up the books she has been reading and walks out to go for a walk. As Rose walks, she thinks about all of what she has read, as well as what the dream means that she had earlier that night.

She knows that the dream had to come from something or someone other than her, but who and why her? She did not know the answers, but she knows that she needs to call an emergency meeting of the council to try and fix Earth before it is too late.

Rose Kincade

The council gathers that morning in the main chamber reserved for public debate. Rose's intention is to include everyone to try and find an answer to the current crises.

"We have an issue that needs to be addressed now." Rose says once the members have all taken their seats.

"And what is so important that it has to take place in the main chamber?" A member named David asks.

"Earth." Rose says to the council members seated around her.

"Earth has been there for more than four billion years. It will be there for at least another four billion years." A council member named Susan says.

"True. But will it support life in the future?" Rose asks as they look back staring wildly at her. "Last night, I had something come to me and ask for my help in repairing the Earth, so it does not die." Rose tells them.

"Who or what is it that came to you?" Jasmine asks.

"I do not know for sure. But if we do not act, the Earth will die, and we will be responsible for letting it happen." Rose says looking around at the blinking eyes of the council members. "I know how to fix the problem that is killing the Earth. But I need people to help with the human issue as well."

"How do we fix what is killing the Earth?" Sylvester asks Nancy, another member of the council.

"We have a tunnel to the center of Mars that will be facing Earth in the next few hours. I will gather all the nuclear materials. All of the nuclear fallout, waste, and warheads along with all the nuclear rods in the power plants that remain on Earth and drop them into the tunnel here on Mars. Effectively doing two things; First, will be to get rid of the radiation from the surface of the Earth, so it cannot continue to do harm. The second will cause Mars own core to melt and be able to spin freely like it once did." Rose says.

"But that might kill you." Linda says as she stands to protest the plan.

"I am the only one capable of moving that much material all at once. We have no choice. I have no choice in this matter." Rose answers as the room breaks out in conversation.

After several minutes one of the council members asks, "When can we get the public involved in this? I, for one, do not want to be responsible for allowing Mother Rose to commit suicide."

"I notified many of the news medias that we will be having a special conference before we started. I am sure that at least some of them are outside right now." Rose says, ready to get this over with as quickly as possible.

Someone in the back of the room leaves to check on if there might be reporters outside waiting. When she returns, she is proceeded by not less than fifteen reporters who all look thoroughly confused. After they take their seats, the issue is restated to the reporters who all have cameras trained on Rose as she speaks.

"Earth, our original home." Rose starts. "The birthplace of all living things in this solar system." Rose pauses for effect. "This once gorgeous blue-green planet is dying, she is in trouble and needs our help, now." Again, she pauses. "It is our responsibility to help fix what has happened to our birth planet. And we can fix both worlds at the same time."

The news reporters are hanging on every word as Rose speaks.

"But your plan is suicide for you." David says from the back of the room.

"This may be true. However, should I choose my own life over the lives of millions and a planet? Especially if we can repair two worlds in the process?" Rose asks the room.

The council members again break out in vigorous discussions as Rose stands silent.

"Earth can be saved, and in doing so, we can help Mars to become the world it once was millions of years ago." Rose says looking around the room. "I have the power to remove all of the nuclear materials, poisoned waters, and deadly gases from Earth. I can then move these things to mars and bury them deep into the core of Mars. This will cause the core to melt, and with help from the gods, it will spin once more, allowing Mars to build an atmosphere once again. Hopefully, one thick enough that it will enable humans to walk freely around outside."

One of the reporters stands to ask a question, and Rose points at her in response. "If your plan works, how will it help the humans on Earth?" She asks before retaking her seat.

"The part of the plan I just mentioned is just the first part. Once we have removed everything that is radioactive, then the hard part starts. We will have to send rescue parties to Earth to start planting crops, build homes, schools, and hospitals. There will need to be those who go into the wilds to help humans understand why we are there." Rose says making sure to keep eye contact with the cameras as well as the people in the council chamber. "Now, we won't need to help everyone. When I was on Earth not long ago, there were tribes of people doing very well on their own. We can offer our help to bring them back into the twenty-third century. However, if they refuse, we must walk away and let them be."

Council-member Alysia stands to indicate she has a question. Seeing her standing there, Rose points to her, giving her permission to ask, "Say everything works as planned. Who is to say that the wild humans want to be helped, and if they fight us, what do we do then?"

"Well, as many of you know, I was on Earth not long ago to rescue my daughter, Elizabeth. While I was there, they were already building a society on their own. Unfortunately, their society is similar to that of pack animals. That being said, I believe by working with them one on one, they will accept our help to rebuild humanity into the next, better society that it can be." Rose answers.

After several more questions to assure everyone that this plan can indeed work, it is set for a vote for later that day. Once the vote is tallied and passes, it is then set for a public vote the following week.

***

"While I was getting some things for dinner tonight, I happened to overhear several people talking about the upcoming vote." Amadahy is telling Megan when Rose walks through the door.

"Oh, what are they saying?" Rose asks, causing Megan to drop a potato as she spins on the spot.

"Rose!" Meagan yells, trying to catch her breath.

"Hi, Mom." Amadahy says. "Most everyone I heard is for it. But there are several that want more assurances before they give their support."

"People are talking about the vote all over." Megan says now that she has regained her composure.

Just then, Rose feels Elizabeth calling to her through the energy. But before Rose has the chance to do anything, Elizabeth is standing before her in the apartment.

"Mother, you cannot go through with this plan of yours. If you have to be so deep in the shaft to make sure everything falls in correctly, YOU WILL NOT BE ABLE TO ESCAPE!!! And then what? How will you get out of there then? Or, were you planning on leaving everyone alone again?" Elizabeth says without Rose having done anything to help her appear.

Rose is so shocked that Elizabeth is standing there, without having used any energy of her own, that the only thing she can do is just stare wildly at Elizabeth.

"Well? Are you going to answer me or just keep looking at me with that stupid look?"

"Elizabeth Rose!?" Megan says walking forward out of the kitchen. "How dare you talk to your mother that way? Don't you know that she loves us all and that if there were any way to do things differently, she would?" Megan adds as tears are falling freely.

Elizabeth is not sure what to say about what Megan has just said. Looking to Amadahy for help, Elizabeth also breaks down into tears, finally bringing Rose to her senses.

"Elizabeth, baby girl. I love everyone so much, and I do not want to leave anyone. I have thought of every way this can go, and if I am not in the tunnel, then Mars becomes the radioactive world." Walking over to Elizabeth and hugging her and Megan tightly. "I don't know why, but I must be in the tunnel for all of this to work out correctly."

"Mom." Amadahy says, running over to Rose, Megan, and Elizabeth and joining the hug.

"How did you get here, Elizabeth?" Rose asks once they all separate.

"What do you mean? Didn't you call me here?" Elizabeth asks, looking at Rose, Megan, and then Amadahy in turn.

"I never had the chance. I no more felt you calling me, and you appeared in all of your anger." Rose says.

"Now that you say that, I thought it was strange that you did not make your face that you get right before someone pops in." Amadahy says as she sits on the couch.

"Your right. Now that I think about it, Rose looked just as shocked as I did the first time, I saw Elizabeth appear from nowhere." Megan says, sounding pleased with herself.

"Mom, you really did not call me here?" Elizabeth asks, looking shocked and worried.

"It's nothing to be worried about, baby girl. We all knew that you have the white energy as well, and it was only a matter of time before you really started using it." Rose says hugging Elizabeth again.

"But then, how do I get back if I brought myself here?" Elizabeth asks.

"Well, that is something I can help you with." Rose says, smiling at Elizabeth. "You just close your eyes, think about waking up in your own body, and you should be home."

Elizabeth gives it a try, and soon she becomes transparent. Hearing the room gasp, she opens her eyes. "I am seeing things from here, there? Aw, there, here? Aw, I am seeing everything in two places." Elizabeth says, starting to look like she is going to pass out.

"Elizabeth, breathe. Think about being where you are." Rose says in a motherly tone.

Elizabeth calms down, and in a minute or so, she is gone. Rose decides to check on Elizabeth to make sure she is okay. Closing her eyes, Rose finds herself in Elizabeth's kitchen. She looks around but does not see her anywhere.

"Elizabeth!" Rose calls out, hoping she responds. Rose walks to the back part of the house where she knows Elizabeth's bedroom is. "Elizabeth, are you in here?" She calls, but still no response.

Just then, Bobby comes running in, yelling, "Grandma!"

"Hi, Bobby." Rose says, bending down to be at the same level as Bobby. "Where is your mom at?" She asks, hoping he would know.

"She went to Megan's house a while ago. She left James in charge, but he left right after mommy." Bobby says as his eyes fall to the ground.

"Well then, is Sarah here too?" Rose asks, hoping Bobby was not all alone.

"Yes, she is in her room, finishing her homework. Mommy said if we were good, she would take us to the amusement park tomorrow, so we are making sure our homework is finished." He tells Rose smiling widely.

"Well then, let's go see if she is finished so we can go check on your mom, Okay?" She says, returning his smile.

Rose and Bobby walk to Sarah's room, where they find she is just putting the last of her homework in her bag for school. They stand there, watching her finish putting her things away since she has not even noticed them enter her room. Suddenly she stops like she has remembered something and then slowly turns to the door.

"Grandma!" She yells, throwing her school bag aside and lunging at Rose. She catches her around the middle and knocks the wind out of her as she latches on tightly.

"Hi, Sarah. Are you all finished and ready to go for a walk with me?" Rose asks, coughing a bit.

"Yes, yes, oh, yes." Sarah replies, turning loose of Rose to run and grab a windbreaker.

Rose has Bobby run and grab a coat as well before they walk to the front door. Rose opens the door for the children to walk outside before Rose follows them out and down the street. The kids lead Rose up the street and around the corner before they stop in front of a door that Rose does not recognize. As Rose is about to knock on the door, it opens, revealing Elizabeth.

"Mom?" Elizabeth says in shock. "What are you doing here? Why are Bobby and Sarah with you, and where is James?"

"James left right after you did. Grandma came by to go for a walk with us." Bobby says quickly.

"Mom?" Elizabeth says with a smile.

"I was coming to make sure you were okay, but somehow I ended up at your apartment with the kids. I couldn't just leave them there alone." Rose says apologetically.

"Well, thank you. I made it back okay, thanks to you." Elizabeth says, smiling.

"I watched over her while she was gone. But when she started freaking out that she was in two places at once, I had no idea what to say. You can imagine my surprise when I started hearing you talking to her." Megan says after stepping around Elizabeth.

"You could hear me talking to Elizabeth when she started freaking out about being in two places?" Rose asks in amazement.

"Not just me, Maribel heard you too." Megan says, pointing into the apartment.

"Well, you have an experience, and an ability I did not know was possible, Elizabeth." Rose says, smiling.

"It is something I don't want to experience again, ever." Elizabeth says, smiling before stepping out of Megan's apartment. "I am going to take the kids home now. You are welcome to walk with us if you like." She adds before kissing Rose on the cheek.

"I need to get back and let everyone else know you are okay." Rose says.

"Grandma, what about our walk?" Sarah asks while batting her lovable puppy dog eyes.

"How about I come back tomorrow and go to the amusement park with you? How is that?" Rose asks.

The children agree with enthusiasm, and after Rose says her goodbyes, she vanishes to inform Megan and Amadahy that Elizabeth is okay.

✱✱✱

Before anyone knows it, the day of the vote has come and gone, and Rose's plan passes seventy-eight percent to sixteen percent. The remaining of those who voted asked for other options. After the results are released, the council requests a public meeting where the fine details can be revealed.

The details of the plan are all ironed out over the next few weeks. Rose will return to Earth to release the radiation from all the places around the world. Once she has it free, she is to launch it into orbit, where it will wait until Rose returns to Mars to drop it into the large mine that leads to the center of the planet.

After that, those who are interested in helping the humans on Earth will first build shelters for the people while also planting gardens. These people will then go into the wilds and invite the humans to come to these shelters to learn how to grow their own food. They know that there are several places that did not get hit by the fallout: Most of South America, the southern tip of Africa, southeastern Asia, Australia, and Japan, along with most of the Southern Ocean islands. But on the rest of the planet, they will plant trees, shrubs, and other plants and reintroduce healthy alga to help reboot the Earth's oxygen production.

It takes Rose and a team of nearly two hundred approximately eleven months to locate and launch all of the nuclear materials into space from around Earth. Mostly because the humans seem to be much more violent near higher concentrations of radiation than those who live out in the wilds.

Once Rose and the team have launched all the nuclear materials safely into space, they start focusing on the other types of pollution, and deadly gases left behind in the wake of the devastation.

After nearly a total of two-years, seven-months, and thirteen-days, everything that can hurt or kill life on Earth has been safely removed to space. Encapsulated in a field that Rose generated to keep everything together, it starts to move towards Mars.

***

Rose is standing at the mouth of the mine entrance getting ready to walk to her position deep inside. "Honey, please don't do this!" Megan cries, grabbing Rose's hand.

"Megan, my love. You know this is the only way. I have explained why none of the other methods will work." Rose says, fighting the tears that want to escape.

"But we both know you won't be coming back; I have seen it, and so have you!" Megan yells, while the tears fall freely.

Rose starts crying as well. "I know. But if I don't do this for our world, something horrible will happen."

"We can find another way to get the radioactive stuff into the core of Mars." Megan cries, pulling on Rose's arm.

"There is no other way; I must guide it all the way down. If I don't, Mars's core will never melt and start spinning." Rose says as her tears start to fall like never before. Rose rips her hand loose while a field suddenly appears, stopping Megan from giving chase. Rose disappears down the long tunnel leaving Megan sitting next to the entrance crying.

Soon, Rose reaches the spot where she is supposed to turn and guide the nuclear material down from. Concentrating with all of her might, the radioactive materials start falling towards Mars and the mine. Within minutes, streaks of hot metals fall through the shaft opening disappearing from sight.

Those watching see what can only be described as a stream of golden molten metal pouring into the mine opening from outer space. The sight is so breath taking that not one person speaks for the ninety-eight seconds that it takes for all of the materials to fall through the thin atmosphere and into the mine shaft.

Megan, Amadahy, Elizabeth, and the rest of her family, as well as Rebecca, James, and their children and Sarah and her husband's watch, hoping beyond hope that Rose will reappear from the tunnel. Nearly half an hour after the flames disappear from sight, the shaft starts to rumble and belch dust from deep inside.

The group of onlookers all fall to their knees, knowing that Rose will not walk out of the mine on her own. Albert grabs Elizabeth and hugs her tight as their daughter Megan hugs both of them. Rebecca and James also hug tightly as do Megan and Amadahy. The children all look as though they are lost, not knowing what to feel or do. Some of the children cry uncontrollably while others are just staring at the entrance wide-eyed.

The next morning, with Rose's family and friends still there crying. A team of mine workers heads into the mine to search for Rose. They know this mine very well since they are the ones to have dug most of it over the last hundred and fifty years. They know of several side tunnels that Rose may have wandered into by accident and gotten lost in. Over the next few weeks, the workers search every square inch of the mine that they can get to. They discover that nearly two-thirds of the mine has collapsed. The old mineworkers start trying to excavate some of the old tunnels leading deep into the core of the planet, only to be stopped by the intense heat.

A memorial service is held for Rose after the search is called off. Most of the planet turns out except Elizabeth, Megan, and Amadahy. They feel that Rose is not truly dead, nor is she gone from this world forever. Each of them insists that they can still feel her presence and life force. Elizabeth tries several times to focus on

Rose Kincade

Rose to try and contact her, but when she starts to feel it might
work, things seem to go nowhere.

Epilogue

Helping Humanity

"**W**E HAVE LOST AN EXTRAORDINARY individual that this world will never forget." Linda of the council says, starting the meeting. "We will never be able to truly replace her in our hearts, on this council, or for those who called her family. However, our meeting today is not to remember Mother Rose, the first of all Martians. But rather to continue with the assistance of restoring Earth to a healthy world that can support life in all of its glorious forms." Linda pauses to look around the room at the council members and members of the public who are in the hall. "As you know, the first part of Rose's plan is now complete. The second part called for us to rebuild civilization while also restoring much of the vegetation. We were supposed to teach the humans how to grow food, build homes, and provide a level of education to jumpstart their growth back to the twenty-third century. However, it has come to our attention that there are many more humans than we initially believed. Furthermore, their technologies are at a level far more advanced than we thought capable."

A member of the media stands to ask a question. After Linda points at her, she says, "So what does this mean for the plan? Are we just throwing it out and letting the more advanced humans deal with the animal-like ones?"

"Not exactly. We would like to propose an alternative to the original version. North America, Europe, and Eastern Eurasia are the worst hit of all the continents. Much of South America, Africa, Australia, and Japan look as though they have grasslands, small forests, and even farming communities. We have even spotted several large cities in South America, South Africa, and Japan. It also appears that the oceans are full of life as well." David says, reading most of the information from papers in front of her.

Another reporter stands to ask a question. Linda points to him, and he says, "We still have not heard the new plan. Please, let us know what you are considering."

"Well, much of it is still the same, however, rather than just sending a representative into these large cities. We would like to perform observations on these municipalities to see how they treat outsiders if we can communicate with them, and if they have any weapons that we need to be wary about. The council members have already voted and passed the idea. The only thing left is to hold a vote of the general public." Linda says.

Much of the meeting goes on like this for most of the day, with people asking why the council members feel the need to change the plan that Rose came up with. After being told that Rose just did not know about everything and that is why they believed that the plan needs to be changed, those in attendance started walking out one-by-one before the end of the meeting.

The new plan went to vote and received one of the widest divides to date of any vote. It barely passed with only fifty-one percent for the change, forty-eight percent against the change, and the last percent choosing to abstain.

The council picked nearly a dozen AI's to watch the large cities around the world twenty-four hours a day. They also had several more start seeding Earth with different types of seeds that have been growing on Mars. Seeds such as pine trees, oak trees, maple trees, and aspen trees, several different shrubs for both the woodland and desert areas, as well as a few different types of grasses that have been growing well around Mars.

***

A new flyer is released among the different communities of Mars that reads; Volunteers needed for the Human taming project on Earth. Excitement and Adventures await you. Sign up today.

"Mom, have you seen this flyer that the council has put out trying to get volunteers to go to Earth?" Amadahy asks Megan, waving the paper in the air.

"To my horror, yes," Megan says, closing her eyes at the sight of the paper being waved in her face.

"They make it sound as though they are planning on trying to keep humans as pets. Some of my human friends are very upset about this flyer." Amadahy yells, slamming the flyer down on the counter.

"Trust me. They are not the only ones who find themselves seething here. Sarah is upset as well, not to mention nearly everyone else I know." Megan says, sitting down at the table.

As Amadahy opens her mouth to say something else, there is a knock at the front door. Raising an eyebrow, very reminiscent of Rose, Amadahy goes to the door and opens it to see who it could be.

"Hello. My name is Justice Daniel. I am with the Rosium Consortium, going door-to-door with a survey over the current political situation. Would you mind if I asked you to fill one out for me?" Justice says, sounding more like a hustler than a professional.

Rose Kincade

Amadahy feels Megan touch her back and steps to the side so that Megan can see the woman at the door. What Megan saw both scared and confused her.

The woman in the doorway is about 6'3" and can't weigh more than a hundred and fifty pounds. She has polished and waxed her horns so that they practically glow. Her hair is cut short and is styled into one of the weirdest looking afros. It looks like someone had played a cruel joke by cutting the afro exactly in half just below the ears. This woman has on blueberry colored lipstick and is wearing a black metallic business suit that seems to change to blue or green depending on how you look at it. Each of her fingernails is painted in a black metallic color that also change to blue or green, depending on how you looked at them. As for the shoes, they look out of place. They look like classic snakeskin pointed boots, though each scale was a different color.

"And what the hell pray-tell is the' Rosium Consortium'?" Megan asks, grabbing the door for support.

Amadahy, who seems to have only just caught the words" Rosium Consortium," blinks wildly at Megan for a moment before turning back to the woman in the doorway in time to see her smile falter for a moment.

"Why, ladies, are you telling me that you are not aware of the great movement known as the Rosium Consortium? If you have some time to discuss it, I would love to tell you all about how we got started over a nice cup of coffee." Justice says, with what one could only describe as an evil grin.

Megan and Amadahy look at each other for a moment before looking back at Justice, their eyes crimson red as they speak in unison." You will tell us what the Rosium Consortium is here. You will not lie to us, or we will know." They say with their voices echoing loudly throughout the building, causing several of their neighbors to come running out.

Justice backs into the wall, looking scared as the color drains from her face. Hearing the doors open on either side of her, her eyes start darting around, trying to look for an escape route. Trying to speak, she can't seem to find the strength to do anything but stand there. She can feel her heart pound so hard that the room appears to pulse with every beat of her heart. Suddenly she recognizes that she is allowing herself the indignity of relieving herself of her bodily fluids.

Megan's and Amadahy's eyes, still in that crimson color, drift down as they realize that Justice is peeing herself in front of them. As they see the puddle grow under the terrified Justice, their eyes start to return to their familiar golden yellow color. Looking around, they see a crowd of people beginning to walk up on them.

"I am sorry!" Justice yells as she turns and pushes her way past the growing crowd.

"That woman has been lurking around here for a few days now. I am glad that someone has finally done something about her." One of the people in the group says.

"She said something about a Rosium Consortium. Does anyone know what that is?" Amadahy asks, looking around the group of people.

"Well, it is a group of young people who believe that Mother Rose is some kind of God rather than a person. Most of them are harmless, but some of them..." Another woman says, finishing with a shiver.

Megan and Amadahy look at each other in wonder and amazement at the statement. They have both known Rose a couple of decades, at least, and though she can do things that they can only imagine, she is no God.

***

The council members are going over the report of AI's that have been watching nearly two-dozen large cities in the three countries. All of the cities seem to be set up the same way, at least in the basic layouts. At the center of each city is a large stone building that looks more like a medieval castle with a large stone wall around it. This is surrounded by the main city. Here you can find apartment buildings, office buildings, and businesses that one would find in any typical city. Another large wall surrounds all of this. Surrounding the main city, you find the agricultural area. Here they grow the crops and livestock needs of the town. This, too, is enclosed by a large wall. Cities that are close enough to each other have railroads between them as well.

"It looks as though, out of the twenty-one cities we have been watching, only eight send people out into the wilds to help the other humans." Says the council member known as Amalia and the only human council member.

"Over the last year, three of those cities were forcing residents out for some reason while only bring back babies from the wilds." A council member known as Linda says.

"Honestly, I believe that we need to take an active approach to helping these humans as Rose intended." Sarah of the council of six says.

The rest of the council of six, who had come to Mars to check on the progress of the human race assistance efforts, agreed with Sarah. This caused several of the members of the Mars council members to raise objections to their presence in the meeting.

"Objections overruled. The council of six are protectors of both Mars and Earth. They have every right to be involved in this meeting." The leader of the council announces to the room.

After relief efforts get underway. The humans in the cities accept the help from Mars and all of the other aliens involved.

As Amadahy is helping out with the relief efforts in a city in central America, she hears a story about a group of people who left Earth after the great war. These people could fly without ships but with wings on their backs, and flu in large black ships when they left Earth. She was told that these people called themselves Dragon Knott's.

✳✳✳

Emma was patrolling the outer solar system with three other AI's Edificie – a military Galaxy-500 that Earth built and gave Mars in 2048; Aisuru – a Japanese built semi-truck that was nearly three times the normal size trucks found around the world at the time; and Camypañ – a Russian heavy troop transport, and the only AI with any kind of weapons.

As they fly through the outer asteroid belt, they start getting strange readings on their radar systems. As they get closer, Emma realizes she has seen these signals before. She saw these same types of signals when she was on Nandime.

"Everyone, stop. I know what these readings are," Emma says to the rest of the group.

"Really? What are these readings, and why do you sound so scared?" Aisuru asks as the group stops.

"The last time I saw readings like this was when I was on Nandime," Emma say, scrutinizing the readings she is getting.

"Okay, but why are you so scared of these readings here?" Camypañ asks begging to sound nervous himself.

"It's because these readings indicate a large armada of ships," Emma starts, "Though, these ships all look as though they are powered down at the moment."

"We need to report this," Edificie says with panic evident in her voice.

"Wait. We all have stealth which is why we are out here. I think we should activate it a go in for a closer look." Emma says.

"I agree. We need to acquire three key pieces of information on this armada," Camypañ says, trying to hide the fear in his voice.

"First is who are they. I can identify them by their ships. While I was on Nandime, I learned about every type of space capable ship and who built them along with who flies them," Emma says.

"Good. The second thing we need to know is how many of each kind of ship they have," Camypañ says.

"I bet I cam figure out the last important thing. Would it be their intention?" Aisuru asks with a nervous tone in her voice.

"Yes, it is. There are several other things we can gain from them if we are careful, but those will be our main goals for now." Camypañ says.

"Okay now, Camypañ, I want you to provide cover for the rest of us. Aisuru, I want you to focus on how many soldiers there are on each ship. Edificie, I want you to try find out what kinds of weapons each ship has. I will and try to make contact with them from a location inside the solar system to try and give you all as much time as possible." Emma says.

The group says "Okay" and they all start flying in the direction on the unknown armada, making themselves invisible as they go.

Once at the location of the armada, they realize that what they have found is not an invasion force, but a ship graveyard. Over ten-thousand ships of varying sizes. All of which looks as though they have been through hell and back.

The group decides to finish their patrol and take what they have found back to the council.